P.L WAITES

Sweet Torture

First edition

ISBN: 978-0-7961-5996-0

Editing by Sierra Winson

This book was professionally typeset on Reedsy.
Find out more at reedsy.com

Dedication

To the reader who dares to feel

This isn't just a story—it's my heart on these pages. It's the constant beat of love and loss, the strong pull of desire, and the sweet taste of hope. This journey is full of intense emotions, with lots of passion and pain.

Every word is a heartbeat, every chapter full of feelings. You'll feel the intensity, the wild ups and downs of my love, my fears, my dreams. As you read, know this is only the beginning.

Stay with me through every twist and turn. Feel what I feel. Love what I love. And maybe, just maybe, you'll come back for more.

With all my passion,
Your potential book boyfriend
Tristan Crane

From The Author

Dear Reader,

I wanted to explain why I wrote this story in a really simple way. It's because I wanted to make sure it's easy for everyone to read, especially if you have dyslexia.

I used this writing style so that it could help you get into the story without any trouble. Reading should be fun and not hard work, so I hope you enjoy every page of this book.

Thanks for reading!

Best,
P.L Waites

Finally Seeing Him

Elona

With my heart racing, I approached the familiar house with its elegant architecture and well-kept garden. I raised my hand to knock on the door, butterflies dancing in my stomach. Cris and I hadn't seen each other over the school break because she had gone with her father on a business trip. While she got to enjoy her break, I was stuck at home, bored. I was excited to see her. Part of the reason I was so excited was that I'd had a crush on Uncle Tristan, her father, since I was sixteen. Whenever I saw him, butterflies fluttered in my stomach, and I would get nervous around him. He was attractive, and his stare could be intimidating.

The door swung open to reveal Cris, her auburn hair falling in waves around her shoulders. Her bright green eyes held a hint of mischief as she grinned at me. "Elona, you're right on time. Come on in!"

We settled down in the kitchen. I sat on a barstool at the kitchen counter while Cris poured us some grape juice. We were in our final year of high school, yet to embark on a new chapter of our lives next year.

"My dad left to attend some meetings, so I was bored," I said as she placed the grape juice in front of me. My dad was into real estate, but I was always grateful for the time he still took to be with me. We had a great father-daughter relationship that I didn't want to ever lose.

"I was going through some research on colleges to attend," she said, placing the juice back in the fridge before turning to face me. "It's really difficult to choose which college to apply to. Journalism is my dream, but I don't want to leave my father here. I worry about him."

I felt sorry for her; we were both really close to our fathers, so I understood how she was feeling. When I moved here, I had the privilege of meeting her mom, Estelle. Cris resembled her mother, but she had her father's forest-green eyes. Her mother had passed away three years ago, and it had been difficult for both of them. My mother passed away when I was five years old, and at that moment, I didn't want to think about it because I was supposed to be cheering up my best friend.

"I'm sure he would want you to live your life and have fun," I said, smiling weakly at her.

"You've seen how he buries himself in work. I'd suggest that he starts dating again, but I highly doubt he would," she said, letting out a heavy breath.

"It's his choice, after all," I replied, taking a sip of my juice. I had to admit that I had a tiny crush on Tristan, but not enough to actually want to pursue him.

"I guess you're right," she conceded.

"I've been thinking about something I might pursue as a career," I said, keeping my hand on the glass.

"Please, spill it!" She was always so eager to know.

I smiled nervously. "Well, I've been thinking a lot about my future lately. I want to pursue a career in modeling."

Cris' eyes widened, a mix of surprise and excitement. "Wow!" she exclaimed, taken aback. "You've got the looks and the confidence for it, no doubt. But you're still a bit shy."

I couldn't help but blush at her words. "Thanks. It's just that I've been researching agencies and talking to people, and I really believe I can make it. I'll never know if I don't try, and maybe that shyness will fade over time. I'm still thinking about it, but for now, please don't tell anyone until I've made up my mind and talked to my father about it."

Cris' grin widened. "I promise, I won't tell anyone. I have no doubt that you'll be great, Elona. And you'll have me cheering you on every step of the way."

"That means a lot, and you know I'll do the same for you," I said with a smile.

"Of course. Now, I just need to get my dad back into the dating scene," she joked.

We heard the front door open and close, and I knew who it was. My heart beat wildly in my chest at the sudden feeling of nerves and excitement.

I tensed when I heard Tristan's voice behind me. "Good afternoon, girls," he said, and Cris smiled at him over my shoulder.

"Hi, Dad. You're home quite early," she said.

Tristan appeared beside me, and I caught a glimpse of him. He was undeniably attractive, with sharp features and a charisma that seemed to radiate effortlessly. It was as if he was accustomed to the spotlight, even within the walls of his own home.

"How are you, Elona?" he asked, looking at me with those forest-green eyes that haunted me in my dreams at times. I cleared my throat.

"I'm well, Uncle Tristan," I replied with a smile, glancing down at my juice as warmth spread across my cheeks. This sensation was unfamiliar to me, a depth of feeling I hadn't experienced before.

"That's wonderful to hear," he responded, his voice laced with velvety smoothness. "Have you been researching which college you want to apply to?" he asked Cris as he reached into the cupboard for a glass. I couldn't help but notice his lean muscles through his black Armani three-piece suit. That didn't help me, either.

"Yes, I've been looking into it, but we have some homework too. We have an essay to write. Is it okay if Elona stays over for dinner? Her father's out at meetings, and it's a Friday night. I can order pizza for us," she said.

When my eyes found Tristan again, he was sipping water from his glass, watching me intently until he stopped. "That's fine with me. In the meantime, I have some work to catch up on in the study," he said as he placed the empty glass in the sink and walked away.

My heart raced, and for the first time, I truly saw him, not just as Cris' dad, but as a man. And as his eyes met mine for a fleeting moment, I realized with a jolt that my tiny crush on him was way more than just that.

The sensation was overwhelming, and I couldn't deny the attraction I felt towards Tristan. The way he carried himself, the depth in his voice, and those mesmerizing green eyes made it hard for me to focus on anything else. I couldn't believe I was sitting in his home, about to have dinner with my best friend and her incredibly charming father. My emotions were in turmoil as I contemplated this newfound, and slightly forbidden, crush.

I couldn't help but replay every moment, every word, and every glance we had shared. It was as if a switch had been flipped, and I found myself irresistibly drawn to him, far beyond what I could have ever imagined.

I wondered if he could ever see me as more than just Cris' friend. Would he ever notice the way my heart raced when he was near or the way my cheeks flushed when he spoke to me? My infatuation felt like a secret I carried around, hidden deep within my heart, only occasionally surfacing in stolen glances and bated breaths.

But I knew, deep down, that this crush was an unattainable dream. The age gap, the family dynamics, and the respect I had for Cris' father all formed an insurmountable barrier. It was a painful realization, one that often left me in a state of inner turmoil.

I tried to redirect my focus toward other aspects of my life, like my modeling aspirations and our upcoming graduation, but Tristan's presence remained a constant distraction. It was as if he occupied a significant space in my heart, one that was not easily vacated.

Homework

Elona

I couldn't get that look out of my head—the one Tristan had given me. His stare was now ingrained in my mind, quickening my heartbeat and deepening my feelings for him, intensifying my crush. It felt wrong, especially considering my age and my close friendship with his daughter. I was sure he felt nothing for me, but that stare gave me different vibes.

I was staying over for dinner, and it would be just the three of us. Maybe I should just go home after we finished our homework. Cris and I sat in the lounge, our English books spread open before us. Positioned on the rug, we had cleared the coffee table of its contents to create a makeshift workspace. It was always the lounge, the kitchen, Cris' bedroom, her dad's study room, or my house where we did homework. Cris was great at creative writing, so ideas flowed easily for her. I, however, tended to be more practical than creative.

I stared at my blank page, tapping the pen against it. I had no clue what to write about. The instructions were to write a short story of a thousand words, but I didn't want it to feel forced. I looked up at Cris, who was writing away. I let out a heavy sigh and then looked down at my blank page again.

The only subject available for writing that I could think of was Tristan. Omitting his name ensured secrecy; not even Cris would suspect. This essay was crucial for our grades, so I delved into describing him. As I poured my emotions onto the page, Cris finished her work before me.

"I'm done. I wrote about my mother," she said, and I looked up at her with sympathy. She was very close to Estelle, and there was a hint of sadness in her eyes.

"Writing helps sometimes," I told her as her eyes glazed over.

"Yeah, it's just the first time I've written about her. Even though I say I'm okay, I keep those feelings inside. I don't even tell my father because I know he misses her and still grieves, even after three years. Who am I to tell him to date? It's wrong, and I won't force him to move on so fast. He should take the time and space he needs to heal on his own terms," she said, wiping away a lone tear that ran down her cheek.

"That's why my father hasn't dated in years. Everyone processes grief and moves on at different speeds. It may take longer for some. Both of our fathers loved and lost their soulmates. I hope one day we both have that kind of love they shared with them. A love that's true. It will be okay, but you won't forget her, and neither will he," I said softly.

"Hopefully, we can move on from the pain," she smiled. "Anyway, I need to order some pizza," she said, standing up and heading to the kitchen.

I leaned back against the edge of the sofa, my legs crossed as I still held my pen in my hand. "What's your essay about?" My heart leaped in my chest as I jumped, startled, and looked to my side as Tristan walked around the sofa behind me. He looked at me, his waistcoat and jacket removed, leaving him in a white shirt with the top unbuttoned. His shirt was tucked inside his black dress pants.

He looked at me again with those forest-green eyes. "Um...we're writing an essay, and the topic can be about anything. It gets added to our grades," I replied, trying to be nonchalant.

He now stood close to me, but as I looked up, my gaze fell on his crotch. The bulge was big, but I quickly looked back at my essay. "So, what topic did you choose?" he asked.

"I chose to write a little story."

"What's it about?" he asked.

"It's about a girl falling in love with someone and how she hopes to be with him someday," I said, glancing up at him—well past his bulge this time. He was already looking at me with a smirk. I wasn't sure what it meant.

"Keep up the good work, and you can succeed at anything," he said, then walked around the coffee table and stood in front of me. I looked at him as he folded his arms over his chest and noticed what he was staring at.

He was reading Cris' essay. My heartbeat slowed this time because this was a sensitive topic—his deceased wife. I looked up at him as he read it. I could see how his facial expression changed. Pain was etched deeply on his face, a sight that shattered my heart for both him and my dear friend. His wife's passing came in the aftermath of a tragic car accident on a stormy night. Losing control on the slick roads, she collided with an oncoming vehicle. Despite Tristan's desperate arrival at the scene, she lingered briefly, fighting against her injuries, before succumbing to the inevitable.

He was devastated at her funeral, and everything about it was heartbreaking because this family was built with so much love. I understood why Tristan didn't want to date; he had already lost the love of his life. I hadn't seen them for three months after the tragedy, but Cris and I had communicated via text. I wanted to give them the space they needed to grieve. She would always text me just to tell me that she would hear him sob at night, which devastated her because she didn't know how to comfort him.

As time went on, things became better, but not to the extent of fully healing to move on. As I continued to watch Tristan read Cris' essay, I could see the devastation becoming evident on his face as he forgot I was sitting there, watching his mask of being strong slip.

"I called the pizza place. I'm starving," Cris said, pulling Tristan's attention away from the essay. He stepped to the side, looking at his daughter. He tried to compose himself, making sure the mask was back on. He looked at me as Cris packed up her things, his pain still etched a bit on his face. He knew that I had seen his mask slip away, and then he walked into the kitchen without another word.

Awkward Discussion

Elona

I packed up my things when I finished writing the essay. Closing the book, I left it on the coffee table. Cris did the same, packing her book into her backpack. I was concerned about Tristan after seeing him read Cris' essay; I noticed a shift in him. However, he knew that I saw.

I stood up from the floor as Cris texted someone on her phone. Glancing towards the kitchen, I noticed Tristan sitting at the dinner table, scrolling through his phone with a neutral expression. I couldn't imagine keeping my composure after feeling sad just by reading about someone I had lost.

I missed my mother, though not overwhelmingly so. Occasionally, a tear escaped, but her passing occurred when I was young, and the ache had softened over time.

"You can have a seat at the dinner table," Cris said.

I hesitated, knowing Tristan was there, and my crush on him had somehow intensified. Taking a deep breath, I found the courage to walk over to the kitchen. As I approached, Tristan was deeply engrossed in his phone.

I pulled out a chair across from him, and as it screeched on the floor, he looked up at me. His green eyes captivated me, and just as I thought his gaze would hold mine, stopping my heart in the meantime, he lowered his gaze back to his phone. I took a seat, feeling awkward as I clasped my hands on the table. My phone was in my backpack, so I had nothing to do. Fortunately, Cris entered the kitchen soon after.

"Dad, table manners," she said.

"I just need to respond to this email, and then you'll have my full attention," he said, looking up at me. "Both of you." My heart stopped because his gaze seemed to pierce right through me. Then, too soon, he was back on his phone. I swallowed, my throat feeling like sandpaper. I needed something to drink.

"Here you go," Cris placed grape juice in front of me and her father. She went back to get her juice and returned, placing it beside me on the table. The doorbell rang.

"That must be the delivery guy," she said, hurrying out of the kitchen. As I took my glass of juice, I noticed Tristan putting down his phone and picking up his glass too.

I looked up at him, and he was already staring at me as we took a sip. We both placed our glasses back on the table simultaneously. He cleared his throat.

"Please, don't say anything to Cris about me reading her essay," he said.

"Um," I licked my lips, and his gaze lowered, following the movement of my tongue. "I promise I won't tell her anything," I replied, and he looked into my eyes again.

"Thank you," he said just as Cris walked into the kitchen with two boxes of pizza. "Dad, I know how much you love pizza, so I ordered two. You must be starving," she said, placing the boxes on the table.

"I'm starving," he said, but his gaze remained locked on mine. I wasn't sure if he was doing it on purpose, but I could be wrong. He had never looked at me like that before.

"Dad, you need to go out more often—and not just for work. I mean dating," Cris said as she sat down beside me, opening both boxes. The aroma hit my stomach, making it growl.

We began eating, and I tried not to look at Tristan. "My dating life has stopped, and if I were to date, you would know," he replied. I still refused to look up at him.

"How would I know?" she asked.

"Do you really want to know?"

"Don't answer my question with another question. Of course, I want to know," Cris pushed further.

"Well..." I looked up at him as he smirked, holding a slice of pizza in his hand. I was curious to know, so I watched him study the pizza.

"Please, spit it out, Dad. We're dying to know." Why did she have to bring me into this? He looked up at me, still smirking.

"You'd hear me fuck a woman," he said. I sputtered as I choked on my pizza.

"Dad!" I reached for my glass of juice and gulped it down, finally able to breathe again. I felt Cris patting my back. "See what you just did to Elona?"

"Are you okay?" he asked. He was no longer smirking but concerned.

"Yes, it just went down the wrong pipe," I said, coughing some more before continuing to eat and looking away.

"Well, soon you'll be doing it, so I might as well talk about it," he said. My eyes found his again. He was chewing, and I watched his Adam's apple move as he swallowed.

"I doubt Elona will do it soon. She's a fucking saint," Cris said, and I turned my head toward her because now she was discussing me.

"Cris, this is about you and your father, not about me," I chuckled, feeling the heat creep up my cheeks. They must be bright red by now. Tristan and Cris have a way of speaking their minds freely, though I prefer to remain respectful to my father. But I loved their kind of relationship too—not that my relationship with Dad was any different.

"Soon, Elona will also indulge in sexual things." When I looked at him, he was watching me intently. "She'll experiment, and she might love some things." In that moment, our eye contact pulled me toward him, as if it was just the two of us.

"I'm eating, Dad. Next topic," Cris said, snapping him out of the trance. He took a napkin, wiping his hands and mouth before his phone rang on the table.

"Can't we just eat in peace without your work bothering you at dinner time?" Cris asked.

"Sorry, I have to take this," he said as he stood up and walked away.

Cris sighed, "He always does that."

"He's burying himself in work because that's what he knows since your mother..." I stopped myself from saying anything more.

"It's okay, you can talk about her. I know he's buried himself in work since she passed away. It's been three years, and it's time I start hearing him fuck someone. At least then I'll know he listened to me and is dating someone," she said, her shoulders sagging. As much as I wanted to be that person, I knew it would never happen.

"He will, in due time. It's getting late, and I need to get home," I said as I stood up. "Thanks for the pizza," I added.

"I love having you around," she said. "Next time, we should camp outside in the backyard before we drift apart next year, going on our next journey in life."

"I'll still come over no matter what," I reassured her.

I gathered up my things and left, walking home and thinking about what's to come. Next year, we'll be going our separate ways with our chosen fields of study. My heart felt heavy because I probably wouldn't be seeing Tristan much, even though they live down the street from me. But with Tristan always busy with work and Cris leaving, I wasn't so sure. Now and then, he would come over to my house to hang out with my dad because they're friends too. So, I hoped to see him here more often.

The Essay

Elona

I was relieved when I got home yesterday. I couldn't believe that Tristan had said all of those things. As I sat in my classroom with Cris in the next row, daydreaming as she waited for the lesson to start, I couldn't help but think that she was putting up a happy front because that essay was something new for her to allow someone else to see. Tristan had hidden it well too when he read her essay.

"Good morning, class, please settle down!" Miss Johnson said. She was a beautiful teacher, with light blonde hair and light blue eyes. She had a sweet personality, but she had a stern side to her too. We loved her. Sometimes the guys could be a bit too much, but Miss Johnson was always there to keep them in check.

Once the class had settled down, we sat eagerly waiting for the day to begin. I was nervous about my essay because I had written it about my crush and desire for someone who was forbidden. "As you all know, the essay that you've written has to be submitted today. If you haven't completed that essay yet, you have plenty of time in class. This essay is part of the competition and counts toward your grade. When you win the competition, it will be featured in a local magazine in a column dedicated to creative writing essays, and that will also help you get into selected colleges," she announced.

I sucked in a breath, hoping that my essay was good enough, but now I felt as if it wasn't. "Now is the time to work on your essays, edit, and make them better," she smiled and walked over to her desk. "Please hand it to me after class," she called out over her shoulder before taking a seat behind her desk.

I grabbed my backpack that was on the floor beside my desk. I took out all of my books, looking for my creative writing notebook where my essay was written. "Shit," I muttered under my breath. I couldn't have left it at home because I hadn't taken anything out of my backpack when I got home yesterday, which meant...it could only be at Cris' house. Shit.

I looked at Cris, who was watching me, and mouthed, "What is it?" I just shook my head and faced the front again.

I kept myself busy with another piece of creative writing until class dismissed, which sucked because I was worried about that essay. I stood up and packed all of my books that I had left on my desk when I searched for my essay. "Is everything okay? You seem panicked," Cris asked as she stood beside me while I zipped my backpack closed.

I turned to face her as the other students left the classroom. "I might have forgotten my essay at your house, and I'm panicking because it has to be in today," I let out a breath.

"Why don't you speak to Miss Johnson? Hopefully, she'll give you until tomorrow." She smiled at me apologetically. I nodded.

"I'll do that, thanks," I smiled, but deep down I was still worried.

"I have to go to SNT. I'm so excited yet nervous, and this is the start of my career next year," she beamed excitedly. "I won't be able to walk back home with you."

"It's okay, I'll be fine," I smiled. "Good luck, I'm dying to hear all about it."

"I'll call you once I get back home," she smiled.

"Sure. Let me talk to Miss Johnson. See you later," I said as I moved past her. SNT was where Cris had always wanted to do journalism. The full name was Starlight News Tribune.

I stopped in front of Miss Johnson's desk, and she looked up at me with a smile, the stack of essays in her hand. But before I could say anything, Cris handed in her essay and then left.

"I forgot my essay at home, and I wanted to know if I could hand it in tomorrow, please?" I asked.

"Of course, you can. The essays will be assessed tomorrow, so you have until tomorrow to hand them in," she replied.

I let out a sigh of relief. "Thank you so much, Miss Johnson. Enjoy your day," I smiled.

She returned the smile, "You too, Elona." I was so relieved that I had more time, but now the only issue was that Cris wasn't at home for me to get it.

When I finally got home, I searched my bedroom one last time in case it was there. I searched the entire place. I heard the front door open. "Hey, kiddo. How was your day?" My dad asked as I was searching in the lounge. I was kneeling on the floor but stood up as my father approached me. He was wearing his black suit with a white shirt, his black tie loosened at the top. His one light brown curl hung over his forehead. His laptop bag was in his hand.

He placed a kiss on my forehead and walked toward the kitchen. "It was okay," I replied as I continued to look around the lounge.

"What are you looking for?" he asked.

"My essay, but I think I left that book at Cris'. I'll call her," I said.

"I need to get a few emails out, and then we can have some takeaway." I stopped by the kitchen as he smiled at me.

"Sure," I replied with a smile, and then I ran up the stairs to my bedroom. I grabbed my phone and typed a message for Cris.

Me: May I come over?

Crane: Forgot something?

Shit. I had sent the text to Mr. Crane by accident. I saved Tristan as "Crane" in my contacts. Of course, I would press the wrong contact since Cris was below him.

Me: Yes. Sorry, I thought I had texted Cris.

Crane: I have your essay with me. If that's what you're looking for, I'd like to hear your explanation of what you wrote.

Shit. Shit. Shit. My heart was about to leap out of my chest. This was not happening. I paced my bedroom as I replied.

Me: My creative writing essay? It's for a competition.

Crane: The part where you wrote about me exploring your body, how you can't imagine me with another woman in bed.

Crane: The part where you'd like to find out...I didn't expect that from you, Elona.

Shit! Think of something, make up something, Elona.

Me: I'm not talking about you; I'm talking about someone else.

Crane: Who is someone else? Last time I checked, I have a letter "C" tattooed on my arm. That was in your essay.

Fuck. I was screwed.

Me: I can explain...It's not what you think.

Crane: Oh, it's exactly what I think it is. I'm coming over so you can explain to me. I'll let you know how I explore because my ways of exploring are more than you could ever imagine.

Me: My dad is home. I wasn't serious about it!

Crane: That didn't stop you from writing inappropriate things about me. You wouldn't want Cris to find out either.

Me: My dad is home. I'm sorry.

There was no reply from him, and I paced as I nervously bit my thumbnail. My phone chimed, and I opened the chat. He had sent me a selfie of himself—he was so fucking hot. I could see that he was in a suit. It was as if he was looking at my soul through the selfie.

Crane: Consider it tutoring of the body, then. I'm walking out of my house now.

Me: There's no need to come over.

Crane: You don't seem so innocent and sweet in your essay compared to in person.

Me: Please.

Crane: I love the way you're begging me. Perhaps you need something in that filthy little mouth of yours.

Did he really just say that? Oh my gosh!

Me: It's only an essay. My dad is home, so you really can't come over.

Crane: As I said, consider it tutoring. I'll give you my knowledge of how I do things. Hopefully, it will help you win the competition.

I clutched the phone against my chest. He would be here any minute because he lived down the street.

A few minutes later my phone chimed against my chest as I paced.

Crane: Open the door. I'm outside.

I stood frozen in place. A second later, my phone rang in my hand, and his picture popped up. I threw my phone on my bed as if it had burned me. As the ringing stopped, the doorbell rang.

"Shit," I muttered under my breath as I hurried out of my bedroom. As I walked down the stairs, my dad was already by the front door.

There stood Tristan. He looked over my dad's shoulder at me and smirked.

"Here she is," my dad said, turning to look at me as he heard me.

"Hi, Elona," Tristan greeted.

A Switch In The Mood

Elona

I was slowly climbing down the stairs as Tristan looked at me, smirking. My heart was beating fast. I silently hoped that he had only come to return my book and would leave promptly. After all, the entire situation was embarrassing enough now that my secret was out.

"Come inside," my dad told him.

No, that was not what I wanted. Shit!

"Great," Tristan replied, stepping inside the house in his black suit, which nearly made me drool. He had my book in his hand. I was relieved about that. My dad closed the door behind him.

"So, how have you been, Tristan?" my dad asked. "Would you like coffee? Beer?"

"None, thanks. I'm actually here to tutor Elona on some schoolwork," Tristan said, smirking as he looked over at me.

I could feel the heat rising to my cheeks. What the hell is he doing?

"That's nice of you. Where's Cris?" my dad asked as he walked to the kitchen. Tristan was about to follow him, but I stopped him by placing my hand on his arm. He looked at me, his gaze burning into mine.

"What are you doing?" I whispered sharply.

"I told you, I'd be tutoring you on your essay," he replied, keeping his gaze on me a little while longer before walking into the kitchen with my book. I hoped he wouldn't tutor me in front of my dad. Oh gosh!

I quickly followed after him. "Cris went to SNT. She should be back in a while," Tristan replied to my dad.

"I'll let you both sit here while I catch up on some work in the study," my dad said, then left after making himself a coffee.

I sat down at the dinner table, but Tristan pulled out the chair next to me and sat down. He placed my book in front of him, opened it to the page with my essay, and reached into his jacket pocket to take out a pen. I clasped my hands in my lap, nervous, not knowing what to expect from him at all.

"You'll have to change some things. First, the tattoo with the letter 'C'—change it to a 'T'," he stated. I didn't move, so he drew a line through the 'C' on the page and wrote a 'T' at the top. "Now, I don't understand why you'd write an essay about me, let alone about your desires," he said. When I looked at him, he was smirking as he skimmed over the paragraph. "Let me write a new essay for you. It won't be anything sexual because you won't win this competition with that, but you can write about love. I think you might have a crush on me, and I'm flattered," he continued to smirk. "I'm glad I got your essay just in time. So, 'T' is a man you have a crush on, and you want him, but there are certain obstacles... I'll just finish it, and you can rewrite it in your own words," he continued to write as I waited.

I watched him write, unsure where this was going, but I waited until he was done. When I looked at the page, it was full of new paragraphs. "Thank you, Uncle Tristan," I said.

"Well, let me tell you what I would do," he said, turning to face me as I looked at him. "I would kiss you gently, and then maybe passionately. My hands would explore your body. You would get goosebumps all over. You would beg me for more and I would carry on until you really want me to take it further. I would..." He paused as thoughts seemed to run through his mind, then added, "But that person wouldn't be you. It would be a woman my age. You're too young to even be thinking about me," he said, his tone shifting in a split second.

"I'm eighteen," I interjected, not wanting him to change his mind about me—or was he playing with me, making me think he wanted me?

"You may be eighteen, but I'm older than you. I can't see myself being with you, Elona. You have your whole life ahead of you, and your mind can't be clouded by thoughts or fantasies about me." He held my gaze, and his expression darkened as if a storm was brewing.

"Then why did you even come over here in the first place?" I asked.

"Simple. I didn't want you to make a fool of yourself. If Cris had read your essay before I did, it would've been very easy for her to connect the dots. You were writing about me. There were hints in it that gave it away. You can't think about me. Ever." He was serious now, his lips pressed into a straight line.

I licked my dry lips, and his gaze followed the movement of my tongue over my bottom lip. I felt like I had done something terribly wrong and was now being punished for it. "I need another mug of coffee; this work is draining me," Tristan said, and we both snapped our heads toward my dad as he entered the kitchen.

"We're done. I have to get back home now," Tristan said, standing up. I was still trying to wrap my brain around this tutoring session. He turned to me and said, "I hope you win."

"I'll walk you out, Tristan," my dad offered, and they both left the kitchen.

My shoulders sagged in defeat, and I leaned back against the chair. What the fuck just happened? He changed his tune in a split second, all because of my age. Why did I even think of writing a silly essay about him? Now I know I can never have him because he's my best friend's father, and he's my dad's friend. He's simply not interested in a young woman like me. It's time I stayed the hell away from him if I want to forget about this incident.

His Words

Elona

As I remained seated while my dad escorted Tristan out, a sense of defeat and frustration washed over me. My eyes caught sight of my book, and I leaned forward, bringing it closer to me. His handwriting was neat, something I would keep and treasure forever. I started to read what he had written.

Love Beyond Reach

In the intricate tapestry of human emotions, there exists a facet that ignites the soul with a fire that defies reason and logic. It is the intoxicating, heart-wrenching, and utterly captivating experience of falling for someone you cannot have. Such a forbidden love transcends societal norms and boundaries, leaving you in a whirlwind of intense emotions that threaten to consume your very essence.

A chance encounter, a stolen glance, and a heart that betrays all reason. The story begins innocently enough, a narrative spun by the impulse of fate. Two souls, entwined by destiny, yet bound by the shackles of circumstance. It is in this complexity that the true essence of forbidden love takes root.

The object of your affection, the one who fuels the fire within you, is tantalizingly out of reach. Perhaps they belong to another, already committed to a love that predates your entrance into their life. Or maybe their heart harbors secrets they dare not reveal, lest the world crumbles around them. In either case, you find yourself at the mercy of an unrelenting desire that gnaws at your very core.

Every stolen moment, every fleeting touch becomes a treasure, cherished and hoarded away in the depths of your soul. You walk a tightrope, teetering on the edge of self-control, struggling to keep your emotions in check. The simplest gestures from them—a smile, a word, a casual touch—send ripples through your heart, threatening to drown you in a sea of longing.

The agony of forbidden love is etched into every fiber of your being. It is a constant battle between heart and mind, desire and morality. You question the righteousness of your feelings, tormented by the knowledge that pursuing this love could cause immeasurable pain to those around you. Yet, you are powerless to resist the gravitational pull of your emotions.

As the days turn into weeks and months, you find yourself entangled in a web of secret meetings and whispered confessions. The thrill of the forbidden intensifies your passion, like a drug that both poisons and exhilarates. Each stolen kiss, each secret rendezvous, is a testament to the depths of your love and the lengths to which you are willing to go to be with them.

But there is a price to pay for such love. It is a price measured in stolen moments, hidden tears, and shattered dreams. It is a love that exists in the shadows, forever denied the light of day. And as the world outside continues to spin, your love remains a silent, pulsating ache in the recesses of your heart.

In the end, the forbidden love you cannot have becomes a haunting melody, a bittersweet symphony that plays endlessly in your soul. It is a reminder that some loves are destined to remain unfulfilled, that the heart can be a cruel master, demanding that which it cannot possess.

And so, you are left with a choice. Do you continue to dance on the brink of forbidden love, risking everything for a chance at happiness? Or do you summon the strength to let go, to release the object of your affection, and find solace in the knowledge that, in love, sometimes the most profound acts of courage come from walking away?

In the end, it is a choice that only you can make, a decision that will shape the course of your life and define the depth of your character. But one thing is certain— the memory of that forbidden love, the intensity of the emotions it stirred within you, will linger in your heart, a touching reminder of the power of love, even in its most forbidden form.

I leaned back against the chair and let out a breath, my feelings heightened by this essay he had written. Was that meant for us? Me? I wanted to know, but I feared making a fool of myself again, so I decided to keep my distance.

"How was the tutoring session?" my dad asked as he entered the kitchen. I quickly closed my book so he wouldn't see it, though he wouldn't know anything from just a glance. I had to make sure that my original essay was destroyed.

"It was okay. He helped me where I was stuck, and this is for a competition. I think Cris has a better essay, though—she wrote about her mom," I said, looking over at my dad, who was standing behind the kitchen counter, sipping his coffee.

"That must have been difficult for her to write. They were a very close-knit family. I do hope Tristan finds someone to be in his life. I'm taking him to the bar tomorrow evening just to catch up. I think we both need it. Who knows, maybe he'll run into someone," my father smirked. My stomach sank with a feeling of nausea at the thought.

"How about you?" I asked.

"I'm okay. I live for my work and for you. Maybe someday I'll make that move," he shrugged.

"I want to go into modeling," I blurted out.

"Are you sure about that?" he asked.

"Yeah, I've been doing my research, and I'll be applying. I also need to do a photoshoot so that I have my portfolio," I added.

He chuckled, "I always thought you'd end up being a model. I never told anyone that. I'll support you in whatever you want to do, but don't do anything that'll break my heart," he said.

"Thank you, Dad," I smiled.

"I think Tristan might know about agencies. His company has partners on board with all these kinds of things. But find out from him—he'll know."

"I might just do that," I replied, though in truth, I wouldn't. I didn't want Tristan Crane to know that. "I guess I'll go upstairs and go over this essay," I said, standing up and grabbing my things from the table before heading to the stairs.

He's the last person I'd ever tell about my modeling. I won't even ask him about agencies—I can handle that all by myself, just like I've been doing so far. He can see me in magazines or on runways when I'm there.

New Friend

Elona

I had been tossing and turning the entire evening because of the essay Tristan had written. Was he admitting his feelings for me? I tapped my pen on my creative writing book. I had rewritten the essay in my own handwriting the previous night and handed it in this morning. The students were chatting softly amongst themselves in class while Miss Johnson went through papers at her desk.

"I heard that our dads are going to the bar tonight," Cris said softly. I looked over at her. She had a smirk on her face. "Do you want to sleep over tonight at my place?" she asked.

"I don't know if I should. I mean…I'm not sure if your dad would be okay with that," I replied.

She scoffed, "My dad won't mind. You've slept over with me since we were little. What's changed now?" she smiled as if I were crazy.

I shrugged. "We're older now. Maybe he wants you both to have your space."

"Elona, you're sleeping over, and I'm not taking no for an answer," she demanded.

There was no way I was getting out of this one, and butterflies fluttered in my stomach at the thought of being in the same house as Tristan for an entire evening. "I've sent in the essays for the competition," Miss Johnson said as the class quieted and she stood in front of the classroom. "However, for those who handed in their essays late, your essays couldn't be submitted since yesterday was the cutoff date." My heart sank. "But you'll still get a good

27

grade for it because the essays were brilliant, and you all make me proud," she smiled.

"I hope I win because then all my hard work will pay off for my journalism," Cris said softly as the classroom door opened. There, in the doorway, stood a figure that seemed like it had been plucked straight from the pages of a gothic novel.

Miss Johnson looked toward him. "Oh, Eric, come on in," she said to him.

Eric was a tall and enigmatic figure. His jet-black hair cascaded in unruly waves over his forehead, partially obscuring his sharp, piercing blue eyes that seemed to hold a hint of mystery. His pale complexion contrasted starkly with the sea of ordinary faces in the classroom. Dressed in a dark, fitted jacket and pants, he appeared to be more suited for a midnight stroll in a cemetery than a high school classroom.

As Eric walked in, his every step seemed to carry an air of intrigue and fascination. He moved with a certain confidence that suggested he was accustomed to standing out, even in a room full of curious gazes. His presence felt like a shadowy enigma amidst the fluorescent lights and mundane surroundings.

I exchanged a quick glance with Cris, and we both couldn't help but be captivated by this new addition to our class. What had brought this mysterious figure to our final year of high school? What stories and secrets lay hidden behind those deep, contemplative eyes? Eric's arrival had injected an unexpected dose of excitement and curiosity into our classroom, and I couldn't help but wonder how this enigmatic presence would influence the rest of our school year.

"I saw that he moved down the street from us," Cris said softly.

"Really?" I asked.

"Yes, I was curious when I saw him, but now I'm even more curious," she responded as she looked at where he had taken a seat by the window. The class was whispering amongst themselves, still intrigued by Eric.

"The winner has been chosen for the essay," Miss Johnson continued. Now all of our attention was on her. "Crislynn Crane, you are the winner. It was such a beautiful and heart-touching essay," Miss Johnson smiled at her as the classroom cheered Cris on. I looked over at my best friend. She covered her mouth in disbelief. I smiled in return. She deserved it because that would help with her journalism career after high school. As I thought about it, I realized I needed to take photoshoots to create a modeling portfolio for myself.

Cris and I walked home after school, but we saw Eric in front of us...alone. "Let's make friends," Cris said as she walked away from me.

"Hey," I stopped her by holding onto her arm. We both stopped as she turned to look at me. "Maybe he wants to be alone."

"Chillax, I'll just talk to him," she said, and I let her do what she wanted. She walked over to him, and they walked in step on the sidewalk. I trailed behind them. "This is Elona," she said, and Eric turned around to look at me.

"Hi," I smiled. He gave me a faint smile. I walked beside them now.

"Elona lives down the street too, so if you want to hang out with us, don't hesitate," Cris told him.

"Thank you. You can call me Spooky. That's my nickname," he said.

"That's such a cool nickname, I like it," Cris said.

As we got closer to Cris's house, Tristan pulled up in the driveway. We came to a stop across the street. My heart was beating at a rapid pace because of Tristan.

"This is where I live. See you later, Elona," she smiled at me, then crossed the street as Tristan got out of his car. "See you around, Spooky!" she called out over her shoulder.

"Is she always like that? Outgoing?" Spooky asked. My eyes landed on Tristan. His black suit hugged his lean muscles, and he looked over at Spooky and me, his brows furrowed. I smiled at him, but he looked between the two of us. He didn't even return my smile as he followed Cris down the driveway toward their front door.

My heart sank. "Yeah, but she's a nice person. She makes me smile during tough times too. She lost her mother three years ago, so it's been kind of difficult for her," I replied as we began to walk in step again.

"Thanks for the heads-up," he said.

"Well, you can hang out with us even at school. We like to make friends, and if there's anything you need, just ask."

"I think I'll be fine," he smiled.

We stopped in front of my house. "I'll see you around," I said. He looked at me with his piercing blue eyes.

"Thank you, Elona," and then he left. I glanced one more time down the street toward Cris's house. It was empty.

When I got into my house, my dad was in the lounge, sipping coffee and scrolling through his phone. "Hi, Dad."

"How was school today?" he asked as I walked further into the lounge.

"It was okay. Cris and I met a new friend, and he lives down the street from us. He moved in recently, and he's in our class," I said, plopping down on the sofa.

"It's great to meet new friends… Speaking of friends, Tristan and I are going out to a bar tonight. We both need it," he said, looking at me as he sipped his coffee.

"Yeah, you do. I'll be sleeping over at Cris's tonight," I replied.

"I'm glad to hear that. You haven't slept over by her in a while. I'm glad you're getting out of the house more often," he smiled at me.

"Yeah," I returned his smile.

"Have you asked Tristan about the agencies for your modeling? Just so you know your options if you haven't yet."

"No, Dad. I prefer that he stays out of my business, with all due respect. I want to do this on my own," I said.

He smiled. "You're more like your mother. She always wanted to do things herself without anyone's help, and I'm proud of you," he continued to smile.

"Thanks, Dad. I better pack a little bag for my sleepover tonight," I said, getting up from the sofa and heading upstairs to my bedroom.

Part of me was excited to spend the evening in Tristan's house, and part of me was nervous. At least I would see him. But something had shifted inside him when he came over to tutor me. My crush on him was wrong, and what he had told me via text and in person was wrong too. I knew it was a problem for him to change.

Bar

Tristan

As I sat on the plush barstool, the cool glass of whiskey in my hand offering little solace, I couldn't help but let my thoughts drift to Elona. It was impossible not to. She had grown into a stunning young woman, and each day she became more captivating, more confident, and more irresistible.

The pain was still fresh in my heart, a constant reminder of the void left by Estelle, my beloved wife, who had been taken from me too soon. The warmth of her laughter, the way her eyes sparkled when she looked at me—those memories were etched into my soul. It had crushed my spirit, and I didn't know if I could ever make it without her. She was my one true love, and that drunk bastard had driven into her. It was a rainy evening, and my wife had lost her life due to that person. He had died too. Unfortunately, I couldn't punish him because I had wanted to make him suffer in prison.

I tried to be there for my daughter, Cris, and I tried to be strong in front of her. Once I was in my bedroom, I would sob. My heart felt as if it had been ripped out of me and I wouldn't have it back again until there was some sort of shift between Elona and me. I had read her essay and knew that when I saw that C, she was talking about me. I had a C tattoo, which I got when Cris was born. I was stunned. Elona had a crush on me, and I could see the way she looked at me. That day had shifted everything, and I really saw her for who she was—beautiful inside and out. Yet, despite my longing, I understood she was beyond my reach. Life, however, seemed determined to taunt me with its unfairness. It felt unjust that Elona, a radiant embodiment of beauty and youth, was tantalizingly close yet unattainable to me. She was like a distant star, burning bright but forever beyond reach.

David, Elona's father and my close friend, sat beside me, a sympathetic look in his eyes. "Tristan, I know it's hard, but you can't keep torturing yourself like this."

I sighed, taking a sip of the whiskey. "I can't help it. I can't just move on from what has happened."

David's voice was filled with empathy. "Estelle wouldn't want you to be unhappy forever. You are still a vibrant man, and life is meant to be lived."

I glanced at David, grateful for his support but unable to shake the guilt that tugged at my heart. "I can't just move on, David. Estelle was the love of my life." And the thought of his daughter.

David leaned in closer, his tone gentle. "I know, and no one expects you to forget her. But you can find happiness again, in your own way."

My gaze wandered to the memories I wished I could escape—those moments when I saw Elona with that young man whom I had never seen before, strolling down the street, smiling, and having a conversation. A pang of jealousy twisted in my chest. It was irrational, unfounded, but I couldn't help it. I asked Cris who he was. Apparently, he had moved into a house with his parents down the street. I was relieved when she said there was nothing going on between him and Elona, but there was always a possibility, and I didn't like that.

David nudged me, trying to lighten the mood. "You know, there are plenty of beautiful, vibrant women out there who would love to spend time with you."

I managed a small smile, though it didn't reach my eyes. "Maybe, David, but not anytime soon." None of them were Elona.

The evening continued, whiskey flowing and laughter in the air, but my thoughts remained consumed by her, the beautiful, unattainable Elona.

As the evening wore on, the bar grew livelier. Conversations swirled around us, punctuated by bursts of laughter and clinking glasses. David and I continued to nurse our drinks, and my thoughts of Elona refused to wane.

Suddenly, a woman took the seat next to me, her presence pulling me from my reverie. She had striking auburn hair that cascaded down her shoulders like a waterfall of fire. Her emerald-green eyes sparkled with mischief as she turned to me with a confident smile.

"Mind if I join you?" she asked, her voice smooth as silk.

I glanced at her, surprised by the unexpected intrusion but not entirely opposed to the company. "Sure, have a seat."

She extended her hand. "I'm Maggie."

I shook her hand, offering a polite smile. "Tristan."

David, ever the social butterfly, chimed in. "David over here. Tristan is an old friend."

Maggie raised an eyebrow, her gaze curious. "Old friend, huh? You two look like you're having quite a serious conversation."

I chuckled softly, the weight of my thoughts lightening for a moment. "Just some catching up and reminiscing."

Maggie leaned in closer, her perfume intoxicating. "Well, I hope I'm not interrupting anything too personal."

David winked at her. "Not at all. In fact, Tristan here could use a bit of distraction."

Maggie's laughter was melodic, and I couldn't help but find her company refreshing. We talked about everything and nothing, sharing stories and laughter. She was vibrant and full of life, a stark contrast to the heaviness that often enveloped me.

As the night wore on, Maggie glanced at me, her eyes searching. "You know, Tristan, it's okay to find happiness in unexpected places. Life has a way of surprising us."

I nodded, her words sinking in. "You're right. Sometimes, we just need to be open to the possibilities."

David, ever the encourager, chimed in. "That's the spirit, Tristan! Maybe it's time to take a chance."

Maggie grinned, a hint of mischief in her eyes. "So, Tristan, are you up for a little adventure tonight?"

I couldn't help but smile, a glimmer of hope beginning to shine through. Perhaps, just perhaps, there was room in my heart for more than just memories.

As the night wore on and the chemistry between Maggie and me grew, the memories of Elona still lingered in the corners of my mind. I couldn't help but think of her youthful beauty, her vibrant laughter, and the way her eyes sparkled with life. But with each passing moment, Maggie was becoming a captivating presence in her own right.

Maggie leaned in closer, her voice low and sultry. "How do you say we continue this conversation somewhere a bit more private?"

I hesitated for a moment, my thoughts flickering back to Elona, to the boundaries I had set for myself. But a surge of desire and the longing for a connection beyond my memories pushed me to nod in agreement. "Sure. My house is just a short drive away."

With a coy smile, she slid off the barstool, her fingers lightly tracing my arm. "Lead the way."

We left the bustling bar behind and walked toward my car. The anticipation was palpable. Maggie's hand found mine, her fingers intertwined with mine, and the touch sent a thrill through me that I hadn't felt in years.

As I opened the passenger side door for her, she turned to me, her eyes filled with desire, and I found myself leaning in to kiss her. The kiss was electric, a release of pent-up emotions and desires that had been dormant for far too long. Maybe I could move on and forget about Elona too.

Under The Stars

Elona

The night air was cool and crisp as Cris and I sat on the steps of her house, staring up at the canvas of stars that stretched endlessly above us. The world around us was quiet, save for the occasional rustle of leaves and the distant chirping of crickets. It was the perfect backdrop for the kind of conversation only best friends could have.

Cris turned to me, her eyes reflecting the distant stars. "You know, sometimes I feel like we're just tiny specks in the grand scheme of things, like those stars up there."

I nodded, captivated by the depth of the night sky. "It's humbling, isn't it? We have all these dreams and plans, but in the grand cosmos, we're just a tiny part of it."

Cris chuckled softly. "Yeah, but that doesn't mean we shouldn't chase our dreams with all our might. I mean, look at you, aspiring model extraordinaire!"

I grinned, my heart warmed by her support. "And you, future world-changing journalist. We are going to make our mark on this world." I nudged her playfully, a mischievous glint in my eye. "Remember that time in chemistry class when you accidentally mixed up the chemicals, and the entire lab smelled like rotten eggs for a week?"

Cris' face turned a comical shade of embarrassment. "Oh, please, Elona! Let's not bring up my lab mishaps."

We dissolved into laughter, the sound ringing through the quiet night. For a while, it felt like we were the only two people in the world, our friendship forged under the canopy of stars.

Cris grew thoughtful, her voice soft. "Even in the midst of all this beauty, sometimes life can be so confusing. We're at the cusp of adulthood, and there are so many choices and uncertainties ahead."

I nodded in agreement, my own worries and aspirations swirling within me. "It's like we're standing on the edge of a vast galaxy, Cris. The possibilities are endless, but it's also a little terrifying."

Cris reached over and squeezed my hand. "We'll navigate it together, just like we always have."

As we continued to chat, the night sky became our confidant, our witness to the laughter, dreams, and insecurities we shared. Under the twinkling stars, our friendship deepened, and I couldn't help but feel that no matter what the future held, as long as we had each other, we would find our way through the infinite mysteries of life.

"You see that constellation right there? I think it looks like a giant ice cream cone."

Cris giggled, her voice carrying a note of mischief. "And that one over there? Definitely a celestial pizza slice." We burst into laughter, our voices filling the quiet night air once more.

Cris turned to me, her expression more serious. "We've been through so much together. High school is ending soon, and we'll be going our separate ways. But I want you to remember that no matter where life takes us, we will always be best friends."

I smiled, touched by her words. "I feel the same way. No matter what happens, you will always be my partner in crime."

I did feel guilty about my crush on her dad, but I couldn't help it. I just had to push it away as far back as I could because it was only a phase. It would pass, and then I would be dating someone else, forgetting about Tristan completely.

Bright lights entered the driveway, and my heart beat fast as Tristan pulled up. "I hope he had a good time," Cris said.

I smiled as he got out of the car and briefly glanced at us. I sighed with adoration as I took in his attire. He walked around the car and opened the passenger side door. A woman got out. I was curious. As they got closer, his hand rested on her lower back. She smiled, and he held my gaze for a brief moment as they approached us. "Girls," he said.

"Hi, Dad. Glad to see you finally have someone," Cris beamed as they walked past us. My heart sank into the pit of my stomach. He stuck to his word this time. I'm very young, and we would know when he had moved on with someone. That was tonight. "I'm so happy that he is doing this. I won't have to worry when I go to college. I just want him to be happy and live his life without dwelling on my mother."

"I'm sure he will be fine," I replied through my disappointment. But maybe it was for the best. I wouldn't want to lose my friendship with my best friend.

"So, about the portfolio, I will gladly take photos of you. You will be a stunning model. Let's get to my bedroom and see what outfits will fit you. You need to start somewhere," she said as she got up, and so did I.

I was hesitant to enter the house. Was it a bad idea for me to be sleeping over here tonight while Tristan had a woman over? It was making me suffer on the inside the more I tried to ignore them.

With a deep breath, I followed Cris inside, and we went to her bedroom. Her room was a treasure trove of creative chaos. Scarves in a kaleidoscope of colors hung from hooks on one wall, photos she had taken on the other. Outfits were scattered on her bed, and a full-length mirror stood in the corner, waiting to reflect the transformation she was orchestrating.

Cris handed me a deep blue dress with a daring slit. "This could be perfect. Try it on." I hesitated, my reflection in the mirror casting doubt upon the idea. Cris, always the encouraging friend, smiled. "Elona, you've got the figure for it. Trust me."

With a deep breath, I changed into the dress. It hugged my body like a second skin. As I stepped back into view, Cris's eyes lit up. "You look stunning. This dress was made for you."

Posing was another matter altogether. I felt self-conscious in front of the camera, and I couldn't quite shake the fear of exposing my vulnerability. Cris, sensing my unease, assured me, "You've got this, Elona. Just be yourself."

As she clicked away with her camera, I tried different poses. I felt awkward at first, but Cris's direction and words of encouragement helped me ease into the role. "Hold your head high. Confidence is key."

With every snap of the camera, I started to feel more at home in my own skin. The dress felt like a part of me, an extension of my newfound confidence. I spun around, letting my hair fall gracefully, and let Cris capture the essence of this transformative moment.

Cris cheered me on. "You're a natural! The camera loves you."

As I looked at the photos on the camera's screen, I couldn't help but smile. It was a liberating experience, a moment of unveiling confidence I never thought I possessed. With Cris by my side, the journey into the world of modeling seemed a little less daunting.

Cris grinned, her eyes twinkling with pride. "You are going to set the world on fire with your beauty and talent." I believed her. And in this room filled with colorful scarves and dreams, I started to believe in myself, too.

Later, as we settled in for the night, the sounds from next door were a haunting reminder of Tristan's new companion. I tried to distract myself, but it was hard not to wonder about the life he was moving toward.

Cris must have sensed my unease. "I guess we should have slept over at your house instead. Who knows how long this will go on for? He wasn't joking either, that we would know when he has moved on," she chuckled softly.

"It would've been better at my house," I replied, though my heart was breaking with every sound that woman was making.

"I think we should go clubbing tomorrow evening. We can have some fun. Let's invite Spooky too," she beamed.

"I don't think my dad will allow me to go to a club."

"We are eighteen! We are no longer little girls. I won't take no for an answer," she said as she made herself comfortable in her bed and stared at the ceiling.

"Fine," I responded.

"You are amazing! I'll try to get some sleep through these activities that are going on. Sleep well," she said, and I wished her goodnight too.

I hoped that Tristan would just tone it down with that woman. He had made his point, and I was ready to move on because I would never have him, despite how I felt. There were too many things at stake, and I didn't want to lose the two most important people in my life.

Cake

Elona

I couldn't sleep for the rest of the evening. I'm sure how many rounds Tristan went with whomever she was. I should not care because we wouldn't ever be together and it would be wrong. Tristan can date whomever he wants and I don't have any say in that because I'm his daughter's best friend and he's my dad's friend. I can only have feelings for him at a distance.

Cris was fast asleep. I got out of bed and walked out of the bedroom, closing the door behind me. I was barefoot as I looked down the hallway. It was quiet. I tiptoed as I went to the kitchen. I looked inside the fridge, dressed in shorts and a tank top. What the hell do I eat? There were a bunch of veggies and... I sighed as I went through everything. There was no fruit and then I closed the door of the fridge.

"Here," I jumped in fright. I turned around with my hand against my chest as my heart beat wildly in my chest.

"Uncle Tristan," I whispered. He was holding a banana out to me. I looked at him, he was smirking as he held his gaze on me. He was close, almost in my personal space.

"Sorry that I scared you," he said as I took the banana from him.

"Thanks," I said as I inspected it. He moved further into the kitchen. This kitchen was a bit smaller to move around in. They had two kitchens but the smaller one had been used since Estelle died. The bigger kitchen was at the other end of the house. Usually, when they had family over, they would use that section of the house. This part is just a perfect fit for Cris and Tristan because it was only the two of them.

He washed his hands by the sink and I noticed that he was only wearing his boxer briefs. He was bare-chested and I couldn't take my eyes off him.

"I doubt you saw the chocolate cake in the fridge," he said as he stood in front of me. I moved out of the way as he opened the fridge and took out a little container. There it was…the chocolate cake. It was my favorite. "I have saved it for you because I know how much you enjoy it and Cris would finish it all in no time." He placed it on the counter before turning around. It was like I couldn't speak. I was taking in every inch of his body.

He came closer to me, his bulge was huge even though it was flaccid. Fuck, I should snap out of it because he just fucked someone. My breath hitched as he stepped closer to me, his chest came into view, closer to my face, "Sorry," he rasped as I looked up. His hand extended above me but his forest green eyes held mine, they became darker as if time had stood still.

I moved my gaze to his Adam's apple, it bobbed as he swallowed. He moved away, smirking as he grabbed the plate that he was reaching for, and he turned around. My eyes landed on his ass. I snapped out of it. I was still holding the banana in my hand.

He turned around but this time, he had a fork with a piece of cake on it and he moved closer to me. "Open," he demanded. I complied, opening my mouth, he brought the fork close to my mouth until it was inside. Closing my mouth around it, he slowly removed the fork while he held my gaze.

The cake was lovely, I chewed, but his hand came towards my jaw, his thumb moved over my bottom lip, removing the smudge of icing, his eyes following his movement until they held my gaze again. I swallowed. "That cake is my favorite too," he said, his thumb lingering. "The cake reminds me of you…sweet and lovable," I swallowed again. I was not sure what to say or do.

"Thank you," I breathed.

He chuckled before removing his thumb and turning away from me. "You can have the rest of the cake. I was here to grab a banana but I thought that you needed it more than me. I hope that I wasn't too loud for you though. I mean…Maggie can be loud," he said.

"Um, I guess you have to do what you need to, Uncle Tristan," I replied, as that really snapped me out of my trance. That was a mood killer right there talking about the woman he just fucked countless times in one night. He turned around to face me again.

"Tristan...you can call me Tristan," he said. I nodded.

"Tristan, I think that it's a good thing that you have moved on. You did tell us that we would hear you and we did. I just hope that you enjoy yourself and–"

"There you are," Cris said as she brushed past us to get to the fruit bowl that was at the other end of the kitchen counter. She grabbed an apple. "So, I hear that you have moved on," she said. I bit my bottom lip, as I looked at the kitchen counter.

"Yeah, and I am having fun. Thank you for encouraging me," he replied. I felt a tinge of disappointment but there was nothing that would happen, so why do I hope that there would be? I have to remind myself that my friendship with Cris is too precious to lose and my relationship with my father is way more precious because he is my only parent.

"I'm happy to know that. Maybe in the future, you can warn us because we do not need to hear all of that," she said, as bubbly as she is.

"I got it. I didn't think that you would have a friend over," he looked over at me and I moved my gaze to Cris.

"My bad," she replied. "Oh, Elona and I are going out to the club tomorrow, so don't wait up for me."

"No, you're not going to a club, especially not for the first time. Do you even realize the kind of creeps that hang around there?" he scowled at her, his tone stern.

"Dad, we are going, we are eighteen. Let us live," she responded.

"Over my dead body, neither one of you will be going. Does your father know about this?" This time he was scowling at me and I felt as if I was a little girl being scolded.

"No, he doesn't know yet," I replied.

"You will not go. Cris, I am against this and you need to listen to me. I will be worried sick about you both."

"Relax, Dad. I'm sure that your lady is waiting for you in the bedroom." She tried to get him to leave the kitchen.

"I don't give a fuck about her right now. My concern is for both of you. I will go with you if that is the last resort so that I can keep an eye on both of you."

"No! Fine, you win, Dad. Geez, you need to relax more, you will give yourself a heart attack before you get a chance to get older." she scoffed. She brushed past us as she left the kitchen, clearly upset with Tristan. He watched me.

"You won't be going either. I will make sure of that," he demanded, and then he moved closer to me, my breath hitching. "Are you going to eat that?" he asked.

I looked at the banana in my hand, "Um...no."

He took it from me, his hands brushed mine as I looked up at him, "Good, because I was about to eat this earlier. I just didn't want to see you hungry as I watched you from the dinner table, scratching around for something to eat. I hope that the cake satisfies you." he smirked before he left me.

I let out a huge breath, so he was sitting at the dinner table, about to eat that banana but saw me instead and gave it to me. He was watching me. All the while, I thought that he was in the bedroom fast asleep. My heart was still beating wildly because of what had taken place. The glances that we shared, the intimate moment where he removed the icing from my bottom lip, and his lingering touch. I was wet in my panties...I wanted him.

This was the first time that I really saw him not wearing much. That is an image that I cannot get out of my head, it's ingrained into my mind. He just made it worse for me. Maybe if I hadn't left the bedroom, then I wouldn't have felt this way. My crush on him was growing deeper and I wanted to stop it from escalating to something more than I could handle. I can't have him and I need to move on somehow.

I took the plastic container and sat down at the dinner table which was partially dark, to eat the cake that he had left for me. At least this is something that I can enjoy from him. But it was only a reminder of his touch every time that he inserted the fork into my mouth. This was not going to help me.

Desires

Tristan

I returned to my bedroom, my mind a whirlwind of thoughts. Elona's presence in the kitchen had ignited a storm of emotions—a relentless yearning I was determined to quell. She was very young, my daughter's best friend, and my closest confidante's child. Entertaining such desires was a dangerous game I couldn't afford to play.

Maggie, the woman who had accompanied me home, had been patient enough. She was lying on the bed, her legs crossed sensually as she gazed at me with sultry eyes.

"What took you so long, Tristan?" she purred, her fingers tracing circles on the bedspread. "I have been waiting for you."

I tried to push Elona's image from my mind as I approached Maggie; her alluring presence was a stark contrast to the turmoil in my head. I leaned in to kiss her, but my heart wasn't in it. My thoughts were consumed by the young woman who I had just left in the kitchen.

Maggie, direct and assertive, pulled away, her brows furrowing. "What is wrong? You've been acting so distant tonight since we got here."

I sighed, torn between my desires and the barriers that prevented me from acting on them. "It's nothing. I just have a lot on my mind lately."

She sat up, her expression shifting from sultry to frustrated. "A lot on your mind? Seriously, Tristan, I came here to be with you, not to compete with your thoughts."

I knew she was right, but my heart was heavy with the weight of my unattainable desires. "I'm sorry. It's not you; it's me. I should have told you before that I'm not in the right headspace."

Her annoyance was palpable. "So, what? You're just going to push me away like this?"

I tried to explain, though I knew the words would do little to console her. "It's not about pushing you away, Maggie. It's about being fair to you and not using you as a distraction."

She crossed her arms, her frustration was evident. "A distraction," she nodded in agreement. "I should've known; I thought that we could do this again and see where we go from here. After all, it was fun." She got up from the bed, her tone bitter. "You know what? I don't need this. I came here to have a good time, not to deal with your emotional baggage."

She started to get dressed. I know that I cannot be with Elona as much as I desire to be with her. But maybe Maggie is what I need. What if I never find happiness again?

As I contemplated the limitations that reality had imposed on my desires, Maggie's words echoed in my mind. She was frustrated and felt like a mere distraction, but she wasn't wrong. My thoughts still wandered back to Elona, despite my attempts to suppress them.

With a sigh, before Maggie could reach the bedroom door, I decided to stop her. I gently gripped her wrist. She was tense, and her expression was guarded as she looked at me over her shoulder.

"Maggie, I'm sorry. I didn't mean to make you feel like a distraction. You deserve better than that."

She turned around to face me, and I let go of her wrist, her eyes softening just a fraction. "I get that you have a lot on your mind, but I don't want to be a burden either. If you are not ready for this, it's okay. Just be honest with me."

I appreciated her understanding and wished I could offer more clarity. "I am being honest. It's not about you; it's about the circumstances. I just need time to sort things out."

She nodded, her disappointment still evident, but she seemed willing to give me space. "Alright. Just let me know when you are ready. I'm not going anywhere."

I gave her a small smile, grateful for her patience. "Thank you. I promise, when I'm ready, I will make it up to you. At least stay for breakfast."

She nodded. "I will." She smiled at me, the disappointment breaking.

We ended up getting back into bed, and we fell asleep.

* * *

After a while of sleep, we woke up, and then we took a shower in my en suite bathroom. I took her hand in mine, and I led the way to the kitchen. It was a sunny Saturday morning. It already felt scorching. I heard the girls talking, and I tried to put up my walls. As we rounded the corner and entered the kitchen, I stopped in my tracks; nothing had prepared me for seeing Elona in denim shorts and, fuck, a bikini top. The strings were tied at the back, easy to untie. Her back was facing towards me, and Cris was chatting away beside her. Elona has amazing legs, and I wanted to touch her skin so badly.

"Ahem!" I snapped out of it as I realized that Maggie was now beside me.

"Good morning, girls," I said, putting my walls back up as I let go of Maggie's hand.

"Good morning, Dad. I hope you both had a great night." Cris smiled at the both of us as I went to the fridge and got juice out, and I took two glasses out of the cupboard above.

"Oh, it was fantastic," Maggie replied, and as I turned around, Elona looked briefly at me over her shoulder before turning back to a fruit salad that they were making. I went to the dinner table and took a seat. Maggie took a seat across from me, and I poured juice into our glasses.

"Elona and I are going to be in the backyard. It's a great day for a swim too. I'm also inviting Spooky over."

That was something that I didn't want. "No," I replied.

"What do you mean?" Cris asked as she looked at me with huge eyes.

"He is not allowed on our property; we don't know him," I replied, my jaw clenching. I didn't want that...asshole here. I don't want him close to Elona either. I took a sip of my juice, and my gaze caught Elona's as she already looked at me.

"Dad, he is new, and we made new friends. I can't believe that you would not allow him here." Cris was upset about it.

"This is my house, and I need you to respect that. You can see him at school," I stated.

She let out a heavy sigh. "Great, he is such an ass," she muttered to Elona.

I didn't give a shit about it, but no boy is allowed under my roof. Maggie remained quiet, but I was waiting for the girls to be done so that I could make breakfast for Maggie and me.

"Oh, we are going to the club tonight, Dad." My heart nearly stopped. It was even worse after I told them not to even go to the club.

"No, you are not going anywhere," I said.

Maggie looked at me as if I were crazy. "Dad, why are you always like this?" Cris was furious with me.

"I would say allow them to have fun. We all did that when we were young too. So allow them to explore," Maggie chimed in.

"Thanks, Maggie. I like you already," Cris said, and Maggie smiled.

"I'm sticking to my answer; you are both not going, and I will make sure of that." I scowled at Cris.

Cris shook her head in disappointment. "Come on, Elona." She walked around the kitchen counter with a glass of juice and a bowl of fruit salad. "We don't need to be here," she said. Elona followed after her without looking my way, her head hung low.

I let out a sigh as they left the kitchen. "They are old enough to go to a club; you cannot always protect them from these places, you know." Maggie took a sip of juice.

"I know, but they are girls, and it's their last year of high school; they should be focused on their books, not fun," I said as I got up and walked into the kitchen.

"Just let them go one time. Make that deal with your daughter," she said as I began to start breakfast, which included eggs, bacon, and toast.

"I will think about it," I replied.

As much as I don't want them to go, I know that I can't always keep them in the house or keep them from harm. But I would prefer that they stay away from danger and men lurking around. Elona was my main reason for them not going. I wasn't even sure where I was going with Maggie, but she seemed to have a great heart for the girls—almost motherly. I needed to get rid of my desires towards Elona, and if Maggie was the one to make me forget, then I would try to be more with her.

Cris likes Maggie, and there would be no risks in a relationship with her compared to if I were with Elona, but still... My desires are stronger for Elona. I have to fight it with all that I have.

Swimming

Elona

The summer sun blazed overhead as I took a leisurely dip in the pool. The cool water caressed my skin, offering respite from the heat. I couldn't help but feel a sense of freedom and euphoria as I swam, my body moving effortlessly through the crystal-clear water.

Cris was sprawled out on a sun lounger nearby, a book in hand but her attention far from its pages. Her auburn hair, pinned up into a messy bun and her sunglasses hid the knowing glint in her eyes. Tristan was out of my sight, lost in the grandeur of the luxurious house. I didn't like that Maggie was still here, but who am I to say anything when nothing is happening between Tristan and me?

As I pushed myself through the water, my senses were heightened, attuned to the world around me. I couldn't help but feel a pang of disappointment because of Tristan and Maggie. That is when I heard the approaching footsteps from the house, each one echoing in the stillness of the afternoon. It was Tristan. My heart quickened, and a mix of nerves and anticipation sent ripples through my chest.

He dressed casually in a linen shirt and blue jeans, casting a brief glance in my direction as he neared the sun lounger where Cris rested. His eyes flitted over me for the briefest of moments, but it was enough to send a flurry of butterflies dancing in my stomach.

"Cris," he said, his voice soft and tender, "I'm going to take Maggie home. I'll be back soon."

Cris glanced up from her book, her demeanor cool and nonchalant. "Sure, Dad. Take your time." she grinned, and I knew what she meant by that, ugh.

Tristan nodded and turned to head back inside, but not before casting another fleeting look in my direction. His eyes met mine, and in that moment, there was something unspoken, a connection that transcended mere words.

I watched him walk away, the rhythm of his steps fading into the distance, but his presence lingered in the air. Cris seemed lost in her book, oblivious to the charged atmosphere around us. My heart pounded in my chest, and I couldn't help but wonder about the secrets and desires that hid just beneath the surface of our interactions.

"You're like a fish in that water," Cris said and I shifted my gaze to her.

"Maybe in another lifetime, perhaps I was a mermaid," I smiled.

"Oh, I have an idea!" she rested her book on her lap with excitement. "Why don't you do a swimwear photoshoot, it doesn't have to be here but we can do it at your house." she grinned.

"That is not a bad idea at all," my smile widened. "Brilliant idea," Cris was a genius.

"You know, men will be falling at your feet because you are beautiful, you're sexy, you have a body. Modeling is the perfect career for you, so I want to help where I can...It's weird seeing my dad eyeing you like that, considering you're my friend. I get it's just how guys are wired, but it still grosses me out. Promise you'll give me a heads-up if he gets too creepy, okay?" Her blunt honesty caught me off guard; I thought she hadn't noticed. Maybe we should stick to safer ground—I can't risk losing her, especially with these feelings for Tristan swirling around.

"Well, why don't you join me for a swim?" I said, changing the topic.

"I'm reading this hot novel, and I don't want to put it down. I need to get my fill of it," she smiled as she got back to her book.

As I swam on, my mind drifted to this new revelation. I really had to be careful. I think I need a distraction from Tristan. Hopefully, next year, when I'm in modeling and Cris is doing journalism, then I won't be seeing him as often as I am right now. I cannot cross the dangerous territories and my feelings...I need to keep to myself.

* * *

I was still swimming lazily through the pool, my eyes fixed on the water's shimmering surface. Cris was still stretched out on the sun lounger, the novel now resting on her lap. I don't know for how long I've been in the pool, but it must've been for a long time because the distant echoes of my heartbeat seemed to amplify the silence that enveloped the backyard.

I heard the door creak open and glanced over my shoulder, the anticipation building within me as Tristan reemerged from the house. He seemed a bit more relaxed now, a faint smile playing at the corners of his lips.

Cris glanced up, her tone teasing but with a hint of mischief. "How is Maggie, Dad?"

Tristan's gaze met Cris briefly, but then, his eyes flickered in my direction once more, the contact so fleeting that it was almost imperceptible. "She's fine. Just a little tired from last night." I rolled my eyes.

I pretended to focus on my swimming, the heat of the sun on my back doing nothing to quell the warmth that spread through me. It was thrilling, the unspoken tension, and I could feel the energy in the air shift.

Cris sat up on the lounger, her curiosity getting the better of her. "I'm just glad that you are moving on. You know, Dad, Elona is an excellent swimmer. She has been doing laps for a while now."

Tristan's gaze met mine once more, and there was something in his eyes that sent my heart into a frenzy. "Is that so?"

I couldn't help but feel a rush of embarrassment and excitement. "Yeah, I love swimming," I replied, my voice coming out steadier than I had expected. I spend a lot of time swimming in the pool at home.

Cris seemed oblivious to the true nature of the connection between her father and me. "You should join her, Dad. It's a beautiful day."

Tristan hesitated for a moment, his eyes locking onto mine with an intensity that made it difficult to breathe. "Maybe later," he finally said.

"I need to get something," Cris said as she stood up from the sun lounger.

I continued to glide through the pool, the water caressing my skin with every stroke. The tension between Tristan and me lingered like a secret, unspoken yet undeniable. Cris had disappeared into the house to retrieve whatever it was, leaving me alone with Tristan.

As I reached the edge of the pool, I could feel Tristan's eyes on me, a magnetic pull that was impossible to ignore. I hesitated for a moment, the water dripping from my glistening body as I hoisted myself out of the pool. The sensation was electrifying, knowing that he was watching, his gaze following my every move.

He stood by the poolside, his demeanor composed yet his eyes betraying a hint of longing. "You are really an excellent swimmer, Elona," he remarked, the same words as Cris, his voice low and husky.

I couldn't help but blush, the heat of the sun mixing with the heat that seemed to simmer between us. "Thank you," I replied, my words tinged with both gratitude and uncertainty.

He stepped closer, his eyes locked onto mine with an intensity that sent my heart racing. "You have a natural grace in the water. It's captivating."

My breath caught in my throat, and I glanced away for a moment, feeling both vulnerable and exhilarated. Cris' absence, even for a few moments, had created a vacuum that seemed to draw us together.

Just then, Cris reappeared from the house, carrying a tray with chilled drinks. She seemed unaware of the charged atmosphere between her father and me, her focus on the refreshments she was bringing.

"I thought you two might be thirsty," she said cheerfully, her attention on arranging the drinks.

Tristan and I exchanged a quick, almost desperate glance as if the moment had slipped through our fingers, and the unspoken desires had to be concealed once more.

Cris's presence seemed to break the spell, and Tristan took a step back. "Thanks." I moved towards the other sun lounger and dried my hair with a towel. I could still feel his eyes on me.

Once I was done, I took a glass from the tray, trying to regain my composure. "You always make the best lemonade," I said as I took a sip.

"Everyone loves it," she smiled.

As we sipped our drinks and engaged in casual conversation, I couldn't help but wonder about the longing in Tristan's eyes and the unspoken desires that had almost found their voice under the sun's unrelenting gaze. It was a chapter in our story that I knew would continue to unfold, even if the words remained unsaid. But I had to keep it the way that it was for a reason. It wasn't long until he went back inside of the house and I felt a pang of disappointment. Will these feelings ever go away?

Clubbing

Elona

Tristan disappeared into his study room. He had work to do. I rolled my eyes. My dad's kind of like that too, but he tries to be cool about it. He gives me space to figure things out, unlike how strict Tristan was with Cris. But knowing Cris, she's a rebel through and through. She'll do her thing regardless of what Tristan said, and I often get caught up in her schemes.

"You know what? We're going to the club whether my father likes it or not. He cannot treat me like a little girl anymore. I'm getting older and I'm nearly out of school. Maybe he should just have another evening with Maggie so that we can sneak away," she was fuming as she pulled up her skinny jeans. We were in her bedroom. I was just sitting on her bed, watching her fume.

"I wouldn't want to get into trouble, but I know we have to start somewhere by testing the water. I'm just careful." I replied.

"We are going to your house after this. You are going to get dressed, put on skinny jeans and a crop top, make your hair nice and we will have fun. Screw what my father has to say," she said as she pulled on a denim jacket.

"Cris, I don't think that it would be okay if we did this," I said hesitantly. I was trying to get out of it. Her hair was in waves, and she stood in front of the mirror applying mascara.

"Elona, live a little bit. You will be a model soon and these are places that you will also be at, so start to get used to it. See it as a way of me helping you. I'm inviting Spooky too," she grinned as I watched her in the mirror.

I scoffed, "You really are something else," I shook my head at her.

Once Cris was done, we walked down the hallway, past the study room. The door was ajar and I could briefly see Tristan sitting behind his desk. He was looking at something on his desk, his head resting on his hand. He seemed frustrated. I hurried after Cris. She called out to her father, "Dad! I'm going to be at Elona's house, don't wait up!" she took my hand and dragged me out the front of the house.

We sprint out the driveway because Cris was dressed a bit inappropriately and I knew that Tristan would have a fit if he had to see Cris this way. Luckily, she had a denim jacket on. We got to my house. Luckily, my father wasn't at home, but I might still get into trouble. My father worked extremely hard, but I didn't want to throw this in his face, of becoming a bad girl, especially now that Cris is taking risks.

Cris ended up putting clothes out for me, telling me what to wear. I felt uncomfortable because she set out a black mini skirt which I had tossed at the back of my closet a few years back because it was inappropriate. I know that when I'm a model, I need to get even more confident in my skin and be revealing. Cris threw a white halter neck crop top at me. This was going to be part of a photoshoot that I had planned to have here in my room to add to my portfolio, but now I don't even know if I want to wear it again. Next thing, black knee-high boots are being thrown on the floor in front of me. "I will end up looking like a slutty schoolgirl," I exclaimed at Cris as I bent down and got the boots.

"It's the whole point of partying. Come on, get ready while I send Spooky a text." She was being impatient.

I started to get undressed, I was feeling...nervous. This was not me, but it will soon be me.

* * *

Cris held my hand as she guided me through the crowd at the club, the music was blaring and the strobe lights flickering. I've been dodging the elbows of the crowd on the dancefloor. The heat was unbearable, but we managed to get to the bar. This was a bad idea.

"So, what would you like?" Cris asked.

"Um, soda, please."

"No, you can order something different. We are legal. Never mind," she said as she turned to the bartender who was cute, and she placed our order, which was tequila. I tried to cover my belly but then I really felt my clothes, searching for my phone. "What is it?" Cris asked.

"My phone...I don't have it. I forgot it at my house," I panicked. My father would get a heart attack if he didn't know where I was.

Cris retrieved her phone out of her skinny jeans pocket. She held her phone up, "I got mine, but we won't be needing it," she shoved it back into her pocket. "Oh Spooky, you made it!" She squealed as she looked over my shoulder.

I turned around to look at him. His gaze found mine with a shy smile. When I actually looked at him, he was still the handsome young man I saw for the first time in class with those eyes. I smiled back at him. "You look great," he said shyly.

"Thanks," heat crept up my cheeks and I turned around as the bartender placed our tequila shots on the bar counter. Spooky ordered a beer.

"You're a photographer, right?" Cris asked Spooky.

"Yeah, not professionally yet, but I would like to be one. It's my dream," he replied.

"Great, Elona needs a photographer. You two should talk about it," she encouraged.

"It's really no big deal," I blushed.

"Yes, it is. This is your future career we are talking about," Cris chimed in. "Please, talk," she held my gaze.

I sighed, "Okay, fine."

I told Spooky about my modeling career that I wanted to pursue, and I need a photographer with better equipment to take my photos for the portfolio so that it would look more professional.

"Count me in. I need more photos for my own portfolio too, if you don't mind. It will also help me with practicing my photography skills," he smiled, and then he took a sip of his beer.

Cris ordered more tequila shots, and it was loosening me up a bit. Men were looking at me as if I was a piece of meat, but I didn't care as I actually felt confident. Cris pulled me onto the dance floor, my loose hair falling in soft curls. As I moved my hips to the rhythm, I truly lost myself in the music. Men began to join us, their behavior surprisingly respectful. I glanced over to where Spooky was, still at the bar, watching us from a distance. He kept to himself, not one to get tangled up in our fun.

I like him... I mean...the person that he is. A good friend. What the hell am I saying? I barely know him.

I was drunk, but I didn't care. I felt great though, confident. I have to loosen up with the type of model that I will become. There are times when I will be posing in lingerie and then perhaps nude too. I need something strong for that because with this I don't think I will be that confident.

I was grinding my hips with someone behind me, his hands on my hips. Spooky was now beside us, he was not dancing, but rather trying to tell us something. He leaned into Cris, telling her something in her ear and she froze as she scanned the crowd and then that is when I saw him.

Tristan was livid as he stood in a far corner watching us in his casual linen shirt and blue jeans. He then started walking through the crowd...towards us. I swallowed, not sure what to do, but his eyes remained on me.

Fuck.

Not What I Had Expected

Tristan

I had to get away from Elona in the backyard. Every ounce of her body in that bikini of hers made me want her so badly. I just had to get away and then I tried to bury myself in work as I always do. As I went through some documents, my mind kept trailing back to her. I ran a hand through my hair out of frustration because this is wrong on so many levels. That is when Cris had called out to me that she would be at Elona's house. I felt relieved yet disappointed, but it is for the best that they were at her place instead.

My phone rang and it was an unknown number. It could be work, so I answered, "Crane."

"It's Maggie, I wanted to know if you're available later for drinks or just to go somewhere and have dinner?" she asked. I let out a sigh as I leaned back in the leather chair.

I contemplated what to say next. Elona came to mind. "Fine, we can have dinner somewhere, but this is not an evening to have sex or anything. I just want it to be pure dinner, understand?" I asked.

"Of course," she replied. She was understanding and I appreciated that. I didn't want to fuck anyone and I was avoiding David, Elona's father, for that reason. He tries to encourage me to be with someone who I'm not ready for. I simply don't go around fucking anyone. I respected my late wife, but my thoughts constantly drifted to Elona, where everything unraveled. She became the distraction I craved, causing all my respect for my deceased wife to slip away.

"Thanks. I'll text you the details. Just text me your number, it seems that you called me from an unknown number," I said with annoyance and I hung up. Did I really want to do this? Yes, all because of Elona.

I checked the time and it was already 7 PM, so I would be meeting up with Maggie at 8 PM. I trust Cris enough for her to be home no later than 10 PM from Elona's house, unless she sends me a text, letting me know that she is sleeping over at Elona's tonight.

My phone chimed and it was a text from Maggie. Immediately, my phone rang in my hand– it was Steve, a good friend of mine and David's. He owns a club called Galaxy. Sometimes, David and I would hang out there when we were younger. The three of us had been inseparable since leaving college and Steve had always wanted to open his own club, luckily it was legal. He's doing good for himself. Ever since my wife died, I hadn't stepped foot in a bar or club until David forced me last night. Now, it feels like a big mistake.

I answered the phone, furrowing my brows as to why he was calling me. "Steve, what can I do for you? Is everything okay?" I asked as he would never just call me.

"I don't know if you are aware of this, but your daughter is at the club and she's been drinking," he stated.

"Cris? Are you sure that it's her?" I asked.

"Yes. I'm one hundred percent sure. There is no mistaking– she looks like your wife," he replied.

I let out a huge breath and leaned forward in my chair. I rubbed my face with my hand. "I will be right there–"

"Oh, and one more thing, David's daughter is here too. I think that you might want to inform him if he doesn't already know."

"Thanks," I said and then I hung up. I clenched my jaw, I wanted to throw my phone across the study room because I clearly told Cris not to go and yet she went behind my back and I would rather let David deal with Elona because she is the last person that I want to unleash my anger on.

I stood up from the chair, grabbing my phone and keys, and I left in a hurry. I literally drove to the club like a madman. I tried to call David, but his phone went to voicemail. I was pissed off with Cris. She will be punished accordingly.

* * *

I got to the club, scanning the crowd as I stepped into a corner. There was no use walking through a crowd and missing them. I hope that Cris and Elona have not taken any other substances because it will be something that I won't easily forgive. They had already been drinking, so I might just let that slide. It was always a challenge to spot anyone in this crowded place. The club was consistently packed, a testament to Steve's success, and that was something I was proud of him for.

I left my spot and walked to the other corner. There were stairs going up too, but that was mostly for the VIP section, but who knows, maybe they might've just sneaked up there or someone could've invited them up, but they are young, and I don't think that Steve would let anything happen if they were on the second floor, especially with the businessmen who frequent there. It was a space that Steve made sure to have reserved for us businessmen.

As if the universe spoke, my eyes caught Elona. She was dancing with a man behind her, she was wearing a white halter neck top that barely covered her flat belly and her hair was loose in waves. I found Cris scanning the crowd and Spooky was beside her and the anger inside of me was so close to erupting, I was trembling. I moved my gaze to Elona again. She was frozen in her spot this time as she held her surprised gaze on me.

I moved out from the corner, and approached them. Cris finally saw me and her expression turned to guilt. She'll face a tough punishment because this was a test she dared to put me through, and she's never witnessed my full wrath before. As for Elona, she was the last person that I wanted to actually look at at this moment, but I did want to punch the guy behind her, he moved away before I got to them as I saw me approaching.

"Dad! I can explain!" Cris said raising her voice above the music.

"Fuck an explanation! Get the fuck out of this place! Both of you. Now!" they both jumped at my tone. As they both moved past me, I turned my gaze to Spooky. "As for you, if I ever see you with them again, I will inform your parents, are we clear?" I asked, my jaw clenching. His eyes widened with fear... real fear.

"Please, don't tell my father," he begged.

"Then stay away from them." I glared at him.

"Yes, Sir," he hung his head before leaving.

The girls were waiting for me at the exit. Elona was dressed in a fucking mini skirt, and I was more pissed off that my daughter was dressed more appropriately than her. I'm still trembling, and I don't want to unleash my anger on Elona, I will leave that to David.

I just hope that David will be home by the time I drop Elona off. I really want to deal with Cris without Elona around. Maybe this was a good thing for me because now this was a distraction for me in some way. Having Elona around is a distraction, but the behavior of the men around her only intensified my feelings, which caught me off guard.

Wrath

Elona

I was feeling nauseous, my stomach turned as we walked in the parking lot towards Tristan's car. I started to trail behind Cris and Tristan. He was walking as if on a mission, but he ended up slowing down the closer we got to his car. I hugged myself as I felt chilly. Tristan stopped and turned around to look at me, waiting for me to catch up to them.

He was still furious and I hate the way he looked at me as if I had done something horrendous that cannot be forgiven. This is the first time that I had ever seen him this way. He doesn't even look at Cris this way. Is he disgusted with what I'm wearing? If he only knew that it was his daughter that put out these clothes for me to wear. Will he look at me like this when I'm a model, posing for the camera in revealing clothes even nude? Ugh. I hope that he never sees me anywhere once I get into the modeling industry because I don't want to see that look again. I would gladly move away after high school and never see the way that he was looking at me at this moment again.

"Hurry up!" he demanded of me. As I got closer to him, bile rose and I hunched over as my stomach convulsed, releasing its contents. "Fuck," I heard him mutter under his breath as I continued to vomit, I felt my hair being pulled back and my back being rubbed gently.

I finally stopped vomiting and a handkerchief was held out to me, I looked up into Tristan's eyes, which were still dark with anger but there was a hint of softness in them. I took it from him and I wiped my mouth. "Keep it," he said as I now realized that Cris was the one beside me, who held my hair and gently rubbed my back. "I take it that was the first time that you had alcohol," he stated, but there was a hint of amusement on his face which quickly disappeared.

"Yes," I replied, which was barely a whisper.

"And I guess that this is not the first time for you," he shifted his gaze to Cris beside me.

"No, Dad," she let out a sigh.

"I'm sick of your attitude right now," he said to her, and then he moved closer to me, making sure not to step into my vomit. The next thing I knew was that I was being scooped up into his arms. I wrapped my arms around his neck and I lay my head against his chest, taking in his amazing scent. I wonder what scent he uses. I closed my eyes as he carried me to the car.

I felt like I was in heaven, being carried by Tristan until he placed me inside the back of the car and closed the door. I rested the back of my head against the headrest, closing my eyes as they both got in the front of the car and drove away. I drifted in and out of sleep, feeling incredibly unwell. Never again will I touch tequila. I held my stomach as we drove, paying little attention to whatever Tristan and Cris were discussing. Darkness consumed me.

* * *

I was shaken awake, it was dark and all I could do was release a groan, "I don't feel well." I was holding something in my hand and I looked down, it was his handkerchief.

"Well, make sure that you don't puke on me," I turned my gaze and I realized that it was Tristan beside me, holding his hand out for me, and I placed my hand in his. I stepped out of the car. "Can you walk?" he asked, concerned this time.

I moved a bit slowly so that he could close the car door and I looked at the house. "This is not my house," I groaned.

"Well, your father is not answering his phone," he stated.

"I have the spare house keys on me," I said.

"We won't be going to your house, your father can pick you up here," he responded.

"Please, could I stay here for the night, I don't want my father to find out about this," I begged him. I looked into his eyes.

"Can you walk?" he repeated.

I looked down at my body and shrugged. As I started to open my mouth to say something, I was swooped up into his arms yet again and I was carried into his house. He kicked the door closed behind him, Cris was nowhere to be seen, so she must be in her bedroom. Tristan laid me down on the sofa. He stood up straight and walked away down the hallway. I closed my eyes as I rested my head on the soft arm of the sofa. I covered my eyes with my arm, never letting go of his handkerchief, just hoping that I would fall asleep and never wake up because I feel like shit. I just hope that I do not throw up again anytime soon. Darkness consumed me again.

* * *

"Here," I removed my arm from my eyes, I squinted at the faint light of the lamp on the other side of the sofa. I guess I must've fallen asleep. Tristan held out a glass of water to me and I sat up straight, shifting my position, placing my feet on the floor. I still had my boots on so I guess that he didn't care about me ruining his sofa. I took the glass of water from him. I was nauseous just looking at it. He sat on the coffee table in front of me. He looked at me with anger and concern. He was hunched over, his elbows rested on his knees, his hands clasped in front of us.

He licked his lips and as he wanted to say something, there was a knock on the door. My heart began to race wildly, my nausea becoming worse. He stood up and walked over to the door. I leaned forward and placed the full glass of water on the coffee table. I sat back, playing with his handkerchief.

"Elona," My dad commanded as he stood further away from me. Tristan stood close to the kitchen. His hands were in his pockets, his jaw clenching, he didn't even look at me. "So you went behind my back to the club," he stated.

"Dad–"

"You might as well carry her out," Tristan chimed in, my eyes darting back to him. They were darker and that anger was back that I felt so small.

"She will walk, she is a big girl." My father scoffed and he made me feel so pathetic, "I...I will deal with you at home, so let's go." he said sternly and I hesitated because I was never one for trouble. "Make it snappy!" my dad clapped his hands, making me jump, he was angry alright. I stood up and followed him out, without any other word or a glance back at Tristan.

Tristan called my dad after I begged him not to and for me to stay the night. But what did I expect? He was being a parent and he definitely wouldn't want to sit with a young girl like me who was careless and followed her friends' bad decisions. Maybe I should've just told Cris that I wouldn't be going with her, but she's like a sister to me and I wouldn't want her to be all by herself in these places.

My father will definitely have to punish me for this too. I just have to brace myself for it even though I feel like shit.

Grounded

Tristan

I was still furious. I wanted to tell Elona something that she wouldn't like. She had been saved by her father because I would've hurt her feelings. I don't know if she would've handled it well enough to not take it too personal, but at that point I had to bite my tongue with her. I nearly gave in to her when she begged me if she could stay the night and not tell David. I just couldn't do that, not after this evening. This will be a lesson for both of them. I opened the door to Cris' bedroom. She was lying across the bed on her stomach, her feet hanging off the bed.

"Cris–" She turned around and sat up straight.

"It was all me. Elona didn't have to be punished too. I was the one who wanted to go; she didn't want me to go alone. It's all on me—I forced her to come with me," she said, her eyes glazing over.

I moved to her desk, and sat on it slightly, folding my arms over my chest, furrowing my brows. "I told you not to go and ...you went behind my fucking back, how fucking disrespectful is that to me?!" I roared at her. She swallowed. "You could've put yourself and your friend in danger. If something had gone wrong, I at least hope you would have called me. I'm glad that Uncle Steve owns that fucking club." I let out a breath.

"I'm sorry, Dad," she said softly.

"That won't make up for what you just did. How can I trust you again after this?" I asked.

"I won't do it again and, besides, I'm at the legal age, so technically, next year I will be out of your hair."

"And yet you are still fucking going on about it. You don't understand. You are fucking grounded for a month, and you won't be seeing Elona for the entire month either," I said.

"Dad, she did nothing wrong and we are inseparable. Please Dad, allow me to see her," she begged, and those pleading eyes reminded me of Estelle, although Cris has my color eyes. I licked my lips as my heart missed Estelle. I shook my head.

"No, the only time that you will see Elona is at school and when you both walk home together. But you will not hang out together after school. You won't have anyone else over, you are only to leave this house if there is something important that I approve of beforehand," I warned.

"But Elona is important, she is like a sister to me, Dad," she said so sweetly. That alone was reason enough for me to avoid even glancing at Elona in a way I shouldn't.

"You are grounded, don't make me take away other things as well, you can at least text and call Elona as a way of hanging out after school," I held her gaze one last time before walking towards the door.

"I won that essay contest, I didn't want to tell you, but it was about mom," she said. I froze in my spot in the doorway. I took a deep breath, not sure what to say to that because things took a shift in my emotions because of Estelle. I walked away without another word not even congratulating her.

I went back to the study room to continue burying myself in work as best as I do in these circumstances of pain. I sat on the leather chair, my elbows on the desk and I ran my hands over my face. Tears escaped, running down my cheeks. Will this pain ever stop?

I remember reading a paragraph from Cris' essay that was on the coffee table when they had to write the essay. I remember those words and they struck my heart all over again.

The Radiance of a Beautiful Mother

A mother is often the heartbeat of a family, the pillar of strength, and the embodiment of love. Her beauty extends beyond physical appearance, radiating from the depths of her selfless devotion to her daughter and her husband. Whether in the simple act of preparing a favorite meal or offering a comforting embrace, a mother's love creates a sanctuary in which her daughter finds solace and security. The loss of such a beautiful soul leaves an indelible void that cannot be filled.

I simply couldn't read it any further. And then Elona happened. I leaned back in my chair, and took the phone out of my pocket. Fuck. Maggie spammed my phone with a ton of missed calls and texts. I was oblivious to these texts and missed calls when I tried to call David in my study room to have him come pick Elona up. It had been silent since I left to get the girls at Galaxy.

My phone's screen lit up again and Maggie's name appeared. I let out a sigh and answered, "Maggie, I'm so sorry but something came up with my daughter. We can have dinner next time when things are better over here," I said. I was more in a mood for not doing anything at all, but if thoughts of Elona kept overtaking my mind, Maggie would've been a good fuck, but not even that would make things better, because Elona would always be there.

"Is she okay?" she asked with concern.

"No," I lied, Cris was perfectly fine except for the part that she was grounded.

"I hope that whatever it is, she will be okay soon. We can have dinner next time, just call me," she said.

"Thank you," I replied and then I hung up, not wanting to prolong the phone call. I placed my phone on the desk. My wedding ring which I still kept on my finger, caught my attention, I slid it off my finger, inspecting it. There was an inscription engraved on the inside, *Yours for eternity*, "What have I done, Estelle?" I said softly as if my wife was here with me. Watching over the mess that I put myself in because of a young woman who is not even out of school yet. I pulled the drawer to my desk open, and I placed it there, keeping it safe.

I feel as if I have disappointed Estelle. Maybe she wasn't happy with me and with Cris acting out. Perhaps she misses her mother, maybe that was the reason she brought up the essay. She was walking on eggshells when Estelle passed away. I was too broken and tried to hide it. I guess my ugly sobs in my bedroom at night were what she heard because, the next morning, she would be concerned yet said nothing. She didn't want to make me sob all over again.

It was since her mother died, I got better at hiding my emotions by burying myself in work. Yet, it still hurt like a fucker. I never stopped and asked how she was when she started to get some life back into her a year after Estelle passed away.

We never spoke about things in detail, but she was such a happy child even up to this day. Maybe she had been bottling everything up, but I think that while she is grounded, we can put a stop to that and talk about things.

Punishment

Elona

I felt so sick as we stepped into the house. My father was silent. I squinted at the light in the lounge as we entered. My father closed the door behind me. I was waiting for some sort of punishment from him. I just didn't like what Tristan had said to my father, that I should be carried because that felt like he was disgusted with me. Well...I don't blame him. I do feel disgusted with myself, especially with what I was wearing.

"Sit down," he demanded, and I sat down on the sofa. He walked to the recliner which was across from me. I took a deep breath. "Why did you do this?" he asked as he held my gaze. He was clearly disappointed in me.

"Cris was going to go and I didn't want her going alone, I wanted to make sure she was safe. What I'm wearing was her idea. She put out these clothes for me and I was going to wear them for modeling, but after this event, I don't think I want to look at these clothes anymore because I feel disgusted. I drank Tequila and it was the first time that I drank, so...I just wanted to be there for her because I didn't want anything to happen to her. She is a sister to me and I felt that it was necessary to protect her. You know how she can be... Sometimes she can't be left alone. She forces things against a person's will even if she has to do something on her own. Spooky was invited but he was a more mature one and kept a protective eye on us."

"I want to meet this Spooky," he said, and I was surprised by his reaction.

"You do?" I asked. Suddenly, I felt awake and better, but not better enough.

"Yeah, I want to meet all of your friends," my shoulders sagged. Is this his way of trying to see what friends I hang out with?

"Well, Spooky is a great friend, he is all to himself. He also does photography. I asked him to take some of my photos for my modeling portfolio. He wants to pursue photography." I said with a smile.

"Well, I want to meet him tomorrow. Make sure that he is here at 1 PM. You can start your photoshoot here." I couldn't believe what I was hearing.

"Are you serious?" I asked.

"I am one hundred percent serious. This is for your future. You are becoming a young woman who will soon leave the nest and, as much as I want to protect you from the world out there and to stop you from making bad decisions, I won't be able to control you or make those decisions for you. I can only offer you advice." He chuckled and shook his head, " I don't know what Cris must be going through right now because Uncle Tristan will punish her," he chuckled again.

I wanted to text Cris to see if she was okay, but my mind drifted to Tristan again and the way that he looked at me, his words being a reminder. "So, you won't be punishing me, right?" I had to make sure.

"I won't be punishing you." he smiled at me. "But please change and throw those clothes away," he said, and I returned his smile.

I jumped up but it was a bad idea. My stomach turned and I took a deep breath, easing my nausea. "Thanks, Dad," I said softly, and then I walked up the stairs to my bedroom.

Once I got to my bedroom, I went to the en suite bathroom and threw up again. I wanted to sleep and get better. I don't think that I will be able to send Cris a text after this, I felt too sick. I changed into my pajamas, which were shorts and a tank top and discarded my clothes in the corner of my bedroom. That will be going into the trashcan tomorrow.

I got into bed with my phone on my bedside table and I was out like a candle.

* * *

I heard my phone chime beside me on the bedside table and I reached out to it. Squinting my eyes from the sleep that I was deeply in, I saw his name on my screen...Crane. I don't know if I was seeing it properly, but I blinked my eyes, and it became clearer. It was Tristan. I clicked on his text.

Crane: Are you okay?

I furrowed my brows at that question. Am I okay? I typed a quick reply to him.

Me: Why do you care?

I placed my phone on the bedside table again and it chimed. I reached out to get the phone, it was him again.

Crane: Do not answer a question with a question. Are you okay?

I was so exhausted that I just discarded my phone on my bed and darkness consumed me.

* * *

I squinted as the sun shone through my window. I forgot to close my curtains. My head was throbbing, but I guess I could manage it. I lay on my back, stretching and yawning. I looked at the bedside table for my phone. I remember having the text dream about Tristan. I reached out for my phone so that I could send Cris a text about how her punishment went. I didn't feel my phone and I sat up straight, it wasn't there.

I threw my blanket off me and there my phone was, lying on my bed. I sighed and then I went through my text, to mine and Cris chat, but I saw Tristan's text above Cris, the text from Tristan was from 2 AM. I went into our chat and there it was, the texts from my dream.

It wasn't a dream, and I didn't even reply back to him. Why was he so concerned about me after he literally called my father to get me? I was mad at him for that part. I was also embarrassed about the way that I had responded to him via text. I was all about respect. I just left the text unanswered and typed a text to Cris instead saying that Spooky would be coming over today and how my way of punishment went. I then texted Spooky to come over today and that he should be prepared for my father.

As much as I wanted to forget about Tristan, it was difficult. But I know that we can't pursue anything. It is just wrong to all of us. I should move on and find someone my own age as difficult as it would be because this can only be a phase, right?

Tough Decisions

Tristan

I couldn't stop thinking about Elona last night. I wanted to know if she was okay. Part of me was concerned. Hell, maybe the whole of me was concerned about her. I texted her and I didn't expect her responses to be the way that they were. It was unlike her, but I guess I deserved it. I was a bastard to her last night, thinking about it she probably had a right to be angry. This is what happens when I'm pissed off. Maybe it's a good thing that I'm punishing Cris, so that not only does she not see Elona, but I don't see her around as well and that will hopefully help me to stay away from her and move away from something that was risky...too forbidden.

"So, when are you going to see Maggie again?" Cris asked me. I looked up at her. She was sitting across from me at the dinner table, taking a sip of orange juice, her pancakes with syrup in front of her. My fences went up with the mention of Maggie because I don't want to see her again, but I know Cris will be persistent about it.

"Is this your way of trying to sneak away to see Elona?" I asked as I scowled at her. I reached for my mug of black coffee and took a sip while I held a business document in my other hand. I placed the mug on the table.

"No, but that isn't a bad idea," she said in thought.

"Don't you even think about it," I warned her.

She giggled, "Relax, Dad. I'm kidding. I just want you to go out and have fun too. Live a little bit," she said, concern laced in her voice.

"I am living." She rolled her eyes at my response.

"At least I will be stuck with my schoolwork and my journalism while Elona gets to have a fun photoshoot at the house, and I'm not there for it," she sighed as she inspected her piece of pancake before she placed it into her mouth.

"What photoshoot?" I asked, my brows furrowed.

"A-A photoshoot that she has to do for whatever-whatever she wants to pursue," she fumbled over her words as she was trying to figure out what to say, and I knew that there was more to it. But the way I felt was like my heart was beating at a rapid pace, and I was about to explode if there was anything that was going to happen with a photoshoot. "I was supposed to be there at her house where the photoshoot will take place, but I'm stuck here," she let out a sigh.

I got up immediately and as I nearly walked to the front door, I had to stop myself because this would raise questions from Cris. I can't have that happen. I turned around, took the mug from the table, and went to the sink, pouring the rest of my coffee down the drain, and leaving the mug in the sink thereafter. I wanted to go and see what this was all about. "What kind of photoshoot is it?" I asked, trying to be calm, as if I was not that interested, but I was failing miserably. This is the effect that Elona has on me, and it is bad. I still can't help the way that I feel. It's like...no other woman can do it for me but her. No other woman is good for me but her.

"I'm not sure, why are you so stressed?" She asked me and I turned around, she was already looking at me.

"Work," I replied as I rounded the kitchen counter.

"No wonder you are dressed in your suit. Just take it easy, Dad. Stress is not good, and you need a break. Ever since mom died, you have been working non-stop and I never saw you go on vacation or at least take a break on a weekend. I find you in the study room every weekend." she sighed.

"I am fine, I'm going to pop in and see Uncle David... we have some work matters to discuss." I lied about my reason for going to Elona's house. I wanted to see what was going on over there and if David was actually at the house while her photoshoot was happening. I stopped beside Cris and leaned down, placing a kiss on the top of her head.

"Great," she said as she let out a breath because she couldn't leave the house and then I left.

I was so eager to get to Elona's house, I walked as fast as I could down the street. David's car was in the driveway. I let out a breath of relief because he was home. When I got to the front door, I knocked. I was here...at Elona's house once again. What the fuck is wrong with me?

As I considered turning around to walk away, the front door opened. "Tristan? Is everything okay? Is there any more trouble regarding the girls?" David asked me. Elona was in trouble alright.

"Not at all. Cris is grounded for a month, and I wanted to come over to just relax," I lied.

He scoffed, "Since when do you come over to just chill anymore? You work on the weekends too, since Estelle.... you know what I mean," he said.

"Can't I just have a break and chill with my friend?" I asked, eager to get inside the house as I burned my gaze into him.

"Okay, sorry for asking, it's just...I'm not used to this. Come on in," he finally moved out of the way. I was supposed to go to my company, but that had changed, and it was scorching outside. I didn't care, I just took off my jacket and placed it neatly on the sofa. "Would you like a beer, Scotch, Whiskey, or water? " He offered as he walked into the kitchen.

"None, thanks," I said as I shoved my hands in my pants pockets after rolling up my white shirt sleeves.

I heard laughter coming from the backyard, the sliding door was open. I furrowed my brows, "Elona is doing a photoshoot. I have allowed her to do this. Spooky is a wonderful guy," he smiled, and my gaze landed on him.

"What is he doing here?" I asked. My brows furrowed.

"He is the photographer for Elona," I bit on my teeth as I wanted to tell him shit. I wanted to explode. "I trust him with Elona, and he is very down-to-earth. Hopefully, they will be more than just friends in the future. He is someone that I can see Elona being with. He is very respectful too," he said as he smiled, and I had to fight not to lash out at what he was saying about Spooky...what kind of nickname is that, by the way? Maybe this is really for the best that she has someone else to be with. But my feelings and my heart are saying something different from what my head is.

I followed after David towards the sliding door. I was eager to see what was going on. We stopped by the sliding door and my heart nearly jumped out of my chest. I clenched my jaw as I watched Elona, who was dressed in a leopard print bikini, standing on the step inside the pool. Her hair was wet as she smiled at Spooky who was talking to her and looking down at his camera in his hands. It was just the two of them and I wanted to separate them as far apart as possible.

"Hey," I snapped out of it as David lightly hit my shoulder to get my attention. "You are staring at them as if they shouldn't be together, and I understand what this looks like, but who cares, if they decide to date then I give my permission. I would rather have him take her photos than a hungry man who looks at my daughter like a piece of meat." he turned his attention back to them. I swallowed. I have to tread carefully. "I know that I won't always be around to protect her, but there are men out there, and I will kill anyone that lays a finger on her that shouldn't be," he said, and then he walked back to the kitchen.

I was not sure what he had meant by that. I hope that he does not suspect anything about me or the way that I look at her. I was torn by him and my daughter and my feelings for Elona. This will be a dangerous situation, but I can't get her out of my head no matter how much I try, I absolutely do not want spooky around her, but that is something I can't prevent. What the fuck do I do?

Sweet Torture

Sweet Torture

Tristan

I remain at the sliding door. David was in the kitchen which was spacious. I could still hear Elona and Spooky laughing and I tried my utmost best to not look their way as David turned around to look at me. He stood behind the kitchen counter. I didn't know what to say because I'm here for Elona, and now I can't do shit. I'm barely even trying to be calm.

"Are you okay?" David asked, looking at me with concern.

"Yeah, I'm fine," I replied, and before I knew it, Spooky entered as he and Elona were talking.

She entered after him, but as she moved past me, holding a towel around her, she tripped, and I reached out, catching her. I held her body against mine, my gaze falling onto her parted lips. Trying my utmost best not to lean in and kiss those lips. Her hand was gripping my shirt, and then I moved my gaze up to her eyes. They were huge with shock.

"How was the photoshoot?" I heard David ask.

I cleared my throat and let her go, but my gaze still held hers. "Are you okay?" I asked softly. I could feel myself softening up from the way that I felt just moments before. She somehow had that effect on me.

She nodded, "Yeah." she replied and moved away as Spooky and David were talking. If they weren't here, I might've kissed her, I could feel my dick strain against my pants and I turned away from them, looking out the sliding door so that they wouldn't see my erection and just then in a split second, it was flaccid when I heard Elona laugh with Spooky and all my anger and... jealousy crept up.

"So why don't you go to the movies tonight?" David asked. I turned around to face them. Spooky and Elona were each sitting on a barstool at the kitchen counter while David was leaning over it, his elbows resting on the counter.

"That is not a bad idea," Spooky said, "I enjoy good films," I walked towards them, and took a seat beside Elona, and she pulled the towel further over her. I could sense her nervousness.

"I think that you both should focus on schoolwork, especially after what happened last night," I chimed in, my gaze burning into Spooky.

"I think that Tristan is right about that," David said, and I was relieved that he agreed with me.

I could see Elona's shoulders sag. I will never allow them to go out together alone. I wasn't going to have Cris join them either because, at this point, I don't trust her due to last night.

"I guess that I better go," Spooky said, and then he looked at Elona. "I will text you," he said as he stood up from the barstool. The anger was back. I didn't like that one bit. I clenched my jaw and I looked at David.

"I better get back home," I told him.

"But you hardly chilled, you basically just got here," he seemed surprised.

"I need to check up on my daughter, and make sure she hasn't attempted to leave the house while she is grounded," I lied and got up from the barstool.

"Very well," David stood up straight.

"I will see myself out, I will walk with Spooky. See you soon," I said.

"Pop in anytime when you need to," David smiled at me and I knew what he meant by that. He wanted me not to bury myself in work all the time. He wanted me to chill with him more often. That includes the bar because that is his favorite place to hang out. Since Estelle passed away, I have never liked to hang out at the bar or club. There were women hitting on me and I didn't have time for that.

I didn't bother to look at Elona when I left. Once Spooky and I were out of the house and on the sidewalk, I stopped him. "I don't want you to distract Elona from anything. Stay away from her and don't even bother to text her," I warned him.

"Mr. Crane, I'm her friend, and I can see her whenever we can see each other. That means we will also see each other at school. You cannot stop me from texting her. You are not her father, and you are definitely not my father," he said, and this just pissed me off further.

"I don't know who you think you are talking to; I am way older than you and you will respect me. So do as I say," I stepped closer to him. He doesn't move.

"I don't know why you have a problem with me being friends with Elona, why not tell me just to stay away from Cris? I may be a person that people think that they can bully and threaten, but I don't care, I have been there and been through it all, and it made me be this person that I am today. I know that you may be feeling something for her, you care for her because you have always been there since she was a little girl, and you are treating her as your daughter, so I understand that part. But I am only her friend," he said and that took me aback. I never expected him to say all of that.

"What do you mean by saying that I feel something for her?" I asked.

"Well, I can see the way you look at her, but who knows I might be wrong," he shrugged, "Can I go home now?"

I have to play it safe because I cannot fail in this regard because it is too risky. "Yeah, but I mean what I said, stay away," I warned, and then I turned around without saying another word to him and walked back to my house.

I have to be extra careful around people. I don't want to be killed by my friend because I'm after his daughter and I don't need any more problems in my life. I think that it is best that I stay away for now so that I do not make things obvious because I do know that I had a few slip-ups in front of them that I had to quickly cover. This was the beginning of my sweet, unbearable torture.

A Slip Of A Finger

Elona

I didn't expect Tristan to come over to my house yesterday. I nearly thought that he would kiss me, the way that he looked at me was sending electricity throughout my whole body. I know that I can't have him. I'm trying to move on and focus on myself with modeling and being a friend to Cris and Spooky. I didn't like it when he told us not to go out. My father agreed with him. But I guess that he was correct, we did need to focus on our schoolwork.

Cris and I usually would walk to school in the mornings together, but she texted me that Tristan would take her to school this morning. I walked alone as Spooky informed me that he would meet me there, which was weird because we usually walked together as well. Am I missing something?

When I arrived at school, Spooky and Cris were waiting for me at the entrance. "It's by time you came, it's like..." she checked her phone before looking up at us again, "One minute left, so we have to hurry," Cris said as she walked in front of us. Spooky and I walked in step.

"I'm sorry that I didn't walk with you this morning. I had to leave the house earlier than usual," Spooky said.

"It's okay," I replied.

"I really don't like her, and I hope that he doesn't think that she will be my future stepmother," Cris said with irritation as she stood, facing the admin department which was across from our class. I looked in the direction and saw that Tristan was standing at the desk of Miss Jennings. She was the school secretary, she was attractive, and I have no doubt that she had his attention.

He was leaning over the desk which was high, and he was writing something down. She was smiling at him, being all flirtatious.

"I guess that it's your father's choice. At the end of the day, he can choose whom he wants to be with," Spooky said with disdain.

"Come on, I can't even look over there," Cris entered the classroom, and as I was about to follow after them, Tristan stood up straight, placing the pen on the desk, and then he turned around. He froze in his spot when he saw me and then his gaze moved over to Spooky, his brows furrowed. I dragged my feet and entered the classroom, turning my back to him.

I didn't see him flirt back with Miss Jennings and I know the type of man that Tristan is, although I feel as if my heart had sunk for a split second, but this is school, he can do anything here because Cris is attending this school, so anything is possible besides the whole dating thing that Cris is going on about. I know the type of woman that he would want. He sure hates a woman that throws themselves at him.

I sat at my desk and Spooky had moved from the other side of the room, sitting in front of me now. "Why don't we do another photoshoot?" I asked him, "I mean...I need one last bikini photoshoot, and then we can do something else such as the park or walking home kind of theme." He was sitting sideways, facing the windows on the opposite side of the classroom, and then he looked at me.

"Well, I had an idea last night, the whole part of the movie theater. It was going to be that theme. It would've looked amazing for both of our portfolios, but your father had to kill that idea," he moved his attention to Cris when he mentioned the last part.

"Well, you are my photographer, and my dad knows what they are for, so it's just as important. Be at my place later," I said.

"I wish that I could be there, but don't forget to send me some pictures," Cris said excitedly.

"I know that your father is only looking out for both of you and Elona is like a daughter to him, so I don't blame him because I'm a guy. But I'm only a friend, and I'm not interested in Elona and, right now, I'm not that into relationships, but there is someone that I like."

"Who?" Cris squealed, causing the rest of the students to look at her until they turned back to their conversations.

"I'd rather not say," Spooky smiled at her before he turned around in his seat, his back facing me again.

"You have to tell me!" Cris went on about it. I smiled as I took my phone out of my pocket. Our teacher was late for class, so I might as well just send Cris some selfies that I took yesterday after the bikini photoshoot.

My phone was held under the desk, and I quickly pressed on her chat. I sent four pictures, of which three were a bit revealing and one was a bodysuit lingerie that was on my bed. I had yet to take a photoshoot in that bodysuit. I pressed send and then I typed the following.

Me: What do you think?

I quickly shoved my phone back into the pocket of my jeans when our teacher entered. We were not allowed to be on our phones in class or else it would be confiscated for up to a month. I can't have that.

We started the lesson, and I felt a couple of vibrations from my phone, and I looked over at Cris, but she was very focused on the whiteboard in front of the class as Miss Johnson was teaching. She had no phone in her hand and as eager as I currently was, something was telling me to check my phone. So, I took my phone out of my pocket and checked it under the desk. It was from Tristan.

I pressed on his name to check his text, but nothing had prepared me for when I saw that I had sent my revealing photos of myself to him. He already saw me in a bikini twice, so that shouldn't matter, right? My heart stopped for like a minute, and now its beating fast. I do not know what to do or say.

Crane: Fuck.

The Surprise Text

Tristan

I was still thinking about Elona. The feeling of jealousy that I felt when I saw Spooky, who was still with her after I told him to stay away from her just made me angry. I don't know what to do to get him away from her. I was asked to make a fucking speech at the school's career day. I simply agreed because my daughter would be encouraging me to do it. I hate the idea of having to give a speech in front of students who might not even have an interest in business or anything about it. But I did it for my daughter. I signed the paper that I would attend, but nothing irritated me more than Miss Jennings, who constantly threw herself at me. I wanted to leave, I even wished for someone else to assist me. I hate that type of women.

Now, I'm back at work, at a meeting that I've been preparing for. I have billions, and yet I'll work hard. I will not waste my time just because I have money, but I do have a Crane foundation and I do good where my heart leads me to. My mind drifted away to Elona before I was interrupted.

"I see that you would like to expand the hospital, and that is a great investment. Everyone at the hospital will appreciate it, the new equipment that we need, and this is all thanks to you, Mr. Crane," One of the board members of the hospital told me, this was something that was dear to my heart.

"Your wife would've been so proud of the good that you are constantly doing," the other said.

I nodded my head with a faint smile. I knew that she would be. That was important. I have many ideas as to where my vision was going in regard to not only this hospital but the others as well.

Once Estelle passed away, and I started to bury myself in work non-stop, I wanted to invest in the hospital, and I've done that ever since. My phone chimed on the boardroom table, and I reached for it while the meeting continued. There were seven members in the meeting, and they were talking about other ventures.

Elona's name popped up, and I pressed on her text. Nothing prepared me for what I looked at. She was in revealing clothes that showed a bit more than expected, and it woke my dick up. She sent this to me. ME. Was this on purpose? I studied her images, and she was so fucking attractive despite me seeing her in a bikini already, this was the cherry on top. Lingerie.

There was a bodysuit that was on a bed, and I was eager to see her in that one. How it would hug her body...every curve. My erection was straining against my pants, and I needed her, even though I knew that I couldn't. She asked me what I thought.

All I could do was reply with, "Fuck," I then continued to send her texts because she was supposed to be in class, and why was she using her phone in class?

Me: I'm in a boardroom meeting, and you sent these pictures to me.

Me: Do you know what that does to me?

Me: Shouldn't you be in class?

I was eager for a response from her. I was oblivious to the meeting. I looked up from my phone as the members continued without me saying anything. My phone chimed in my hand, and I looked back at the screen, it was her.

Elona: It was meant for someone else. I'm so sorry.

That stirred the anger inside of me.

Me: Who was it meant for? I will beat the shit out of him.

Elona: So, you would beat the shit out of your own daughter?

Me: Watch that little mouth of yours.

Elona: Or what?

I was surprised that she wanted to know what I would do to her. The confidence.

Me: You wouldn't want to know the things that I would do to you.

Elona: What would that be?

Me: I would...it isn't appropriate for someone like you.

Elona: Well, there was my essay.

I found myself smirking as I typed my next reply.

Me: Fucking smart ass.

Me: I want to see you in this.

I sent her the image of the bodysuit lingerie...I really wanted to see her in that.

Elona: Not going to happen.

Me: I will see you later.

I was about to place my phone on the table as the meeting was about to wrap up, but my phone chimed almost immediately. She was fast.

Elona: I will be busy. I have things to do.

Me: Part of those things include me. I will see you one way or another.

She won't get away from me that easily, not after this.

Elona: I'm joining a modeling agency. I will be busy.

My jaw clenched as I read that text over. Modeling agency. No wonder she had been doing photoshoots. I'm not happy about that. It was as if things were just becoming worse.

Me: You won't join them. I don't want anyone else to see your body.

I let out a frustrated breath.

Elona: What I do is none of your business.

This young woman will give me a heart attack.

Me: You made it my business when you sent those pictures to me.

Me: Does your dad know about the modeling?

Elona: Yes, he knows about it.

Fuck.

Me: I will have a word with him.

I'm not going to let David put Elona in an industry that also has men that are hungry for women like her.

Elona: Please, leave him out of this.

Me: I love it when you're begging me. Now, focus in class. I will see you later, one way or another.

The meeting wrapped up, and I was desperate to see Elona. I ended up finishing my remaining work for the day before I left the office. I refused to look at my phone, I was ignoring Elona's possible texts. I checked up on Cris at home, and she was focused on her journalism projects that she had to prepare for, and I was happy about that. I told her that I was going to run some errands, and then I left and went to Elona's house.

David wasn't at home because he was busy with work as he had told me earlier in the day. I didn't knock on the front door. It was already unlocked, and I entered. As I walked further into the house, I heard laughter and when I went to the kitchen, Elona and Spooky were standing by the kitchen counter, each with a glass of juice in their hands. Elona's hair was dry and gorgeously blown out. She was in a black bikini top, her breasts threatening to spill. How I wanted to hold them. She was at least wearing denim shorts.

I cleared my throat to snap out of my desires and blood was rushing to my dick. They both looked at me. Elona's eyes were huge. Did she really think that I was joking? "Uncle Tristan," Elona said under her breath, and she swallowed.

"Well, I have to leave and focus on homework. I'll send you all the pictures once they are ready," Spooky told her as he left his now empty glass on the counter. "See you tomorrow," Elona only nodded, she was glued to her spot in surprise. "Mr. Crane," Spooky said with disdain as he walked past me.

Elona and I continued to stare at each other until I heard the front door close. "Would you like orange juice? Freshly squeezed? My dad is still at work," she said.

I smirked, she seemed all shy in front of me, but via text, she was all confident...let me not get started when she does the photoshoots. "The orange juice would be nice," I replied.

She placed her half-empty glass on the counter, and then she took an orange from the fruit bowl and then grabbed a knife out of the drawer, she started cutting the orange in a quarter. I moved behind her. Pressing my hard dick against her perfect ass. I moved her hair behind her ear, and leaned in, my breath against her. She gasped, pausing at what she was doing. "I don't want him around you, or any other male for that matter. I will get what I want. You will not be pursuing modeling."

I moved my hands slowly down her arms until I reached her hands. She let go of the orange and the knife. I turned her around. I studied her face as I held onto the counter behind her. My gaze was on her lips. They parted, her breathing heavy. Her chest rose and fell. I leaned in closer, inches away from her lips. I held myself there just studying them, I was so close to kissing her, I could feel her warm breath. My sweet torture that will come to an end with just one kiss.

So Close

Tristan

I was so close to getting what I wanted.... what I needed. I wanted her so badly, I want to be inside of her badly, but that has to wait. I need to just focus on this moment. Savor it. She licked her lips and they parted again. I want to suck on them. I wanted to make her mine, so that no one else could have her. I sucked in a deep breath, and I reached for a piece of orange behind her. I pulled inches away from her lips to study her face. Her eyes were on my lips.

"You're so fucking beautiful. I never thought that you would ever occupy my mind the way that you are. I can't stop thinking about you," I rasped.

She gasped and I loved the sound of that. I moved the orange towards her lips, and I squeezed, the juice dripping onto her bottom lip and into her mouth. I kept my gaze on her lips, I placed the orange back on the counter behind her and I leaned in. I was just inches away from her lips, I was going to do this.

I took the plunge and my lips barely brushed hers. "Elona, I'm home!" I pulled away from her immediately and quickly reached to the top cupboard, taking a glass out, and Elona continued with the orange. "Here you are... Tristan?" I turned around to face David, he smiled at me with confusion. I gave him a faint smile.

"I came over to chill, so I decided to wait here for you." I lied, "Elona is just making orange juice," my heart was beating at a rapid pace.

I felt like an awkward teenager. He moved to the counter and Elona turned towards me, but then the orange that she held in her hand fell on the ground, and then she bent over to pick it up. My eyes fell on her breasts that were now really threatening to spill. I could see the darkness of her areola starting to show. Blood rushed to my dick as I stared and as I wished that I could see more, she stood up straight and adjusted her bikini top to my disappointment.

I cleared my throat as she took the glass from me, she kept her gaze on me before turning around. "I like to see you here often. You need to get out more." David said as he sat on the barstool. Elona held out the glass of freshly squeezed juice and I took it from her before she tidied up. "So, how's work?"

"I needed a break, and the meeting went well. They are going to expand the hospital, and they will be getting more equipment. It's one thing that I'm so happy about. I'm just focusing on my next venture." I replied, and I took a sip of the orange juice, which reminded me of moments ago and my gaze automatically went to Elona as she now sat beside her father. She was eating a banana. That banana. I teased her with one before.

I was happy that David couldn't see my erection earlier. It went flaccid as soon as I spoke to him. I thought that this moment would be it. The kiss...but it's like there was always something that kept on happening in order for me not to kiss her and that frustrated me. I wanted her...I needed her. I'm going insane, and I never felt this way before.

"I'm glad," he smiled. "How's Maggie? Have you seen her again?"

I glanced at Elona briefly, her expression had changed. "I don't know. I haven't seen her since the other day, and I don't plan on seeing her again." I told him. Elona seemed hopeful now.

"Tristan, you need to live a little more," he said.

"I am living," I groaned in frustration, he was beginning to sound like Cris now with the whole living life thing.

"You're not living the way that you should be. Let's go out tonight," he suggested. Elona let out a breath as she focused on her orange juice in front of her.

"I just want to chill."

"Okay. There is no use in getting you to go out." He replied before turning his attention to Elona. "So, how was school and how is your portfolio coming along?" he asked her.

"It was okay. I just have some homework to finish and Spooky was over here to do another photoshoot." That son of a bitch is going to make me do things that I regret. I clenched my jaw. "Our portfolios are coming together well. We do want to go to the movies and do a movie theater-themed photoshoot and I think that it would be perfect. Please, allow us to go, it's important for our future," she begged him, and I didn't want that to happen. Yet, I have no say in it right now.

"It is for your future, so you have my permission to go," he smiled at her.

"Thanks, Dad. I will text Spooky." she smiled. I tried to keep calm. So, I gulped the rest of the juice instead. I walked to the sink and placed the empty glass inside and as I turned around, David stood up.

"I just need to make a quick call," he said.

"I will be leaving, so I will see you around," I told him as he walked away, shaking his head in disappointment. I know what he was thinking that my chilling with him was not that long. But I had to lie, and I know that one lie leads to more.

As soon as David disappeared, Elona got up. I moved towards her as she rounded the counter and I stopped her, pushing her against the cupboard, which was a long cupboard that held cleaning materials in there. She gasped and I caged her in.

I studied her face, and I licked my lips to moisten them. "You will not go with Spooky to the movie theater. You will not do modeling. I won't allow you to do that. I want to see you in that lingerie. Only me," I was stern, yet I wanted to kiss her.

"You cannot tell me what I can and can't do. I will pursue my career and I will be friends with whomever I want. You're grounding your daughter, so spooky is all that I have right now. And with regard to the lingerie...that won't happen," she swallowed, she was struggling, she wanted me too, and I would have my way with her.

"You don't know what you're doing to me, and I'm not done with you. I'll finish where I have left off. One way or another," her breathing increased, and I know she was feeling it...the intensity. But she did hit a nerve with me. That involved Cris. It seemed like I had to un-ground my daughter.

I pulled away as much as I didn't want to. David would be in the kitchen anytime and I couldn't risk him seeing us in an inappropriate way. I was not ready to lose him yet as a friend. But I will get what I want. I forced myself to leave. I will kiss her, but now I have something to take care of.

Another Word

Tristan

I didn't want Elona to go with Spooky to the movie theater. That was the last thing that I wanted. I was pissed. That prick better not agree to go. As I walked down the street

towards my house, I contemplated whether to go to Spooky's house and make sure that he would not go. I turned around, and walked all the way past Elona's house until I reached Spooky's.

I walked down the driveway, the garden was not really cared for, and I scrunched my face at it. I love a neat garden. This neighborhood is for luxury, for wealthy people, but this place seemed to be abandoned. I walked up a few steps and I rang the doorbell.

The door opened, "Mr Crane, is everything okay?" Spooky asked, hesitating as he looked past me to check if there was anyone else with me, and then he looked at me again.

I'm even annoyed with him wearing black all the time. "I need you to stay away from Elona. She wants to go to the movies with you and I don't want you to agree to that."

"Um...you are a little too late for that. She already texted me like two minutes ago, and I agreed," he said.

"You will tell her that something came up," I said through clenched teeth, moving a step forward while scowling at him.

"Tristan, that won't happen, she is my friend," he scoffed and shook his head in disbelief.

"It's Mr Crane for you," I warned him, moving closer to him.

"I know that you might be jealous of me being around Elona, and it is actually funny, but I didn't do anything wrong to jeopardize my friendship with her or your daughter. You are not Elona's father and I get that maybe you want to look out for her, but it's more than that and I won't be saying anything about it because I can clearly see why you're so jealous, it makes you...possessive of the person that you want, and it makes you cruel to the ones that you love. I've seen things in my years at school. I'm quite the observer, I don't say a word, but look at how things unfold. I've seen how she looks at you too. Your secret is safe with me, but just know that you will never stop me from seeing her," he smirked at me. "I'll see her tonight, and thanks for the little visit, Mr Crane," he emphasized my last name before closing the door in my face. That prick.

I clenched my jaw and let out a frustrated breath as I ran my hand through my hair. I don't know what I will do with him, but he knows that there is something between Elona and myself where nothing really happened, not even a fucking kiss. I have to be careful because I do not trust him.

When I got to my house, Cris was sitting at the dining table, sipping coffee and scrolling through her phone. "We need to talk," I said, as I pulled the chair out of the table and took a seat. She looked up from her phone as she placed the mug gently on the table.

"Am I free to go?" She asked, her eyes wide.

"Yes, but there is a reason for it," I said before she could get all excited.

"What is it?" she leaned back in the chair, narrowing her eyes at me.

"Spooky and Elona are going to the movie theater tonight, and I think that you should join them. I don't trust them to be alone. I want you to keep an eye on them, and you can have fun, but you need to behave or face the consequences of being grounded again," I warned.

She scoffed, "Dad, I get that you are being overprotective of Elona for some reason, but she can be with whomever she wants to unless Uncle David says otherwise. She will be in college next year, and she will be making her own choices," she smirked as she reached for her mug and took a sip of her coffee again.

I narrowed my eyes at her, "Why are you smirking like that?" I asked.

"Well, whenever you grounded me, you never ground me until the end of the period given to me because you feel too sorry after a while, it was just a matter of time. And I know that you're looking out for Elona as a daughter too, but... I was an only child for so long, you and mom never tried again after me." she looked at me with sadness in her eyes and I just couldn't look at her without feeling as if I would break down. "I'm sorry to bring up Mom, but you having fun and being with Maggie made me feel happy for you, why don't you go and see her? Maybe this time you can be happy again. Maybe I won't be an only child after all." I looked up at her, furrowing my brows because I knew what she was saying...but I don't want any kids. "Elona has been there all the years, she is a sister to me... A sister or sibling that I never had, and I get that you want to protect her, which is a nice thing, but she will be fine. She has a good head on her shoulders and she won't make stupid decisions."

"Like the stupid decisions that you made her do," I stated with disappointment. She looked down, "Do not corrupt your friend, who is innocent and perfect."

She glared at me this time. "It sounds to me that she is the perfect daughter that you never had," she stood up, the chair screeching.

"Cris, sit down. I didn't mean it that way." If only she knew what I really meant.

"I will go as you ask. I will first go and make it up to Elona by taking them out to dinner at your favorite restaurant. Thanks, Dad," she said, and she left, but she still had disappointment written on her face. I let out a breath. I still don't feel satisfied. I wish that I could be alone with Elona again, but there was always something coming up when those moments are interrupted.

As I continued to have this nagging feeling after Cris had left to take Spooky and Elona to my favorite restaurant, I couldn't help but think about what Cris had done, taking Elona to a club. Its not just that, but its the fact that I want to see with my own eyes that everything is as it should be.

My phone rang as I sat on the recliner in the lounge with a glass of Scotch. I reached for my phone on the coffee table. It was David. My heart was beating fast. I hoped that nothing had happened because Cris just left ten minutes ago.

I answered, "David, is everything alright?" I asked.

"Yeah, I see that Cris is no longer grounded, she just came to get Elona, and then they will be off to dinner and a movie as well as the photoshoot with Spooky. I wanted us to grab a few drinks at the bar, are you up for it?" he asked, my jaw clenched when I thought about the photoshoot with Spooky.

"Yeah, I will meet you there," I said and then I hung up. I gulped the rest of the Scotch down, and then I got up, took my car keys, and left.

* * *

Walking into the place that Estelle and I would go to all the time when it was date nights or just to have our fun and special moments of celebrations, it felt like every other time that I would be here, the lights were dimmed. I scanned the room for familiar faces. I was about to have drinks with my friend who might just kill me if he ever found out that I had developed a new type of love for his daughter...love, not lust or infatuation. It was becoming more than that...love. I finally spotted them and I reached the table. I looked at the one who had taken my breath away and who was busy stealing my heart too. She looked at me with wide eyes, she looked beautiful, her hair loose and her lips red compared to earlier, completely oblivious to Cris and Spooky sitting on either side of her.

"Dad, what are you doing here?"

Not Again

Elona

I stared at Tristan as he looked at me. His eyes burned into me, and my lips parted. It felt like everything else had disappeared around us. I still can't believe that he wants me, we were so close to kissing and I wanted more with him. I licked my lips and his eyes followed as my tongue moved over my bottom lip.

"Dad?" Cris snapped me out of it. He looked at her as I reached for my champagne and took a sip. Shit, are we going to get into trouble for drinking champagne? I placed the glass on the table.

"I wanted to join you three," he said as he looked at Spooky too, and I didn't miss the scowl that he gave Spooky before looking at Cris again.

"This was supposed to be my time with my friends, but clearly, you do not trust me," she let out a breath.

Tristan pulled a chair out of the table and took a seat across from me, holding my gaze. "I'm sure that your father wants to get out and find someone that he can have fun with," Spooky smiled as he looked at his glass of champagne.

"I have had my fair share of fun. I do not want to have fun at a bar, I would rather choose this," Tristan replied as he shifted in his seat.

"Well, there is nothing that will be going on, Dad, " Cris said with sarcasm.

"So, what movie will we be watching?" Tristan smirked at Cris.

"Oh Gosh," Cris muttered and buried her face in her hands in disbelief. I couldn't help but giggle and that caught Tristan's attention as he now looked at me. His smirk was still in place and I felt heat all over my body. "Can we just watch a movie in peace?" she asked as she looked at him.

"Nothing wrong with watching a movie with you three."

"You're the one who asked me to keep an eye-" Cris cleared her throat and I furrowed my brows. "You wanted me to be ungrounded and spend time with my friends, so now I'm being watched so that I don't catch on shit," she snapped at him.

"Watch your mouth," he clenched his teeth, scowling at her.

Cris threw her hands up in the air as she surrendered because I could see that Tristan would not leave and part of me was happy about that. Cris checked her phone. "Shit, we won't have time to eat. We have to go before the movie begins," she stood up and so did we.

* * *

The theater was down the street, so we walked. But nothing prepared me for the moment that I felt warmth on my lower back, Tristan was behind me. I savored the moment before it was taken away. I wanted to be alone with him, but things always come up.

As we walked on the sidewalk, Tristan was beside me while Spooky and Cris walked in front of us. It was a cool and beautiful evening. "I must say that you look...fucking sexy tonight," Tristan said, his voice low enough for me to hear. I blushed. I was wearing a black shirt that flared out from my waist, a length just above my knees, and a slightly cropped top that exposed a little of my belly, but it was not that inappropriate compared to the club attire, which was slutty. I also added ankle boots. It was a photo shoot after all.

"Thank you," I replied shyly.

"I still want to see you in that lingerie, I want to get you alone," he said softly.

"I doubt that we can have that time alone."

We finally got to the movie theater. Cris and Spooky ordered some snacks but Tristan and I didn't want anything. We went into the theater and Tristan sat next to me. I was so happy that he was actually next to me. There were butterflies that fluttered in my stomach, but we had these few hours together before going to our houses.

As the movie started to play, my arm was resting on the armrest, and out of the corner of my eye, I saw him resting his arm next to mine. I held my breath as my heart beat fast. And then that was when I felt it, his finger stroking mine. I licked my lips. His hand moved over mine, and he held it there. My chest was rising and falling. I looked at our joined hands, he was holding it. Luckily it was dark. I was oblivious to Cris and Spooky beside me, I didn't care about them at this moment because Tristan was holding my hand.

He took my hand and brought it towards him. He placed my hand on his hard bulge. I swallowed. He kept my hand there, and it felt super hot in this theater. I didn't know what to do, and it felt so unreal that the man whom I had a crush on was now next to me, holding my hand on his erection.

It became too much for me, so I pulled my hand away and I stood up. I moved past him and walked down the aisle all the way to the exit. Cris would think that I had gone to the bathroom. The coolness hit my skin as I entered the ladies' bathroom. I stood in front of the mirror, hunched over the vanity, gripping the edge of the basin as I caught my breath. What the hell just happened? It happened. I felt his erection in my hand. It should be a proud moment for me, right? But it was like a dream that I didn't want to wake up from.

I heard the door closed and as I wanted to compose myself, he appeared behind me in the mirror, watching me with newfound hunger. He held my gaze, they were dark with want...need.

He moved closer to me without breaking eye contact, he was now against me, his hands on my shoulders. "I have been waiting for this moment," he rasped. He moved my hair over my one shoulder, exposing my neck, and he leaned in. "I don't want you to be around Spooky, and I'm still serious about the modeling part too. Don't do it." he breathed against my ear. It sent shivers throughout my entire body, my lips parted, and I closed my eyes. "You are mine, and your body is only for me to see," he pulled the strap of my cropped top down my shoulder. I opened my eyes as I watched him in the mirror. "No photoshoot after this," he breathed along my shoulder, sending goosebumps throughout my entire body and I closed my eyes again. I was wet, and I wanted him now, despite being a virgin, I didn't care, I wanted him.

"Please," I breathed.

"Please what?" he rasped.

"Please don't make me wait," I watched him in the mirror again. He held my gaze, and then he leaned further down, breaking eye contact as his lips pressed against my skin, trailing soft, slow kisses along my shoulder. His hands rested on my hips and his fingers grazed my belly, which was partially exposed. My core was throbbing with need.

He pulled away and then he spun me around. I stared at his lips. He bit his bottom lip, his one hand came up to cup the back of my head. I looked up, he was staring at my parted lips. He leaned in, and I closed my eyes as I was about to finally feel his lips on mine.

The bathroom door opened and we both pulled away from each other as a woman walked in and scowled at us, walking to one of the stalls. Tristan didn't know what to do and as soon as the door of the stall closed, we both let out a breath.

"Fuck!" Tristan muttered in frustration.

"I should go back," I stated, and then I left the bathroom. I'm thankful that it wasn't Cris that entered the bathroom. I don't know what she would've done or if I would've lost her. Just thinking about that made me sad.

"Elona," Tristan called out to me as I walked towards the theater where our specific movie was playing, and I stopped to turn around. He walked towards me, "Don't go back, let's just hang out or go somewhere else. Forget the photoshoot," he looked at me with hope...with desperation. I just didn't want my best friend to get suspicious or anything. "Please," he begged.

The look in his eyes made my heart ache for him, as that look is what I saw on his face when Aunt Estelle passed away, and we were at the grave site, the coffin being lowered into the ground. I will never forget that day.

His Part

Elona

I was really skeptical about staying behind with Tristan. I was being pulled in two directions. I just didn't know what Cris would think, that we had both disappeared. But he was looking at me with that vulnerable expression. I just didn't know what to say to him.

"What about Cris? She will get suspicious that we are both not there," I said.

"I will make up something, I can tell her that you feel sick, we can go to the restaurant and just talk, get to know each other more and we don't have to kiss or do anything that is sexual right now unless you want to," he stated.

"I have my photoshoot. We didn't come all this way just for a movie. The plan was to do a photoshoot," I reminded him.

"Screw the photoshoot," his brows furrowed with frustration. "Please."

"That photoshoot is for my future. I'm pursuing something that I want and you won't stop that. If you want to hang out with me, I will. But make sure that the excuse that you spin to Cris is believable. Just know I need to be back for the photoshoot." I held my gaze on him.

He let out a frustrated breath because he would not get his way all the time. "Fine," he took his phone out of his pocket and he typed a quick text to Cris. "I told her that you were light-headed, and I'm taking you to eat something. We'll be back when the movie is done," he put the phone back in his pocket.

"Thanks," I smiled.

He gestured with his hand towards the exit, and we ended up walking in step down the street to the restaurant that we had been at moments before.

The host was very familiar with him because it was a restaurant that was his favorite. He and Aunt Estelle used to frequent here.

We sat at a table. I looked at the menu, but I wasn't hungry. I just wanted something to drink. I was hot not just from the air but from this moment with him. He was being a gentleman, and that possessiveness switched. I wanted to see more of this man. However, I only got to see the hardworking and fatherly side of him that Cris experienced.

The waiter stood beside us. "What would you like to drink?" he asked.

"I would like a soda, please," I smiled, and then I locked eyes with Tristan before he looked at the waiter.

"I will have some red wine, the regular," he said. The waiter left.

"So what will you order?" he asked, but he was smirking.

"I'm not hungry, just thirsty," I replied.

He smiled as he shifted in his seat. "I never thought that I would actually be alone with you, I mean...away from the ones that we know. I do want to be alone with you where there is no one. But this is a start," he stated.

"Its too risky to be sneaking around."

"That's true, but we'll make it work if you want to be with me. I know how you feel about me, but that is ultimately your decision. I'll always have you on my mind and I'll always want you. I tried so many times to forget about you. Your father forced me to have fun and that included Maggie. I wanted to live up to my statement that you and Cris would hear when I have moved on with someone. You heard that," It hurt me, but I had to try to accept it at the time. That was before now. "I had never planned to be with Maggie again after that. I don't ever plan to be with her. But when it comes to you..." he held my gaze. "You have turned my world upside down. I just can't forget you, no matter how much I try. I need you, Elona. It's not just a want."

I swallowed, not sure what to say. "I feel the same way about you," I replied softly.

"I know that things can be risky, but we can try. The only thing is that we will have to keep it a secret for now," he stated.

"Okay. I guess we could try," I smiled.

He returned my smile, and then he looked down at the menu as his smile faded, "I loved Estelle, she was my everything. She was beautiful and Cris reminds me of her. Estelle loved journalism, and you know that she excelled at it. She was great. Now I see Cris is following in her footsteps with journalism. We were so happy together that we decided to try for another baby three years ago, despite Cris being older. The accident that Estelle was in," he paused, taking a deep breath. My heart was breaking because I knew that he was in so much pain when she passed away. I had seen it on that day that she was buried. "She...uh...we lost the baby too in that accident. I lost not only one person but two. No one knew about the pregnancy, not even Cris," He leaned back in the chair, and finally, his gaze met mine. "We had planned to keep it between us until the second trimester, but she didn't make it that far," his expression was pained and his eyes welled up with tears, "I still haven't told Cris to this day."

"I'm...I'm so sorry to hear that and for you to go through that. I won't tell Cris about that part. I...I hope that in time you find happiness and the pain does take time. Things had gotten better over the years when my mother passed away. My father didn't date anyone either after that and it's been years. She was an artist," I smiled.

"Your father told me, but speaking of artists. Some of your mother's paintings that were kept in storage will be at an art gallery next week. I will be there with your father. I know that you will be there too," he smiled.

"I would love to see those paintings. I remember she painted a dolphin and that is a very faint memory of it."

"I guess we have paintings in common. But we still need to talk about modeling and the agencies. I want to be part of it too in the business aspect of things, no matter how much I hate it. I know that I can't convince you to stop pursuing it," he stated.

"That is correct," I replied.

His phone chimed, and he took it out of his pocket. "It's Cris, she said not to worry about the photoshoot, you can do it another time, and they will be walking home."

I was happy about that, more alone time with Tristan. "So, what do we do next?"

"Well...we can drive around, take a walk in the park. I can take you home or...as much as I want you, there is always a hotel."

I smiled, "Well, it's too soon for that. Perhaps a walk in the park. It is a beautiful evening after all."

"Park it is," he said as he signaled for the waiter to get the bill.

I was smiling like a silly teenager. I just loved to be with him despite the fact that he may be possessive at times, his way of being protective, I guess. I wanted to hold his hand while we walked in the park, but maybe that would be inappropriate as I don't know who might be watching, and then we get caught, which could lead to serious consequences...loss of two friendships and a possibility of severed relationships between both Dad and me and Tristian and Cris. With Cris wanting to pursue journalism, she is a great investigator too.

A Walk In The Park

Elona

After the restaurant, Tristan and I walked to the park, and we kept a bit of a distance so that it wouldn't seem suspicious, especially if we bumped into anyone that we knew. It was a slow walk, and I was a ball of happiness because Tristan and I were trying our hand at dating, and I could not believe that it had come true.

We walked towards the lake, and then we just went over to a nearby bench and took a seat. "Perhaps I should get you home soon. I don't want your father to be worried or ground you," he smiled as he looked over at me. The lamp that we sat under was shining over us.

"I guess so. I just want to know something," I said.

"What is it?" he asked, shifting on the bench so that his body faced towards me.

"The night of the club, it was my first time drinking and Cris was the one that told me what to wear. I felt so ashamed and embarrassed to wear that attire, let alone when you saw me in it. You scrutinized me. You were disappointed and that actually made me feel sad. You sat in front of me on the coffee table at your house, and before you could say anything, my father knocked on the door. I could see that disappointment in your eyes," I held his gaze, but that disappointment was long gone. "What were you going to say before my father knocked on the door?" I asked, I was dying to know.

He parted his lips and looked down, "I don't think that you want to know what I was going to say in that moment, its in the past and I trust that you won't be going to a club again," he looked up into my eyes. His forest green eyes were dark.

"Was it that bad?" I asked, which was barely a whisper.

"Yes," he sighed as he looked ahead.

"What were you going to say?" I pushed further.

"Elona–"

"Please," I begged, and he held my gaze again.

"I was going to say that you were a huge disappointment, and it was a disgrace. I wouldn't want to be with someone that was acting up and dressing that way. But I was going to say that in the moment before I even knew that Cris was the one who dressed you up and that you just tagged along. I know you better than to be a party girl, Elona. That is why...that is why I fell for you," he admitted.

That stung my heart but I swallowed. "You care enough about my attire, but you want me to wear a lingerie bodysuit for you," I stated.

"That is only meant for me, no one else. I hate the fact that you want to pursue modeling. I would do anything for you not to pursue it. Men will look at your body, you will basically be naked, and your private parts will be covered. You might be posing with men with their hands on what's mine and I hate to even think about that," he shook his head, his jaw clenching.

"Then don't think about it," I smirked. I will have fun seeing him miserable whenever I do my photoshoots because I won't be stopping the career that I want to pursue.

"That will be difficult to do," he said softly.

My phone rang, and I took it out of my pocket, "It's my dad," I answered. "Hey, Dad."

"Where are you? I saw Spooky and Cris walking home when I drove back to the house."

"I'm at the park, I just needed some fresh air, but I will be home soon," I said, hoping that I was not in trouble because he sounded disappointed.

"Make sure that you tell Tristan to see me when he drops you off at home," he said and hung up before I could even say anything.

"What is it?" Tristan asked.

"My dad wants to see you when you drop me at home." I placed my phone in my pocket.

"Fuck. I was supposed to meet him at the bar, but I went to the restaurant instead. I can understand that he wants to say a piece of his mind about not showing up."

"He saw Cris and Spooky walking down the street," I replied.

"Then he probably asked them. So we might be in some sort of shit... Well, I'll be in shit by your father," he said and I stood up.

"We need to get moving then. I don't want my dad to wait any longer and I'm supposed to feel sick or something."

Tristan stood up, but he took my hand in his, and he pulled me closer to him, leaning down, his face were inches away from mine. My lips were parted, and I wanted him to make that move. I was nervous as my heart was beating wildly in my chest and my core was throbbing with need.

"I have been dying to kiss you," he rasped.

As he leaned in closer, someone whistled at us and I realized that being in public was risky. I pulled away as his lips brushed against mine. "We can't-we can't do this in public," I said as if I ran a marathon because I was out of breath.

"You're right. I'm sorry. That's just what you do to me each time, " he said with disappointment. "Let's get you home before your father unleashes his wrath on us both if we are not there soon."

We walked in step all the way to where his car was parked at the restaurant. I was hugging myself as I waited for him to unlock the car so that I could get inside. "Are you getting cold?" he asked as he walked over to my side.

"Yeah," I replied.

He took his jacket off, and placed it over my shoulders and I held onto it so that it wouldn't slip off. The lights of his car flashed as he pressed a button on the key. He opened the passenger side door for me and I got inside. The car smelled like him, the delicious scent that I always get from him.

He got into the car. "Are you ready?" he asked as he looked over at me, but I could barely see him as it was dark.

"Yeah, ready as I'll ever be," I replied with a sigh.

I didn't want our outing to be over, I wanted it to last as long as possible. I hope that we get to have another opportunity to be alone together because I enjoy it so much. I felt his hand on mine, which was resting on my lap, and I stared at it. I loved it, this moment of physical contact. I couldn't help but smile. I can't wait to test the waters with him and see where this takes us.

A Slight Confrontation

Tristan

We reached Elona's house. I knew what was to be expected from David when entering that house. I feel like a teenager that was sneaking around, hoping not to be caught all over again. We stopped in front of the house, I turned the ignition off, and I let out a breath as I looked ahead before turning to look at Elona. She was taking my jacket off.

"Are you ready?" I asked.

She smiled at me, "Yes," I returned her smile before getting out of the car.

When I got to her side, I opened the door, holding my hand out for her, and she took my hand as I helped her out of the car. I closed the door, and then she pulled her hand out of mine. I forgot for a moment that we were a secret.

I let her walk ahead of me, but I watched her hips sway as she walked down the driveway, and I just couldn't believe that she was finally mine. We haven't kissed yet, and I wanted to taste those lips. She opened the front door and stepped inside.

"Hi, Dad," she said. I closed the front door behind me and then we both walked further into the lounge.

"Hey," I forced a smile. David was sitting in a recliner, a document in his hand that he was reading. He looked between the two of us. My heart was beating wildly. I didn't want any drama, but I could see by the expression on his face that he was not happy. More disappointed.

"How are you feeling?" he asked her with concern.

"I feel much better thanks to Uncle Tristan, who took great care of me. I just needed something to eat and some fresh air." She lied and smiled at her Dad. It felt so weird that she called me Uncle now that we are dating, but it was all for the secret.

"I'm glad that you are feeling much better," he said, but Elona was awkward, so she went up the stairs to her bedroom after stating that she was going to lie down.

"Thank you for taking care of her this evening," he shifted in his seat, placing the document on the smaller table beside the recliner where the lamp was shining bright. "However, you ditched me to be with them at the movies," his gaze burned into me.

I moved to the sofa and took a seat across from him. "I just wanted to check up on them, they were at the restaurant...my restaurant," I held his gaze. He knew that it was mine and Estelle's favorite. "I just decided to be with them and keep an eye on them. When was the last time I watched a movie? I'm always busy with my work," I leaned back against the sofa, crossing my leg over the other.

"Well, you could've sent me a text, then maybe I could've joined you with the kids. But you left me at the bar waiting for you."

I scoffed, "I'm not your girlfriend who needs to tell you where I'll be, but I apologize for not letting you know, it was at the last minute."

He shook his head. "We're friends, Tristan. Sometimes we need to let those kids just be out on their own and we can hang out. But as soon as you're supposed to have fun with me or to chill, you hardly even stick around for long. You disappear, but as soon as it's with the kids, you show up almost immediately, and then you actually hang out with them."

"I can do whatever I want, David. I'm not restricted to hanging out with you. I may have been a shitty friend since losing Estelle, but I'm also keeping an eye out for the kids and their safety, which you fail to do," I stopped myself from saying more. I just didn't have time for this. I let out a huge breath. "I'm sorry."

"You should be. I don't know what is up with you and having fun. Perhaps you are struggling because of Estelle. Maggie seems like a nice person too. Have you heard from her again?" he asked, his tone changing with interest.

"I'm not interested in Maggie, and she hasn't called me again but left me a text or two which I never responded to. I don't need you to force me to be with someone that I don't want to be with. I felt as if I had disappointed Estelle by bringing her into my home. That was something that I regret. Although it was great, she's just not my type. Just don't force me into anything," I said.

He nodded, "I guess I can back off with that. I apologize if I have forced her onto you. But you cannot wallow in your work all the time."

"Trust me, Cris wants me to start dating. I just need some time," I lied. I don't want him to find out that I just started dating his daughter moments ago. He would rip my head off, so we will be giving it time. I think that the best time to inform him is after Elona has graduated at the end of the year. So we can probably break the news to him next year.

"She only wants to see you happy. I don't blame her," he replied.

"She shouldn't worry about me. I'll be fine. I've been fine," I smiled. But I was lying to him. That would create guilt, but I was feeling alive with Elona. She makes me feel different compared to when I was forced to be with Maggie.

"Thank you for taking care of Elona," he smiled.

"I won't let anything happen to her either," I reassured him. "How are you feeling about her being a model next year if that happens?" I asked.

"Well, I will support my daughter with whatever she wants to do in life. We all have free will in life to make decisions, and it depends on the decisions that one makes, whether it's good or bad, there are always consequences for that. I just want her to be happy, but I know that I cannot always protect her from the world, she is becoming a grown young woman and I don't want to stand in her way of anyone, but if she dares to start dating, then that is something that I'll look into, because I don't want her to be with the wrong man." I cleared my throat and shifted on the sofa. If he only knew that she was dating me. "I'm not too keen on the modeling because of what industry it is. I just want her to be careful most of all, but again...I won't stand in her way"

"Well, I'm not happy that she's going into that industry. A lot is expected, and she is perfect. I don't want that industry to ruin her and I don't want anything to happen to my daughter's friend. If I can provide some sort of security, then I will. There are filthy men out there who have hidden agendas.

As much as I'm against this, I want her to be protected from them. I would prefer that she not model at all if you know what I mean," I responded. I didn't want people to look at her body with lust or anything dirty if she had to go to that extent in the modeling industry. I need to stop that one...way or another.

"Thank you for looking out for Elona, I would appreciate the security too. I think I should check up on her," he smiled as he stood up from the recliner.

"See you around," I said as I stood up and then I left.

I had to be careful with how I spoke about Elona too. I know that there'll be more lies to cover up our dating until we come clean next year. There'll be plenty of time to prepare for his reaction, which could be bad if he doesn't take it well. If Cris had to date David, then I probably would've flipped. But now that I'm in this situation, I know that we have to be very careful because it is not only David...there is Cris too.

Unveiled Harmonies

Elona

I rushed down the stairs and went to the kitchen in a chirpy mood today. I was going to see Tristan. Even though the plan was to spend time with Cris at her house, I was going to be in Tristan's presence. I took an apple from the fruit bowl.

"You're chirpy today," my dad entered the kitchen, giving me a suspicious smile.

"Well, I'm going to be at Cris' today. She wants to work on her journalism assignment. Its like a test of some sort. I found the perfect agency that I want to get into with hard work and dedication," I said with excitement.

"And what is that?" He asked, folding his arms over his chest. Eager to know what it is that I'm about to tell him.

"Well, you know that show that we always see on TV when it's New Year's Eve? The Velvet Secret Fashion Show?"

"Yeah, I'm aware of that."

"I want to be one of them." I was so excited.

"So you really want to parade around in front of the world half-naked?" he asked.

I became uncomfortable about it, especially talking to my father about that, "Well, it is part of modeling, so if that is what will be required of me, then I guess I have to. I don't think I have a limit except for full nudity. I don't think that I want to go that far." I replied.

He nodded, "I'm just looking out for you. Some industries can be full of men preying on women. I just want you to be careful, but I won't be stopping you."

"Thanks, Dad. I love how supportive you are," I moved closer to him and placed a kiss on his cheek. I pulled away, "I'm going to Cris now, I will see you later," I sunk my teeth into the apple and chewed.

"Have fun, not too much fun though," he warned.

I chuckled, if only he knew that Tristan and I were dating. As I walked out of the house, the sun hit me like an oven. Luckily, I was dressed in denim shorts and a slightly cropped top. My hair was tied up in a messy bun.

I was still eating my apple when I stood in front of the door to Tristan's house. Knocking on the door, I took my last bite and threw the rest of the apple in the garden. They always grew apples and other fruits. Well, that is what was advised to me by Cris from a very young age, to throw the apple into the garden so that a tree can grow. Her mother loved the garden, she always used to sit in the garden and read a book.

"Come on in, I have plenty to do, but Daddy will entertain you," Cris took my hand and pulled me inside, closing the door behind me. I chuckled, as it sounded so wrong.

"So, where will you be working then?" I asked as I followed her into the kitchen where Tristan was sitting. Documents spread out on the dining table. He looked up and smirked at me, " Hi, Elona," I returned the smile, my heart was beating at a rapid pace.

"Good afternoon, Uncle Tristan," Cris poured us both some apple juice, and then she walked towards me.

"Why are you so shy today? My dad won't bite," she gave the glass of juice to me. Tristan's eyes were still on me, but this time he took in my appearance. He looked away before Cris could see, as he tried to focus on his work. I took a sip of the juice," Daddy, please entertain her," she said, and Tristan looked up at me, smirking again as Cris left.

"So, I have to entertain you," he leaned back in the chair. "What am I going to do with you?" his eyes moved over my body again and heat crept up in my cheeks.

"Well, there are plenty of things to do," I shrugged as I moved closer to the dining table.

"I have an idea," he stood up from the chair, he rounded the table and I placed the glass of juice on it. He stopped in front of me, holding out his hand and I placed my hand in his. He led me out of the kitchen towards the bigger section of the place where they didn't use it after Aunt Estelle's death. There was a bigger lounge and in the far corner was a piano. There was a large window that overlooked the view, and we stood in front of it. He never let go of my hand. "Do you still remember when you and Cris used to run around here when you both were little?" He asked, his gaze burning into me.

"I remember," I took in the lounge again. This place was huge and gorgeous, some parts in this section looked ancient but beautiful. "It looks as if you have inherited this place," I said as I walked towards a bookshelf. I traced the spine of the books which were full of dust. Most of the furniture was covered with white sheets.

"It wasn't inherited. This was a place that Estelle loved. She was good friends with a woman that used to live here. She was Estelle's Professor. Estelle was adopted by an older couple when she was young. They showered her with love and they were wealthy people. They moved to Germany. Sadly, they both passed away due to natural causes. She had inherited her parents' house, and the one in Germany, and this one. Her professor left it for her because she didn't have any kids. Estelle used to take care of Professor Roberts. She was very old. Estelle wanted us to live in this place. I just couldn't find the courage to step foot in this part of the house because all of our memories were here. The Christmas tree....everything."

"I remember that tall Christmas tree that was filled with lights. It was beautiful." I smiled. "These books must be Aunt Estelle's books?" I said.

"Yeah, I didn't want to touch anything that was last touched by her, I didn't even want to move anything." He turned away as he looked out the window again.

I walked over to the piano beside him. "Whose piano is this?" I asked.

"That is mine," he replied. I looked at him in surprise.

"Really? Is this piano yours? I don't think I've ever heard you play the piano even with all the time I've spent here growing up." The air seemed to hum with an unspoken energy, a subtle tension that wrapped around us like a delicate melody.

Tristan's eyes flickered toward the piano, and a thoughtful expression played on his face. "You know, Elona," he began, "There's something about music that has always resonated with me."

I raised an eyebrow, intrigued. "Really? I never knew you were into music."

A faint smile graced his lips. "There's a lot you don't know about me."

With that, he moved towards the piano. He sat down on the bench and his fingers hovered over the keys as if contemplating whether to unlock the secrets they held. Then, with a decisive nod to himself, he began to play.

The first notes filled the room, a soft and melancholic melody that wrapped around us like a gentle embrace. I stood there, utterly captivated, as the room was filled with the tones of the piano. Tristan's fingers moved gracefully, each note resonating with a depth of emotion I hadn't expected. The pain he had inside of him.

My eyes widened in astonishment. "You play the piano?" I took a seat beside him on the bench.

He continued to play, the music weaving a narrative that seemed to transcend words. "I have been playing since I was a young man. It's something I haven't shared with many."

The beauty of the music held me in its grip, and I found myself drawn closer to him. The harmonies, both haunting and beautiful, created a connection between us that went beyond the spoken word.

As he played, the air seemed to shimmer with the unspoken stories and emotions that only music could convey. The piano became an extension of Tristan's soul, revealing a side of him I hadn't known existed.

When the final notes faded into the quiet ambiance of the room, I just sat here, awe-struck. "That was incredible. I had no idea you were so talented."

He met my gaze, his eyes revealing a vulnerability that was rare to see. "Some things are meant to be kept hidden until the right moment."

He leaned in closer to me as his gaze fell onto my parted lips. His hand cupped the side of my face. My heart was beating wildly, and my core was throbbing. As slow as it was, I closed my eyes, his lips finally pressed against mine. This was it, we were finally kissing. He held his lips against mine as if to never pull away, as if not to wake up from a dream. He pulled inches away from my lips before pressing them gently against mine again. This time, savoring each moment of the kiss. Before it got passionate, he pulled away.

"I wanted to do that for a long time," he smiled "It's a bit risky with Cris in the same house. So we have to be careful," he returned to the piano, but I was dumbstruck that we finally kissed. I couldn't believe it.

The piano, once silent and unassuming, now held the echo of shared secrets and the beginning of a new understanding between us. The music lingered in the air, a reminder that even in the quietest moments, there could be symphonies waiting to be unveiled.

Risky

Elona

Tristan and I remained in the main lounge, where he continued to play another song. I was mesmerized. I loved seeing this part of him. We continued to sit next to each other. He placed his hands in his lap after he was done playing the last song. I enjoyed this moment, but we forget at times that Cris is in the study room, and she could just be looking for us, so we couldn't be that close to each other.

"You said that you have played the piano since you were a young man. How young were you?" I asked.

He stared at the keys of the piano. "I was twelve when I could play it perfectly, but I started as young as five." He looked over at me, his green eyes glowing from the light through the window. "My parents have a love for music, and they wanted me to be this perfect pianist one day, but I just didn't share that dream. I wanted to pursue business and entrepreneurship. I was passionate about that. I did end up being a perfect pianist at a young age, but they somehow supported my decision when I graduated from high school. I was happy that my parents never forced me into anything that I didn't want to do. I would've been unhappy. But it had been a very long time since I had played the piano. I think I stopped when I was twenty-one years old," he said.

"It still seems that you have it. It's like you never stopped playing. You're still perfect." I smiled at him and he returned it.

"I try to be perfect at things. I'm glad that I still have it. The funny thing is that..." he looked at the keys again, sighing, "Estelle had never heard me play before."

"Really? Never ever in her life since you both had been together?" I asked, surprised.

"That is correct," he chuckled as he looked at me. "You're the first person to hear me besides my parents and the audience I played in front of at theaters and music recitals. I guess you see the deeper parts of me, it's like there is something about you that brings that out of me," his gaze intensified, and then he leaned into me, "I want to be alone with you. I have to think of something... to make up a story," he whispered, looking over his shoulder to check if we were still alone, "I want to spend at least a night with you." He pulled away, and my body tingled, my core throbbing.

"I want that so much," I confessed.

"There is a career day tomorrow at your school. I have to give a speech. I don't feel like giving the speech, but if I can see you again, then I will be there. You are my motivation for going. No one will be interested in my speech, they'll be bored, and I feel like that is a waste of my time. I agreed to it because it's Cris' school," he gave me a faint smile.

"I look forward to hearing your speech," I returned his smile.

"So, what will you be wearing on career day tomorrow?" he asked.

"Hmmm, a bunny lingerie outfit with white ears as a headband," I smirked.

"Hell no, I won't allow you to dress that way in front of your school. Hell, in front of anyone else, for that matter-"

"Relax," I chuckled, "You'll see what I wear." I teased.

"Please, don't give me a heart attack when it comes to your attire tomorrow. You'll be the death of me," he let out a breath.

"You need to relax at times," I smiled.

"Here you two are!" Cris exclaimed. "I've been looking for you both. I'm finally done with my assignment. I'm starving, is anyone up for pizza?" She asked.

"Yeah, pizza sounds good," I replied.

"You two look cozy sitting over here. Dad, you're finally back in this lounge since Mom died. I'm happy to see that," she smiled. "You seem to be more alive now."

"Well..." he stood up from the bench and walked towards her, "It's all thanks to Elona, she made me step out of the past and, because I had to entertain her, she brought out the old me...the happy me," he smiled.

"You're a great friend, Elona. You should hang out with my dad more often so that he can get his happiness back. I'm off to order pizza," she said as she turned around and walked away.

Tristan turned back to me, and he held out his hand, placing mine in his and I stood up. I could see that he was genuinely happy. "Let's go sit in the kitchen," he said, and he led the way out of the huge lounge.

***

We got to the kitchen as Cris went through the pizza menu. Tristan had let go of my hand before entering the kitchen so that Cris wouldn't see. "So, Dad, I heard that you'll be giving a speech tomorrow. It was announced this morning as a reminder. I know that you hate to be at schools to give a speech, but you really don't need to be there," she said as she sat down at the dining table.

"I want to do it seem that it will be the first and the last," he stated as he leaned against the wall, folding his arms over his chest. I sat down across from Cris at the table.

"Oh, I've seen The Velvet Secret Fashion Show. Applications are open, and I think that you can apply," she said to me, completely ignoring her dad this time as her excitement took over.

"No, that won't happen," Tristan chimed in. I looked at him and he scowled at me. I let out a sigh.

"Dad, she can do what she wants, her father is supportive about it, so be happy for her." she stood up, " I'm going to make a call. Elona, can you please pour us some juice?" she asked.

"Of course," I replied as I stood up.

As I walked past Tristan, his brows were furrowed, but he stared at the ground. He was not happy. I went around the kitchen counter and I reached for three glasses from the top cupboard, and then I took the juice out of the fridge, opening it. But then I felt him behind me. He placed his hands on the counter, caging me in. He leaned in, his breath against my ear, sending tingles throughout my body. I paused what I was doing.

"Why are you driving me crazy like this? Why are you refusing to listen when it comes to modeling?" He breathed.

I turned around to face him, and he was so close to me, I let out a breath. "I'm doing what makes me happy-" he grabbed my jaw gently, and he crashed his lips against mine. I closed my eyes and his lips lingered against mine. He pulled away, and I gasped as he rested his forehead against mine.

"If you don't listen to me, then I will be there...wherever you go. That is my compromise. I will also text you an address with instructions," he said softly.

"I have ordered the pizza. I hope they won't take forever to deliver," Tristan pulled away from me immediately, and I turned around to continue pouring the juice.

My heart was racing. Tristan shouldn't be risking us this way with kisses. I don't want to lose my best friend, as Tristan and I only began dating. I wish things had been different, but this is where we are right now, and we have to be careful.

The Unexpected Beauty

Tristan

The school auditorium buzzed with energy as I stepped up to the podium, my eyes scanning the eager faces of students, parents, and teachers. Elona and Cris' school had become a vibrant tapestry of dreams, and I felt a profound sense of responsibility to share insights from my own journey even though I didn't want to be here. Elona and David weren't here yet. I continued to look for Elona.

"Good morning, everyone," I began, my gaze unconsciously seeking out Elona in the crowd. When my eyes found her, dressed as a beauty pageant contestant, I was momentarily taken aback. The sheer elegance and confidence she exuded left me breathless. A radiant smile played on her red lips, and I couldn't help but marvel at the unexpected beauty she brought to the event. She was dressed in a blue, glittery dress that hugged her curves, her breasts pushed up, and the length hit the ground. She had a sash over her that read 'Miss Universe', her make-up was beautiful, her long brunette hair was in Hollywood waves, and she had a little tiara on her head. Immediately, I saw her as my bride. I snapped out of that thought. Clearing my throat as I peeled my eyes away from her.

"As we navigate through life, each of us carries a unique set of aspirations," I continued, my words weaving through the attentive audience. "And speaking of unique aspirations, let me take a moment to appreciate the stunning Elona, who has chosen to represent her dreams with such grace and poise."

The room erupted in applause, and I couldn't hide the pride in my eyes as they met Elona's. Her choice to embrace the beauty pageant theme spoke volumes about her courage and individuality.

"Now, as we delve into the world of business and entrepreneurship," I shifted the focus back to the main topic, "it's crucial to recognize that success is not only about financial gains but also about the journey, the values we uphold, and the authenticity we bring to our endeavors."

My words flowed, drawing on the experiences of my own career. The unpredictability, the challenges, and the triumphs, all facets of the entrepreneurial journey. Yet, as I spoke, my mind kept drifting back to Elona, who embodied the essence of authenticity in her choice of attire.

"I have had the privilege of witnessing the power of authenticity in business," I continued, "and it's a principle that holds true in life as well. Your uniqueness is your strength. Embrace it, nurture it, and let it guide you."

The applause resonated through the auditorium once more, and I could sense the connection forged through shared experiences and aspirations. As I concluded my speech, a profound sense of gratitude washed over me.

Elona, standing there as a beacon of individuality, captured not only my attention but also the essence of the message I aimed to convey. I was proud of the beautiful soul she was, inside and out. The fact that she hadn't succumbed to societal expectations and chosen an outfit that reflected her genuine self filled me with happiness. I was happy that she didn't wear the bunny outfit that she teased me with.

As the audience dispersed, I made my way toward Elona, a smile playing on my lips. "You look absolutely stunning," I said, my eyes expressing a depth of admiration and affection. In this moment, surrounded by the echoes of my speech and the authenticity embodied by Elona, I felt an overwhelming sense of contentment.

"Mr Crane, that was an amazing speech," Mr Esau, the school's principal, said to me, breaking our moment. "Elona, you look beautiful, outstanding, I may add," he smiled at her. He was older and partially bald, his glasses made him look even older.

"Thank you," Elona and I said in unison.

"Can I have a word with you for a moment?" He asked me. I felt him pat my back.

"Sure," I replied and glanced at Elona with a smile before stepping aside with Mr Esau.

"This is Miss Jennings. I believe that you both met before," he introduced us. Miss Jennings, who is the school's secretary, was smiling and I didn't want to be around her because of the type of woman that she was.

"Hi," she smiled all flirtatiously.

"We met, she helped me to fill in the form for my speech," I replied. I slipped my phone out of my pocket as I looked in Elona's direction. She was all alone as she scanned the crowd. Cris came with me, but I wondered where she was. I haven't seen Spooky either. But I hope that he got my message to stay away. She smiled at me and I returned it. Her hazel eyes stood out from the lighting and her make-up. I turned my gaze away as Mr Esau and Miss Jennings were talking. I looked down at my phone and typed a quick text to Elona.

Me: Meet me at the Stern Hotel in half an hour.

I glanced over at her. She was looking down at her phone, a smile spreading on her face. Her gaze found mine as she looked at me. She nodded. I smiled in return. Before I was engaged in a conversation, I saw Cris standing with David, laughing. At least she was safe.

"Mr Crane, would you like to have drinks sometime? Some of the school staff will head out to the bar tonight, so if you want to join us then you are more than welcome," Miss Jennings said.

"We would love to have you join us," Mr Esau chimed in.

"I have other plans after this that cannot be canceled," I smiled politely.

"That's a shame," Miss Jennings said with disappointment. "Maybe next time."

"If you will excuse me," I smiled and walked away from them.

Elona was no longer standing where she was. I scanned the crowd, but I didn't see her. I went to join Cris and David. Cris was dressed in formal attire for her future career in journalism. "Dad, that was an amazing speech," she smiled.

"Thanks. Where is Elona?" I asked.

"I saw her walk to the bathroom," Cris said. Well, that sucks. I cannot sneak into the bathroom and have my way with her. We cannot be caught.

So, I remained in my spot and waited for Elona. Except the more I waited, the more she didn't come back. I excused myself from Cris and David. I walked through the crowd again and searched for her, but she was not there. I went to the bathroom, but she was not there either. I took my phone out of my pocket and I texted her.

Me: Where are you?

My phone chimed almost immediately.

Elona: I'm on my way to the hotel. I told my dad that I needed some time alone in the park. He's okay with it.

I smiled as I read it.

Me: See you soon. I hope that you're ready for me.

Elona: Bring it on.

I shoved my phone back into my pants pocket. I walked over to David and Cris. "I have some work that I need to get done at the office. I will see you later." I told Cris.

"Of course," Cris replied with a faint smile.

I looked at David. "Do you mind getting Cris home for me, please?" I asked.

"I don't mind at all. Don't work too hard," he said. I smiled and left.

If only they knew what my work would entail right now. I'll be working hard on Elona, that's for sure. No interruptions. She was going to be all mine for the remainder of the day.

Damage Control

Tristan

As I walked into The Stern Hotel, I saw Elona standing in the lobby. She was the only person that stood out. Everyone's attention was on her, she was just beautiful. I approached her and she smiled at me. I asked her here because I wanted to be alone with her and that is what we would have. Time spent alone and not worrying about whether we'll be caught or not.

"Hi," I smiled at her.

"Hey," she said shyly, returning my smile. "One second."

I went over to the front desk and booked a room for a few hours. Once I got the key. I walked towards Elona, I took her hand in mine, and led the way to the elevator. There were three people who entered the elevator after us and I couldn't wait to get to the room, just to be free and not worry about anyone else that we could run into publicly too.

Once the elevator stopped on our floor, the doors opened and we stepped out. "I can finally breathe," I told her over my shoulder as we walked down the hallway. She remained quiet. I unlocked the door to our room and opened it. Stepping inside, Elona followed after me.

I closed the door behind her, locking it. But before she could walk any further. I reached out and wrapped my hand around her wrist, pulling her towards me. She gasped as I held her by the waist, her hand on my chest. She looked at my lips and I leaned in. Nothing was going to stop me from taking my time to kiss her now. Our first kiss was a bit rushed due to Cris, but now I can take my time with her. I pressed my lips against hers, savoring the moment.

We deepened the kiss. As I forced my tongue into her mouth, she let out a soft moan. Her hand gripping my shirt. My cock wanted her so badly... to feel how she felt inside. I pressed my cock against her and she moaned again. I pulled away from her, studying her face. My one hand rested against the wall and my other hand cupped the side of her face, her lips were parted, and my thumb moved over her bottom lip. "I want you all to myself. I wanted this moment since I held my gaze on you that day in the kitchen when I came from work. That was when I really saw you. Your eyes....they made me really notice you." I rasped. I leaned in again and crashed my lips to hers, but then she pushed me back, and I moved to her silent command. I cupped the back of her head, holding her in place as we continued to kiss passionately, my heart beating rapidly.

Before I could go any further in the room, she pulled away and pushed me backward as I plopped onto the sofa. She looked at me with a newfound hunger. A young woman who was ready to devour me. My erection was visible. She lifted her dress up enough for her to straddle me. "I always wanted this too," she said seductively. Her hands rested on the back of the sofa.

My hands were on her hips but her breasts were so close to my face, having her sit on my cock just made this moment feel as if I was in a very happy place. "I see that you know what to do, you like to take charge, don't you?" I asked as she leaned down and pressed her lips to mine again. "It feels as if you're not a virgin, as if you have experience," I said against her lips. She pulled away. I looked into her eyes. They were contemplating something.

"You're correct. I'm not a virgin and I want this," she said.

"I wonder who you gave your virginity to. I would've beat him up if I knew back then." I chuckled lightly.

She shut me up with her lips, she was eager and so was I. I dug my fingers into her skin. I felt as if I would explode in my pants just by kissing her. She began to move on my cock, "Fuck," I whispered against her lips. "Do you really want this with me?" I asked.

"Yes," she said, which was barely a whisper. Our breathing was heavy.

"Good," I said as we continued with the kiss, and then I stopped, "I don't have any condoms on me, I won't risk anything, no pregnancy. No more kids for me," I sucked in a breath.

"I'm on the pill," she said.

"Thank goodness," I let out a sigh of relief.

We kissed again, and I moved my hands towards the straps of her dress and then lowered them down her shoulder. I leaned in, pressing my lips against her skin. My phone began to ring in my pants pocket, but I ignored it.

As my lips grazed the top of her breasts, I pulled away, looking at her before moving the top of her dress further down, exposing the swells of her breasts. I pressed my lips along the dress neckline where the swells of her breasts were. My phone continued to ring.

"Just answer it. It might be an emergency," she breathed.

I pulled away with frustration. I should've put my phone on silent. I struggled to get my phone out of my pocket but Elona stood up, and eventually, I got my phone. It was work.

I answered, "Crane."

"Mr. Crane, We have a problem. A huge one. You need to be at the office as soon as possible. There's been a cyber hack and not only with the data of clients but also financial hacking-"

"Fuck, I am on my way," I said before hanging up. I stood up, looking at Elona. "I'm sorry, but I have to do some damage control at work. Um...I will text you later?" I felt bad about leaving her like this.

"Yeah, you go and sort out whatever it is. Your business is what's important. I'll wait for your text later," she smiled.

I moved closer to her and I pressed my lips against hers before pulling back. "Thank you," I said.

Before I could get lost in her again, I left. I didn't even want to leave, but I had no choice. I wonder who has hacked my company. I hope whoever has been hacking will be found and rot in prison. This company is my world, and I don't know who had the nerve to even do this to me, because I have no enemies at all. So who could this be?

Drunken State

Elona

I went back home thirty minutes after Tristan had left. I was disappointed because I wanted to have that moment with him as surreal as it is for me. First time to have sex with my crush. The first time that I would have sex. I lied to him about not being a virgin. I just didn't want him to wait just because I didn't have sex before. I didn't want to wait any longer. So I lied.

I walked down the stairs as my father got off a phone call. "So, how was your walk in the park?" he asked as he was sitting on the recliner. He had a long call...work as always.

"It was...refreshing," I lied.

"I'm glad that you needed time alone. You're always hanging out with Cris, and sometimes I do feel as if you two are hanging out too much with each other. Where's Spooky, by the way? I didn't see him at Career Day." He furrowed his brows with concern.

I let out a sigh, "I don't know. He hasn't responded to my text yet. I'm sure that he's fine and something important came up," I shrugged.

"I like that kid, you two are the perfect match."

"Dad, he likes someone else, not me. He said that to my face and I believed him. I don't like him in that way either." I said over my shoulder as I walked into the kitchen.

"Maybe he's lying to you," he followed after me.

"Dad, we know him. I'm not his type, and he's not mine either. So, please drop it. I know you like him but do not try to play matchmaker. Maybe you should try to date again," I said as I reached for an apple in the fruit bowl.

"I'm trying to get into the game of dating. I pushed Uncle Tristan into it, and it seems that it isn't for him after Maggie. I don't blame him after being single for a long time. I doubt that he has moved on from Aunt Estelle," he sat on a bar stool and I joined him. But nothing stung like the mention of Maggie's name. If only my Dad had known that we were dating.

"Just let him be happy with whatever he wants to do and focus on your love life," I tried to change the topic to him.

My mother had been dead for years and my father had also never dated since then. He would always go to the bar, which is his "happy place" but he needed to move on too.

"I know, Kiddo. I just feel better when I'm helping someone else. I also want to see you happy." he smiled at me as I sunk my teeth into the apple.

"I am happy," I said with a mouth full of the apple.

"Then I'm happy," he replied.

"Dad, what would you have done if one of your friends had dated me?" I asked as I looked over at him. I was nervous about his answer.

"Well, that is quite a question. I'm close to Tristan. I can only think of him if he had to date you...." he shook his head, blowing out a breath. "I guess I would kill him with my bare hands...I don't know. But I surely wouldn't allow my friends to take advantage of my daughter and get away with it. I don't know...but as long as it's not happening I'm happy," he looked at me with a smile. "There isn't anything there now, is there?" he narrowed his eyes in suspicion.

"Oh no! It was just a question. Cris and I just brought it up in a conversation out of fun," I lied with a smile.

"Well, I hope you both are keeping it to men other than mine and Tristan's friends," he said, returning my smile.

"Don't worry, Dad," I lied, and I continued to eat my apple.

This was going to be tough, especially when Tristan and I were dating for a long time, my father would have to know. I need to ask Tristan all of his intentions, so I can be sure what happens in the future.

***

I was in my bed, and my father went to have an early night because he had a huge meeting tomorrow. I couldn't help but think about whether everything was okay with Tristan's company. I was also worried about Spooky.

I reached for my phone beside my bed which was on charge. Tristan has never texted me yet. Neither did Spooky. I pressed on Cris' chat.

Me: Any word about Spooky?

Cris: No, but I do think that we should go to his house tomorrow.

Me: Great idea...only if he doesn't respond.

Cris: I'm off to bed. I'll see you tomorrow. My Dad isn't at home yet, something about work emergencies. Anyway, nighty night.

Me: Goodnight.

I checked the time and it was almost midnight. Was Tristan still at work this time? All of a sudden, my phone chimed.

Crane: I'm at your front door...open up before I bang on this door, and we wouldn't want to wake your father up.

Shit.

I stood up quickly, I was in a tank top and my pajama shorts. I didn't care how I looked because I didn't want Tristan to bang on the door. I left my phone on the bed and I hurried out of my room and down the stairs. I unlocked the front door, opening it. Tristan was standing with his hands on either side of the door frame, his hair was disheveled. His tie was loosened, and the top buttons of his shirt were undone. His suit jacket was unbuttoned.

"Tristan," I whispered.

He stumbled inside and he cupped the back of my head, crashing his lips against mine. Walking me backward, I could smell the alcohol on his breath. I scrunched my face as I stopped him with my hands on his chest.

"I need you right now," he said softly.

"You're drunk and you can't be here. My father is asleep."

"That is so much more fun. Have him watch us," he smirked as he leaned into me again, but I pushed him away.

"You need to go home."

"Nope," he shook his head. He crashed his lips against mine and his hands moved to my ass, squeezing them, and a moan escaped me. My core throbbed, and he lifted me up, my legs wrapped around his waist with my arms around his neck. He pressed me against the wall. But I broke the kiss.

"We can't, not when you're drunk. Let's get you home," I replied as he put me down, and I helped him, his arm was over my shoulder as I walked with him out of my house and closed the door behind me.

* * *

We walked down the driveway until we got to the sidewalk. I noticed that his car was not there or down the street. "How did you even get here?" I asked.

"I took a cab. My car is at the bar. Maggie offered to drive me, but I refused, she would've wanted to stay the night and I didn't want that. She wasn't you," he looked over at me with a smirk.

"Maggie was with you at the bar?" I asked and anger surged through me.

"Yeah, she found me there."

We finally got to his house and I opened the door. It was already unlocked, so I didn't need to struggle. Cris was asleep, so I hoped that Tristan would not wake her up because I didn't want to explain to Cris why I was helping her dad inside his own house.

I helped him inside, but he let go of me, and he stumbled all the way to the lounge and plopped down on the sofa, lying down on his back. I approached him, his eyes now closed. I reached for the flannel floral throw that was on the back of the sofa and threw it over him. I leaned over and stroked his cheek.

He didn't stir, he was out like a candle.

I don't know to what extent the emergency was, but it clearly made him visit the bar. I leaned down and pressed a soft kiss onto his forehead before Cris could appear in the lounge and then I left.

I didn't want to explain anything, especially to lie even more. That was the worst part. I hope that Tristan will tell me what's going on at his company. This must be serious.

Finding Spooky

Elona

I waited for Cris so that we could go and check up on Spooky as he still hadn't responded to our texts, even calls. Cris was awaiting feedback for an internship from SNT. She would be able to finish school and automatically work for SNT once she's accepted. So, as she waits for that text, we will be on a mission to find Spooky. I already sent a text to Tristan to find out how he's doing this morning after he showed up drunk at my house last night.

My phone chimed as I walked down the stairs. I took my phone out of my denim shorts pocket.

Cris: I'm sorry to break this to you, but I need to go to SNT. They're having a weekend away for the interns. My dad is also not himself, he has a hangover. But chat soon.

No wonder Tristan hadn't been texting me back. I reached the kitchen. "I'm going out with some friends, don't wait up," my father said as he was dressed in blue jeans and a white t-shirt. A hoodie draped over his arm. It was late afternoon already.

"Okay, Dad," I said as I sat on the bar stool.

"I love you," he called over his shoulder.

"I love you too, Dad."

I was on my phone again, typing a reply to Cris.

Me: Is your dad that hectic? Don't worry, I'll check up on Spooky.

Cris: Yeah, when I went to get some water in the middle of the night. I got such a fright. I thought it was an intruder, just to see my dad passed out until this afternoon. Let me know about Spooky.

Me: 👍

Tristan still didn't read my text. I'll give him some space to get over that hangover. I got off the bar stool, locked up the house, and walked down the street to Spooky's house.

When I got to the driveway, I felt this weird vibe as I slowly walked towards the front door. The garden was not taken care of and the grass was growing tall. I walked up the steps and rang the doorbell. I waited but I felt chills. Maybe it was a bad idea to be here by myself.

I rang the bell one last time because I wanted to get away from here. But still, there was no answer. I slowly walked down the steps and turned around looking at the windows to the top floor of this huge double-story house. The curtains were closed, but when I looked down, before leaving, I saw an open section next to the house. I slowly approached but saw that it was a path. Perhaps Spooky might be in the backyard. So I went to check.

When I got to the backyard, it was deserted. It was as if no one lived here. The pool was nasty too, weeds were growing through the tiled cracks in the landscape. I walked up the steps to the sliding door, I knocked, and waited. There didn't seem to be anyone, but the kitchen looked clean to me. I tried to slide the door open, but it was locked on the inside.

I let out a breath. Turning around, I saw a section further in the backyard where there was a gate in the backyard fence. It led somewhere away from the house, so I strolled towards it.

I got to the open gate, and it led to the lake further ahead. "Hey," I jumped in fright. Turning around with my hand on my chest, my heart beating at a rapid pace.

"Spooky," I let out a relieved breath. "You scared me," I said.

"What are you doing here?" he asked. He was wearing sunglasses with his usual black clothing.

"I was looking for you. You never returned our calls or texts."

"My phone broke."

"Well, you haven't been to school either, so is everything okay?" I asked.

My phone started to ring, and I reached into my pocket, taking it out. It was Tristan, but I ignored it by putting it on silent. I wanted to know what was going on with Spooky. I shoved my phone back into my pocket.

"Well..." he trailed off.

"Why are you wearing sunglasses?" I asked.

"It's nothing, just the sunlight." I looked to the side of the wall next to the gate and there were a few snacks. "I've been chilling over there, it's my favorite place to sit when I need an escape," the corners of his mouth curled up. "Do you want to sit?" he asked.

"Yeah, sure," I said, and then we both sat on the freshly cut grass which was part of the public that needed to be kept cut. "So, please tell me what's going on," I pushed.

The sun started to dip low in the sky, casting long shadows across the grass. An unspoken tension hung in the air. Spooky, still wearing his sunglasses, looked more subdued than usual.

"Elona," he began, his voice carrying an unusual weight, "I just haven't been feeling well lately."

So, that was it? He wasn't feeling well, and his phone was broken. "Well, I hope that you get better soon, it's just weird not having you chill with us."

He hesitated as if grappling with whether to open up. "I also have some things on my mind. Nothing major. You don't need to worry."

But worry had already planted its seed in my chest. "Spooky, we are friends. Friends share burdens. What is really going on?"

He sighed, his gaze fixed on the distant horizon. "It's just... my parents. They are away on business. I would rather not talk about it."

His response left me with more questions than answers, but I respected his boundaries. "Okay, if you don't want to talk about it, then I respect that. But you know I'm here for you, right?"

He gave a small, appreciative smile, but a layer of tension lingered between us. As we chatted about lighter topics, I couldn't shake the feeling that something unsaid hung between us.

"I really like Cris," he said.

"I know you do. But will she return those feelings? You know how outgoing she can be." I stated.

"I know, but I'm willing to give it a try with her and see how it goes," he replied.

"Then you should hang out with us more." I smiled, this was my way to make him leave his house more after this, "Besides, you need to get away from any problems over here. Cris will entertain you," I've used the same statement that Cris had used with me and Tristan.

"She certainly will," he smiled. But then he looked at the sky and then his smile disappeared, "I think I'll go and rest. I'll walk you home," he said as he stood up and held a hand out to me. I placed my hand in his, and he helped me up. He picked up his snacks, and we walked in step. A pang of unease settled in my stomach.

"Are you sure you're okay? You seem... different."

"I'm fine, I just need rest, not feeling well, remember?" he said, but his words held a weight I couldn't quite decipher. As he walked me home, the distance between us felt palpable as if an invisible barrier had sprung up.

When we reached my house, Tristan's unexpected presence on the front steps seized my attention. His face, illuminated by the glow of his phone, wore an expression of anger that sent shivers down my spine. He stood up, scowling at us.

"What is going on here?" he demanded, his eyes locking onto Spooky.

"We were just hanging out, Tristan," I explained, confusion knitting my brows.

Tristan's gaze shifted between us, his anger simmering beneath the surface. "You need to stay away from her. I had no clue where she was, not even her father knew. I won't allow you to put her in danger, it's dark already." he warned Spooky.

As Spooky's sunglasses hid his eyes, I couldn't help but feel like there was more to this tension than met the eye. I gave Spooky an apologetic smile before he left. It was all my fault because I ignored Tristan and put my phone on silent. So, of course, he would worry as it was dark now. But he shouldn't be cruel to Spooky because of me. I felt bad, I just hoped that this wouldn't make Spooky stay away from us.

Needs

Elona

I walked past Tristan up the few steps and I unlocked the front door, opening it. I entered and he followed after me. I could feel the tension coming from him and he closed the door behind him. I felt bad for not answering the phone and making him worry about me but I'm fine and safe at home.

"I don't want you to be anywhere near him," he seethed. I turned around to face him. He was livid, his jaw clenching.

"He's a friend, Tristan. How many times do I need to say that to you? Why are you so worried about Spooky? Afraid that he will steal me from you?" I raised my voice.

"Yes and the fact that I don't trust him one bit. He's bad news," he raised his voice too.

"He has been missing and I went to look for him-"

"In the dark? Alone? You could've asked me to come with you," he interrupted.

"And then you would tell me not to go. I'm sorry that I didn't answer your calls. But Spooky is not well and his phone is broken. He didn't respond to our texts and calls. His parents are away for business. It was enough for us to worry," I tried to explain.

"I will not tolerate you two being together." his gaze burned into mine as he slowly approached me and I walked backward.

"I won't allow you to tell me who I can and cannot be friends with let alone my modeling career," I hissed at him and my back was now against the wall.

He rested his hands on either side of me against the wall, caging me in, and then he leaned in. He was inches away from me. "You are mine and no one will have you," he was stern but yet the tension was so much that I couldn't say anything further, I wanted him, I was soaked in my panties. My lips parted. "Tell me that you're mine," he whispered.

"I'm always yours," I said softly.

His lips crashed against mine, kissing me passionately as I closed my eyes, my hands roamed his chest until my arms were wrapped around his neck, bringing him in closer. His hands found my ass and he pulled me against him, his hard bulge against my lower abdomen. He moaned and he moved against me. His tongue entered my mouth as soon as I gave him the gap to do so. Our tongues danced, lifting me up, I wrapped my legs around his waist.

His lips were inches from mine. "I want you so badly," he rasped.

"Please, just fuck me," I begged.

I couldn't wait anymore, I didn't want to wait any longer. He smiled at me and then he carried me upstairs and into my bedroom. He kicked the door closed behind us and his lips found mine again. He put me down, breaking our kiss. He bit his bottom lip and my stomach flipped, that was a huge turn-on for me. His hands reached the bottom of my cropped top. I lifted my arms up in the air and he removed it, discarding it onto the ground.

His eyes fell onto my breasts and then his hands moved down to my denim shorts, he undid the button and little zipper, slipping my shorts off until it fell at my feet. I kicked off my sneakers and I stepped out of my shorts, pushing it to the side with my foot. His hands reached my lace panties.

"Lace," he breathed, "I love lace," He lifted his gaze to mine again. His hand moved down until it was inside my lace panties, cupping my pussy. I wanted more than this. "You are drenched for me," he said softly.

"Yes," I breathed, my hand gripping his arm. A moan escaped me as his finger found my clit. He flicked his finger over it and I felt as if I could orgasm right in this moment. I clenched my legs together in order to prolong it, but then his finger entered me and my grip on his arm tightened.

"Fuck, you look so beautiful even when you are aroused."

"Please, just fuck me," I begged.

"I love the way you beg me," he continued to thrust in and out of me, my one hand moving to his t-shirt, gripping it. I felt my orgasm building.

"Please," I continued to beg but he wouldn't stop. My orgasm ripped through me, "Ahhhh, shit!" my knees buckled and he caught me before I could drop to the ground. He held me against him as my chest heaved and I came down from the powerful orgasm that I had.

He removed his hand from my panties, "Are you okay?" he asked.

"Yeah," I whispered in my euphoric state.

He helped me to stand up and then he cupped the back of my head, pressing a kiss against my lips, becoming passionate again. His hands moved behind my back as he unclipped my bra, and removed it. Discarding it on the ground with my cropped top and my denim shorts.

His hands moved to my panties and he removed it, letting it fall to the ground and I stepped out of it, as I broke our kiss. My bed hit the back of my knees and I sat down.

Tristan was watching me with this hunger that I haven't seen before as he removed his t-shirt and then he undid his jeans. Removing his sneakers and letting his jeans fall to the ground, stepping out of it. He was left in his boxer briefs. His erection was visible and he was huge. He removed his boxer brief, his cock springing to life and my eyes widened at how huge he really was.

I moved further to the middle of my bed and he climbed onto it. His eyes moved to my breasts and as he moved on top of me, he leaned in and captured one nipple into his mouth, his hand fondling the other. I moaned, closing my eyes and my whole body tingled and wanted more. I felt a sharp sting on my nipple as he bit lightly into it. He paid attention to the other one too before he trailed kisses between my breasts all the way up to my neck, my jaw, and finally my lips. He was fully on top of me now and his cock teased my entrance as he balanced himself on his elbows which rested on either side of my head.

"Are you ready?" he asked softly.

"I've always been ready," I responded impatiently.

He reached between us and he guided his cock into my entrance with a bit of force. I yelped. "Are you okay?" he looked at me with concern.

"Yeah," I held my breath as he pushed further into me. I was a virgin and he didn't know that I was. I had lied to him, so obviously he thinks that he can just penetrate.

"Fuck, you're so tight," he breathed, his face contorted as he also struggled to push inside of me, "Fuck," he let out a breath. A tear slipped and he saw it. "Is it too much?" he asked.

I shook my head, no. Sucking in a breath, "Continue," I demanded.

"I'm not even fully inside of you yet. So bare with me. I know I might be huge," he smirked.

I just nodded and then more tears streamed down my face as he penetrated further inside of me, all the way to the hilt. I moved my hands to his back and I dug my nails into his skin causing him to groan. He started thrusting into me and the pain seared through me. He was only going at a slow pace.

"I'm sorry that this is hurting you," he whispered, his elbows still resting on either side of my head and he leaned down to press a kiss on my forehead as he continued to thrust into me. I wished that it wasn't this painful, but I tried to focus on the pleasure over the pain.

He picked up the pace and I dug my nails into him again causing him to groan. He kept at that pace. "You're mine. No one else's but mine," he rasped.

Another orgasm started to build within my core and the heat caused us to sweat. I clung onto him as my body convulsed with my orgasm, I bit so hard on my bottom lip that I tasted the metallic of my own blood.

My pussy pulsated around him causing him to draw close to his release. "Fuck," he muttered under his breath as I saw white spots. He kissed me. Sucking onto my bottom lip where I bit myself and then he pulled back.

As I came down from my orgasm, he pulled out of me and released his fluids onto my stomach. His face contorted as he continued to come on me. Our chests heaved, and our panting was the only sound in my bedroom. Tristan Crane had sex with me, and my crush on him and to even be with him came true. It felt so surreal.

"Fuck. You're bleeding," he said as he got up from the bed and he looked around for something but he took his t-shirt and he cleaned me up. I looked down and there was some blood on my sheet. I just continued to lay on my bed in my euphoric state. I felt exhausted and I just wanted to sleep. "How are you feeling?" He asked as he continued to clean me up.

"I feel good," I gave him a lazy smile. He discarded his t-shirt on the ground and then he moved up beside me. He took a throw that was draped over the end of my bed and he covered us with it. He wrapped me in his arms, and nuzzled his face into my neck, kissing me.

"Are you sore?" he asked.

"Yes," I was about to drift off to sleep. The lamp continued to shine in my room. It was battery-operated so I left it on during the day too. It was the only light that was shining besides the hallway lights.

"I'm sorry if I was rough," he said.

"Don't worry about it," I responded.

"You're mine forever," he breathed against my ear, "No one touches your body besides me."

"There will only be you, Tristan. It has always been you since I had my crush on you which started a few years ago."

"Really?" he asked with surprise.

I chuckled slightly, "Yeah. I wanted you to notice me too but to my surprise, you eventually noticed me this year."

"I'm glad I did. I don't know what I would do without you. There's something about you that just makes me feel alive and happy again. No one else has that effect on me." he sighed, "I want us to be this way forever...We will not be a secret for long but when you are in college next year then we can break the news to Cris and your father. I don't care if they don't take it well, I'll still be with you no matter what. I've been lonely for the past three years and this is my only chance at happiness, so they need to understand. For the time being, we have to keep this a secret. I'll book hotels in order for us to hang out. We can drive away from close places and just be us somewhere else with no one noticing us," he said.

"I like the sound of that. I may be hesitant about Cris and my dad finding out about us, especially next year but if we want to be together then I think we should approach this carefully. Maybe we can let them know at the same time." I suggested.

"That could work," he said. He nuzzled his face into my neck again and kissed me as I started to drift off to sleep. I'm not sure if I was imagining this but I did not expect to hear what was said next, "I love you," he murmured.

I was so far in my drifting off that I couldn't even decipher if he really said that to me or if I was dreaming. But darkness started to consume me as my body felt exhausted from the sex that we had. I hope that it was not a dream when I woke up in the morning. I still inhaled his scent as I was in complete darkness and I found comfort in that and the way that he held me...I felt safe.

Finding Something

Elona

I reached my hand out with my eyes still closed but I felt an empty space beside me. I opened my eyes but squinted at the sunlight. Tristan wasn't beside me and I sat up straight taking in the surroundings of my bedroom. I rubbed my eyes and yawned. As I stretched I winced as my body was stiff and sore. I was still naked. Tristan finally fucked me and I smiled to myself.

I looked over to my bedside table and there was a folded note laying against the lamp. I reached for it and unfolded it.

Elona,

I don't want you to think that I just got up and left. I'm being careful. I waited until you fell asleep and then I left. I love to stare at you even while you sleep. You are beautiful and you make me forget about things. Please, come over to my house, Cris is away for the weekend and you have me all to yourself.

I love you.

Tristan.

My heart stopped when I read the last part. There it was again. *I love you.* I traced the words with the tip of my index finger. So what he said last night was true. He loves me. I heard that correctly. Smiling, I folded the note and got out of bed. As sore as my body was, I was not used to this but it was great. I do hope that it gets better.

I placed the note into my vanity drawer and I took out my clothes that I would wear today which was a floral sundress. I took my clothes from the previous day and discarded them into my laundry basket which was next to my vanity cabinet. I took a shower and I was reminded of the moment that Tristan and I shared together the previous day.

Water poured all over me as I stood under the shower and washed away that moment. But my brows furrowed. Did my dad come back home last night? He did say that I shouldn't wait up for him. Once I was done in the shower, I grabbed a towel and dried myself, got dressed, and walked out of my bedroom.

The aroma of breakfast filled my nostrils as I walked down the stairs and into the kitchen. "Good morning, Dad," I smiled.

"Hey, I'm starving, so I decided to cook breakfast for us. I hope that you're hungry," he said as I sat on the bar stool.

"I won't say no," I continued to smile as he placed eggs and bacon onto my plate before turning away from me as he switched the stove off. "So, when did you get back home?" I asked as I took a fork and began to eat.

"I got home just after midnight. Tristan tried calling me earlier in the evening when he was at our house. He was worried about you because he couldn't get a hold of you for something that was career-related." he said and I knew that Tristan had lied to him about the career-related part.

"I'm sorry to worry anyone. It's just that Spooky never replied to our texts or calls and we never saw him. Cris and I were supposed to check if he was okay but then Cris had this SNT thing for this weekend, so I went by myself. He isn't feeling well, and his phone is broken but I just hope that he is truly okay." I said, my mind drifting off to Spooky now.

"You're a great friend and so is Cris," he smiled at me.

"I'll be going to Tristan after this, I want to apologize and see why he needs me for the career-related thing," I had to lie to him for my reasons as to why I'll be going to Tristan.

"You usually call him Uncle Tristan," Dad said.

Shit.

"Sorry, Dad," I forced a smile. That was so close.

* * *

After I was done with breakfast, I went to Tristan. I just wanted to get away from home so that my father wouldn't even get suspicious if I slipped up.

I walked up the steps and then I knocked on the front door. Tristan opened the door almost immediately. He reached out and grabbed my wrist, pulling me inside with a smirk. He was dressed in a light blue t-shirt and dark blue jeans. He shut the door and he pressed me against it. He leaned in as he caged me in with both of his hands against the door.

He pressed his lips to mine and I moved my hands up his chest. He pulled inches away, "Good morning." he smiled. I loved this...to see him happy.

"Good morning," I replied, returning his smile.

"How are you feeling?" he asked.

"I'm sore, but all good."

"Well, I'll wait a bit until you're no longer sore." He pulled further away from me and he took my hand in his. Leading me towards the kitchen, he pulled the chair out for me and I took a seat.

He rounded the table and took something from the kitchen counter. When he came closer, he had a plate of pancakes and a slice of chocolate cake. "It's early for cake," I said but I loved chocolate cake. I do not eat any other type of cake.

"Well, I wanted to surprise you with your favorite this morning," he smiled as he sat down.

"Thank you," I said.

His phone rang and he took it out of his pocket. He frowned as he looked at the screen. "Excuse me, I have to take this," he answered his phone. "Crane..." I just sat there not even touching the pancakes and cake. He let out a heavy breath and he ran his hand through his hair, "Fine, and thank you," he hung up.

"Is everything okay?" I asked.

"No, everything is not okay. Someone hacked into my company. So far the person that might've done this is being investigated. The thing is...I've worked so hard for my company and I put all my blood, sweat, and tears into it. The pain that I had since Estelle's death, drove me to work harder. That's what grief did to me. In that time, I became more successful, I hardly even had any rivals. But there are always people out there who want to steal. Stealing other people's hard work." He leaned back in the chair and I could see that hurt. The mask slipped away because of someone else who was stealing from his company.

"You don't deserve any of this. I know how hard you've been working. I see that and you're only starting to have fun now–"

"Please, with you...this is nothing close to 'fun' because with you, I'm serious and happy. I feel alive again. You're not just some kind of booty call for me or a one-night stand. With you...its more than any of that. Sure, there may be fun moments where we can laugh together and go out. But you're a diamond to me that I cannot let you slip out of my grasp. I won't find another woman like you. You remind me of Estelle, the softness, she got whatever she wanted and she didn't let anyone stand in her way but with you, your career choice, I'm still against that. I have to respect you too but I'm here to protect you from the world out there too." He held my gaze and I swallowed.

"I know that you mean well, but I'll be fine." I gave him a reassuring smile.

He looked down at the table, "After working so hard with my company, there were lots of funds and investments. I could buy even more buildings and open up more companies. The gallery where your mother's painting will be...it was flooded due to a pipe burst and we had to push back the date of the exhibition. Don't worry, all the paintings are being kept safe in a storage room. Also, I have lost half of my money due to the hacking. Luckily, my teams have stopped them from taking all of it, including my clients," his eyes glazed over.

"I'm so sorry to hear that," my heart broke for him in this situation. "Are you able to get all of it back?" I asked.

"I hope so. Everything is being taken care of, investigations...everything. I want that hacker to be found and I want my staff to be questioned thoroughly. Monday will be the day that I will unleash my wrath on them. I'm not going to be the lenient boss I used to be. They hit a part of me that poured all of myself into the company," he said and I saw his eyes darken with anger.

"First see who is behind it. It may not even be an inside job but I get it...you have to look everywhere and they can be anywhere."

"Exactly," he replied and I reached out to him, resting my hand on his, giving it a gentle squeeze. "On a different note. I wanted to make love to you again but you need to recover from last night," he said.

I pulled my hand away, " I think so too. It was pretty intense-"

"And painful." he smiled.

"I hurt you by being too tight," I said, which was barely a whisper.

"It's fine. I'm sure that I'm huge according to you, so..." He shrugged. "I guess that is to be expected."

I wasn't going to tell him that he took my virginity and that was the reason for our first time together to be that way, but I was curious about another thing. "How did Estelle and Maggie handle you when in intimate moments?" I asked hesitantly.

"Well, it was the same at first with Estelle. The more we had sex the less painful it got. With Maggie, it was a one-night stand, so we fucked nearly the entire night, she was sore in the morning but nothing compared to you. You were very tight and for a minute I actually thought that you were a virgin but when a woman doesn't have sex in a long time, it tends to get painful again for a woman. Estelle and I were just married and we didn't have sex as much. I had to go to London for a few months and then we had sex again, it felt like the first time all over again for her." He shrugged.

I needed that information. "So it doesn't really get any better unless we fuck all the time?" I was hoping that it would become better even after a while.

"The more we do it, the better it becomes. I will not go anywhere, so you're secretly stuck with me," he smirked.

"Until next year. I just hope that Cris and my dad will take the news well."

"I hope so too. Now, eat up because I plan for us to watch a movie today." He stood up from the chair. But then his phone rang, I started to eat the cake which was delicious. I was oblivious to his phone call because I was enjoying my favorite cake. "I have to go to work to sort something out. I hope that you'll be okay with that. You can stay here, I won't be that long," he said to me with sadness in those eyes.

"I'll be here," I offered a smile. He leaned in and placed a kiss on the top of my head and then he left.

I placed the fork on the plate with my half-eaten cake and I stood up. I walked through the house just to explore. I went all the way to the bigger section of the house, where he played the piano for me and then I went to the study room which was bigger than the other one he started to use after Estelle's death.

I pushed the door further open and it creaked. I stepped inside. It was clean yet the desk was full of dust. I walked by the bookshelves and there were photos of Cris, Estelle, and Tristan. They were so happy. I traced the photo with the tip of my finger. I stepped away from the bookshelf where the photos were and I went behind the desk, pulling the leather chair out. It was covered with a white sheet.

I took a seat. I opened the drawer and then there was a framed photo that was glass but turned on its front. I took it out and when I looked at the picture...my heart sank and tears stung the back of my eyes. It was a framed photo of an ultrasound. The baby was the shape of a bean. The baby that they lost in Estelle's car accident.

The Window

Elona

I left Tristan's house not long after I had seen that ultrasound picture. There was nothing for me to do there, just being by myself. I sat at my desk in the corner of my bedroom and just scrolled through my phone. There was no text from Tristan. I could've gone to check up on Spooky too, but I was already at home and I didn't feel like going over there. That house just gives me the creeps.

I sent Tristan a text.

Me: I'm at home. I hope that things are okay at work. I love you.

I just couldn't believe I had said that. It felt too soon to say that, but we have known each other for a long time. So it shouldn't matter.

My phone chimed and it was him.

Crane: Things will be better. I love you more.

My heart melted at that. I couldn't help but smile.

***

It was becoming dark, and I went downstairs as my father sat on the bar stool at the counter. He was reading a newspaper. There was a box of pizza and my stomach growled. "So, what is interesting in that paper?" I asked as I rounded the counter.

"Nothing too interesting." He folded the paper and placed it on the counter. "How is your modeling coming along? What did Tristan want to talk about with regards to your future career?" He asked as he opened the pizza box and took out a slice of pizza.

I was caught off guard with the future career question. I forgot that Tristan had used that excuse for me to be with him.

"Um, it was only about agencies. Oh, I have submitted my portfolio to a few agencies and one of them is The Velvet Secret," I said. I had to lie about what Tristan said. This was going to be an issue. All of these lies to keep track of. Who of us will slip up? Me or Tristan?

"That is amazing. I hope that all of them accept you so that you have plenty to choose to be with. And as for Tristan, I'm glad that he is also looking out for you," he smiled, and then he took a bite of the pizza.

"Yeah, he sure does," I smiled. The way that Tristan looks out for me is just insane...as if I cannot do something that I want to pursue because he doesn't want anyone else to look at my body.

I grabbed a slice of Pizza and I took a bite. "I will be in the study room working. Have you heard what's going on with Tristan's company?" He asked, taking another bite of pizza.

"The hacking?"

"Yeah, it's something that never happened, and he doesn't have any rivals, not that I even know of. That man worked so hard and for that person, whoever they are, to just do that? It's crazy. I hope they find that hacker." He let out a heavy breath.

"I hope they do," I added.

"I will go to the study room now and get some work done," he said as he stood up.

"So, you won't be going out?" I asked because he usually does.

"Not tonight. I need to get things done for work," he smiled before he walked out of the kitchen.

I finished another slice, and then I went up the stairs to my bedroom. I changed into my pajama shorts and a tank top. I checked my phone on my desk, but there was no text from Tristan, perhaps he was still busy and I wouldn't be bothering him. So I left my phone where it was.

As I walked over to my bed, there was a tapping sound on my window. I stopped in my tracks as there was more tapping. I went closer to my window and opened the curtain. Tristan.

I opened my window wide. "Tristan, what are you doing here? You actually climbed?" I asked with surprise as I moved out of the way as he climbed inside.

He smiled at me as he stood up straight. "Yes, I did. I wanted to see you again. I know that your father is home, so I wasn't going to knock on the door and I wanted to surprise you. Are you surprised?" He asked mischievously.

"Yes, I am surprised." I smiled, and then he leaned in, cupping the sides of my face with both of his hands. He pressed his lips against mine. I closed my eyes as he pressed me against the wall beside the window. I gasped, and he took that opportunity to slide his tongue into my mouth. His hands moved down, cupping my breasts, and then he pulled inches away from me as his hands moved further down my body until they got to my shorts. He slipped them off with my panties, and it fell around my bare feet and I stepped out of it.

"This will be quick," he whispered as his hands moved between my legs, his finger found my clit, flickering it. I let out a moan, and he pulled away. "You will have to be quiet," he rasped.

I bit my bottom lip, "Please, I need you now," I begged.

He removed his finger from my pussy, and then he undid his jeans, freeing his cock. He pulled me closer to him, and then he lifted me up, with my arms around his neck and my legs wrapped around his waist. He pressed me further against the wall, and he reached down between us, aligning the tip of his cock with my entrance, and then he pushed in slowly. I parted my lips, throwing my head back against the wall.

"You're still so tight," he whispered, and he never stopped pushing into me. He was deep inside of me, all the way to the hilt, and then he began to move his hips, penetrating me. I held onto him so tight, it was so intense. His pace picked up, and I bit my bottom lip, trying not to make a sound because my father was downstairs in the study room.

He pounded into me, and it was a mixture of pain and pleasure. He breathed against my ear as he pounded into me and my orgasm was starting to build up. "Shit," I whispered.

He looked at me, and he pressed his lips against mine. My orgasm took over me, he never stopped. He continued to keep his lips against mine, to keep me quiet, and then he pulled away, pulling out of me. He pressed his forehead against mine as he came, biting on his teeth to stay quiet. His fluids were now on the bottom of my tank top.

Both of us came down from our orgasms, panting. "How are you feeling?" He asked through his panting.

"I feel great," I replied, our chests heaving.

He placed me on my feet and I walked over to my closet, taking out a new tank top and I got dressed. He was sitting on the edge of my bed, and he looked at me as if he wanted to devour me again.

"So, how are things at the company?" I asked as I sat down beside him.

He reached out to me, and then he moved my hair behind my shoulder. "Things are being sorted out." He smiled at me.

"I'm glad that things are finally being sorted. I don't wish for this to happen to you again. You deserve only the best," I smiled, and he leaned in, placing a kiss on my lips, but that turned passionate and then the next thing, he was fucking me on my bed. I could get used to this.

His elbows rested on either side of my head, he buried his face in the crook of my neck as he continued thrusting into me. My hands roamed his back, digging my fingers into his skin. He groaned as he looked at me, his eyes were dark with pleasure. He made me orgasm for a second time and not too long after me, he pulled out and came on my bare stomach. I was happy that it was not on my tank top because then there would be more laundry for me to do. My tank top was shoved up to my breasts.

Our chests heaved as we caught our breath. He held me in his arms, and we just spoke about things. "Has Cris texted you yet?" I asked. My head was on his chest and I listened to his heartbeat.

"Yeah, she loves it over there. She's a very intelligent young lady and I'm proud of her," he said.

"Me too."

"As for you…" He started.

"Please, let's not talk about my career. That is for me, and you do not need to worry about it. It's what will make me happy," I said.

"So, you're saying that I don't make you happy?" He asked, and I moved my weight on my elbow so that I could get a better look at him. He wasn't happy about it.

"You do make me happy more than you know," I said as I leaned in and placed a kiss on his lips. I pulled away but he still wasn't happy. "Don't think anything bad, please."

"It's difficult not to when you're going into that industry, showing off your body to the world."

"Just relax, please. I can handle this," I tried to reassure him, but he scoffed at me.

"Really? You can handle it. There are vultures in that industry, and I'm trying to protect you," he held my gaze.

"Let's change the topic, shall we?" I said.

There was a knock on my door. "Elona," my dad called out from the other side of the door. My heart raced.

"Get up!" I whispered to Tristan as I stood up from the bed and put on my shorts.

"Just a minute, Dad!" I called out to him. Tristan was slipping on his boxer briefs and I moved towards him, "You have to leave," I whispered.

"Fuck." He muttered under his breath and he struggled to get into his jeans, but he grabbed his sneakers and climbed out of the window just in time when my dad opened the door.

"Is everything okay?" He asked, and I heard a loud thud outside. I hoped Tristan was okay. "What was that?" My dad asked.

"Probably just a cat. Everything is fine," I smiled as I moved towards my bed, and he looked at it, his brows furrowing. My bed was a mess from Tristan and I. Usually, it was neat and tidy when my dad would enter my bedroom, or I would be in my bed.

"Okay, I'm heading to bed. Sleep well," he said as he began to close the door.

"Night, Dad," I smiled.

Once the door closed, I let out a breath, and then I moved to the window to see if Tristan was still there. But he was gone. I went to my desk and sent him a text.

Me: That was close. We have to be more careful next time. I love you.

Crane: I might've hurt myself climbing down. I love you.

Me: I hope it's not serious. It was loud.

Crane: Don't worry about me. I'm fine. Sweet dreams.

I smiled at the text. My heart was still beating at a rapid pace. I thought that I would have a heart attack if my father had opened the door without saying anything and then the chaos would have begun. We have to be more careful. The hotel seems to be a better idea to be safe. I don't want us to get caught in this kind of way. I want us to tell my father and Cris at the same time next year, so we have to pretend that nothing is going on between us, even though it's difficult.

Breadcrumb

Tristan

I sat at my desk as I stared at the laptop screen in front of me that was displaying a line of codes. The recent cyberattack on my company had thrust me into a position I hadn't anticipated. I took a sip of my lukewarm coffee, the bitter taste matching the bitterness that had settled within me since the breach.

There was a knock on the door and I looked up from the screen "Mr Crane, any progress on the investigation?" Stan, my IT specialist, asked as he approached my desk, concern etched on his face.

I rubbed my temples, feeling the weight of my responsibility. "Not yet. They are good, Stan. Really good. But I won't rest until I find who is behind this."

Stan nodded, "As you should. We will find this person," he said, and then he walked out of my office, back to his workstation.

I looked at the laptop screen again and then my phone rang. I averted my gaze at my phone. Maggie's name appeared on the screen. It was like all the air had been sucked out of me. My heart tightened, and a mixture of emotions surged within me. Anger, guilt, and regret. I ignored her.

I couldn't allow any kind of distraction, not even Elona right now, because my main mission was to get this hacker. I cannot afford to lose more than what this person has stolen. I refocused on the laptop screen, analyzing the intricate web of code. Every second counts, the longer our systems were compromised, the more damage could be done, but Stan was brilliant at containing anything. I just wanted to make sure that asshole doesn't find a way to do this again to me.

The IT team worked tirelessly to restore the security. But my mind was not at ease. My phone rang again with Maggie's name appeared on the screen. She was being persistent. I continued to ignore it, my jaw clenching as frustration mounted. My priority was my company, the employees who depended on its stability, and the livelihoods at stake.

"Mr Crane," Stan called again, his voice urgent, "I found a trace. It might lead us to the source."

I shot out of the chair, my weariness momentarily forgotten, but winced due to the fall that I had from climbing out of Elona's window yesterday, I landed on my back. "Where? What did you find?" I asked.

Taking my phone, I followed Stan to his workstation, I took a seat in the chair next to him. Stan's fingers danced across the keyboard, navigating through lines of code with practiced precision. I leaned in, my eyes narrowing at the screen, eager to grasp any lead that could unveil the perpetrators behind the cyberattack.

"Mr Crane, check this out," Stan pointed to a specific section of the code. "This is where they breached our firewall. But look here, it's not just a straightforward attack. They have left a breadcrumb, a trace intentionally meant for us to find."

I squinted at the screen, trying to decipher the intricate patterns of code. "So, they want us to follow this trail?"

"Exactly," Stan confirmed. "It's like they are taunting us, leading us down a rabbit hole. But the thing is, this might be a diversion. While we are busy chasing this, they could be exploiting another vulnerability."

My frustration deepened. The attackers weren't just skilled, they were strategic and playing a psychological game. "How do we know this trace is legitimate and not another layer of deception?"

Stan nodded, acknowledging the challenge. "That's the tricky part. However, I 've cross-referenced it with multiple systems, and the anomaly is consistent. It's a risk, but if we follow it cautiously, we might get a lead."

I sighed, grappling with the decision. "Let's do it. We need to take that risk. I want to know who is behind this, and I want to know now."

Stan nodded and started initiating the trace, his fingers flying across the keyboard with a focused determination. As the progress bar on the screen filled slowly, the tension in the room was palpable, I couldn't shake the feeling that every second counted.

Amid the concentrated silence, Maggie's calls persisted in the background, a nagging reminder of a personal storm brewing alongside the professional one. But at this moment, my focus narrowed to the relentless pursuit of justice for the company.

Finally, the screen flickered, displaying a series of IP addresses. Stan turned to me, a mix of excitement and caution in his eyes. "Mr Crane, we got a lead. The source seems to be originating from an offshore server, but it's a starting point."

I clenched my jaw, the nameless adversaries now having a faint identity. "Let's track them down. I want to know who thinks they can threaten what I've built."

As we delved deeper into the digital labyrinth, the office became a battlefield of data, each keystroke a strategic move. The relentless pursuit of justice had begun, and I was determined to emerge victorious, both for the sake of the company and for the semblance of control slipping through my fingers.

The incessant ringing of my phone cut through the focused hum of the workstation. Irritation simmered beneath my skin as I glanced at the caller ID, it was Maggie again. The timing couldn't have been worse, and my patience had worn thin.

I excused myself from the bustling activity of the IT room and retreated to my office. The muted glow of city lights filtered through the windows, casting a somber hue over the space. I answered the call, the tension in my voice palpable.

"What do you want, Maggie?" I snapped, my frustration bubbling to the surface.

"Tristan, we need to talk. It's important," Maggie's voice held a hint of urgency.

I clenched my jaw, my tone curt. "Now is not a good time. I'm dealing with a crisis at the company."

Her voice persisted, undeterred. "Tristan, it can't wait. We have unfinished business."

I took a deep breath, my patience hanging by a thread. "Maggie, I've moved on. I have a girlfriend now. Whatever 'business' you think we have is over. Don't call me again."

There was a long pause on the other end of the line, the weight of my words sinking in. The silence stretched until I could almost hear Maggie processing the reality of the situation.

Finally, she stammered, "You... you moved on?"

I nodded, forgetting she couldn't see the gesture. "Yes, Maggie. It's time for both of us to move on. Goodbye."

Without waiting for a response, I ended the call, my hand gripping the phone tightly. The air in the office felt heavy with the unresolved tension, but I refused to let the ghosts of the past disrupt the fragile balance I was desperately trying to maintain.

As I returned to the IT room, the glow of the computer screen awaited, the digital battlefield demanding my attention once more. The unfinished business with Maggie had no place in the present, not when the company's survival hung in the balance.

If this doesn't get solved, then I will just leave it and work hard on securing everything so that hackers cannot do this again. I know for sure that I don't have any business rivals or enemies that I can think of. But I will get my finances back that I've worked so hard for. This stress is just becoming too much for me now, and it does play a role in my health. So, I won't let it get to that extent.

Visitor Surprise

Tristan

I was eager to see Elona as I walked on the sidewalk towards her house. When I got to her house, David's car was parked in the driveway. It was Monday, so Cris was home after school. I was at work early this morning, but I needed a break after I had been at the office the entire day yesterday. I knocked on the door, waiting for Elona to possibly open it. I hadn't even texted her last night due to things that were going on at the company.

"Tristan, come on in. We have a visitor," David smiled. I furrowed my brows wondering who this visitor could be.

"A visitor?" I asked as I stepped inside.

"Just head to the kitchen and you will see," he said as he closed the door behind me.

I hope that he was talking about Elona because I have no idea who he was talking about. My heart dropped as I entered the kitchen, my jaw clenched, and I scowled as I looked at the back of the woman who was sitting at the kitchen counter. The one woman that I was avoiding. "Come on, take a seat," David patted my back, snapping me out of it. I sucked in a breath before I walked closer to her. She turned around, and a smile was visible on her face.

"Tristan, I'm so glad to see you," David sat on the other side of her.

"Maggie," I stated as I took a seat beside her on a bar stool.

I rested my elbows on the counter, clasping my hands. "I wanted to see you, I missed you. David is great company, so I came over here because we are still friends," she said.

I clenched my jaw, not liking this. "Well, I came here to see David, not you," I replied.

"Have you heard anything back from Dakota Agencies?" David asked as Elona walked to the fridge.

"Yes, they are interested in me," She replied, and then she took a bottle of water out and closed the fridge, turning around to face us. She held my gaze, but she wasn't happy to see me sitting beside Maggie. Well, she has nothing to worry about because Elona has me already, no one else will have me. But I don't like that she is still going through with this modeling shit. I have to try to stop it one way or another. I continued to hold her gaze.

"That's amazing," David said. She finally broke eye contact as she looked at him.

"You're so beautiful, any man would have their eyes on you. You'll be amazing. I have no doubt about that," Maggie chimed in, and I wanted to tell her shit, but I bit my tongue.

"'Thanks, I have no doubt that they will have their eyes on me," she replied, moving her gaze at me, glaring. If she wants to play it that way, she has one thing coming. Anger rose within me, because not only is Maggie pushing it now, but so is Elona. I already have things going on that need my attention. "I will be going to see Spooky soon," Elona said, and then she took a sip of water. Double hit to my gut. Was she doing this on purpose?

"When is he coming over again? He's a great young man." David said, and it took everything inside of me not to snap at them.

"I have no idea," she replied, and then she walked out of the kitchen. I stood up too.

"I'll be leaving, I need to check up on the situation," I lied.

"So have you found the person?" David asked. Maggie was quiet for some reason, which meant that she had lied that there was business to talk about. But what was she doing here? Probably asking David about me.

"No, it was a dead end after I had thought that we had a lead," I let out a sigh.

"I'm sorry, I hope that you get that son of a bitch," David said.

"Yeah, me too. But I need to go," I replied and then I walked into the lounge.

I was not prepared to be stopped, "Tristan, wait," I stopped in my tracks, turning around to face Maggie.

"What is it? I thought that I had made it clear that I moved on, and I have a girlfriend," I scowled at her.

She bit her bottom lip as if she was offended by that, "Who is she?"

"That's none of your business," I hissed.

"I think that you're lying about having a girlfriend. You know how much I want to be with you. That night was so incredible and special that I have fallen for you, Tristan." She reached out and grabbed my arm, but I yanked it out of her grasp. I heard Elona's footsteps as she walked down the stairs. I turned to look at her, but she was glaring at us as she walked out the front door.

Turning back to Maggie, I said the following, "I have a girlfriend, respect that. I wasn't interested in you back then and never will be. That night was a one-night stand, nothing more, and it was definitely not special to me. You were just an easy fuck to get things off my mind that night... I don't have feelings for you, so do not bother me or call me ever again. Block me," I warned and then I left.

I hurried out the door but Elona was standing on a step as she typed on her phone, her back facing towards me. She turned to look at me but as she wanted to leave, I closed the door behind me and grabbed her wrist. I pulled her towards me and pressed her against the wall of the house.

Her lips were parted, and I placed one hand on the wall as I leaned in. "Do you enjoy doing this to me? Spooky, and modeling?" I asked softly, but it was filled with anger.

"You can't stop me from doing those things, and what about Maggie? What is she doing here? Are you two still talking to each other? Fucking each other?" she asked.

"Watch that filthy little mouth of yours," I warned, "I'm not talking to her, and I'm definitely not fucking her. She happened to be here. But I will not allow you to go to Spooky. If you want me that much, if you love me that much, you would respect me for what I ask," I demanded.

"Well, you demand, you do not ask. There is a difference." She was being stubborn.

I grabbed her jaw and I crashed my lips against hers, not giving a damn who on the street saw us. I pulled away, my chest heaving "You will be the death of me. I want to see you tonight, but I have work things to take care of. Do not think for one second that you will go to Spooky because you won't go there. You know what happened the last time. I would prefer you to hang out at my house with Cris. She's at home, but that's up to you." I searched her eyes for hope that she would come over.

My gaze moved to her lips as she licked them and my erection strained against my pants. "I will see about that, but I cannot promise anything."

"If you were in my house, I would fuck some sense into you. You drive me crazy, and I cannot sleep at night without thinking about you and stroking myself. That's what you do to me. I...I can't get enough of you. You... You are like a drug that I'm addicted to. I don't say this lightly, but that's what you do to me. Please take my advice and stay the hell away from Spooky and the modeling agency. I have to go." It took all of my strength to pull away from her. She just stood there with parted lips, looking at me.

I turned around and walked down the driveway to go back home. I would work in the study room, but I wish that she would come over so that I could at least have her to myself for a few minutes. I want no one else but her. She's the one for me. Never in a million years had I ever thought that I would say that again after losing Estelle. I'm confident to say that now. I do want to spend forever with her and I will make that happen, no matter who gets upset with us being together. I will not let her slip through my fingers.

She is my precious rare jewel that no one will have. She is mine and she needs to know that. But why the fuck was Maggie hanging out with David? Most probably to find out things about me since I have said that I've moved on. That will be a conversation for another day with David. Maggie will not get her way with me, and especially not today.

Sneaking In

Elona

I was stunned by what Tristan had told me. I turned around and walked back inside my house. I wasn't sure what Maggie was doing here, but seeing Tristan with her again made me so mad that I felt betrayed. I walked up the stairs to my bedroom and took my phone out of my denim shorts pocket. There was a text from Cris.

Cris: Please, have a sleepover by me tonight. I know that it's a school night, but I'm bored, and I haven't seen you this weekend. Please say you will.

I smiled at her text and this would play in Tristan's favor.

Me: Yes, I will.

I packed a little bag. I was not going over there now. I would go tonight when its a bit dark. I finished my homework until it was time to go to her. Cris was not at school today.

***

She opened the door. "I missed you!" She exclaimed and took me into her embrace.

"I missed you too," I said as she pulled away from me and stepped inside with my little gym bag and my backpack for school tomorrow.

"My dad is still working. Did you eat something?" She asked.

"What about me?" I looked in the kitchen and there Tristan stood with a glass of orange juice in his hand. He looked at my bags and then at me.

"I told Elona that you were busy working. She's sleeping over tonight," she said, and he looked at me with a newfound hunger. I felt the heat of his stare all over my body. The corners of his mouth curled up into a smile. He was happy about it and I smiled at him. "We'll be in my bedroom. Night Dad," Cris said.

"Good night, Uncle Tristan," I said, he still smiled at me hungrily, and then I followed after Cris.

Once we were inside her bedroom, I got undressed in my tank top and shorts. I plopped down on the other bed in her bedroom. She had two single beds. "How was your SNT weekend?" I asked.

My phone chimed and I looked at the screen.

Crane: You are sexy.

I smiled at the text, and then I focused on Cris who was talking about her time at SNT. I didn't even reply to Tristan. "I know that I'll love it there. It's the best choice that I'm making. I got to rest today, it was much needed." She said.

"I'm happy that you're doing what makes you happy," I smiled. "I got into the Dakota Agency."

"Yay!" She exclaimed, "That's amazing. We'll do what we both love." She lay down on her back, a lamp shining on the bedside table between us. I placed my phone on it. I got undressed and climbed into bed. "You'll be a gorgeous lingerie model." She sighed, catching me off guard as I looked at her.

"Well, I have my boundaries, and who knows, I might get into The Velvet Secret," I winked.

"They're amazing. I can't miss their fashion shows every New Year's Eve. You have to get into that. I saw how my dad even looks at you, he literally checks you out. I mean... he shouldn't be eyeing my female friends. It's just weird," she says as she checks her phone. Immediately, I blushed, but then I couldn't say anything because I didn't know how she would truly feel about me already dating her father.

"I did apply to them too, but I'm not setting my heart on it," I said.

"I don't know if I'll even have time for dating, but I want to date," she looked up at the ceiling.

I was lying on my side and looked at her. "I'll be dating soon," I replied. I just hope that I don't lose this friendship that we have when Tristan and I tell her that we're dating.

"Yeah, you'll get many guys easily," she yawned, "Let's continue that conversation tomorrow. I'm tired as fuck," she said, "Good night," she turned on her side and switched the lamp off.

"Good night," I replied. I just struggled to fall asleep because my mind was drifting to Tristan. Do I sneak out and go to his bedroom?

I decided against it and eventually, I fell asleep.

* * *

I felt something dip beside me on the bed. I stirred and blinked my eyes open. I got such a huge fright, "Tristan," I said, my heart beating fast. He was above me, it was dark.

"Shhh. Keep quiet," he whispered, his hands resting on either side of my head. I looked to the side to see Cris fast asleep, her back turned towards us.

I looked back at Tristan hovering above me. "We can't, not here," I whispered.

"Trust me," he replied.

He leaned down and pressed his lips against mine, kissing me passionately. His tongue entered my mouth as soon as I parted my lips, our tongues dancing together. He sucked my bottom lip before he moved down, trailing kisses along my jaw and neck. I gasped because it was both risky and thrilling that we might be caught this way, but I didn't care at that moment. I wanted him, my core was throbbing, and I was soaked for him. He pulled back. I could hardly see him in the dark.

"This will be quick," he whispered.

He moved his hand towards my shorts, and he slid them down with my panties. He threw it to one side on the bed. He was bare-chested and in his boxer briefs.

His finger found my clit and I gasped, nearly moaning, and I bit my bottom lip, "You're soaked," he rasped, and then he removed his hand from me and freed his cock.

I felt the tip of his cock at my entrance, and he pushed in. I arched my back, closed my eyes, and gripped the sheets on either side of me as he pushed in all the way to the hilt. I was full...full of him.

"Fuck, you feel so good, so tight." He groaned. I moved my hands to his back, and I dug my nails into his skin. He reached behind him for both of my hands, and he pinned them above my head against the headboard, he held them there with one hand.

He began to move, slow at first and then faster. "I want to come inside of you, but I need you to be on birth control," he whispered, and it took all the restraint in him not to just explode inside of me.

My orgasm was busy building up, "I'm on the pill," I blurted out.

"Thank fuck," he said as he picked up the pace even more and the bed squeaked with every thrust.

I bit my bottom lip as I orgasmed, my body convulsing, my eyes closed as I rode it out as silently as I could.

"I'm going to come," he groaned and just then, as I opened my eyes, my chest heaved in my euphoric state. Cris changed positions and she was now facing us. My heart beat faster as it was now too risky.

"Fuck," Tristan tried to keep quiet as he filled me up with his fluids. "Fuck," he repeated softly. He rested his forehead against mine as we panted, chests heaving. "Are you okay?" he asked.

"Yes," I whispered.

"Come to bed with me," he said, and I nodded.

Tristan climbed off the bed and pulled the boxer brief over his flaccid cock, but it was still huge. I quickly put my panties and shorts on. I stole one more glance in Cris' direction. She was still fast asleep, and then I followed Tristan out of her bedroom. That was so intense.

Study Room

Elona

I followed Tristan down the hallway. I was so happy that Cris didn't wake up. That would've been something else. I could just imagine waking up to see my father fuck my best friend if the situation were the other way around. What if that had to be the other way around? How would I have felt about it? Let alone how Cris would feel. I snapped out of my thoughts as Tristan turned around, grabbed the back of my head, and crashed his lips against mine, kissing me passionately as he pressed me up against the wall. My thoughts were forgotten.

I moved my hands against his chest and he slid his tongue into my mouth. He pressed against me and his cock was hard again. As my hands moved around his neck, his hands moved to my ass, squeezing as I let out a moan. He lifted me up, and I wrapped my legs around his waist.

He continued to kiss me passionately as he carried me, but this time we walked past his bedroom and further down the hallway. I think I know where he was taking me. Far away from Cris so that we could continue without getting caught. I pulled away, chest heaving, his eyes were hooded. The hallway light was on, "Where are you taking me?" I asked.

"My big study room." The corners of his mouth curled up.

I leaned in and pressed my lips against his again. I remember being in that study room the other day when he had left me to tend to work. Next thing, he opened the door and walked inside with me, kicking the door closed behind us.

He put me down on the desk and I leaned back, my hands resting on it behind me. "I want to fuck you in every room of this place. What used to be a very sad place, is no longer that when it comes to you. You make me feel like a new man. I want to mark every room with you." He said as he looked at me with hunger, but then his eyes caught something beside me. His brows furrowed. I turned my gaze to see what he was looking at.

My heart dropped as the ultrasound was on his desk. I'm sure that I put it back before I left the last time. I can't even remember. I swallowed. Cris doesn't know that she lost a sibling. It's Tristan's secret. He pulled away from me as I looked at him, he moved to the other end of the desk, and he took the ultrasound. Looking at it, his expression hardened.

"Cris must've been in here. She knew that this study room was off limits, and it was because of that," he said with a hint of anger in his voice.

I don't even know what to say because I just cannot remember if I had left it there. "I...uh... I was in here when you left the other day. I wanted to explore and I came in here. I saw the ultrasound, and I was sure that I had put it back. I'm so sorry. "I hope that he won't get mad at me for snooping around in his things.

He sucked in a breath as he continued to look at it. "I was about to fuck you in this study room which I have abandoned for three years, this room catching dust. I didn't want to be reminded of the pain, but somehow you made me want to move on. Now, seeing this," he looked up from the picture and found my gaze, "This is something that I also tried to bury. You found it, and if I want to move on, then I should just do that. But this is like a blow to my gut right now," he moved around the desk and I got off, turning around to face him. My heart was aching because I didn't know what to expect now as he placed it back inside his drawer, closed it, and took a seat on the leather chair that was still covered with a white sheet. He looked at nothing.

"I'm really sorry," I said again for what it was worth.

"I... I would appreciate it if you didn't snoop around in my things until I'm ready to share them with you," he looked at me, burning his gaze into me as if he was angry, and then he got up from the chair and walked around the desk. Standing in front of me, he cupped the back of my head and crashed his lips against mine again. He bit my bottom lip before kissing me passionately. I tasted the metallic of blood. He pulled away and turned me around. "Bend over, let me teach you a lesson," he commanded, and that turned me on.

He lowered my shorts with my panties and he massaged my ass cheeks. My hands were resting on the desk, I flinched as his hand came down hard on my ass, leaving a sting behind. He massaged again, "Will you learn not to snoop around again?" He asked.

I licked my lips, and gasped again as his hand came down on my ass, "Answer me," he demanded as he massaged.

"Y-yes," I replied.

"Good," he rasped as he stood behind me, and then his cock aligned with my entrance, I was still drenched with my juices mixed with his cum. I squeezed my eyes as he entered me without stopping, and he began to pound into me. This was my form of punishment for being in the study room when I was not supposed to be in it.

His fingers dug into my skin as he held me by my hips and my abdomen was pushed into the edge of the desk as he continued to thrust into me at a rapid pace, pounding all the air out of me. I moved my hands to the opposite end of the desk and as I wanted to grab that edge, his hands snaked around to my breasts, and he held me that way, never faltering with his thrusts as pleasure took over.

He pulled me towards him, making me stand up straight, his cock still inside of me. His arm covered one breast while the other held my breast as he thrust into me at a slower pace this time, his breath against my ear.

"Fuck, you're going to be the death of me," he breathed against my ear, and I let out a moan, throwing my head back against his shoulder and his arm moved to my neck, closing his hand around it, he began to squeeze until there was no air left to breathe, he picked up the pace yet again and it was so thrilling to experience it in this way.

"If you can't breathe, just tap on my arm," he said.

My orgasm was building up, and my eyes rolled back as I was struggling to breathe. My hands grabbed his arm.

"Fuck, I'm going to come," he groaned. He squeezed tighter and my body convulsed as I orgasmed, my mouth parted but no air getting in.

"Shit... fuuuuuck!!!" He roared as he filled me up with his fluids. My vision began to blur as he removed his hand from my neck, and pulled out of me. I gasped for air, coughing, placing my hand against my neck as my legs gave way. Tristan kept me from falling to the ground, "Elona, can you breathe?" He asked as we were now both on the floor with him still holding me against him. I was still coughing and getting the air I needed. He cupped the side of my face.

I nodded, "Yes," I whispered through gasps.

"That was too much for you, I apologize," he searched my face as concern laced his voice. He leaned in and placed his forehead against mine, "I'm so, so sorry."

"It was...intense, and I loved it," he pulled away, looking at me with surprise. "You did?" He asked.

"Yeah," I was able to breathe again, and I moved so that I could pull my panties and shorts up, I needed to shower all the sex off me.

His flaccid cock was still free, and he pulled his boxer brief over it and then he stood up. "I had never done that before. You're my first. I mean..." He held his hand out to me and I placed mine in his, helping me to stand up. "That's what you do to me. I can't get enough of you. Like I said before, you're like my drug, and you bring this out of me," he said.

"I love the gentleness and the roughness. But as much as I want to do this for the entire night, I wouldn't want Cris..."

The door opened and we both looked towards it, my heart pounding in my chest.

Sensitivity

Elona

"Here you are," Cris said. She entered and her brows furrowed as she saw Tristan with me. "Is everything okay?" she asked suspiciously.

"Yeah, I found Elona in the kitchen–"

"I couldn't sleep," I interrupted Tristan.

"I took her for another tour as she hadn't been here in this study room since three years ago," he added.

"Well, I was in the kitchen about to get water, hoping that I would find you there. You didn't come out of the bathroom either, so I decided to see where you were. I can make some hot chocolate for us instead," she offered as she still looked between us suspiciously.

"I would love that," I smiled. "Thank you for the tour, Uncle Tristan," I said, almost cringing as I said that before I followed Cris out the door.

"I'm noticing something," she stated and I heard the study room door close behind us as I could feel Tristan's gaze burning into the back of me. I hope that it's not what I think it is that she's noticing.

"What is it?" I asked.

"Well, when my father is with you, he goes back to that section of the house, and he lights up like a Christmas tree. So, I think that you should come over more often. He takes you as a daughter, but something happened that made him close off from trying for another baby, especially when I talk about it more often, but I get it...my mother died and that stopped it. So, I guess he's taking you as his own daughter. I'm happy to see him this way."

"What way?" He asked from behind me as we entered the kitchen. I walked over to the dining table as Cris went to the cupboard. I pulled the chair out and took a seat.

"That you're happy. You take Elona as your own daughter. Soon we will have our own careers and then you will be alone again. You need someone, Dad, and also, I would still like to be a big sister, but that's up to you, of course." She said as she prepared our hot chocolate.

Tristan pulled a chair out from the table, and he paused, his expression changing. I know the reason that Cris does not know.

"I will not have this conversation about babies again. It will never happen," he snapped.

"Relax, Dad. Geez. No need to get all angry about it."

"Then stop pestering me about it all the damn, fucking time," he barked at her, which made me flinch, and then he stormed off, out the kitchen.

Cris was quiet and I could see her sadness. She was starting to blame herself for what she had said to him, making him lose his light at this moment with this sensitive topic that she knew nothing about. I respect Tristan enough not to want a baby, and she shouldn't force that on him because it's still something he was getting over. But most of all, I'm glad that he was beginning to move on with me.

"I'm sorry that you had to witness that," she said as she continued with the hot chocolate.

"It's normal," I tried to make the conversation light. "I need the bathroom real quick," I said as I stood up from the chair and walked out of the kitchen.

I went straight to Tristan's bedroom. I knocked on the door before I opened it slowly. His bedroom was partially dark except for a lamp that was burning beside his bed. I closed the door behind me after I stepped inside. Tristan was sitting on a recliner which was in the corner of his bedroom close to the window. He rested his elbows on his knees, his hands clasped and he stared at the floor.

I sat on the edge of his bed across from him. "Are you okay?" I asked softly.

"You shouldn't be in here. Cris will notice when you're away for long," he replied, but but coldness laced his voice this time.

"Please talk to me, I know it was about what Cris had said in the kitchen. I want you to know that I'm always here if you need to talk about it or anything," I encouraged.

"Elona, I do not want to talk about that." He snapped his head up to look at me. His eyes were darker, I wasn't sure if it was because of the room or his own anger, "I have told you already about that part of my life which I'm trying to move on and yet, here you are too, bringing it up. I don't want kids. Cris is the only child for me, and she will always be. I did take you as my own daughter before I developed feelings for you that day in the kitchen when I truly noticed you." He still held my gaze.

"Maybe you should explain that to her instead of just making her think that you should have another one and... I think that you should tell her the truth about what happened in that accident. Maybe she'll understand and not beg for a sibling," I said.

"I'm not ready yet," he replied.

"It's been three years. When will you be ready?" I asked. I wanted him to get it over and done with, not just for him, but for Cris too. She needs to know what happened. Hopefully, she would leave Tristan alone about that topic.

"I think that we should not have this conversation. It's something that I have to deal with on my own. Like I have said, I don't want kids and I hope that you'll understand that moving forward in our future. In fact, this is a great time to get it out of the way so that we both know where we stand when it comes to kids. I. Don't. Want. Kids. If you feel that you want one in the future, then perhaps you should reconsider being with me. If you love me enough, maybe we can make this work, and just respect my decision about what I would like," he said.

It crushed my heart that he would say these things, but I know what I want. "I do not want kids either. So you have me forever. That's something that you don't need to worry about. You do know that the pull-out method that you did is not one hundred percent effective. But luckily, I'm on the pill. Remember a few years back, I was in excruciating pain, I held my stomach in a fetal position, and you found me that way. You were freaking out and Cris was standing there crying because she didn't know what was wrong with me. You ended up calling my dad. It was because I had very bad period cramps, they were irregular every month, and I had been basically forced to be on birth control pills since I was fifteen. My dad and I kept it between us. I'm sure you and Cris think that it was just something that I ate, but I asked my dad not to say anything. It was meant to be private. That day made me decide that I did not want kids, that pain alone was unbearable and I sure as hell do not want to go through something ten times worse than that. So, you don't need to worry about kids when it comes to me. I'm your type of girl," I said. I was determined to make this work.

He looked down at the floor, taking in what I just mentioned. I was waiting for a response, but there was a bit of sympathy on his face. He licked his lips, "You should go. You've been long enough in my room for Cris to come looking for you and find you in my bedroom." He looked at me.

I swallowed as I stood up, "That didn't stop you from fucking me in her bedroom earlier," I said, his eyes falling down on my body, but he was taken aback by my response. I turned towards the door and walked out.

Maybe I came across as a bit rude when I said that, but maybe he just needed time to soak in what I said and for him to find the strength to open up to Cris about what happened. I should have an open mind and just be patient with him. At least we both want the same things and that's what matters.

Be Discreet

Tristan

I was not ready to have a conversation about the accident with Cris. I knew that Elona only meant well, but I was just not ready yet. I sucked in a breath as I heard them laughing down the hallway. I was standing at the dining room table, packing my files into my laptop bag that I'd spread out on the table earlier. I'm supposed to give them a ride to school, but David called me earlier and said that he wanted to drop Elona at school himself because he wanted to take her for breakfast before he goes away for a two-day meeting. When I heard that, I was excited because I could go to her house and have my way with her.

"Good morning, Dad," Cris smiled as she walked to the kitchen counter and grabbed an apple from the fruit bowl. Elona smiled at me, and she looked so fucking good in that check skirt, just above her knees. Her pink top was tucked into the skirt. I wanted to fuck her in that. "Are you going to give us a ride to school?" I looked away from Elona, clearing my throat.

"No, I need you to stay behind. There's something that I need to talk to you about." I moved my gaze to Elona, "Elona, your dad wants to take you for breakfast this morning, so he'll get you here," she furrowed her brows, remaining silent.

"This sounds serious," Cris said as she approached the dining table.

"It is serious," I replied as I took my laptop bag and placed it on the ground. I stood up straight, Elona was holding the strap of her backpack that hung over her shoulder.

"What have I done now, Dad?" Cris sighed.

"Nothing. I just need to talk to you," there was a car that honked its horn.

"That must be my dad, see you at school. Goodbye, Uncle Tristan," Elona said, I wished that could stop calling me uncle, but it was all for show. I didn't want her to leave. Her perfume lingered where she was standing. It filled my nostrils. I need to know what scent she is wearing because I love it.

I snapped out of my thoughts and pulled a chair out from the table, I took a seat and Cris did the same, sitting across from me. She clasped her hands in front of her on the table. "So, what is it?" she asked, her brows furrowed.

I shifted in the chair and cleared my throat. "This may not be easy, but there's something else that you should know about the accident that involved your mother," I said, looking at her. "Your mother was pregnant at the time of the accident. She was early in her pregnancy, and we didn't tell anyone about it yet. We wanted to wait until it was the right time. That night it was storming, she was bleeding so much in the accident, and...just thinking about your sibling that we were losing. It was like such a huge punch to my gut as if something was ripping my heart out as your mother died and that precious little baby." Tears welled up in my eyes, that hurt was back in full force. My tears spilled over and ran down my cheeks. "I kept this a secret because I didn't want you to know. No one else knew about it besides your mom and I," I wiped my tears away with the back of my hand. I wasn't going to tell her that Elona also knew. "I'm sorry that I didn't tell you. It's just so painful with all that had happened that day. I didn't know how you would take this information," I looked at her to see her reaction, but she just stared at nothing.

She swallowed, "I found the ultrasound in your study room, and I left it on the desk by accident. I usually go to that section of the house when I miss Mom. I wanted to work on my SNT over there in hopes that Mom would be closer to me. I rummaged through your drawer and found it. I wasn't sure whose ultrasound it was, but I saw the date on it. It still didn't make any sense to me until now. Is that... Is that the-"

"Yes, that is your deceased sibling," I replied. She looked down at the table. "I'm sorry that I hadn't told you sooner."

"I get it now. That time when mom died, you were sobbing uncontrollably when you thought I was asleep at night. You were so broken, and I understand now, it was because we lost them both. I have wanted a sibling so badly since I was young. I was begging you both, and just when you both were going to have another child, that accident happened, and I'm so sorry for pestering you all the time for a sibling," she looked at me with sadness in her eyes.

"As long as you know about it now. I don't want you to feel bad about it. It's a sensitive topic for me. I know that you need to soak all of this in, and it will take some time. But I don't want another kid and I hope you understand that," I said.

She nodded, "I understand," she reached out to me and placed her hand on mine. "We will be fine," she gave a small smile as her eyes glazed over. "Thank you for having this chat with me, Dad. Now, I need to get to school. I'll be going with Elona somewhere after school today." She said as she pulled her hand away.

"Just let me know when you both are home. I have to sort out the hacking thing that's going on at work," I said as I got up and she did the same.

"Is that still not solved yet?" She asked as she slung her backpack strap over her shoulder.

"No. We hit a dead end, and now it's back to investigating it," I said as I took my laptop bag and car keys, and then we left.

* * *

Once in the car, I wished that Elona had been with us, but David had his own plan this morning. "Would you go with us to a photoshoot for Elona this week?" Cris asked.

"Where will it be?" I asked. Immediately, my heart beat wildly in my chest. I wasn't happy about this.

"It will be at the Dakota Agency. Spooky will be joining us too."

"That son of a bitch," I muttered under my breath as I held my gaze on the road ahead.

Cris chuckled beside me in the passenger seat, "Why is Spooky such a problem? The poor dude has done nothing but be respectful. But I love to see how his presence just makes you go crazy, Dad."

"Just watch your mouth...I don't want to hear anything about him," I said through clenched teeth, but that only made her laugh harder. I don't find it funny at all.

"Fine, Dad. But you cannot avoid him for long though. I know you will be at the photoshoot because you love Elona as you know, so you will definitely be there to protect her. I know you, Dad, you are always one to protect the ones that you love and when you genuinely care about someone. That says a lot about your character. But please, stop checking my best friend out, I see the way you check her out, and it's just weird."

I couldn't believe what I heard, but at least she didn't know about Elona and me. I have to be more discreet about it when it comes to Elona and sneaking around. I admit that what I did last night, fucking Elona in her bedroom, was too risky, I cannot do such a thing again. But Elona just drives me crazy. She makes me do crazy things.

"Trust me, I don't have that sort of eyes for her. I'm protecting her, that's all," I replied. I don't know if that was a good enough reply. I need her to be distracted from that.

"Fine," she said as she scrolled through her phone.

Finally, we pulled up at the school. I was relieved when she got out of the car because I needed to breathe again. I loosened my tie because that moment was so close to her being suspicious enough to know the truth. She noticed, she could be one hell of an investigator just like her mother, but I have to keep my shit together until Elona graduates. I don't know how she will actually react, but now it will be too soon for this to get out. I can't have her telling David either. There is still half a year to go and it feels so damn long. I want to have my way with Elona and to have our freedom. But I have to control myself much more than I am now. It would work out for us better if there was control from myself.

Being Me

Elona

I was thinking about Tristan and Cris while I had breakfast with my dad. He was going for a two-day meeting and I would be alone. He had asked Tristan to keep an eye on me and I knew what that would entail when it came to Tristan. When Tristan asked Cris to stay behind to talk, I knew what that would be about because when she came to school this morning, she was not her usual happy self. She didn't talk much to anyone, she was just sad. I hope that it went well between the two of them.

Spooky came late to class, and it was the first day in a while that he was back, but he still had on his sunglasses. What is really up with that?

As the three of us left the classroom and walked down the hallway. Everyone was silent. "So, how has everyone been?" I asked, breaking that silence. It was only the chattering of students around us.

"Well, there has been something that my dad kept away from me for three years and I found that...thing before he actually told me about it this morning. I had a sibling who died in that accident with my mother. They were happy about it, but we lost them both. My mother was early in her pregnancy." We came to a stop close to the administration office. "Gosh, I don't know how to feel. I want to cry, and I want to be there for my dad. I don't think that he's over that." She said as her eyes glazed over and my heart pulled.

"I'm so sorry about that," I said with sadness lacing my voice.

"Well, there's nothing we can do about that now. It's been three years," she replied. "I think that going with you to Dakota Agency will shift my emotions to something happier," she forced a smile. "So, how about you?" She turned to Spooky who was looking past us.

"I feel a bit better. That's all I can say," he replied.

"What's up with those sunglasses? You haven't taken them off," Cris inquired.

He shrugged, "I have conjunctivitis," he continued to look past us, and I followed his gaze.

My heart stopped as Tristan was standing at the desk of Miss Jennings, leaning over the desk as he wrote something. She had her hand on his back as she stood next to him. The green-headed monster resurfaced. This was the issue with keeping our relationship a secret. No one knows about us and I can't do anything about it. This was unbelievable.

"Not her again," Cris sighed.

"She's so cringe," I replied, but I wanted to rip her from my boyfriend.

"Tell me about it," she said as she started to walk away.

When Miss Jennings sat down behind the desk, Tristan stood up straight, placed the pen on the desk, and then reached into his pants pocket, taking his phone out, and his gaze found mine. He paused as if not expecting to see me here. His gaze shifted to Spooky, who was standing beside me and his expression changed, his brows furrowed as he looked away and answered a call.

"I can't stand that man," Spooky said as he started to walk away.

"I don't blame you," I replied as I walked in step with him. "So, how are you? I understand if you don't want to speak in front of Cris," I said. I wanted to get my mind off Tristan and what I had witnessed from Miss Jennings. I'm surprised she hasn't done that to my father as yet, because he hardly came to school.

"I'm fine. No need to worry about me," Spooky replied.

"You can reach out to me anytime you want, and I will try to be there. I just don't want you to think that we don't care about you," I kicked a pebble on the asphalt as we walked to the side of the school building, the sun burning into me. It was hot as hell.

"I know," is all that he said. Cris was standing under a tree next to the school building, enjoying the shade as she scrolled through the phone.

"So, you two are finally done watching that show," she stated without looking up.

"What show?" Spooky asked.

"The one where Miss Jennings was all over my father. Apparently, the staff is going for drinks tonight and my dad makes a pretty good donation to the school once a year as part of making it better since I'm attending it. I wouldn't be surprised if she asked him to join them, and I love my father for the man that he is, he refuses." She said, still on her phone.

"He clearly hates me for no reason," Spooky chimed in.

Cris sighed as she finally looked up from her phone. "He does that for good reason. I think he sees you as a threat to us. We're both young women, and he doesn't want us to be taken advantage of, hurt, or anything bad to happen. He's only being a good father. It was only Elona and I for years, and he had never seen us be friends with guys and that kind of sets it off. A father is protective, and he takes Elona as his own daughter," she said.

"Yeah, right," he muttered under his breath, I heard that. Cris was oblivious. My heart stopped because I hoped that Spooky hadn't seen anything. What if he's suspicious too about the way that Tristan goes overboard with me and his reaction towards Spooky whenever we are alone together?

"Elona, are you ready to go? I can't wait to get to The Dakota Agency." She smiled, but I knew she was also putting up a strong front.

"Yeah, I will see you around," I smiled at Spooky and he nodded.

"Let's go for lunch," that voice made me upset behind me.

"No, Dad. I told you that Elona and I would be going out, so we'll be home later," Cris replied, and I turned to face him. I was forcing a smile this time.

"Maybe next time, Mr Crane," I was being sarcastic.

He scowled at me, he always showed up when Spooky was around. "I would prefer that you both eat something and maybe I can accompany you both," he looked between Cris and me.

"Dad, we'll be fine. Maybe you should have a drink with Miss Jennings and let us do our things without someone looking over us. We need to be independent," she replied.

"So, that's what happened when you went to the club without my permission, and look how that turned out," he hissed.

I shook my head and walked past him and Cris. I wasn't going to be late for the agency, and I wasn't going to let Tristan stop that. "Wow, Dad, you had to go there, especially after the conversation we had this morning. See you later," Cris said, and I heard her jogging towards me from behind. "Sorry about that, I hate it when he does that."

"It's okay. I'm used to it by now," I responded. But I wasn't happy at this moment.

Today will be my day with the agency, sharing this precious moment with my best friend, and no one will take that away from me, not even Tristan. He should support me in this and not try to take my dreams away. Tears stung the back of my eyes when I thought about it. I took a deep breath just accepting this as it was. He would never support my dream. He tried to stop that. I saw right through him a few moments ago, and it doesn't look pretty to me. It hurts me, not to mention the Miss Jennings scene in front of me as he allowed her to touch him. I wasn't going to have that get me down. We're a secret for a reason and I can't say or do anything to Miss Jennings. So, I'll do me... being a model.

Getting To Know Spooky

Tristan

I wasn't happy when Elona and Cris walked away from me. I wasn't happy that they had disrespected me in this way. A man looking out for Elona and that is what David had trusted me with...in this case, her modeling. I knew that keeping an eye on Elona would mean more than just these things. I would have my way with her because she would be alone at home.

Spooky started to walk, but I grabbed his backpack which was draped over his shoulder, "Where do you think you're going?" I said through clenched teeth as I pushed him back against the wall of the school building. I grabbed a fist full of his collar. Those stupid sunglasses are always in place. I took it off with my other hand, throwing it to the ground.

"Let go!" He struggled against me, but I was stronger.

I furrowed my brows as I loosened my grip on him, I pulled away as I saw that blue eye. He adjusted his t-shirt collar and jacket. Not sure why he still wore a jacket in the heat. "What happened to you?" I asked, genuinely concerned this time. This was not what I had expected.

"Nothing is going on," he huffed as he began to push past me, but I stopped him by pulling him back to the wall again.

"I will not let you walk away until you tell me what the fuck is going on with you. Who gave you that?" I asked, eager to know.

He let out a sigh, "Why do you even care?" He looked past me.

"Do not ask a question with another question, so answer me. Who did that to you?" I asked, still holding him against the wall.

I let go of him in case that would help him talk. "I need to go home," he said.

"Get in my car, and then I can take you home. Or we can have lunch because clearly, those two girls ditched me. So, what's it going to be?" I asked.

He let out another sigh, "Fine, let's have lunch," he said, and then he picked up his sunglasses from the ground and put them on again before we walked to my car. We got inside, and we drove in silence to my favorite restaurant. I was eager to know what was going on with him.

* * *

Once we got to the restaurant, I led the way to a table in the far corner and a waiter placed menus in front of us. "The usual, Mr Crane?" He asked. Spooky didn't open his menu.

"Yes, please. Make that times two." I replied and looked back at Spooky, my reflection staring back at me in his sunglasses. "What would you like to drink?" I asked him.

He shrugged, "Chocolate milkshake, please," he said. At least he has manners. I moved my attention back to the waiter. "A chocolate milkshake and my usual," I said.

"Got it, Sir," the waiter took both menus and left. I adjusted my suit jacket and shifted in my chair to sit comfortably.

"So, what's going on?" I started, holding my gaze on him.

"After all the things that you did to me in order to keep me away from Elona, you care enough to take me to lunch and ask me about my situation," he stated.

Well, there was certainly a concerned shift within me when I saw that blue eye, and I wasn't going to let it go, "Are you going to tell me or not? If it's a bad situation, I may not be able to help," I replied impatiently.

"Whatever you say or do won't change a damn thing."

"Something tells me that your father could be abusive towards you." I leaned back in the chair. "He punched you, didn't he?"

"So what if he did? You can't do anything about the situation."

"What if I can? Stop being so stubborn and just talk to me," I was so impatient that I was starting to lose my shit, but I tried to remain calm.

"He beats me up sometimes. He has anger issues and whenever I don't want to do something, or when I'm just in my room all the time, he comes up to beat the shit out of me. I haven't been to school recently because I wasn't in the right frame of mind. I was forced to go to school this morning because he was at home. He usually travels. We moved here because he got a new job...well, he started his own company gradually before we moved. He was fired from the previous company due to his anger. He takes it all out on me and that's what I've known ever since." He shrugged.

That was like a knife through my heart. I don't wish that kind of thing on anyone. "What about your mother?" I asked.

"She died when I was young," that twisted the knife further into my heart. "He was the death of her. I have a stepmother now, whom he adores and never beats, but she doesn't even feel sympathy towards me. That's what it's like being in a household where no one cares about me." He said, and I continued to hold my gaze on him as the waiter came back with our meal. I just needed to soak this in. Elona, Cris, and Spooky all have that in common. They lost their mothers. They go through pain and I felt bad for him.

The waiter left, and I finally pulled my gaze away from him as I looked at my meal. "What about other family members?" I asked, looking up at him again as he dug into his steak.

He shrugged, "I have no idea. I guess because of my father's shit, he has been on his own for a long time. I never got to meet my family. I don't even know about my mother's side of the family as my father kept us in this box. It wasn't too bad, but it did get worse. I wasn't even able to attend my mother's funeral. I was locked up in my room. My father didn't wait long after my mother died to marry my stepmother. I can't help but think that they must've had an affair," he said.

I was staring at my food now, soaking this news in. He's not safe there. But I don't trust him around Elona either. I wanted to meet his father and see if all that he was saying was true. I mean...that blue eye was enough evidence.

"You can call me if you need me, but you need to keep your distance from Elona," I said.

He scoffed, "I don't like Elona in that way. The only person that I have my eyes set on is Cris. She's the one that I like, and she pulls my heart towards her. I don't even think she likes me in that way. It was never Elona, and you tried to keep me away from her for nothing. Now that you know it's Cris that I want, maybe you can back off and allow Elona and me to be friends," he hissed.

I was taken aback, my Cris is the one he wants. I didn't see that one coming. My daughter of all people. "I will not allow my daughter to date you who comes from a family that will put my daughter in danger. How will you even protect her from your father if you cannot even protect yourself?" I snapped.

"I doubt she even wants me, but I'll never allow her to be in my house. That's one place where I wouldn't want her to be. I don't even want her to meet my father. If she wants me...if that ever happens. We'll be kept a secret. I'm sure that you and Elona are a secret," he said and started eating.

I clenched my jaw, and then I let out a sigh. "Thanks for telling me all of this," I replied, not bothering to say much about Elona and me.

I needed to see his father, and hopefully, I can do that today. But first, I'll make a turn at Dakota Agency and see what's going on over there. It seemed like I would have to take Spooky with me. This was a lot to take in in such a short time.

Photoshoot Nightmare

Elona

Cris and I went to The Dakota Agency so that I could do a photoshoot, and just get my things sorted. The building was huge, and we went all the way to the second last floor. As we got out of the elevator, the floor-to-ceiling windows were everywhere. It was breathtaking as we took in our surroundings with so much awe.

"I could be here forever," Cris said as she turned in a circle to look around.

"I'll love it here," I smiled. I looked ahead and there was a desk in the corner, a lady sat behind the desk, and we walked over. She looked up from her book, pausing to write something down with a pen in her hand. "You must be Elona?" She asked. She had black-framed glasses on and her brunette hair was neatly combed to the back.

"Yes," I smiled.

"Please, have a seat. The boss will be with you soon," she replied.

"Thanks," I responded as Cris and I took a seat on an orange sofa, I placed my backpack on my lap.

"I cannot wait to see you do the photoshoot. This time in a real studio. What's the theme?" She asked.

"I think it's just casual. They'll be providing the clothes and I get to keep them."

"That's such a great perk."

"Elona?" A woman with blonde hair approached with a page in her hand.

"Yes," I said as I stood up with my backpack in hand.

"The boss wants to meet you," she turned around and walked away. I followed after her while Cris stayed behind. I left my backpack with Cris.

We reached a door, and she opened it for me. I stepped inside and the door closed behind me. There were floor-to-ceiling windows and the figure of the man standing, looking out of those windows. His hands were in his pants pockets and then he turned around.

He was an older man, with a streak of gray hair on the sides. He seemed intimidating but had attractive features. Light green eyes. "Elona," he said as he rounded the desk, and then he came to a stop in front of me, studying me. "I love your outfit. I think that this will be great. See it as a schoolgirl theme." He reached his hand out and placed it on my hip. Chills ran down my spine, and I wasn't comfortable at all.

Was I doing the right thing? Is this what it would be like every time I model? Him touching me? Where is a female who needed to work with me? I stepped back out of his reach, his hand falling to his side, and his gaze penetrated into me. I swallowed.

"When you work in my agency, you'll comply with everything I say. If I want you to be partially naked, you will be. If I want you fully clothed, you will be. You're a very attractive woman and I believe that you'll sell easily."

"Sell easily?" I asked.

"Your body speaks for us," he moved closer and walked around me. I could feel his eyes burn all over my body. Why was I feeling so uncomfortable as I never felt this way with Spooky when he did my photoshoots? He stood in front of me again. "I saw your portfolio, and I wanted you the moment I saw you," he lifted his hand and moved a strand of hair behind my head.

"Wanted me? In what way?" I asked, my brows furrowing.

He chuckled, "To be my model."

"Right," I let out a breath.

His index finger now traced the collar of my top until it traced the top of my breasts, I was so uncomfortable. "We'll do a photoshoot in this attire, and then you'll strip down into lingerie. Maxime will get you changed. I look forward to working with you. That'll be all," he said as he turned and rounded his desk.

I swallowed and walked as fast as I could to get out of there. My heart beat wildly. I don't like that man as much as he can be attractive. Was Tristan right about this all along? He knows better than me. I hate that he touched me, but is that expected in this industry?

* * *

As I did my photoshoot with the clothes I had on from school. The boss walked to where we were. Cris was now sitting on a chair in the corner, taking pictures of me and then doing her own thing on the phone.

"She needs a touch-up of makeup," Maxime told the makeup artist. I allowed them to do their job, but that stare from the boss was making me uncomfortable again. I didn't like it. I just wanted to go back into my shell and never come out. I sucked it in and just did what was needed of me.

"If you want this badly, you need to do what is expected," he called out.

"Where's the schoolgirl lingerie?" Maxime called out. One of the fashion designers ran our way and handed it to Maxime. She shoved it against me as the makeup artist had just finished. I didn't like this vibe. Didn't Maxime like me? "Strip," she demanded.

I looked around the room and there were the photographers, who were a man, the lighting crew, who were men, and the fan girl besides the other women who were taking care of me. My eyes found the boss, and he was watching me expectantly. "Well, what are you waiting for?" Maxime snapped.

I shook my head, "I prefer to get dressed in private with no men looking at me," I still held my gaze on the boss.

"Mr Luca..." Maxime said, expecting him to intervene.

"This is the modeling industry, men will be around, looking at you and your body. You heard Maxime. Strip," he demanded. I looked over at Cris who was now sitting upright, her brows furrowed as this played out in front of her. She wasn't impressed with them, she was ready if anything had to happen and I was so grateful to have her here with me.

I sucked in a breath and began to take off my top, which left me in a pink lace bra. All of a sudden, the boss was behind me as my hands trembled. His hands on my shoulders. "Relax," he whispered.

I tried but I couldn't. His hands moved down my arms, his way of making me feel comfortable. It wasn't helping. Gosh, I wish that Tristan had been here, he would've done something by now.

He hooked his fingers into the top of my skirt, and I breathed. I wanted to pursue this career, I got into the door of it, and now I have to do this. "I'll do it," I blurted out.

"What the fucking hell!" I heard.

"Dad!" Cris chimed in as we all turned to look their way. Cris was placing a hand on Tristan's chest, he was fuming. He clearly saw that. I was relieved. But he'll tell me that he told me so. Spooky was beside them too. That was a surprise as Tristan didn't like him.

"Mr Crane, lovely to see you here," Mr Luca said as he removed his hands from my body, and I was even more relieved. I still had to get this lingerie photoshoot out of the way. "We can go to my office if there's anything you want to talk about. This building is yours after all."

Wait...this building is Tristan's?

The Industry

I was livid when I saw that creep touching Elona, he was about to put his fucking hand into her skirt and I could see how much Elona was trembling. Cris was holding me back before I could go and rip that son of a bitch to threads. All eyes were on me, and I was happy because that made Mr Luca stop what he was doing.

"Let go of me," I said through clenched teeth to Cris, and she removed her hand as Mr Luca started to walk out of the studio. We'll have a nice chat about this.

"Just relax, Dad," Cris was trying to calm me, but I didn't give a shit. I stormed out after Mr Luca.

I loosened my tie as I entered his office. He was standing at the door and closed it behind me. When he turned around, I grabbed him by the collar and shoved him against the door. "You keep your filthy hands off her, do you understand?" I hissed in his face.

He laughed, "Relax, this is the industry, and it's not like she is anything to you, or is she?" He asked.

"Just do not touch her," and then I let him go. I ran my hand through my hair, trying to remain calm. He walked around his desk, pulling his suit jacket closed.

"I think she means more to you than you let on. Is she family?" He asked as he took a seat.

"Yes, she's family. No one does that to my family," I pointed my finger at him when I said that.

"Take a seat," he demanded, and then I did.

"I bought this building for the purpose of doing good. I didn't expect a pathetic jerk like you to end up being the boss in this company and treat women that way. That's not how you handle a woman, especially on their first day. She's young and who knows how many other women you have done this to," I glared at him.

"Mr Crane, I will not repeat myself, but men work with women in this industry too. They can be hair stylists, make-up artists, photographers, you name it. They will end up seeing her naked. She knew what she was signing up for. If you have a problem with that, maybe you should stay away and allow the young lady to do what she wants." He said, and I didn't like that one bit. This was the reason why I didn't want her to be in this industry in the first place.

"That's no excuse to be acting like that. I can end you by removing you from this building. Better yet, replace you."

"Mr Crane, I am the boss. No one can replace me. There's no proof that I've done anything. Go ahead and ask everyone who has been working with me. I'm waiting. In the meantime, allow the young woman to do what she wants. You're just the owner of this building. No sense in fashion or the industry. So, good luck with everything else, and seem that she is your family, I'll keep my hands away from her. Don't think that any other men will keep their hands to themselves, they will always be touching her in this industry whether you like it or not. She's attractive and sexy, and they'll see her as such. Now, if that is all, I have work to do," he dismissed me as he looked down at the papers in front of him. My jaw clenched but he was right. I'm the owner of this building and I have no clue in depth about this industry. I have to do something and I hope that Elona will change her mind about being in this industry.

"This won't be the last that you'll see me," I warned him as I got up from my seat and walked out of his office. I was eager to get to Elona.

***

When I got to the studio, she was not there. Spooky was sitting beside Cris as they were talking about something on her phone. I walked towards them. "Where's Elona?" I asked.

Cris looked up from her phone. "She went to the changing room down the hallway that you just came from," she said. "She...she's a bit shaken up-"

"I'll deal with it," I reassured her, and then I walked back down the hallway.

I saw *changing room* on the door and opened it. As I stepped inside, I heard a gasp as Elona turned around, hugging herself as if she tried to cover herself. She was in a schoolgirl lingerie that this agency provided her with.

"It's only me," I said, and she relaxed more before turning around, her back facing me. I closed the door behind me, and then I approached her. She was standing in front of the mirror with bright lights around it.

As I took in her appearance, she looked sexy, but I was not here for that. I stood behind her and placed my hands gently on her shoulders, but she sniffled as she wiped her tears away. "I thought this would be easy," she said.

I gently turned her around, "I saw what he did to you and this is the reason why I've been warning you about this industry. They will always be in this industry, no matter what agency you take. You might be lucky with a few that don't have men like Mr Luca. But I don't think you should go through with this." Tears escaped, and I cupped the sides of her face and wiped the tears away with both of my thumbs.

"I will continue with this. I won't give up. It was my first day and this is my dream. I just didn't expect it to be this way. I can do this," she said.

"I don't think you should," I tried to steer her away from this.

She shook her head, no. "I stand by what I say. I will do this. I want to be part of The Velvet Secret and this is a start for me. So, I hope you can still support me as I will endure the treatment over here," she looked at me with determination and hope. Fuck, there is nothing I can do now to keep her away from her dream.

"I'll be with you on every set, okay? That way no one dares to touch you the way that Mr Luca had and he won't do that again because I will break his hands," I said, and she smiled. "There's that smile," I was still livid inside, but I had to be supportive of her too.

"Thank you. Please, stay over tonight with me," she said.

"How can I say no to that?" I smiled. "Now, get dressed," I demanded.

The door creaked open, and I turned to see who it was. It was Cris who was looking concerned and suspicious yet again. "Um..." she seemed awkward. Fuck, I stepped away from Elona as fast as I could, so that she wouldn't be more suspicious. I'm failing miserably with Cris. But I'm trying. Elona looked at her. "How are you feeling after that douchebag did that?" she asked.

"I feel shaken up, but I'll get through it and I'll come out at the top," Elona forced a smile.

"I wish I could say that's the spirit, but I'm concerned. I just don't want anything to happen to you."

"I'll be accompanying her on each set. No one will have their hands on her. I promised Uncle David that I would keep an eye on her and protect her. That's exactly what I'll be doing," I said.

"Well, as long as it's not the type of other, "keeping an eye on her" then by all means."

"I'm not those men," I tried to argue about it.

"Hmmm," is all that she said before looking at Elona. "How about we go out to get some ice cream or something?" Cris asked.

"I would like to be at home if you don't mind," Elona replied.

"Of course, I understand that." Cris smiled, concern still etched on her face.

"Can I get undressed, please?" Elona asked.

I shoved my hands in my pants pockets and walked towards the door, "We'll be waiting for you outside the door," I said over my shoulder. Cris followed after me.

When we stepped out of the changing room, I closed the door. "Dad, please take good care of her. You saw how she was. I'm worried. So, knowing that you'll be there for her makes me happy. I don't want anything to happen to her because of that man. And... never mind," she shook her head, "I'll see you around. Spooky and I will go and grab some ice cream," she said with a faint smile, but my brows furrowed at what she wanted to say.

She should know that she can come to me with anything. We were nearly caught in a compromising position, but at least my excuse would be that I was comforting Elona. On a different note, Spooky and Cris having ice cream together doesn't sound like a bad idea, in fact, it made me smile. Perhaps, I can cut that kid a little slack because he's interested in my daughter after all. I needed to have a talk with his father, whoever he was.

Bathtub

Elona

Elona was quiet the entire drive back to her house. I wasn't going to pressure her into talking to me due to what had happened. She was determined to do modeling, and I have to do everything that I could to protect her, not only for my own reasons but also because David had trusted me to take care of her.

I followed Elona up the steps, but her hands trembled as she tried to put the key into the lock, but it fell to the ground. I crouched, picking it up for her, and stood up straight again. I looked at her with concern as her gaze fell on the keys in my hand.

"I can unlock," I said as she looked up. I gave her a reassuring nod before she stepped out of the way.

I unlocked the door and stepped inside. David wouldn't be here, and I should be happy about it. I was excited the entire morning, but that changed due to The Dakota Agency. What the hell was I going to do about it? I do know other agencies, but to have Elona be taken care of is a different case when it came to that industry with little to no one to trust.

Elona had followed in after me and I closed the door behind her. She placed her backpack on the sofa and I moved closer to her, taking her hand in mine. I led the way up the stairs, "Where are you taking me?" She asked. That was the first time she had spoken since we left the agency.

"I want you to relax and forget about today," I said as we walked down the hallway and stopped in front of the bathroom door. I looked at her, and she gave my hand a little squeeze. We entered the bathroom and I let go of her hand. I leaned over the bathtub and turned the faucet open. I stood up straight as my phone began to ring in my pants pocket.

I looked at Elona who was staring at the bath. "You'll relax in the bath," I gave her a reassuring smile before looking down at my phone again. Fuck. Maggie just never stops. I ignored the call, I was not going to turn it silent because I have a daughter who needs to be able to reach me in case anything happens. "It's nothing important," I smiled at her before shoving the phone into my pocket again.

I moved closer to her as I helped her get undressed. I was as gentle as I could be. This time, sex was not on my mind, I wanted her to feel relaxed and hopefully forget about things. Once her top was off, she was left in her pink lace bra. She hugged herself now. I was being extra careful because this was the same position that she was in earlier. "Do you trust me?" I asked softly.

"Yes," she replied, which was barely above a whisper.

"I'm going to take your skirt off. Just remember that it's me, okay?" I was handling her as if she was fragile, someone that was afraid.

"Okay," she replied with a heavy sigh.

I gently hooked my fingers into her skirt and pulled it down along with her pink lace panties. They dropped at her feet and I hadn't noticed that she had taken her shoes off, it was probably while I checked my phone. I gently unclipped her bra and I slipped them off her arms, discarding it on the floor.

I moved past her, leaning over the bath again to turn the faucet off. When I turned back to her, I held my hand out, and she placed her hand in mine. She stepped into the bath and relaxed. I reached for the bubble bath in the bottom shelf of the vanity cabinet and threw some into the bath, creating some bubbles.

My phone was ringing like crazy, and I continued to ignore it as I was focused on Elona. I wasn't going to join her in the bathtub, she sat up straight as she looked at me. "Are you not joining me?" I took off my jacket and placed it on the little bench in the corner, rolling up my white shirt sleeves to my elbows as I walked back to her.

"No. I want to take care of you." I said as I crouched on the other side of the bath. I took a sponge and I gently washed away the remnants of the day. "Just relax," I whispered and she complied as she exhaled a breath.

* * *

Once I was done, I helped her step out of the bath and wrapped a towel around her. "You must be hungry," she said as she took over from me and dried herself. It seemed as if she was getting her confidence back.

"Well, I had lunch with Spooky so–"

"You did?" she was taken aback. She seemed much better now as the corners of her lips curled up.

"Yes, is there a problem with that?" I asked with confusion.

"Well, you hate him. So, why would you actually have lunch with him? Are you getting a soft spot for him?" She teased and I didn't like that, but if it made her smile, then I would let her tease me.

"I don't have a soft spot for him. I'm keeping him at arm's length. Besides, he told me that he likes Cris," I shrugged.

"So, that's the reason why. That means that you're no longer worried that he might steal me away from you...which won't happen," she added.

"Maybe. But I do need more time to trust him. Just don't push it," I warned her, and then I walked out of the bathroom as she followed after me. My phone was still ringing off the hook.

"I think you should answer that," She said, "I'll get changed and meet you downstairs," I looked over my shoulder, catching a glimpse of her before she disappeared inside her bedroom.

I took my phone out of my pocket, it was Maggie yet again. I answered the phone "What the fuck don't you understand when I made it clear that I have a girlfriend?" I hissed into the phone as I walked down the stairs.

"Firstly, do not talk to me like that. Second of all, David told me that you do not have a girlfriend, so who is lying?" she asked.

I let out a frustrated breath, "He doesn't know that I have a girlfriend, and it's none of your business. I don't appreciate you calling me and demanding these things of me. We will not be together as much as you try."

"You're missing out on something amazing," she carried on.

"No, I'm living my life the way that I want with my girlfriend, and you don't come close to her. She's better than you'll ever be, so back off and leave me the hell alone, or I'll report you for continuous harassment," I hung up before she could say anything.

I blocked her immediately, something that I had not thought of doing before. That woman was obsessed. If she ever thinks that I would want her, she's mistaken.

"Who was that?" I turned around as Elona walked down the stairs in denim shorts and a normal t-shirt, this time with flip-flops.

"It was work," I lied.

"So, nothing about the hacking thing?" She asked as she walked to the kitchen and I followed after her. She took two glasses from the top cupboard and placed them on the kitchen counter as she turned to the fridge and took the juice out.

"It was a dead end, but we're not giving up. There's another company willing to invest in us so that whatever I lost can be restored," I said as I took a seat on the bar stool.

She poured juice into each glass, and she moved mine towards me. "Thank you," I said. "The art gallery will be reopened. The damage is sorted. The exhibition will be on Friday. You and your dad need to be there. The paintings of your mother will get the spotlight they deserve," I said.

Her eyes lit up as she now sat beside me. "That's wonderful. Thank you," she smiled as she looked over at me. I placed my hand on hers.

"I'll always give anyone the spotlight they deserve. Even if that means you want to model. But I'll accompany you on it all."

"You cannot do that all the time. I'll be okay. I just have to get used to it and I will. I was just taken aback by Mr Luca and Maxime," she looked down at her glass of juice.

"Well, what Mr Luca did was unacceptable. That shouldn't have happened," I said as I took a sip of my juice.

"I know. But I should be the one to handle all of this. It is my dream after all," she shrugged.

"I will also be accompanying the school on the camp that's coming up soon."

She looked at me with huge eyes.

"You're what?"

"Yeah, the school asked me. That's why I was at school. I had to sign some papers too." I smiled.

"At least I won't be away from you," she replied.

"We still have to be careful."

"That's no problem for me, but is that going to be a problem for you?" She asked.

"It will be difficult, but I have to try," I smiled.

I was so glad to see her smile and be herself again. I kept the conversation going. I would be spending the night with her. I just had to spin another story when it came to Cris. She cannot know that I would be spending the night with Elona. What story would there be for her? I hate to lie all the time, but we had to keep at this until Elona graduated.

More Lies

Tristan

I enjoyed being in Elona's presence, her confidence that was back just made me admire her even more. But my mind drifted back to the industry. What person is out there that is trustworthy? Do I know anyone with whom I have interacted before that I could trust so that they could keep an eye on her when I couldn't?

"What would you like to eat?" She snapped me out of my thoughts as she slid off the bar stool and rounded the kitchen counter. I sent Cris a quick text to inform her that I would be out for the rest of the night and that she shouldn't wait up. I would be spending the rest of the night in bed with Elona.

"I would say I want you, but that's not the case right now. I just want to have you relax tonight and, since I'll be here for the night, I will hold you. We don't need sex." I said as I took a sip of my juice. She took something out of the fridge and when she placed it on the counter, it was strawberries. I looked up at her, she was smiling at me seductively. "What is that smile for?" I asked, returning the smile.

"Well, since you don't want to have sex with me, we can share strawberries." She turned around and took something out of the cupboard and then turned to face me. She placed a jar of Nutella on the counter. She then walked around the counter sitting back on the bar stool next to me. She opened the Nutella, I was inspecting what she was doing, and then she brought the bowl of strawberries closer.

She took a strawberry, dipped it inside the Nutella, and brought it towards me. I opened my mouth as she held her gaze on it. I sunk my teeth in as she let go of the strawberry. She then leaned in closer and opened her mouth, taking the other end of the strawberry into her mouth, our teeth sinking further into it until our lips met as we sucked the juice that ran down from the corner of my mouth. She pulled back enough to chew, while I chewed and swallowed, as I now leaned closer, I cupped the back of her head with my hand and I crashed my lips against hers.

My other hand rested on her hip, and I dug my nails into her skin, causing her to moan. I forced my tongue into her mouth as we kissed passionately. Her hands moved to the back of my neck. My erection was straining against my pants. She pulled inches away from me. "I thought we would be relaxing tonight," she breathed.

"You clearly don't plan on relaxing," I rasped and crashed my lips against hers. My hand moved from her hip, up towards her breasts and I cupped one, fondling it. She moaned into my mouth. I bit her bottom lip, she was driving me insane. I don't know what I would do with her.

I pulled back, looking at her breasts which were covered with her t-shirt. "Fuck, I want to rip this off," I groaned impatiently.

"I have a better idea," she said as her hand moved down all the way to my hard cock. She grabbed it and massaged it. "I need you," I said.

She started to undo my pants, freeing my cock. She leaned in, and then she took me into her mouth. I threw my head back. "Fuck. Your filthy little mouth feels so good." I breathed, my chest heaved with every suck and twist she did with her mouth. I cupped the back of her head and I started to thrust into her mouth. "Oh, fuck, you feel so good." I went deeper into her mouth, going all the way, "Take all of me," I said. I reached the back of her throat. Her face was red, and she gagged as she pulled away. Her eyes were watery.

I placed my hand under her chin, "Are you okay?" I asked.

She nodded, "Yeah," she then reached over the kitchen counter as she rested her other hand on my leg, and then she took the jar of Nutella. She dipped her finger inside and scooped a good amount of it out and covered my cock with it. She gripped the base of it with her hand and started licking the Nutella off my cock until she started sucking me again. She was so damn good, I bet from her previous experience she had been taught that. Which made me wonder if she had a boyfriend before that I didn't know about.

She sucked me so hard it snapped me out of my thoughts and I let out a moan. "Fuck, I'm going to explode," I cupped the back of her head again as I thrust into her mouth and her hand rested on my leg. I was not giving her time to breathe at this moment, my other hand gripped the edge of the counter and I rolled my eyes to the back as I filled the back of her throat with my cum. "Fuuuuuck!!!" I roared not giving a shit who heard me outside. "Fuck," she was milking me clean until she gagged, and I stood up, pulling out of her mouth, she gagged some more.

"Are you okay?" I asked as I cupped the sides of her face. She licked her lips and nodded. "You're fucking great," I said. She pulled away and walked around the counter, getting a paper towel to wipe her mouth from my fluids.

I tucked my flaccid cock into my pants. "You might need a shower...Nutella," she smiled as her mouth was now clean.

"Only if you join me," I said.

"I've already bathed thanks to you."

There was a knock on the door. "Are you expecting anyone?" I asked.

"No," her brows furrowed.

"Let me check," I said as I stood up and went to the door. It was already getting dark.

I opened the door and to my surprise, it was not who I had expected it to be. "Dad, what are you doing here?" Cris asked, her brows furrowed.

"I'm here to check up on Elona after today's events," I lied partially, opening the door wider, and stepping to the side as she entered.

"So are you done with being out the rest of the evening?" She asked, looking at me over her shoulder as I closed the door behind her.

"I'll still be going out," I lied. I still didn't want to disappoint Elona by going home just because Cris was seeing me here. Perhaps I could leave and come back later when Cris was back home.

She walked to the kitchen and I followed after her. "You are looking wild," she said.

Elona looked at her with huge eyes and then it quickly changed to confusion.

"What do you mean?" Elona asked as she placed some frozen pies in a bowl. Well, now I see what Cris sees.

"Your hair is wild," Cris said as she sat on the bar stool.

Elona quickly adjusted her hair. That was all my fault. "Oh, uh, I was sleeping and just woke up when your father popped in to check up on me," she lied.

"As per Uncle David's orders for me," I chimed in.

"Dad, go out and have fun," she was chasing me away and my eyes met Elona's.

"I love you," I mouthed, and she smiled before looking at Cris who was talking.

"See you girls in the morning if I do," I said.

I left, just giving them privacy and not making anything obvious. I took my phone out of my pants pocket and typed a quick text to Elona as I walked to my car which was parked in the driveway.

Me: I'll see you later. I didn't want to be obvious in front of Cris. I love you.

I hit send and shoved my phone back into my pants pocket. That was close, and I didn't expect Cris to show up this late. I guess I have to tell her not to wander around at night in the street. She should be at home where it's safe. But at least she hasn't caught on to anything this evening. I was almost caught out because of my text...how many more lies do we need to spin before we tell them the truth?

Gallery Night

Elona

It was the night of the exhibition that my father and I had to attend. This was something that I was eager to be part of because it was my mother's sketches. I wanted to see them again, but it was a distant memory of her painting. Tristan didn't get to spend the evening with me because Cris decided to sleep over by me. The only issue was that Tristan left his jacket in my bathroom which Cris found when she had to use my bathroom.

I lied and said that it was my father's. I took the jacket and quickly hid it away in my closet. That was another scare of almost getting caught. I thought that my heart would beat out of my chest, thinking that she had figured it out with his jacket. I think that she was being suspicious about it.

As my father and I entered the gallery, it was packed. I wore a black dress that was glittery at the bodice, and it flared out from my waist, the length barely hitting the ground. My hair was in Hollywood waves and draped over one shoulder. The top part of my dress had one strap, while my other shoulder was bare and I held a black clutch bag.

"I see her paintings," my father said.

"I'm eager to see them," I replied. I followed my father through the crowd until we got to the section where my mother's paintings hung. She was such a brilliant painter.

That dolphin painting I remembered like it was yesterday hung up there. It was my favorite. As I remember my mother in my thoughts, tears stung the back of my eyes. I missed her. Although I was little when she passed away due to an illness, I still remember her in certain things.

"Are you okay?" My dad asked.

"Yeah, just thinking about mom," I replied.

"Me too," he looked back at the paintings. I took in all of them. My father was awfully quiet, she was the love of his life. That's another reason why he hadn't moved on, but he does go out and have fun, as he says. My father was a handsome man and any woman would want him, but I guess he wasn't ready for any commitments either, as Tristan had been before me.

"I'm glad to see you both are here," I turned to see Tristan smiling at us. He looked dashing in his tuxedo. "These are the paintings your father gave us permission to display and sell," he said as he looked at the dolphin painting behind me before his gaze fell on me.

"We couldn't miss this. Thank you for doing this, Tristan," my dad said.

"This needed the recognition that it deserves," Tristan shoved his hands in his pants pockets and I scanned the crowd behind him.

"Where's Cris? She said she would be here." She didn't even text me today. She only let me know last night that she would be here.

"She's hanging out with Spooky at the house." His smile was forced, and I guess Spooky needs time away from people with whatever is going on with him.

"I'll get some Champagne, would you like one?" Dad asked me. I was taken aback.

"You never allow me to drink," I said.

"Well, you are eighteen after all, and you already had alcohol," he meant that night at the club.

"No, thanks," I replied, and then my father disappeared into the crowd, leaving Tristan alone with me.

He looked at me with hunger as he took in my appearance. "You look fucking hot. I can just rip that off you,"

I chuckled, "Well, you better not make it obvious because Cris is already one person who is clever. Thanks to your jacket in my bathroom, I had to lie that it was my father's."

"I forgot that I left it there. I didn't expect Cris to show up and spend the night with you. That was a huge disappointment for me." He let out a sigh.

"Don't worry, we have plenty of time together. Your jacket is safe in my closet," I replied.

He took one hand out of his pocket and held out his hand towards me. "Give me your hand," he said softly. I did as he said, and he placed a card in mine. "Go to the hotel after this. I'll meet you there tonight. Tell your father that you are going to be somewhere with The Dakota Agency." His gaze held mine and I wanted him. My core throbbed with need. I bit my bottom lip, his gaze falling on it. "If you keep on biting that lip, I will bite it for you in front of everyone. That's how crazy you're driving me and I can't get enough of you," he rasped.

"I'm back. Look who came here," Tristan composed himself as my gaze shifted to no other than Maggie, who was smirking.

"Hi, Handsome," she greeted Tristan.

"What the fuck are you doing here? This is by invitation only," he hissed at her.

"Tristan, give this lady a break. All you ever do is push her away when she wants you. Give her a chance, but that is no way to speak to a lady." My dad intervened.

I just couldn't stand to see her. "I'll be going to the ladies' room," I excused myself, and Tristan looked at me apologetically.

When I entered the ladies' bathroom, I stood in front of the mirror, looking at myself. Sighing, I opened my clutch bag to take out my lip gloss, which was pink. The door creaked open and closed with a click.

"You're looking so radiant this evening," I looked at Maggie in the mirror as she started to powder her nose. Ugh.

"Thanks," is all that I said.

"I don't know why he's acting like such an ass tonight. Does he have another woman that I don't know about?" She turned to me.

"Um, I don't know," I shrugged. I don't even know what to say, since we were a secret.

"Have you seen him with another woman?" She asked, her brows furrowing. Well, she did not know we were dating, so I lied.

"No, he doesn't have a girlfriend or a woman that I know of," I lied.

"Great," she was so happy as she turned back to the mirror. I placed my lip gloss inside my clutch bag. "He was with me two nights ago. Perhaps the type of environment that he is in or the people that he's around makes him act like a jerk. Do not let a man string you along and talk shit to you in front of people, because that is not a man." She warned me and left. Then why do you want him, Maggie?

My heart had stopped when she said that Tristan had been with her two nights ago, and that was when Cris came over unexpectedly. I assumed he had gone back home. You're a fool, Elona. He went somewhere because he lied to Cris that he would be out thinking that she would be back at home and sneak back to be with me, but that didn't happen since Cris made herself comfortable in my house for the remainder of that night.

So, where did they meet each other that night? Was it at the bar? I didn't even want to think about whether anything had happened because my overthinking was kicking in and adding anger to it with possible hurt. But I needed to get to the bottom of this before I jumped to any conclusions. I took a deep breath to get it together, to face the crowd out there, but I knew that I would see them out there too. I really needed to talk to him, but that would only happen at the hotel, so I texted my dad.

Me: Dad, I forgot to let you know that I'll be going with The Dakota Agency for the rest of the night. Don't wait up for me.

My phone chimed immediately. It was my dad.

Dad: Be safe. I love you.

Me: ❤

I left the bathroom and walked through the crowd, I was scanning through them to see where Tristan was. I saw him standing at the bar with my dad and Maggie. He was still looking pissed off. I don't even know if what she said were true. I needed to know from him what took place.

That Night

Tristan

I was miserable as fuck. Who invited Maggie here? It was strictly for the people on the list. David, Maggie, and I were standing at the bar. I took a sip of my Whiskey. I had to stay here at least until most of these people were gone. It was my idea for the exhibition. I scanned the room for my assistant. But I did not even see her. I tried looking for Elona too, but I didn't see her either.

A hand was now against my chest and I turned to see that it was Maggie and her claws. "Get your hands off me," I said through clenched teeth as I yanked her hand away from me.

"What's bothering you so much?" She asked.

"Give this woman a break, Tristan," David chimed in.

"I'm going to find out if my guests are happy." I excused myself because I didn't want to be here.

"Before you go, David and I were talking the other day about us. Since the two of you guys haven't shared a woman before, I want to do that with you and David who has already agreed. So what do you say?" Maggie suggested.

"What the fuck is wrong with you? I will never share a woman," I blurted out.

"It doesn't hurt to have more fun. Besides, she's right we haven't tried that," David shrugged.

"What is this?" I was disgusted. "No-"

"So, that means you won't share me then," Maggie stated.

"Fuck, no... I mean, no I won't have you because I have a girlfriend," I hissed at her while David turned and sipped his drink. "You two are welcome to fuck each other." I stormed away through the crowd. What kind of a fucking joke was this? A threesome? Not something that I'll ever consider, I have Elona, and she's more than enough for me.

As I left through the crowd to take a break from everyone, let alone from what Maggie had suggested. I walked to a secluded section that wasn't meant for the public. Most of our things were stored here for the evening. I heard heels and I turned around and I saw Jessie, my assistant, walking with a clipboard in her hand.

"Oh, Mr Crane, the evening is going smoothly," she smiled as she walked over to some documents that were on a chair. She wore a formal black dress, black leggings, and ankle boots, and her blonde hair was cut into a pixie hairstyle. I loved her as an assistant. She didn't care about me or my attitude at times. She never had any hidden agendas towards me because she was not interested in me. That was the type of assistant that I had always looked for. My previous assistants always tried to throw themselves at me and because of that, I fired them. I just couldn't work like that.

"That's great to know," I replied, and then she grabbed a document, clipped it to the clipboard, and left. I paced the section, my shoes echoing on the shiny tiled floor. I wanted this evening to end so that I could go to the hotel and be with Elona. I heard heels again. It had to be Jessie forgetting something.

As I was about to walk, I stopped in my tracks when Maggie appeared. She was smiling seductively at me as she walked closer to me. I scowled at her. "You shouldn't be here, this is only for my staff."

She continued to make her way closer, and I moved back until my back was against the wall. She placed her hand against my chest, and then she traced the buttons of my jacket. "I know that you don't have a girlfriend, and I will get my way with you. You're losing a good thing and I hate that you're wasting this," she said.

"Well, I would prefer to lose it, because I do have a girlfriend," before I knew it, she leaned forward until her mouth was close to my ear.

"Don't think for a second that you will get rid of me, because I'm here to stay," she whispered, her breath against my ear sending shivers down my spine. "I know you don't have a girlfriend because Elona told me that you don't have one. I mean David doesn't even know that. Which means you were lying to me. Besides, did you forget the other night that we were together? " And then I felt her lips press against my neck and I grabbed her, yanking her away from me.

"What the fuck?!" I barked at her. She nearly stumbled back when I yanked her away from me. I wiped her kiss off my neck. Her eyes were huge. "You spoke to Elona about me? She doesn't even know I have a girlfriend and David doesn't know shit," I hissed, partially lying, still wiping her kiss off me. "Leave me the fuck alone," I pointed at her, "Next time, I'll be getting a restraining order against you," I said before I left.

What the hell was wrong with these kinds of women? I do shit to no one, and yet they all want to be with me. Well, not as obsessed as Maggie was. I regret having a one-night stand with her. I did that just to get Elona out of my mind, hoping that it would help, but it didn't. I'm such an ass for listening to David who encouraged it in the first place.

*****

I got to the hotel, eager to forget about my evening. When I entered, the lounge was quiet, and I walked further inside to find Elona half asleep on the sofa. I smiled at her as I took my jacket off and threw it onto the recliner. She sat up straight. "How was your evening?" She asked, still dressed in her gorgeous dress.

"It was…okay," I wasn't going to explain about Maggie. I didn't want that to dampen the mood.

She stood up from the sofa and I closed the space between us, placing my hands on her hips. "I want to fuck you in this dress, but I don't want to ruin it," I said as my eyes fell on the swells of her breasts. My erection was straining against my pants. She didn't seem to be in the mood, but I was going to try.

"What's wrong?" I asked.

"Just tired," she gave me a small smile.

"We don't need to do anything tonight. We can just cuddle," I suggested.

She moved out of my hold, and then she turned to face me. Her eyes narrowed.

"Why is that on your collar? Was that from her? Or a guest?" She asked with hurt in her eyes.

I furrowed my brows in confusion, "What do you mean?"

She scoffed, "Clearly you know what's on your collar."

I unbuttoned my shirt and took it off to check what she was talking about. "Fuck," I muttered under my breath. It was Maggie's lipstick in the shape of her lips, a bit smudged on my collar. I let out a heavy breath. Did she plan this?

"Clearly, something happened," she was accusing me of something now. I discarded the shirt on the floor. I'm not wearing that again.

"Are you accusing me of something?" I turned her way, taking a seat on a recliner, resting my elbows on my knees, clasping my hands, and watching her.

"Well, Maggie said that you were with her the other night. That night when Cris slept over at my house. Were you with her that night?" She asked, her voice laced with hurt. I looked at the floor. I wished so badly that Cris had not been there and ruined our evening that we were supposed to have together. I went to the bar to wait until Elona had to text me that Cris was gone, but then I got that text of disappointment. So, then I continued to sit at the bar.

"Were you two together that night?" She asked. I continued to look at the ground. "Answer me, it's that simple," her voice broke a bit and I just didn't want her to think the worst of me and I didn't want her to be hurt by me not responding and making her think whatever she wanted to. "Please, answer me," This was the first time that I heard her with any hurt laced in her voice.

I looked up at her, the look in her eyes was full of hurt, and I guess she was hoping that Maggie was wrong. I sucked in a breath as I held her gaze.

"Yes, I was with her that night."

Love Bite

Elona

I stood there as if he had stabbed me in the heart when he said those words. I should've known that Maggie would always be there when he didn't get his way with me. He ran to another woman. I'm so stupid to think that Tristan Crane wanted me. I'm young, and I'm stupid according to him after he did this.

"You-you were with her? Maggie? Where? I need answers. Explain everything to me," I demanded.

He looked at me with such guilt, his eyes were sad, and I didn't care because he broke my heart. "Before you jump to any conclusions. I was at the bar," he stood up this time, approaching me, bare-chested since he had taken his shirt off.

"Don't come any closer to me," I held out my hand for him, trying to stop him from getting closer to me, and he stopped in his tracks.

"I had a drink, and she sat in the empty seat next to me. I didn't want her to be there, and I wasn't going to leave either, because why should I leave? I was comfortable being there while I waited for you to text me that Cris had left, but to my disappointment, you texted that she would sleep over and that disappointment led me to have another drink. Maggie was talking about shit knows what, because I had blocked her out. She also tried to come onto me, but that made me leave. I went home since Cris decided she was spending the night with you. There was no need to pretend that I was going to be out for the entire evening." He let out a breath.

"But your shirt...how can I believe you when there is ..." I can't even say it.

"Elona, she came onto me, whispered in my ear that you told her I didn't have a girlfriend. I've been telling her the whole fucking time that I have a girlfriend so that she could back off, but now she won't because you screwed that up," I flinched as he hissed.

"How was I supposed to know what to say to people when we are a secret?" I asked, tears welling up in my eyes. "I hate to be kept a secret, especially when she's around. How do you think I feel?" My voice broke.

He moved so fast towards me, that he was in front of me in no time. Cupping the sides of my face, he leaned in close and looked into my eyes, "Trust me, I hate it too. I want to scream to the whole world that you're mine. But we have to wait. There are only a few months left until you graduate. Your father will kill me if he has to find out now. Just please, trust me. I have never been with another woman while being with you. You know me, Elona. You know my past, you know everything so far." Desperation laced his voice.

"Promise me that I'll be your one and only woman now and in the future. You won't leave me for anyone else. We'll have a future together," I needed to hear that.

"I promise. I don't want anyone else. No one makes me feel the way that you do. I promise to spend the rest of my life with you. I promise to marry you in the future. You are the only one that makes me crazy and do things that...that I never thought I would. I love you and I always will," he crashed his lips against mine, closing my eyes, I placed my hands on his arms, and he walked me back until I was pressed against the wall.

His tongue invaded my mouth as I gasped. Our tongues dancing. He pressed his hard bulge against me and I moaned into his mouth. Pulling away, our chests heave. He turned me around, and then he unzipped the top of my dress until it fell to the floor.

"Fuck," he muttered under his breath.

I heard him unzip his pants. I was left in only my black lace bra. And then I felt him against me, he moved my hair over one shoulder as he breathed along my ear, my neck, and shoulder. He moved his hands to the front and cupped my breasts. As he now trailed kisses along my shoulder.

He started fondling my breasts, pressing his hard cock against my ass. "Do you feel that? That's what you do to me, even when you're not around. You consume my thoughts, and it drives me insane. I cannot get enough of you," he breathed against my ear, it sent goosebumps throughout my body. "Only you do this to me."

"Thinking about me didn't stop you from fucking Maggie that night when I slept over. You went at it all night. Surely, I'm not the only woman that makes you feel this way," I breathed, my core was throbbing, and I was drenched. I wanted him to fuck me already. "Ah," I gasped as he sunk his teeth into my shoulder.

"Forget about Maggie and any other woman. Trust me, I was fucking her with you on my mind. I imagined that I was fucking you that night. Now, I get to really fuck you," he rasped, and then his hands moved down towards my lace panties. He slid them down, letting them fall to the floor around my feet.

He massaged my ass cheeks, and then he pulled me back a bit, "Push your sexy ass out," he demanded. I rested my hands on the wall in front of me, pushing my ass out. That's when I felt the tip of his cock at my entrance. I braced myself for it. And then he pushed in. I bit my bottom lip as he pushed all the way into the hilt. I was full of him. He wrapped his arm around my breasts and pulled me up straight against him, my hands still against the wall.

Gasping, he started to penetrate me slowly at first, and then he picked up the pace. I squeezed my eyes closed as the intensity of this position was too much. It felt as if I was being ripped into shreds, but it was mixed with pleasure, and that all too familiar feeling started to build up.

His other hand moved around until they cupped my pussy. He slipped a finger between my folds, finding my clit, and then he flickered while pounding into me. Sparks went off inside of me and I just couldn't take it, it was just too intense. "Fuck!" I blurted out as my body convulsed with my orgasm.

"Shit," he groaned behind me, "That's it, milk my cock," he hissed. My muscles clenched around his cock as I continued to orgasm. "Fuck!"

"Ahhhh!!!" I was barely coming down from my orgasm when pain sneered into my shoulder. Tristan's teeth sunk into me as he came, filling me up with his fluids.

He finally pulled away. "Are you okay?" He asked through his panting. My knees wanted to buckle. I started shaking, my hands were still against the wall and Tristan held me in place. He pulled out of me and my knees gave way, holding me, he went with me to the floor, never letting go of me.

He nuzzled his face in the crook of my neck. My back was against his chest, "I'm exhausted after that. It was amazing," I said tiredly as he pulled away.

"Shit," he muttered under his breath and his fingers traced the part where he bit me.

I looked over my shoulder. "What is it?" I asked.

"I bit you, and now you're bleeding. It was a bit too hard. You have a mark for... I don't know how long."

"I can cover it up," I replied.

"I hope you can, otherwise we'll have to lie about that too," he suggested.

"We don't have a choice," I let out a sigh.

"Let's get this cleaned," he said.

He stood up with me, holding me in his arms as he carried me to the bathroom. I loved this part of him, where he took good care of me. The gentleness that I saw was what made my heart swell. He won my heart when I first started to have a crush on him a few years ago. He won my heart this year and even now, after the recent events with Maggie. He wants me...only me.

Cozy

Elona

Tristan had carried me to the bathroom. The bathroom was white and so neat. He placed me on a little bench. We were both naked. I studied his body. That C tattoo that I had written about in my essay before we started secretly dating. He had told me to change it to a T in my essay, and then he went to go and change the whole essay. That was basically the first time he had admitted to having feelings for me. Those were our first memories. He crouched in front of the vanity cupboard, taking out the first aid kit. I wonder how bad the bite mark was. Would anyone be able to see it? Especially when I have to do my photoshoots?

I let out a heavy sigh as he came towards me, "What is it?" He asked as he moved behind me.

"I'm just thinking about my photoshoots. I don't know how bad that bite mark is," I said.

"Well, I'm sure your makeup artist will be able to cover it up... I'm sorry about that. You make me do crazy things," he said behind me.

"I don't blame you," I smiled. "I supposed that Maxime will be able to cover it up. I just hope that I won't be yelled at by her. Mr Luca gives me the creeps, I mean... I didn't expect that from him when I had to see him in his office. I felt... like I was making a mistake. If it was the wrong agency. But I will get there. I have to toughen up," I said.

"If I had my way, I wouldn't have you in that industry because of those creeps and I would always be around to keep a watchful eye on you. This is what you truly want, and you made that perfectly clear to me as much as I hate it. I'll support you as much as this is difficult for me because of the industry. I'll be a supportive boyfriend and be with you every step of the way. You're also correct in toughening up towards them. Don't let them touch you."

"I have no choice but to toughen up."

"This is going to sting," he said, and then I winced as he cleaned my bite mark.

I felt his breath on my skin as he blew over it, sending goosebumps all over my body, and then he trailed soft kisses along my shoulder. "I love you," I said over my shoulder.

"I love you more than anything. I can't even express it. I know I'm an ass who has a hot head, and call me whatever you want, but when I love, I love deeply. I'll go to the ends of the earth for those who I love. You changed my life in ways that I never thought would happen. I thought that I would always be stuck in this place of grief and work myself to the bone. I've had more lenient breaks from work ever since I really saw you for you. This beautiful young woman who is beautiful both on the inside and out." I felt him pull away further, sticking a band-aid over my bite mark, and then he appeared in my view, my gaze on his ass as he packed the first aid kit away and washed his hands.

"It still feels so surreal that we're together." I looked at him in awe. "Never in my wildest dreams have I thought we would ever be together. I would daydream about you. How you might be in bed and to be Mrs Crane," I smiled at the thought.

He turned around to face me, but his cock was hard again. I moved my gaze up, he was smirking. "How am I in bed? Does that meet your expectations?" He asked as he moved closer to me, holding out his hand to me.

Heat rose to my cheeks, "Well," I placed my hand in his and stood up. "It's amazing. Better than what I thought it would be," I replied as he crouched in front of me. He had a paper towel in his hand and cleaned me up before standing up and discarding it in the trash can. He faced me again, holding his hand out to me again.

"I like that. It tells me that I'm not out of touch." He continued to smirk as

I placed my hand in his again, leading me out of the bathroom and into the bedroom. "Would you like room service?" He asked as he let go of my hand and I climbed onto the bed, I reached for the throw that was on the edge of the bed and covered myself with it.

"I'm not hungry, just exhausted from the event," I leaned back against the headboard.

Tristan sat beside me, he held his arm out, inviting me in. I moved closer to him as he took the throw and covered his lower half with it too. I rested my head against his chest, listening to his steady heartbeat. His cock was now flaccid as he held me in his arms. I draped my arm over his abdomen.

"You know I won't do anything to destroy what we have, right?" He said.

"I know you won't and I trust you. After what you said to me earlier, Maggie can say anything to make me believe the worst of you," I replied.

"Please, do not listen to her. She's a snake and I don't even trust her with my life."

"Will you ever show anyone else that huge part of the house?" I asked.

"Soon I will, thanks to you. Once everyone else knows about us, I'll start to clean that place and start over. I want us to make it ours. Cris will be out of the house when she goes to SNT next year. It will just be me. I want you to move in and enjoy what's mine. I want to be able to play the piano more often while you watch me. I want to make you breakfast in bed and worship your body as much as I can. I want to watch you sleep. I want that fresh start with you, my future Mrs Crane," he rolled me over, and now I'm on my back with him on top of me. "I'm glad that I have you." He leaned down and pressed a tender kiss on my lips.

His phone rang in the distance, "Maybe that's Cris." He pulled inches away, "Did you let her know that you would be away for the rest of the night?" I asked.

"No, let me answer that," he said as he climbed off me and walked out of the bedroom.

I didn't want to move the position that I was in, and I knew that we would go at it for the rest of the night. After a while, Tristan appeared. "I texted Cris that I would not be at home. She'll be out with Spooky again tomorrow."

"So, are you okay with her hanging out with Spooky?" I asked as I sat up straight, grabbing the throw and covering myself. He had put on his boxer briefs that we left in the lounge. He still had his phone in his hand as he was busy typing.

"Yeah. I mean he likes her," he shrugged.

"So, it's okay for him to hang out with her, possibly date her, and it's not okay for us to be friends?"

He looked up from his phone. "At least I know his intentions are not with you but my daughter." He walked towards the bed and placed his phone on the bedside table and got on the bed again.

"So, we can be friends now?" I had to make sure because I didn't want him to jump down my throat again or be mean to Spooky.

"Yes, friends only," he held my gaze. I couldn't help but smile at that.

"Thank you. You're starting to soften up towards him and I like that you're trying," I said.

"It's not easy, but what can I do?" He shrugged. "I'll be taking you home tomorrow morning to pack a little bag. I want to take you somewhere for the day since the camping trip has been moved to two weeks' time in order for your school to prepare more. I'll check up on Cris tomorrow morning. I told her I had work to tend to for the rest of the night regarding the hacking. She doesn't seem to care, which is great that she isn't in her suspicious mode. Your father called me to keep an eye on you tomorrow and bring you home from The Dakota agency. That lie has worked. But he has something to take care of this evening," he said, looking at nothing.

"What was it that he had to take care of this evening?" My brows furrowed.

"Maggie...she got sick, so he took her to the hospital."

"I wonder what could be wrong with her," I said, trying to figure it out.

"He said that she was vomiting. But I don't give a shit about her. My focus is you," he pulled me in and trailed kisses along my collarbone and I giggled as he tickled me.

This was the side that I liked most about him. These moments are where he opens up and shows the soft-hearted Tristan Crane that lies buried beneath all that hard exterior. Knowing that I'm the reason for that just made my heart swell. But one thing that I do not like was that Maggie was always around when she was clearly told to back off, and now she was with my dad, hanging out with him. I don't like that one bit either.

Cover Ups

Elona

Tristan and I went back to his house. He wanted to take me somewhere tonight. But I wanted to make sure that my best friend was okay. I was still wearing my dress from the exhibition since it was a last-minute hotel meeting with Tristan that I had to lie about to my Dad. I wonder if he would be home since Maggie got sick. I just hope that he wasn't hanging out with her because I can't stand her.

I entered the house after Tristan, "Dad!" Cris stood up so fast from the sofa.

"Mr Crane," Spooky said as he shifted his position on the sofa. His eyes found mine, "Elona," he gave me a small smile before looking towards Tristan again.

"What's going on here?" Tristan asked. Cris was fidgeting with her hands as if she was guilty of hiding something. That was always her giveaway.

"Nothing," she smiled. I furrowed my brows as I looked between her and Spooky, who was now sitting with his elbows on his knees. His hands clasped as he looked to the floor.

"Well, I have to see that Elona gets home safely, as per Uncle David, but I need to shower and change. It had been a long night," Tristan said.

"So, I get to have my friend to myself for a while," her eyes lit up. I smiled in return. "You look gorgeous by the way," she said. I just wished that Tristan had warned me before the time to pack in clothes because now I'm dressed this way... too overdressed.

"Thanks," I responded.

"Can I have a little word with you, Spooky? What's your real name?" He asked.

"Eric, Sir," Tristan was blown away by being addressed as Sir.

"Meet me in the kitchen," Tristan said before walking away to the kitchen with Spooky following after him.

"So, how was The Dakota Agency? Tell me all about it," she came to me, grabbed my hand, and led me to her bedroom.

If only she knew what her dad and I did last night, "It was okay. We spent some time at a hotel. Just getting to know each other as models," I lied as she closed the door behind me and I sat on one of her beds. "It was a last-minute thing. I decided to go. So, what's the deal with Spooky?" I asked, changing the topic before I would say something that didn't add up.

"Well, we kissed and had fun," she said as she sat across from me.

"What kind of fun?" I narrowed my eyes at her.

"Well...we had sex. He's okay in bed. I just think we can improve. It was his first time though," she blurted out. I nodded as I soaked that in. That was too much detail for me to know. If only she knew how great her father was in bed, how he handled me.

"Wow," I muttered, trying to act surprised as I snapped out of my thoughts.

"You don't look surprised." Fuck.

"It's a surprise but... I didn't know that you were interested in him. I knew he liked you." I shrugged.

"I wanted to give him a try."

"Just don't break his heart, because I know the kind of person you are. You like to take risks, you like partying. You like to be on the wild side."

"Spooky is more like you...the conservative person who respects all rules... .hell, who doesn't even break a rule. Something needs to change with that. Maybe when you work with The Dakota Agency more often you'll meet a guy, and then you can do whatever you want. Mr Luca is a good-looking guy but there needs to be some boundaries and who knows, maybe he has a son or something you can explore things with. You're a virgin, and you never had a boyfriend. It's time to start living. If Spooky can do it, then so can you," she said.

"I'm not ready yet. You'll know when things have changed." I gave her a small smile.

She looked at me suspiciously. "Well, there's something that I want to address and it's something that will mean a lot to me."

My heart beat fast, "What is it?" I asked.

"My Dad's birthday is coming up in three weeks' time and I want to arrange a pool party here at the house. The thing is, I want it to be a surprise. He hasn't celebrated his birthday since my mom passed away, because you know that it was our tradition as a family. So, I want this year to be different before I leave the house when I start my time at SNT. I need help in planning this. He cannot know about this beforehand. It needs to be top secret." Secret...We were top secret.

"Of course," I smiled. "I would like to help," I said.

"Great!" She squealed with excitement. "It's a pool party and, hopefully, I can invite some of his work employees. I didn't know who else to invite. Oh, your Dad is a must to be invited." She said as her eyes widened and lit up even more.

I let out a little laugh as I enjoyed seeing her being excited about something that had to do with her father. They deserve all the happiness that they lost, and I do hope that Tristan was not hard on Spooky.

"My Dad would love to be part of the surprise party. I hope that he stops having so much fun and at least settle down the same way that you want your father to settle down."

"Yeah, it was a mission to get him to have fun with your Dad. I was so happy when he was with Maggie, but now, he just pushes her away. What is his happily ever after?" she said. Maggie again. Why was it always Maggie?

"I know that it will not be her. I can tell that he doesn't like her and I know that he wouldn't want to be pushed into a situation or relationship that he doesn't want to be part of. He will move on when he's ready," I tried my best to give her a smile, but it was small.

She shrugged, "I guess you're right. I wouldn't want him to be with the wrong woman who is only after him for the money and not love him for who he is. He needs love and patience. He can be difficult."

That I know he was. But slowly, I got to witness that man's softer side when he showed it. Knowing that I'm also the reason that he was softening up to things and what he used to find joy in, made me happy that I'm the one for him.

"I know, but he will get there with time."

"You speak like someone who knows all about it," she smiled.

I shrugged, "I guess I learn and observe people."

"Very true. Let's go down and see what they're up to. Let's hope they are not at each other's throats. You know how my Dad gets," she stood up, and I followed her out of the bedroom.

I was happy that she didn't suspect anything. I needed her to keep her mouth shut when it came to me and that I used to be a virgin. Well, according to her, I'm a virgin who never had a boyfriend before. But if that came up, it was a lie that I might need to tell Tristan. I wished that I had never lied to him about being a virgin. I don't know how he would react to that, but it should be nothing...right? Now, we have to plan his surprise birthday party, which I hope he would take well.

More Lies Added

Tristan

I knew by the way that Cris and Spooky were fidgeting that something happened. When I walked in by that front door, I caught a glimpse of them kissing. I won't lie but I'm so happy that it wasn't Elona that he was with. It was a huge relief for me. I could tell that more happened. They were alone together yesterday and I hope that my daughter was on birth control.

I took the juice out of the fridge. "Take a seat," I said to Eric. Eric sounded better than that stupid nickname. He took a seat looking guilty as fuck as if he did something bad.

I poured juice into my glass and then the other, and pushed it towards him, setting the juice down on the counter. "I know there is something going on between you and Cris. You don't have to deny it. I know my daughter." I watched him intently. "If something more happened between you two yesterday, I would prefer that she be on birth control. I don't know if she is for that matter and I don't know if she had done this thing before because I never spoke to her about it. She can break rules, and sometimes she can be difficult to contain like a blazing fire. Where she got that from is beyond me, because she sure as fuck didn't get that from me or her mother. If you do have sex with her, I have a box of condoms in my bedroom bedside drawer. That's protection. I don't want to become a grandfather anytime soon and you're both young. I know that your father will not take that well at all. I'm teaching you these things to be responsible and have protection. Do not make the same mistakes that I...other people have made."

"I will take your advice, and thank you for the talk," he said, genuinely interested.

"I want you to take good care of my daughter and not break her heart. That's one thing that I will not tolerate from you. I don't want to see my precious, beautiful daughter hurt. So, I hope you know what you're getting yourself into when it comes to her." I said, still watching him intently. He doesn't cower.

"You have my promise that I will not break her heart. I like her way too much. I would rather let her break my heart than be the one to break hers. I know that I come from a damaged family, but I long to have the love and stability that I have always wanted within a family. I will never be the man that my father is, because I'm far from that. I know the type of person that I am, I will not hurt a fly. You have my promise, Sir."

I was taken aback by that. What young man says these profound things to the father of his ...girlfriend? This young man impresses me all the damn time, and I was such an ass to him. That just makes me feel guilty. He has gone through a lot and I had added to that thinking that he wanted Elona, but it was the opposite. He wanted my daughter.

"As long as I know that she is loved, taken care of, and not to be hurt by you. You have her and if she's happy with you, then by all means, date her. If she's out of line, come to me and I'll set her straight. I wouldn't want her to break your heart either," I took a sip of my juice.

'That means a lot to me, Mr. Crane."

"Tristan, please," I said, his eyes were huge now. "You earned it, you can call me Tristan."

"Thank you... Tristan," I gave him a small smile.

"How are things at home?" I asked, curious to know, his blue eye was gone already, which was why he was no longer wearing sunglasses.

"It has died down, mainly because my father went away for business. I get to be a bit free. But once I graduate, I plan to move away. I want to pursue photography and that's why I worked with Elona so that I could also build up my own portfolio. I just want to be far away from my father. I know what you said to me the last time about protecting her when it comes to my father. I won't let her set foot in my house. I would rather be here with her...with your permission, of course."

"You have my permission to be here. Just use protection when you do the deed."

"Got it, Sir."

"Also... don't tell Cris about what you might know about Elona and I. Please, keep that to yourself. I don't want relationships and friendships to be ruined. When the time is right, we will say it ourselves."

He nodded, "I won't say a word. It was never my place to say anything. So, don't worry about that." He took a sip of his juice. I was so relieved by his answer.

"Good."

"So, what are you interrogating Spooky about?" Cris and Elona entered the kitchen. I couldn't stand that nickname.

"I was just having a word with him about dating you. I know, Cris," her cheeks turned red as she blushed.

"I hope that you weren't being too harsh on him," she said as she walked past Elona. Her brows furrowed, looking at Elona's back.

"Uh, no. I gave permission to date," I said.

"Thanks, Dad." she smiled. "Why do you have a band-aid on your shoulder?"

Shit...now to lie about that. "Uh, I hurt myself, I stumbled down a few steps on my heels last night," Elona lied.

"Oh, you poor thing. I hope someone was there to help you up... Mr Luca maybe."

Anger resurfaced within me because of what he tried to do with Elona, putting his filthy hands on her. I'm glad that there was no actual Dakota Agency event last night. Even if there was, I would be there and this was a conversation that I needed to have with David. I needed him to know what could possibly happen when I'm not there to look after his daughter even if Elona would toughen herself up.

"I'm fine. It's nothing to worry about." Elona smiled at her.

"I'll take a quick shower. I'll be accompanying Elona to another event. So, don't even wait up for me," I lied.

"Tristan Crane, the bodyguard." Cris smiled. "Who would've thought that you would be a bodyguard to Elona?"

I shrugged, "It's David's orders," I replied.

"Just take good care of my best friend, Dad," she said as she sat down beside Eric on a bar stool.

"I will always try my best. Give me a few minutes," I said to Elona, and she gave me the most gorgeous smile. I just couldn't wait to have her to myself.

I would be taking her to a place that I haven't been to since Estelle passed away. It was one of our favorite places to be at. Elona just brings all the feelings out of me that I buried away for a reason three years ago. They were popping up like flowers in springtime. I welcomed those feelings that Elona was bringing out of me and the way that she drove me crazy. I want it all with her and I don't want that to change.

A Little Confession

Tristan

We entered Elona's house. David's car wasn't in the driveway yet. So, he was either still with Maggie or somewhere else. Just as I was about to close the front door, his car pulled up in the driveway. I was disappointed because I wanted to at least have a quickie with Elona before we left.

"I will take a shower and get my things," Elona smiled and went upstairs before David entered.

"Hey," he said, his voice laced with exhaustion.

"How have things been?" I asked as he closed the door behind him. He was still in his attire from last night's exhibition. It seemed that he hadn't been home since then.

"It has been a long night." He walked to the kitchen and I followed after him. I sat down on a bar stool while he took a glass out of the top cupboard. "Would you like Scotch or Whiskey?" He asked.

"No, thanks," I would be driving, so I didn't want any alcohol in my system. I didn't need it though.

He poured himself Scotch, his back facing towards me. "I was at Maggie's place the entire night after she got sick. She wanted me to stay with her," he said, and took a sip of his Scotch, turning around to face me.

"You didn't have to stay with her," I said.

"Well, how could I not? She's alone and has no one else to take care of her. She was out of it. I'm exhausted because I needed to be awake to make sure that she was okay."

"But she's not your responsibility. I wouldn't do that unless you like her or something."

"I can have fun but like...she's far from my type." He scrunched his face in disgust.

"I'm glad to know that you've seen that. I think that she manipulates men easily. We are wealthy men and we do not know her background. She's always hanging out at that bar. Don't do that to yourself. There are so many women out there. Some are rare, so don't fuck that up." I tried to steer him away from Maggie.

"I'm not looking for any commitments, although there's one person that I have noticed...like really noticed but...she's off limits to me," he let out a sigh before taking another sip of Scotch. "She's beautiful, vibrant...full of life. How can I be with her when she's so much younger than me? I doubt that she even looks at me that way and I just think it's wrong," he said in thought.

I furrowed my brows, "Younger than you in terms of how far apart are we talking?" I asked.

His gaze fell on me as if he realized what he was talking about. Clearing his throat, he said, "I'm twice her age."

"You are twice her age," I said in thought. I'm twice Elona's age. "So, this means that she's in school or college?"

"She'll be attending college." I furrowed my brows. Who the hell could that be? David and a young woman? That's a first. I should be speaking last about that. I never thought in a million years that could happen to me either.

"Elona will be going back on some outing with The Dakota Agency, so I'll be accompanying her again." I lied.

He nodded, "Thanks. I know that I'm a shitty father right now. I appreciate that you're being there for my little girl and taking good care of her. She needs that support and while I'm not there to be with her, you are there. I couldn't have asked for a greater friend." He smiled through his exhaustion.

I forced a smile because everything he said hit me like a punch. I was fucking his daughter, I was lying about it and once he found out about us, I'm not sure how he would look at me again, and I doubt he would be my friend.

"I'll always be there for her...she's like a... daughter to me," that last part was just damn awkward to say.

"So, how is she doing over there with the agency?" He asked.

"I would say she does well, but there's this creep, Austin Luca, that wants to touch her. That man is sending me bad vibes and, if I'm being honest, I don't think that I'm even happy about her going into this industry because of the type of men that are out there who want a piece of her and...who touch her. She's clearly uncomfortable with it, but yet she's so determined because it's her dream. I just don't trust those men and I can't always be there to keep a watchful eye over her." I said with so much anger lacing my voice.

"I agree with all you have said. But we cannot always hold her back or protect her from anything. Once she's done with school, she'll be on her own and finding herself. That's what we had to do. All we can do for now is protect her, but like you said, we won't always be around for that. I think that she'll be able to look out for herself."

"She was anything but looking out for herself when I saw him touch her. She was standing there, not liking it but not saying anything to stop it. What does one do with that?" I was now angry because David seemed to be oblivious to that.

"Tristan, I like how you care. But if he takes it further with her. She'll know what to do. It was her first day, she needed to get used to things and know how to handle these things. If he takes it further with her, she can report it. But that's the industry that she chose to be in. It's her dream and I can only do so much as a father. It's her dream and I won't stand in the way of it." He said as he gulped the rest of the Scotch down and placed the empty glass on the counter.

I didn't like what he was saying, but I had no choice but to actually agree with it. She could report it when it gets out of hand, and they would always be touching her because men work with her. I could just kick myself for being an ass to Eric when he was doing photoshoots with her because now there are far worse men she was going to work with. It just made me even more guilty of what I did to Eric.

I furrowed my brows as an idea formed, "Do you think that my company can open a modeling agency and I can put the right people in place who aren't perverts? I can easily fire them when things get inappropriate." I said I was being desperate here.

He laughed, shaking his head, "Tristan, I know that you are looking out for Elona, but you are literally wanting to do this for her. No one else. You're willing to have an agency just for her and that is... that's just weird, and I think that she will be fine," he said.

"So, are you ready?" Elona asked, appearing beside me.

"Of course," I replied.

"You look like crap, Dad," she said.

"I feel like crap, once you both leave, I'll rest. I could sleep for an entire day," he yawned. "You two should enjoy the outing or whatever it is." He rounded the counter and stopped by Elona, placing a kiss against her forehead. "I love you," he said before he walked out of the kitchen.

Elona turned to me." Let's go," she smiled with excitement, and then I got off the bar stool, taking her little bag of clothes, and I followed her as we left the house.

I couldn't wait to show her this place. I know that no one would notice us, no one that we know would be there. But I might just walk into some people that I'm familiar with over there. People who knew me and Estelle. Most of all, I cannot wait to spend another evening with Elona.

Away From Home

Tristan

I ended up taking Elona to the South Hamptons. It was one of my favorite places to be. We stayed in a hotel and I wanted to take her to see some places and to go for a walk. I felt like the happiest man on earth. I would be even happier when our secret was out after her graduation.

I waited for Elona as I sat on the sofa in the hotel lounge. Reading the texts on my phone from work that I didn't have time to go through. Nothing new has been going on, but the investigation was still ongoing to find the person who hacked my company. They wanted to stop the investigation, but I wasn't going to stop that. It was my business that was affected by the loss of money and I will not let it go that easily.

"I'm ready," I looked up from my phone. Elona was dressed in denim shorts, flip-flops, and a cropped top, her hair was tied up into a messy bun on the top of her head.

"You look gorgeous as always," I smiled as I stood up from the sofa, sliding my phone into my jeans pocket, and making my way to her.

"Thanks," she grinned, I wrapped my arms around her waist, pulling her against me.

"Are you ready to hit the streets?" I asked.

"Yes, I'm ready for some sunshine," she replied as I leaned in and pressed a sweet kiss on her lips.

I pulled away, taking her hand in mine, and led her out of the hotel room. As we stepped on the sidewalk, we held hands. We wouldn't bump into anyone here from back home. I wanted us to be free, and we get to be free here.

The cafés were packed as we weaved through the people. "Tristan is that you?" My heart nearly stopped as I looked to my side, seeing an older woman sitting at a table on the sidewalk. She was having some tea from this café. My smile widened as she was one of the people over here who was so kind to me and Estelle.

"Moreen, it's great to see you again," I went over to her, dragging Elona with me. We stopped at the table. I continued to hold Elona's hand. Moreen's eyes moved to Elona.

"Who's this young woman?" She smiled. Moreen was a gray-haired woman. She looked well in her age.

I looked over at Elona, my heart swelling with the love that I have for her. "This is my girlfriend, Elona," I smiled.

"Nice to meet you," Elona said. I turned back to Moreen.

"You are so pretty. I can see why Tristan is so in love with you. He doesn't have to say anything. It's written all over his face." She smiled. "Please, take a seat. I would love to catch up," she said.

I pulled a chair out for Elona, and she sat down comfortably. I sat next to her across from Moreen. The breeze was cool against my skin. I looked over at Elona. "Would you like to order anything?" I asked.

"No, thank you." She smiled. I could tell that she was nervous. I reached out to her under the table and I took her hand in mine, just holding it.

"I'm so happy to see you again after three years. I was wondering if I would ever see you again and to my surprise, you're here," Moreen smiled. "How's your daughter?" She asked.

"Cris is doing well. She'll be getting into journalism next year just like her mother. This is her final year of high school." I smiled.

"Oh, she's such a beautiful child. I bet the two of you will make beautiful babies too," she smiled at me and Elona.

"We won't be having kids. Cris is my last," I forced a smile and I just don't like to talk about this topic.

"How about Elona? Do you want kids? Do not let a man rule you for what you want," she said.

"I'm on the same page as Tristan. I have a lot to live for. A career that I cannot afford to fall pregnant and other reasons, but as long as Tristan and I are happy, and we have each other, that's all that matters," I looked over at Elona, proud of what she had said, she always managed to surprise me. I'm glad I found someone who was on the same page as me and wants the same things as me. Who doesn't want kids as well. That's more than what I've asked for. Elona was the one for me, there's no questioning that.

"I hope that you'll both change your minds," she smiled at us.

"I think that society telling people what's to be expected is none of anybody's business except ours. If we don't want kids, then that is our thing. If we change our minds, which I doubt, then so be it with kids, but we will not bow down to what society has to say. All we ask in return is to respect our decisions as a couple. It's not like people out there will pay for the baby to be taken care of and so on. There is responsibility, and we do not need to explain ourselves to anyone." This was something that I hate about society, thinking that they could tell a couple what would happen and encourage them to have kids when they don't want or are not even ready and also without knowing the reason for not wanting kids. This was something that always frustrated me.

"Very well. As long as you both are happy, that's all that matters," Moreen said. I smiled because she didn't argue with that.

This topic had dampened my mood, so now I want to take Elona back to the hotel and just worship her body. The reason for being here was for our moods not to be dampened either. I looked over at Elona, who was sitting uncomfortably. "Are you ready to go?" I asked as she looked over at me.

She nodded, "Yes," she smiled. I turned back to Moreen.

"It was nice seeing you again, Moreen, but we have to leave," I said.

"Please, do not stay away for so long. It was nice seeing you and meeting Elona," she smiled at us.

"I'll do my best to be back." I said as Elona and I stood up, "Take care, Moreen," I said and Elona said goodbye to her before we left.

"I hope that we do not get to run into people who will just want to catch up. The reason why we are here is to be together," Elona said as we walked hand in hand down the sidewalk back to the hotel.

"I apologize. It was all my fault for sitting down and catching up with her. I didn't think that she would bring up that topic."

"It's okay as long as we both know what we want, that's all that matters. I don't care what anyone else says or thinks about us. They can have kids of their own for all I care," she grinned.

"That's my girl," I smiled.

Elona and I were like teenagers in love walking towards the hotel. I haven't felt this happy and carefree in such a long time. I'm so happy to take this leap with her because I would've still been a single, miserable man who buried himself in work. As I look back, there was a massive difference. I'm staying out of work more often because of Elona, and everyone else was trying to get me to take breaks or vacations, but Elona was the one who changed it all for me.

Hotel Room

Elona

Tristan's mood had changed since Moreen had brought up the topic about kids. I had to agree with everything that Tristan had said to her. I most certainly don't like it when people try to take control of my life because they think it's best. It's wrong and weird. Tristan and I walked hand in hand towards the hotel building. I felt free and not a secret for once. I loved this with him. I cannot wait for us to be able to be carefree when we tell Cris and my father.

"I wish that we could do this more often, every day for that matter," Tristan said as we walked on the sidewalk.

"Me too. I'm sorry that Moreen had to bring up that topic. I know you didn't want to run into anyone." I looked over at him.

"I could've chosen to go somewhere else, but this place is of significance to me and I want you to experience these things with me." We came to a stop in front of the hotel entrance. He held my hand in his, "I love doing this with you, and just imagine how it will be once we are no longer a secret next year." He smiled. "I will show you off to the entire world, I don't give a crap what anyone else has to say about us. Age is only a number, and it doesn't affect me."

I smiled at what he said, my heart swelling. He reached into his jeans pocket and took his phone out. "What are you doing?" I asked as he now stood beside me, leaned in, pressing his lips against my temple while holding his phone out in front of us, and he snapped a picture. "You took a selfie?" I turned to face him.

He shrugged, "Why not? I can have a picture of us on my phone," he smirked. "Come on, another one or two?" He smiled. He was like a little kid, all excited about those selfies.

"You better send them to me," I said as I got into position. He pressed his lips against mine and snapped another selfie, another one was of us smiling.

"Let's go inside," he said, shoving his phone into his pocket and then took my hand as we entered the hotel.

* * *

When we got to our hotel room, Tristan grabbed me after unlocking the door. He cupped the sides of my face and crashed his lips against mine. He reached behind me, and we stumbled inside, never breaking our kiss. He slammed the door closed behind us, and he pressed me against the wall. Gasping, he slid his tongue inside my mouth. I moved my hands to his chest and my heart beat at a rapid pace. I pulled away, my chest heaving as I panted.

"I need the bathroom," I said.

"Make it quick because I want to have you all to myself," he leaned in and pressed a soft kiss against my lips before pulling away again.

"I'll be back in no time," I grinned, and then I disappeared into the bathroom.

I had a plan, and it was something that he had asked me to do a while back. This would be a surprise that he would not forget. After changing into my black lingerie bodysuit from that picture, I accidentally sent to him and got his attention when he was in his boardroom meeting. I stared at myself in the bathroom mirror. The bodysuit hugged my body like a glove. It was the first time I wore it.

I sucked in a breath and then walked out of the bathroom. When I got to the bedroom, he was sitting on the edge of the bed, typing on his phone. I stood in front of him, my black heels were what made him look up, taking in my appearance, and when his eyes found mine, they were dark with hunger.

"Fuck. Me," he muttered as he placed his phone on the bed beside him.

I moved closer to him, and he rested his hands on my hips. He looked up into my eyes before studying my body.

"Surprise," I said with a grin.

"This is a great surprise. I know I have asked to see you in this, but I had actually forgotten about it." His hands now roamed my body as if I was something delicate and that fascinated him. "This is perfect on you," he said.

"I'm glad to know that it's perfect on me," I said seductively, and I moved even closer to him, standing in between his legs, his hands moving behind me, cupping my ass cheeks, and then I leaned in, pressing my lips against his. My hands moved around his neck as he let out a groan.

"This will be a long night, so be prepared," he said against my lips.

"I'm ready," I whispered, and then I climbed onto his lap, straddling him. Taking the end of his t-shirt, pulled it over his head, and discarded it on the floor. I leaned backward until he was now on his back, my hands on either side of him, my hair falling like a curtain on either side of our faces.

"Are you sure you want to be on top?" He asked, his hands still on my ass cheeks.

"I'm sure," I'm nervous and hope that I would satisfy him. I moved against him, feeling his hard bulge.

"If you don't hurry up then I would have to fuck you myself," he breathed, getting impatient. He reached between us and undid his jeans, his cock springing free.

I gasped as his finger pushed the fabric of my bodysuit to the side. I was soaked and throbbing. His finger moved between my folds "You're already drenched, there's no more waiting now," he said as he flickered my clit.

"Please," I breathed as I felt the pressure building up.

"I love how you're begging me," he grinned.

"So, are we doing that again? I beg and you get satisfaction in that?"

"Why not?" He continued to grin.

I reached between us, removing his hand, and then I took his cock, aligning it with my pussy and I sank down onto it slowly. I bit my bottom lip as his hands rested on my hips. "Fuck," he muttered. He was filling me up all the way, and then I started to move slowly. He helped me by moving his hips.

I leaned down and pressed my lips against his, he bit my bottom lip, and then he began to thrust into me. I threw my head to the back as his thrusts became rougher and faster. "Fuck me just like that." I breathed.

The bed was creaking loudly as the headboard banged against the wall. My toes were curling with the pleasure that was coursing through my entire body.

"I'm going to cum," Tristan's voice strained. His face contorted and his eyes squeezed shut as he pulled me closer to him as he filled me up with his fluids, causing my eyes to roll to the back as I reached my climax.

"Shit," I breathed as my chest heaved, climbing down from my orgasm.

We were both breathing heavily and exhaustion took over me as I laid down on him. Closing my eyes as we both were still catching our breath.

"You surprise me," he said tiredly. "I didn't know that a shy girl had this much experience," he said. I climbed off of him, and then I rested my head against his bare chest. His arm was wrapped around me. I still felt guilty for lying to him about being a virgin.

"Did you...did you have a boyfriend, or who did you have sex with before? Do I know him?" He asked hesitantly. I could feel him holding his breath, his heart still beating rapidly in my ear as I continued to lay my head against his chest.

"Um...no, it's not someone you know. It was just a fun thing," I lied.

He let out his breath, "Is he still around? How old is he?" He asked.

"Um, he isn't around anymore and I'm not sure how old he is. I think he was a senior. He moved away." I lied some more.

He pressed his lips against the top of my head. "Good," he said. "How old were you?"

"It was last year...I seventeen." I lied.

"Did he treat you with care and respect?" He asked.

"Yes," I said softly, hoping that he would stop these questions.

"Good."

I didn't know how he would react if I told him the truth about being a virgin when he had me for the first time. Knowing his temper, I'm not sure if lies as innocent as that would change his thoughts about me. So, I had to lie some more. I felt bad about it, but I didn't want to lose him either, because of a simple lie that I told him just to have sex with him. These lies would not become easier with all the other lies we were telling everyone else about us. It's a matter of keeping up with them and making sure we both know what to say to people for now.

Surprise On The Doorstep

Tristan

Elona and I arrived back at our houses this morning. I decided to head to work late. I wanted to take my time and be the boss who deserved to have time for himself. The little trip was good for myself and Elona. We relaxed and had sex most of the night. Elona was exhausted and that was because of me. But I enjoyed our time together.

I scrolled through some emails in the lounge before going into the office. There was still no new information regarding the hacker, but my team had secured everything so that this wouldn't happen again. There was a frantic knock on the front door. Looking up from my phone, my brows furrowed.

"What the hell?" I muttered to myself as I shoved my phone into my pants pocket, and walked to the front door. "If you don't ease down, this door might just break," I hissed as I opened the door.

My eyes widened as Eric stood in front of me, tears running down his face, he was bruised up. He ended up sobbing as he nearly fell to the ground. I caught him just in time, holding him close to me. He grabbed a fist full of my black suit jacket. I sat down on the ground with him, just holding him. He was sobbing this ugly cry and it broke my heart.

Tears welled in my eyes and I blinked them away. "It's okay. I'm here." I said to him as I moved his hair to the back. I placed a little kiss on the top of his head as if he were my own son in need of love and care. "I'm right here," I tried to soothe him. "You're safe here." His sobs began to subside, but he remained in my arms as if he were afraid to let go. So, I allowed him to stay in my arms.

I wanted him to feel safe here. I wasn't going to allow some asshole to do this to him. I may have been an ass to him at the beginning, but this was something that made me change towards him too. A lone tear ran down my cheek as my heart broke into a million pieces for him. Not just the abuse that he had to endure from his father, but from myself too. I knew that he had forgiven me for it and, in this way, I could help him. I wiped that tear away.

He slowly pulled out of my arms, "I'm sorry," he said as he wiped his tears away with the back of his hands. "I didn't mean to show up unannounced like this." He sniffled.

"Eric, you did the right thing by showing up here. My door is always open for you, though you're lucky that I'm still at home. I do think that you should go to the hospital to get checked–"

"Please, Tristan. I cannot go, they'll call my father. He won't like that at all," he begged me with fear in his eyes.

"You don't deserve this. You need to be checked, and you can stay here for as long as you like."

"I can't. My father will expect me to be at home," he responded.

"I will not take no for an answer. You will stay here. I'll take off from work today so that I can be here for you. Does Cris know about any of this?" I asked.

He shook his head, no, "She doesn't know."

"She'll find out sooner or later. Trust me, she's a good detective. Come on, let's get inside before anyone else sees us this way." I stood up and held my hand out for him, and he placed his hand in mine and I helped him get up.

He stepped inside, and I closed the door behind him. "You may sit on the sofa, I'll get you something to eat," I said.

"I'm not hungry," he took a seat on the sofa.

"You need to eat something. Are you in any pain?" I asked as I moved further into the lounge, closer to him.

"I am. A little bit," he said, hugging himself.

"Let me guess, you have pain over there," I stated and he just nodded his head. "Well, you need to get checked out," I said before going to the kitchen to get some painkillers and water for him.

I needed to have a nice word with his father. I cannot delay this. That man should know who he was dealing with. I will not let anything happen to Eric on my watch. I went back to the lounge with the painkillers and a glass of water, placing it on the coffee table. I sat on the recliner across from him, watching as he took the glass of water and painkillers.

"Thanks," he said as he leaned forward with a wince, placing the glass on the coffee table. He got comfortable on the sofa again.

"So, what happened this time?" I asked.

"I didn't hear him call me for breakfast this morning because I had earphones in my ears and the music was on full blast. He barged into my bedroom as I got ready for school, and then he beat me up. I can't go to school when he does this to me. People will see what he does to me and then some of them might even make fun of me. I just can't live like this anymore. I pray so much that this year can go by fast so that I can move out," tears welled up in his eyes. This just shattered me all over again, but I wouldn't allow him to see that side of me. I had to be strong.

"You can stay here. I mean that. I will not allow you to go back home, but I need you to go with me to your house tonight so that I can have a word with your father and I don't give a damn what he says. I can report him. You have this place and a girlfriend who cares about you. So, do this for yourself and for her. There are only a few months left until you graduate, so stay here," I stated, hoping that he would agree to this.

"I will go with you. If things don't go your way, and I get beaten up again, it's on you this time," he said. He really didn't want me to go to his house to confront his father or for things to get worse. But this was a conversation that needed to happen.

"Fine, I'll take full responsibility for that. As long as I know that you're safe here in my house." Eric's pain echoed in the silence of the lounge. His eyes were a mix of hurt and yearning, and my heart couldn't ignore the desperate plea for understanding. It was a moment when life demanded more from me, and I knew I had to give it.

"Eric, I may be an ass, but I can also be a father figure," my voice carrying a weight I hadn't realized was there until now. "A father's love isn't measured in power or dominance. It's not about control, it's about protection. It's about being a steady force in the storm, a guiding light even when the path is unclear."

I held his gaze, trying to convey the sincerity that filled my words. "A father should be a sanctuary, a place where you find solace and unconditional acceptance. It's a love that doesn't demand perfection but embraces flaws. No matter what mistakes you make, a father's love should stand unwavering." Eric's eyes flickered with a mix of emotions, and I could see the vulnerability etched across his face.

"You don't deserve to be treated like this," I continued, "A father should lift you up, not bring you down. He should be your biggest supporter and your loudest cheerleader."

I felt the weight of my own experiences, the ache of losing my wife, and the struggle of being a single parent seeping into my words. "I can't change what happened to you, but I can be here for you now. You don't have to face any of this alone."

As I spoke, I saw a flicker of understanding in Eric's eyes, a realization that perhaps there was another way, another kind of love that he deserved.

"Love should never hurt. It should be a balm to the wounds, a force that heals, not inflicts pain. You are worthy of that kind of love, and if your father can't give it, then I will. Consider me your sanctuary, your steady force, your protector."

I let the words linger in the air, hoping they would settle in Eric's heart. In that vulnerable moment, I revealed a part of myself that I had shielded for so long. It was a fatherly love, raw and honest, a love that aimed to heal wounds and build bridges to a brighter future.

You can get some sleep in Cris' bedroom. I'm sure she'll be surprised to see you here, and I think you should tell her because she will find out."

"Thanks, I'll deal with Cris when I'm ready. I appreciate what you said. It means a lot," he forced a smile as he stood up, and then he walked away down the hallway.

I remained seated in the recliner, thinking about his situation. It's funny how things have changed based on circumstances. My heart was still aching for him. He doesn't deserve this at all, and I will put a stop to it and save him from this. His father won't know what hit him when I go and give him a piece of my mind.

Confronting His Father

Tristan

I allowed Eric to rest. I went up to Cris' bedroom earlier to check up on him, he was fast asleep. But now I was just sitting in the lounge thinking about this situation. I wanted to beat that bastard to a pulp so that he could feel how it was to be beaten up. Anger rose up within me, and I was not going to leave this the way it was.

"I think I should head home," I snapped out of my thoughts. Eric came into view.

"Um… I think that you should stay here," I said as I shifted in the recliner. "You know what will happen when you go back."

"I cannot be here because he will look for me. I don't even have a phone because he broke it the last time I was MIA." He let out a heavy sigh.

"Don't worry about it. You will have me." I stood up and then walked past him.

"Where are you going?" He asked as I opened the front door. I stopped to turn around. He was confused.

"I'm going to your house," I said. "You can stay here, or you can go with me," I gave him a choice. He sighed and then walked past me, out the door. I followed after him, closing the door behind me.

I was still wearing my Armani suit. I was just too attached to this situation. "Please, don't do anything that will make things worse for me," he said as we walked in step down the sidewalk.

"The thing is…he will pay attention to me and I will not let this go easily. I can report him easily. You have a story and have experienced loss and things that not many people know about. He needs to pay for what he has done," I responded.

We got to his house and it just made me cringe with the way it looked. His father doesn't even hire someone to take care of this property. It said a lot about the person he was. There was a silver car parked in the driveway and I knew that the time had come to put a stop to this shit once and for all.

I followed Eric inside the house. "Why the hell are you here? You're supposed to be in school. I work my ass off to put you in that school," I heard his father loud and clear as I slowly walked towards the kitchen where Eric disappeared. I did admire the house inside. The marbled tiles were shiny, and this was way better than my own house. Grey and white throughout the house with stairs going up.

I reached the kitchen, which had sliding doors with a view of the pool and the backyard, which was just as cringy as the front garden. When I walked into the kitchen, Eric was standing across from his father, the kitchen counter between them.

His father, Mr Parker, was gray-haired, and he was fuming. "I would suggest that you shut your mouth. Eric doesn't need a parent like you. He's a good young man," I said. His father looked at me.

"Who the hell are you and why are you in my house?" He barked at me. "Did you go and get him for me?" He looked back at Eric.

"I'm here because your son will no longer live here unless by some miracle you change. I know everything about you. You're not fit to be a father, and you think it's okay to just beat him up for anything he does? That's not how a father loves his son. I'm surprised that you haven't been charged for anything, let alone for what happened to your wife." I hissed. My heart was racing in my chest because I was fuming with this disgusting man.

He pointed a finger at me, "You need to leave. I'll call the police for trespassing on my property," he warned. All I saw in him was plain evil.

"Really? How about the evidence of your son that you're laying a hand on? I'm sure that you wouldn't want that to ruin your reputation and I will not stop there. He will live with me from now on. He deserves so much better than this."

"My whole life revolved around him, he was a mistake, a useless one. I never wanted him, he had already ruined all my plans that I wanted with his mother. I lost her because she was so stubborn to listen to me, I told her to get rid of him yet she wouldn't listen." He said as if he was disgusted with Eric. "That ruined me, and you can stand there all you want, but at some point, there is something that will ruin you."

"That's enough. I will no longer listen to this bullshit." I looked at Eric, "Pack your things, you're coming to live with me," I demanded. Eric looked at me with huge eyes. "Go!" He hurried out of the kitchen.

"You have another thing coming," Mr Parker said to me.

"Bring everything you want against me, but this stops here. You are no longer laying a hand on him. If you wanted to get rid of him so badly, then why not just let him leave with me? If there is an ounce of feeling towards him that you still have in you, you will let him go, but most of that space is filled with resentment and anger. Heal if you really want him. You're getting older, so think about that," I said.

He shook his head as he turned around and took a glass that was standing close to the sink, and he poured Whiskey. "All I have ever done in my life was love his mother, but she ruined that by falling pregnant."

"That's why any form of contraception is important, but not all of them are one hundred percent effective. Accidents happen, and not everything can be blamed on the woman. That's just my opinion." I shrugged as I waited for Eric. Mr Parker took a sip of the Whiskey.

"I hope you have fun with Eric while it lasts. He can be stubborn and he doesn't listen. At least that's not my problem any longer," he placed his glass on the counter with a thud, and then Eric appeared.

"I'm ready," he said, carrying two duffel bags.

"Great," I acknowledged as I took one from him and then I walked out.

I heard Eric's footsteps after me, "Don't bother coming back!" Mr Parker called out from the kitchen.

Eric will not step foot in this house again until that bastard wants to change in the future. Eric has his goals and that was what I would help him with. He wants to be a photographer and I have the perfect thing in mind for him. I will be the fatherly role in his life now and with that comes the part of wanting the best for him. I want to see him succeed in life and I will gladly help him with that. I could have a word with Austin Luca from The Dakota Agency for another photographer, which Eric could be able to keep an eye on Elona when I'm not able to, or he could work at SNT, where Cris would be.

His options are endless, and I have no doubt that he would be great. I do hope that he chooses the right one. If he chose to work with Elona then that would be great. That's what I want more, but ultimately the decision would be up to him. I would first allow him to settle in at my place before having that conversation. After all, his father was the one paying for everything, so I might have to be the one to step in financially for him now. I would do it out of the greatness of my heart.

Caring For Spooky

Tristan

When we reached my house, I was still livid with Mr Parker. Why couldn't he just get someone else to look after Eric or take him after what happened to Eric's mother? People like that made me angry. I know I may not be the greatest person, but I have love in me when the people I care about are hurt. Even if I see somebody I don't know get hurt it breaks my heart. I'm a human who felt these things. I could build up my walls and have no emotion because I got really good at that after my wife passed away. But Eric was someone that I have gotten to care about in this short span of time as if he was my own son.

I opened the front door. Eric winced, "You still need to get checked out at the hospital," I said as I let him enter, and then I followed after him.

"I'll be fine. It's nothing that I can't handle. I've been through this countless times already." We walked down the hallway.

"I will not take no for an answer. If that still persists tomorrow, then we are going. No arguments." I stated.

"Yes, Sir," he replied. The more I spend time with him, the more I like this fella. He was about to turn into Cris' bedroom.

"You won't be sharing a bedroom with Cris. Your bedroom is further down the hall," I said, and I walked past him as he looked confused. I stopped at the far end before it reached the bigger section of the house that I had abandoned since Estelle passed away.

I opened the bedroom door and entered. It was clean and everything was white. Sometimes I hire a cleaner to just clean when it is needed. But the bigger side of the house is off-limits to her. I don't want her to touch anything in that part of the house. It was left just the way it was since that accident. Except for the piano that I played and the study room where I fucked Elona.

"Thank you," he said as I placed his things down in front of the cupboard.

"Let me know if you need anything," I said as I walked out of the room.

I could see that he was not himself, but he still had those manners. He needed to see a doctor. I will give him some space today, but tomorrow is a must.

"If you need anything, please let me know. You are welcome to use the kitchen freely too," I said as I shoved my hands in my pants pockets.

"Will do," he said over my shoulder, and then I left him alone.

***

Hours passed as I decided to do my work in the lounge that I had to do at work today. The front door opened. "Hi, Dad. I thought you were at work today," Cris asked, her brows furrowed.

"Well, I changed my mind because of Eric," I nodded in the direction of the hallway. "He will be staying with us from now on. He's in the guest bedroom," I said. She was so confused, and then she walked down the hallway.

Sighing, I dived back into my work. I wanted to see Elona since she walked with Cris after school, but this work just kept me buried in it. Cris came back, her expression had changed drastically as she plopped down on the recliner across from me.

"Are you okay?" I asked as she looked at nothing.

She shook her head, no, "I didn't know that... he went through that. He-he didn't need to tell me anything. I understand why you took him in. Is his father that evil?" She shifted in the recliner, and her eyes finally found mine. There was sadness in them.

"Yes, I went to go and have a word with him. The bastard doesn't deserve Eric. Hell even Eric doesn't deserve to be in that environment and to be treated that way. I had to help him. That's the least that I could do for him." I held her gaze.

"Thank you for that and for doing this, Dad. You sure do have a huge heart. I just wish that he had told me sooner. It makes perfect sense to me now....that time when he wasn't around was because he was beaten up. He was in pain, and we were just going about our days as if nothing was wrong. I'm a shitty girlfriend, Dad," tears welled up in her eyes.

"Cris, none of us knew about this. He chose to keep it a secret for a reason and now that we know about it, we are able to help him." I was trying to fight my own tears.

"As long as we know what's been going on, and we can help him accordingly," she blinked her tears away.

"Yeah," I choked up.

"You care about him a lot," she had a little smile as if she loved the fact that I was opening up more to Eric.

"He's like a son to me, a son I never had. I would treat him as such," tears welled up in my eyes.

"Oh Dad, I get why you feel that way. Maybe someday you will be able to..." She sucked in a breath, "I hope that you find someone to move on with. It may not be Maggie because I can tell that you don't like her. But I hope someone will treat you right." She gave me a small smile.

"Yeah, someone that is everything that I want and more." That was Elona.

"You deserve that, Dad," there was a hint of suspicion in her eyes, but she didn't say anything further, and I hoped that she wouldn't even try to ask me anything. "So, can Spooky sleep in my bedroom?" She asked with hope in her eyes.

"I guess you two have already done that. I think it's best that you give him some space tonight. What he went through was not great, and he just needs to recuperate. Give him that space and then maybe tomorrow or whenever he's ready to share a room with you, then by all means, the rules are to have condoms in your bedroom–"

"Dad!"

"Better safe than sorry. I've raised you better than to make me a granddad. You're young and so is Eric. Focus on both of your careers. Finish school first. Make me proud," I stated.

"Fair enough," she lifted her hands up in surrender, and then she stood up. "Let me see if Spooky needs anything." She walked away down the hallway.

I reached for my phone and typed a quick text to Elona.

Me: Can you come over for dinner tonight?

I hit send and my phone chimed immediately. It was her.

Elona: I will be there.

That caused me to smile like a little kid. I was happy to know that she would be here, not just for me, but for her to be here with her friends. I didn't want her to feel left out, and I'm sure that Eric would appreciate it. I wanted to invite David over too, but I guess he has his own things going on, and I hope he steers away from Maggie. That one was a piece of work. I wanted the best for David too, but not with her in a million years.

Dinner With Three

Tristan

Cris had ordered Pizza, and now she was setting up the table. I was eagerly waiting for Elona to come by. I didn't see her for the entire day. Eric entered the kitchen, and he pulled out a chair as Cris opened the pizza boxes. There was a knock on the door and I knew who that would be.

"I'll get it," Cris said and hurried to the front door as I grabbed a plate.

"How are you feeling?" I asked Eric as he reached for a plate too. I took a slice of pizza and put it on my plate.

"I can't complain. But grateful to be here," he replied, also placing a slice of Pizza on his plate.

"Just let me know if you need anything," I gave him a small smile.

"Hey," there was that sweet voice that I had been longing to hear. Elona rounded the table and sat on one end at the table, and she gave me the most gorgeous smile as she adjusted the chair.

"How was your day? Anything interesting happened at school today?" I asked her, she moved her hair behind her ear with a blush on her cheeks.

"It was okay, the same old." She looked at Eric and her brows furrowed. "Are you okay?" she asked.

"Yeah," he forced a smile, but she could clearly see how he looked. Her gaze moved to the pizza box instead, and she reached out for one slice and placed it on her plate.

"Here are your fluids," Cris stated as she placed a glass of juice beside my plate, and she did the same for Elona, Eric, and herself.

"Any word about The Dakota Agency?" I asked Elona. She paused her chewing. She nodded as Cris took a seat at the other end. The girls were basically sitting on either side of me and Eric as he sat across from me.

"Yeah, I have to go for another photoshoot in a few days' time." She took a bite of the slice of Pizza.

"I will see if I can accompany you on that day. My work schedule might just clash with it, but I'm sure that Cris will take good care of you when you are there, right Cris?" I asked as I looked at my daughter.

"I will be there every step of the way. I just don't like him...what's his name? Luca?" she looked at Elona.

"Yeah," I heard Elona's soft reply.

"He's a creeper and I'll make sure that he doesn't touch you the way that he did again. It must be very uncomfortable, but it's your dream career, and we won't always be around to protect you unless you have bodyguards," Cris took a bite of her pizza. Now, that wasn't a bad idea. Why didn't I think about that?

"How about you, Eric?" I asked as I looked at him. He swallowed what he chewed.

"I will pursue photography. I did send my portfolio to The Dakota Agency but the waiting period is a bit long and I sent my portfolio to another agency. I'll be looking at more." He responded.

"I will see what I can do. I want all three of you to achieve your dreams, whether it's something that I like or not. I can't stop you from going after your dreams, especially if it's something that you are passionate about. I would hate it if you were doing something that you hate and then being miserable at your job for your entire life. But I'm also looking out for all of you," I said as I made eye contact with all of them. Elona was the one who caught my eye as my gaze lingered on her the most.

"That means a lot to us, Dad," I looked at my daughter who was smiling, but it didn't quite meet her eyes. Eric was quiet, this must've been a bad idea.

We all finished our meal and then Cris and Eric did the dishes. "I better get home," Elona stood up and I did too.

"I'll walk you home," I said.

"No, it's okay. Just walk me out?"

"Okay," I responded as I pushed the chair back in. "I'll walk Elona out," I said to Cris.

They all said their goodbyes and Elona followed after me as I opened the front door. We stepped outside, the cool breeze hit my skin, the stars were twinkling, and someday I hoped to lie in the open air with Elona and enjoy the view of the night sky. Perhaps at the camp that was coming up, we could do that.

"Beautiful night, isn't it?" She said as she stood beside me.

"Yeah, but you're more beautiful," I looked over at her, and then her gaze found mine. She was so gorgeous, my cock was straining against my pants. I reached out to her and moved her hair behind her ear, moving closer to her. I cupped her face as I studied her lips. They were parted, and I wanted to bite her bottom lip. "Gosh, you're so fucking beautiful." I leaned in and crashed my lips against hers. Her hands were holding onto my arms.

It was only me and Elona at this moment, no one else, and just like that, she pulled away. "We can't do this here," she whispered. "We need to be safe if we want to be together. I'll text you," she smiled, and then she hurried down the driveway. I watched as she disappeared from view.

I needed to control myself around her, but it just got more difficult each time I tried to, the front door was still wide open when I entered. Eric and Cris were in the kitchen when I heard them talk, and I closed the door behind me. I walked down the hallway to my bedroom, and then I took a shower, washing away the troubles of the day.

After the shower, I got into bed, leaving Eric and Cris to do whatever they wanted, but I wanted to be in this safe haven of my bedroom where I once sobbed the ugliest of cries when my wife passed away. A lump formed in my throat, I had only my boxer briefs on and as I lay on my back staring at the ceiling, the tears started to run down my face and I closed my eyes.

Rain poured all over me, drenching me as I ran to the car where my wife was trapped. The paramedics were on their way and I went to her side, but she was losing consciousness. I reached out to her, grabbing her hand as I panicked within, but still tried to keep myself strong for her. The blood was endless, and I knew that it was the baby we were losing.

My heart was breaking at that moment "Trist...the...the...baby... S-save it," she said softly.

"No, both of you will be okay. You will both make it," I tried to reassure us both.

"Please...take care... of...of Cris," she said as she lost complete consciousness.

"Estelle? Please...Stay with me! Estelle!" Tears mixed with rain blurred my vision as I tried to wake her up, arms wrapped around my waist from behind, and then I was being pulled away. "No! Let me stay with them! Let me go! Save them! Please."

I found myself in a fetal position, sobbing enough for Cris and Eric not to hear me. I felt as if the walls I had built up had shattered all around me because the situation with Eric had made me think about that accident. I wanted to scream but I couldn't. It felt like I wanted to rip out all these emotions of the pain that I felt in this moment, but there was nothing to rip out. It felt like I was reliving that moment right as I sobbed the way I used to after that horrible night.

His Vulnerability

Elona

I hadn't seen Tristan for three days, he only texted me that he was at the company busy with work. It was short and felt off for him, I felt like something could be wrong, but I didn't want to ask any questions because it could be work-related. I was not going to show up at Crane Industries just to see him. He had a hacker problem, so I'm sure it was that.

I reminded him about accompanying me to The Dakota Agency if he would be able to make it. Cris and Spooky had a lunch date after school, so I was left all by myself. Tristan had agreed to accompany me. When he picked me up from my house, he was in a foul mood and he wasn't really talking to me. I felt small. What had happened since I had dinner with them? Was it the kiss? The drive to the agency was silent.

"Are you okay?" I asked as we entered the agency building. He was looking straight ahead as we walked all the way to the studio department. "Is it because I'm doing another photoshoot today?" I asked as we walked around the corner and down a hallway, walking in step.

"Everything is fine," he said. I could still tell that he was not okay. I furrowed my brows.

"If there's something that's going on, you can tell me. We are a couple after all, so we can share things. Just because I'm young doesn't mean I won't be able to handle certain things. I might not be able to advise on certain things, of course. But I want to know what's happening in your life, if you will allow me to enter those parts," I looked over at him eagerly.

"I know," he replied, still not looking at me. I let out a sigh as we came to a stop in front of my dressing room.

I opened the door and we entered, I stood in front of the mirror. "Good morning," Maxime entered like a whirlwind. I wanted privacy. She walked up to me as Tristan took a seat on a chair just watching us. He was dressed in dark blue jeans, a white t-shirt and sneakers. I doubt he even went to work today. Maxime shoved clothes into my arms. "These are for the photoshoot, get dressed, and don't waste any of my time. We'll be in the studio," she said as my make-up artist and hair stylist entered.

This is the career that I wanted and I will do this. I got dressed in a swimsuit, and then my hair and make-up were done. Tristan watched me in the mirror, he was awfully quiet, I didn't like it, and then he took his phone out of his pocket and looked at it instead. "Are you ready?" The hairstylist asked.

"Yeah," I responded as I got up, and then I followed them to the studio.

As we entered the studio, my breath hitched at the sight of Mr Luca standing with Maxime. I hope he doesn't touch me this time. Chills ran down my spine as I thought about the last time. "Don't worry, I'm here," I looked at Tristan who was beside me now, he was glaring at Mr Luca, and I felt safe.

Tristan took a seat on a chair while I got to my spot in the limelight of the photoshoot. "Elona, you look amazing," Mr Luca said to me as he walked over. "I think you should become a swimwear model, it fits you amazingly and this will make the swimwear line sell." He said as he was so close to me, I held my ground and fought to be strong because this was what I wanted.

He walked around me. "Such confidence, now I want to see that confidence in these photos," he stood in front of me. I looked at his chest, his scent was lovely...surprisingly. "Surprise us," he said, and then he moved away, giving the photographer orders to start.

I posed in various ways, getting the perfect angles, going to change into different swimsuits and bikinis. Lights were being adjusted and with Mr Luca not being in my way, I felt confident enough to pull this off. I looked in Tristan's direction, and he watched me as if there was no one else in the world but me. I gave him a shy smile, continuing with my photoshoot until it was done.

When we entered the dressing room, it was only the two of us, and he sat on the chair again. He leaned forward with his elbows on his knees, his hands clasped in front of him. He was just staring at the ground as I got undressed. I was worried about him as I watched him in the mirror.

With a sigh, I walked over to him, I crouched so that he could see me, and I placed my hands on his legs. "What's wrong?" I asked.

I watched as his Adam's apple moved, "I think it's best if I don't say anything," he looked into my eyes and there was pure sadness in them. I didn't expect him to be sad.

"Please, tell me." I was desperate to know what was going on.

"Eric had been beaten up by his father. I went over there because he needed my help. His father is an evil person and I don't see how Eric handled that for so long, just...allowing that man to beat him up." Tears welled up in his eyes and my heart was breaking. "I confronted his father, and he doesn't love Eric, this was all because he resents Eric and to say that Eric was a mistake for existing in this world was beyond cruel. I can't even imagine how Eric must feel for that being the reason he had been getting beaten by his father. I took him in but that night when we had pizza, I just... I remembered the accident of Estelle and that just made me break down again after the three years that I worked so hard to build up those walls because I didn't want to feel broken with grief." A tear ran down his cheek and I reached up, cupping the side of his face, and wiped it away with my thumb.

"This is a very sad...situation," I replied. "You are allowed to feel these things."

"It's like all the walls are crumbling down. I went to work to try and bury myself with all the work I had on my desk, hoping that those walls would come back up, but it was different this time. Eric reminds me of what I lost and what I should cherish." He held my gaze, and that sadness just poured into my soul.

"You will have these memories from time to time and it's okay. If working helps to make you feel better, then I'll give you all the space that you need. Just remember that I'm here for you. If you want to talk, no matter how young I am, I'm here."

"I don't see you as young. Age is just a number." He gave me a small smile.

"You are beautiful and amazing. I'm glad to have you in my life. You are the light in my darkness. You make me feel better." He said as he cupped the back of my head, and leaned in, pressing his lips against mine, our lips just lingering.

"I see you as my dream come true. I still pinch myself to see if this is real," I smiled as I pulled inches away from him.

"Me too. I never thought that I would have such a perfect beauty by my side. You also know what it is to lose someone so close. You never really spoke about losing your mom and I get it...you were very young. But... I hope that I can be here for you in any way you need me. I don't want this thing to end, I have found my happiness and I hope that other people will see that when we tell them." He held my gaze. "I love you, Elona Everett."

I smiled, "I love you too, Tristan Crane."

"I will support all of your dreams, I will no longer stand in your way of what it is that you want to achieve in life. I wanted and still want to protect you from men like Mr Luca out there. But you handled it great today, you showed me that you are confident despite those men being around you. But I want you to have something that's also a form of protection, such as pepper spray. I only want you to be safe," he stroked my cheek.

"Thank you, and that means so much to me. You are improving with certain things, and I'm happy that you are," I smiled.

"At some point, certain things or situations will allow you to rethink what you have done or how you have reacted. Seeing you happy with doing what you love has made me realize what an ass I've been with being too protective, and it doesn't come out as being protective, but more as a possessive ass, which is....ugly," his brows furrowed. "Eric made me realize that too when I discovered about the situation at his house. I just want to focus on being with you and becoming a better man if possible," he smiled.

"Thank you for seeing that and for trying."

"I need to speak to Mr Luca regarding Eric and his portfolio," he said as he stood, holding his hand out to me. "I will meet you here," he said as I placed my hand in his, and he helped me up. I leaned in and placed a chaste kiss against his lips.

I loved this vulnerable part of him that I don't often get to see. I'm so happy that he had decided to share these things with me and I want to be here for him whenever he needs me. I will do the best of my ability to help where I can and remain that light in his life. He needed me and I will not leave his side.

A Leech

Elona

Tristan pulled up in front of my house, my dad's car was in the driveway. The ride to my house was silent, and I knew it was due to what Tristan had been going through recently. I was going to let him go through the motions and I would just be here supporting him.

"Hey," he reached out to me, his hand on my thigh before I could reach for the car door handle. I looked at him. He gave me a small smile of admiration. "You are beautiful, and I'm proud of you," he said as he leaned in, placing a gentle kiss against my lips, and then he pulled away, "I'll be going to work for the remainder of the day, I'll text you when I can," he said. I knew he would be burying himself in his work.

"I will look forward to that text. I'm always a text away when you need me, whether that's to talk or just because." I gave him a reassuring smile.

"Thanks. I love you."

"I love you too," I said, and then I got out of the car and walked down the driveway.

Tristan had left and when I opened the front door, I walked further inside and kicked the door closed behind me. I found my dad sitting in the kitchen by the counter. He was scrolling through his phone. He was still dressed in his suit. I sat on the bar stool beside him. His attention was still on his phone, nothing got his attention easily in this moment, and I just watched him. I could see that he was tired, and I remembered we had hardly got to speak since the gallery night.

"""

"How was school and the photoshoot?" He asked as he finally looked up at me.

"It was great, I was taken care of and being looked after," I smiled.

"Is Tristan treating you well?" He asked.

"Yeah, I'm grateful for his support and for accompanying me to where I need to be," I responded.

"I like to hear that. He has always been a great friend. There were a lot of buyers for your mother's painting. They are all sold," he gave me a small smile.

"That's amazing."

"All thanks to Tristan for doing this special exhibition," he was still not quite himself.

"Are you okay?" I asked, concerned.

"Yeah," he scrubbed his face with his hand, "I'm just tired."

"Work or is it Maggie?" I asked. I wanted to know where he was standing with Maggie.

"Work is rough, and I haven't seen Maggie since that night she got sick at the exhibition. I don't know what was wrong with her, but she told me that it was something that she ate."

"I think it's best that you stay away from her. I know that Tristan is staying away from her because he doesn't trust her. She has been around the block before or many times, I guess. I don't even trust her around you, Dad. I know that you like to have fun, but let it not be with her. I feel like she's in it for the money, she sees some rich dudes in a bar, and then she wants to be all close with both of you. I guess that's how she's trying to wrap you both around her fingers."

"Elona, she's only a friend, she hasn't asked for money or anything. She really likes Tristan...and since when are you calling him Tristan?" He asked, brows furrowing. Shit. "You always call him Uncle Tristan. I taught you better than that young lady."

"Well, he told me to drop the Uncle part. He doesn't want to be reminded that he's getting older," I lied.

He let out a laugh, "That's Tristan for you." I'm glad he bought that lie. He looked down at his phone again as if something was weighing down on him. "There's someone that I like, and I don't know if I'll ever be able to have her." He didn't look up at me.

"Who is it?" I asked. If it was not Maggie, then it would be great to finally see my father settle down too.

"I...she's too far out of my league, she will be attending college in the new year. I don't think she even sees me in that way," he finally looked up at me. I furrowed my brows, I was just caught off guard that my father likes someone who was around my age. "Don't worry about it, I just wanted you to know that Maggie is not that person that I like," he gave me a small smile. I just didn't know what to say about it.

"Well, I do wish you all the best if you try to pursue her." All I could do was support my father, besides, I'm dating his friend, so it can't be any worse than that.

"Thanks," he smiled as he got off the bar stool. "I don't think I'm going to be with her, I don't want to ruin anything. I'll be in the study room if you're looking for me," he said, and he walked out of the kitchen.

I still can't believe that my father was into someone far younger than him. But who wouldn't want my dad? He has good looks too, so whoever she was... I hope that she will treat him right and for the right reasons....if she reciprocates his feelings.

There was a knock on the door, that might just be Cris or Spooky or both of them. I got off the bar stool and went to the front door. When I opened the door, I didn't expect her to be here. "What are you doing here?" I asked with irritation.

"I'm here for your dad," Maggie replied. She seemed fine to me.

"My father is busy, and he's not interested in you anymore. He's with someone else. I suggest that you leave him alone. Find someone that will love you for the woman that you are, and that is not Tristan either, he has his preferences." I said.

"Well, I know that Tristan has his eyes on someone very close, and I will not be spoken to in that way. I'm older than you," she stepped closer.

"Tristan can be with whomever he wants, if you don't get that into your head and leave us all alone, then I will have to take things further with you," I warned her.

She scoffed, "Sounds like something that Tristan would say. I'm not surprised he has rubbed off on you when you spend so much time with him."

"Are you stalking us now?"

"Little girl, listen here. I have eyes and, unfortunately, you are too young for him. So, cut the act with me."

"You must be seeing things, he has someone in his life-"

"Oh, I thought that he didn't have a girlfriend, according to you, so who is lying here?"

"He told me after that because I didn't know," I lied.

"Well, I'm not leaving them alone, so bring your worst," she warned.

"Oh, I will do just that, now get the fuck away from here," I slammed the door in her face.

Gosh, that woman was a leech that would not leave us all alone. I hope that something gets done to her because this was insane and she sure as hell doesn't take no for an answer. She would be back, I'm sure of it. I know that Tristan regrets his one-night stand with her. I don't blame him, he wanted to forget about me, but that didn't help, and he didn't know that Maggie was the kind of woman who wouldn't let go. Something has to give though because this is absolutely insane and she's on both mine and Tristan's last nerve.

Camp

Elona

My father insisted on taking me to school. It was a nice Friday morning with the sun out and shining. My bags were packed for the weekend camp. I was supposed to ride with Tristan and Cris, but my father wanted to take me. I appreciated the time spent with my dad, and also it was a good idea so that Tristan and I would not have any awkward moments in front of Cris.

We entered the school premises, Tristan was standing with Cris behind his car as they spoke. My dad pulled up next to Tristan's car. My heart fluttered as I got out and so did my father. I walked around the back of the car as my dad took my bags out the back.

"Hey," I smiled at Tristan and Cris.

"We are waiting to leave, there are just a few more students to wait for," Cris said.

"These are Elona's bags," my dad placed them on the ground and stood up straight. "Please take good care of my baby girl," he pats Tristan on his shoulder. Tristan was standing with his hands folded over his chest. His forest green eyes lingered on me.

"I will do just that. You have nothing to worry about," Tristan replied.

"Oh, Mr Crane, we need your help with packing the students' bags into the bus," Miss Jennings came rushing over. Ugh, she was like another Maggie, another leech. She was wearing black sports leggings with a cropped top. I must say she's stunning, but she can be too much when it comes to Tristan, she also has a body to die for.

"Ask someone else," Tristan said, scowling at her. I could see that he didn't like this one bit.

"We need you, Mr Crane. Oh, and you will be riding with us on the bus," she said excitedly as she placed her hand on his bicep. That fueled the living hell within me. I looked away at the other students as Cris scoffed.

"I will drive my car, it's more convenient for me and the girls," he replied with irritation laced in his voice.

"No, you will be with us. Those are the rules." Miss Jennings pushed.

"What happens when someone gets sick or injured, and needs to be rushed to the hospital? My car is way faster than a bus," Tristan argued.

"Stop being boring. Nothing will happen to them. Come on," she begged as I looked their way, and she pulled him by the arm, dragging him with her. He yanked his arm out of her grasp as they walked in step towards the bus.

"Well, good luck to him on this camp," my father chuckled.

"He signed up for it after all because of me, so he has to live with it," Cris replied as she looked their way.

"Where is Spooky, by the way? I thought he would be joining," my dad inquired.

"He's at home. He didn't want to be around anyone. He hates camping," Cris said.

"Well, that explains it. I better get going. All the best with camp." my father leaned in and placed a kiss on the top of my head.

"Thanks, Dad," I replied as he pulled away.

"Be safe and come back in one piece. Both of you, or shall I say three of you," he smiled at us.

"Of course," Cris rolled her eyes as she smiled.

"I love you," he said to me.

"I love you too," I responded as my father went to get into his car and I moved out of the way so that he could leave.

"So, are you excited?" Cris asked.

"I guess I am. I'm not much of a camp fan, but as long as I get to spend time with you," I said, but in all honesty, it was for Tristan.

"Everyone, please line up. Girls! Get your bags in here!" Miss Jennings called as it was only Tristan, Cris, and I who needed to get our bags on the bus.

I took my backpack from the ground as Tristan walked towards us. I swung one strap of the backpack over one shoulder and I carried the other two as Tristan took his bags out of the car, while Cris carried hers. Cris and I walked to the bus, and we threw our bags inside but kept our backpacks on us when we eventually got inside the bus.

Cris and I sat next to each other, with me beside the window. I placed my backpack on my lap. Cris was typing away on her phone. Miss Jennings took a seat two rows in front of us and then Tristan walked down the passage, bending over because he was tall, he saw Cris and I sitting together. "Mr Crane, you will be sitting next to me," Miss Jennings said, and he rolled his eyes before turning around.

"That's why my car would've been better," he said with irritation, and then he sat down next to her.

Cris chuckled beside me. "He will have a rough time. This is going to be amusing to watch."

"He's so hot," I heard a student say behind me, I had to try everything not to make it known that Tristan was all mine. I let out a sigh as I looked out of the window as the bus started to drive away. My phone chimed in my backpack and I unzipped it, taking it out. It was a text from Tristan. My wallpaper was a selfie that Tristan took of us together.

Crane: I'm sorry about this. Camps are not my thing and Miss Jennings is not my thing either. I wish to sit next to you but as long as Cris is beside you, I know you both are safe. You look beautiful as always.

I looked up from my phone into the back of his head. I smiled before I looked down at my phone again, I was wearing my denim shorts, a little white cropped top, and sneakers. I typed a reply.

Me: You look good yourself. Don't worry about it.

I added a heart emoji and pressed send. He was wearing three-quarter cargo pants and a light blue t-shirt with sneakers.

"What made you so happy?" Cris asked.

"Just happy to be going to camp, that's all," I shrugged as I lied.

"We will have fun. I just wish that Spooky was with us. It would've been epic. Hopefully, there will be some sort of signal at camp because I want to be able to check up on him," she said as she scrolled through her phone.

"I hope there is too." I wanted to at least text Tristan when I couldn't see him. We'll be in different tents. I'll be sharing it with Cris.

"We'll be playing volleyball too. Are you up for that?" She asked.

"Yeah, as long as I can play the sport," I chuckled.

"You can play volleyball. Remember when we were younger, we literally played that sport in your backyard? I wish that your father never took that net down." She sighed.

"Me too. But he had other plans for that," I replied.

"I'm surprised that he hasn't settled down either. I do see Maggie hovering by his side. Is there anything going on there?" She asked.

"No, he likes someone else. Apparently, she's going to college next year, so that means...she could be our age. He literally dodged the question when I asked him if I knew her," I sighed.

"Well, now look at that. Mr Everett is interested in a young woman. Perhaps my dad knows who she is. At least your father knows what he wants in a woman, unlike my father. I'm even more eager to know who your father is interested in. He did drop you off at school. Isn't that maybe why he could've been here? She could be under our noses," she smiled as if she realized she cracked a code or something.

I chuckled, "I don't even want to know at this point," I said.

What would the difference be if my father and Cris found out about me and Tristan? Would it matter to my father if he liked someone as young as me?

A Quick Night

Elona

The bus came to a stop at our destination. Each row of us had a chance to get off the bus. It was my turn as Tristan and Miss Jennings were the first to get off. I walked down the steps after Cris, and as I was about to put a foot on the gravel ground, I was pushed full force, nearly stumbling to the ground, but luckily I reached out to Tristan, who was standing outside the bus entrance and he caught me.

"Watch it!" He barked at someone.

"Sorry, I didn't mean to," Grace, the one who said Tristan was hot behind me, apologized as she squeezed past us.

Tristan helped me to stand up straight, "Are you okay?" He studied my face with concern, my heart was beating wildly against my chest, and my life had flashed before my eyes at that moment.

"Yeah, she likes you though," I said softly as I dusted myself off with my backpack that was swung over one shoulder, his hand moved to my back, holding it there as we walked in step to the back of the bus where Cris was waiting to retrieve the rest of our bags.

"I don't give a rat's ass who likes me or not. I'm with you and whoever is going to pull this kind of thing with you again, they will have me to deal with, and I will not be nice about it," he said.

"Since when are you ever nice when it does come to these things?" I smiled.

"Are you okay?" Cris asked as we stood beside her. Tristan finally removed his hand from my back.

"Yeah, just Grace being a bitch because she likes your dad," I rolled my eyes.

"She pushed Elona out of the way, luckily I was there to catch her in time. Elona could've had a broken neck," Tristan said as he crossed his arms over his chest.

"That little bitch," she scanned the area and glared at Grace who was watching us. She was standing with her friends far away with their bags, waiting for all of us. "She will definitely get a piece of me."

"You don't have to do that," I said.

"Well, that's what friends are for," Tristan stated as he retrieved our bags.

"I've just checked, the signal is still available here. You are sharing a tent with me, by the way," Cris said as Tristan stood beside us again, placing our bags on the ground.

"Everyone! Gather around!" Miss Jennings called out. She now stood by us as the students gathered around. "Boys will be sharing with boys," she said. The boys were driving on the other bus. "Girls will be sharing with girls. There's a male and female bathroom, please don't use it for anything inappropriate. This camp is to have fun and to get to know each other. Mr Crane, you're going to be helping me set up some tents."

"Fucking hell," Tristan muttered under his breath. "On that note, I have my own tent, and I won't be sharing it with anyone," he made that clear to her.

"Of course!" Miss Jennings said. But she was taken aback.

We took our bags, and then we walked further to where the campsite was. There were lots of trees and bushes, the bathroom facilities were not too far away, and we chose a spot where it was nicer for us. Tristan's tent was a bit further away. I just had to deal with this camp and that he was far out of my reach. We also had to behave ourselves if we didn't want to get caught. I walked to the bathroom, which required me to walk past Tristan.

He gripped my wrist and I stopped, looking at him, he leaned in close, "Come to my tent tonight," he said in a low voice in my ear. I nodded with a smile.

He let go and I walked away. He doesn't want me to be far away from him and I know that it could lead to inappropriate things as Miss Jennings would call them.

* * *

Cris and I finally chilled in our tent. It was late at night, and all we did today was get everyone settled. Making food outside and exploring the grounds. Miss Jennings just gave Tristan some more work to do. Miss Johnson, our base teacher, was mostly helping with food and kept an eye out for anyone being in possible danger.

"Ugh, no signal. I hate this," Cris said as she shifted her position to lie on her back with her phone kept high in the air. Our lamp was hanging from the top of our tent, so we could see each other.

I looked at my phone, "Same here," I responded. I needed to go to Tristan's tent, and it was already late, so I guess I should go now.

"I need to use the bathroom, I'll be back in a while," I said as I placed my phone on my pillow, I put on my sneakers and crawled out of our tent, zipping the flap door closed after I got out.

Lamps were shining in some tents, and the twigs and leaves crunched and snapped under my sneakers as I quietly made my way to Tristan's tent, but then he got out. He smiled as he saw me approach him. I'm still wearing my clothes from today, and so was Tristan.

"Come on," he said softly as he held his hand out to me as he looked around, making sure that no one was watching us. I placed my hand in his, and he led me on a path through the trees and bushes. He had a torch that he had shining in front of us to see where we were walking.

"I think this spot is safe," he said as we walked to a tree that was partially hidden. He turned towards me and pulled me against him, crashing his lips against mine, kissing me with so much hunger.

"Gosh, I wanted to kiss you all day," he whispered against my lips. "We have to make this quick," he pulled away and dropped the torch to the ground as his hands reached my shorts and undid it, sliding it down with my panties to the ground. I stepped out of it, I was already drenched. That's what he did to me.

He pulled me closer to him as he slipped a finger between my folds and I let out a moan. He started to flicker my clit. "You like that?" He rasped.

"Yeah," I bit my bottom lip.

"You're always so drenched for me. I love it," He removed his finger from my clit, and then he moved his hands to my ass as I wrapped my arms around his neck and he lifted me up, wrapping my legs around his waist.

Next thing, my back was pressed against the tree, the tree trunk being rough against my lower back, pressing into my skin. I dug my nails into his skin, and he let out a groan, "Fuck, if you keep doing that, I might just be rough with you and I won't be able to stop you from screaming and everyone else will hear how I fuck you," he rasped.

That turned me on even more. "What's taking you so long?" I breathed. He reached between us and undid his pants. I felt the tip of his length at my entrance, and he pushed in, not even slowly. I bit my bottom lip, closing my eyes.

"Is that alright?" He whispered.

I opened my eyes as he filled me up all the way with his hard length. "Uh-huh," I replied.

"Good," he thrust hard into me as if the breath in my lungs were punched out of me. He picked up the pace as he trailed kisses down my jawline, his breath against my skin as he picked up the pace. The tree trunk penetrated into my skin and then our breathing became ragged as he pounded so hard into me, that I couldn't help but moan out loud just as he said I would.

He ended up pounding at a rapid pace, squeezing my eyes closed as the pressure inside of me was building up, that I would be over in no time with my orgasm.

"I'm going to cum. Come with me," he demanded, and I tried to let go.

"Fuck," he bit down gently on my collarbone, he muffled his groan against me.

"Fuuuuuck!!!" My orgasm washed over me, and my voice echoed in the air as Tristan filled me up with his fluids. He continued to hold me against the tree as I opened my eyes, seeing spots in my vision. His face was still buried in the crook of my neck. Our chests heaved as we panted, climbing down from our intense orgasm.

"You always amaze me," he said between breaths as he pulled away. I could partially see him in the dark. "Are you okay? Did I hurt you?" He asked with concern.

I shook my head, no, "I'm fine. I loved it," he lowered me to the ground, and then I put on my panties and shorts as he zipped up his pants.

We heard the crunching of leaves and snapping of twigs. I looked in the direction of where it could be coming from. "Shhhh," Tristan stood beside me now, and then he picked the torch up, turning the light off. It was pure darkness, the tree branches with leaves were hanging over us as it blocked our view from the moon and stars. We saw the light that was shining our way, moving around not too far away. "That must be the security just checking, we'll be fine," he said softly.

My heart was beating so much that I thought I would hyperventilate. Tristan placed his hand gently on my back and then the light disappeared as it went further away. I breathed a sigh of relief. I was worried about nothing.

"Relax, we're safe," he said as he gently rubbed my back. "Let's go back."

Tristan led me back to the campsite, but I needed the bathroom to clean up before going to my tent. Tristan had waited for me as I cleaned up and then when I was done, we walked in step back to our tents.

"I love you," he whispered as he went to his tent.

"I love you too," I whispered back. We didn't see anyone else and that was a great thing. I got to my tent, unzipped the flappy door, and got inside.

"What took you so long?" Cris asked as I sat down on my sleeping bag, taking off my sneakers.

"I was freshening up." Well, I basically was freshening up after the quickie.

I got into my sleeping bag and took my phone from my pillow, "Your phone's screen lit up, and I checked it to see if you had gotten a text with some kind of signal. But why do you have a picture of you and my dad together as your wallpaper?"

Shit, now my heart was back to beating fast. "Um, it was when he was with me on a photoshoot, and we were being silly, he just wanted to make me as comfortable as possible...you know with Mr Luca being a creep and all, so that made me feel better, and I kept it as a wallpaper to remind me that your father is always there to protect me during those times whether or not he is around me for the photoshoots," I lied. It was becoming exhausting.

"Hmmm, oh well. You two look great together though, father and daughter. We have never taken selfies like that ever since my mother died. That's how badly he closed up, but it's like you're his favorite daughter, and he opens up further around you, he even has a wallpaper up on his phone of both of you too. But don't get me wrong, it's a good thing. I'm off to sleep. Dream sweet, don't let the bed bugs bite," she turned on her side, her back facing towards me.

"Good night," I said softly as my shoulders sagged, and I turned the lamp off, settling into my sleeping bag.

I felt bad that Tristan closed up when Aunt Estelle passed away, and he hadn't put up a selfie of Cris and him together since three years ago. I could clearly see that it did affect her in some sort of way as if Tristan preferred me as a "daughter" instead of her. But only if she knew the truth about us, hopefully she would understand.

Volleyball And Pills

Elona

We woke up a bit early. Cris was herself but seemed to be a little distant. I guess that the wallpaper on my phone really made her think that her father was choosing me over her. That's far from it. I wished that I could tell her the truth, but if she was this distant, then how would she actually react when we told her the truth?

I really don't want to lose her as a friend, we came a long way and to lose that over her father? I don't want to think about it. I sucked in a breath, I was dressed in comfortable black sports leggings and a pink cropped top. Cris took what she needed, "I will meet you outside," she said, before she crawled out of the tent.

I got on my knees and scratched in my backpack. I do not hear them, usually I do, so I throw all the contents out of my backpack. I rummaged through them. It's not there. I move to my duffel bag and I throw all of my clothes out too. I rummaged through them again. Nothing. I get to my other bag and I do the same...but nothing.

"No, no, no, this can't be happening," my heart beat rapidly as I searched through all of my things again. "It has to be here," I said to myself as I began to panic. But I still haven't found it.

I crawled out of the tent and walked to where Cris was. It was a chilly morning, the weather was overcast. I didn't care about anyone else as I walked towards her as she sipped a mug of coffee, she was standing by a little fire.

"Cris, have you seen any pills?" I asked, trying not to sound panicked.

She furrowed her brows. "No, what kind of pills? Maybe I can help look for them." Her demeanor totally changed now as concern etched on her face.

"Have you seen them or not?" I nearly hissed at her impatiently out of panic. I ran my fingers through my loose hair as I looked at the surrounding ground, hoping that it would magically appear.

"Come on, let's go look for it," she said as she walked past me and I followed after her as we looked on the ground and made our way to the entrance of the campsite where the buses were parked. Cris jogged towards Tristan who was looking down at his phone because this was where he got signal. He was dressed in a black t-shirt and other cargo three-quarter pants.

"Dad!" Cris called out as we jogged towards him. He looked up from his phone as we came to a stop in front of him. "Have you seen any pills?"

His brows furrowed, "No, what kind of pills are you looking for?" He asked.

"Elona is looking for them," I heard her say as I continued to search the ground.

"What kind of pills, Elona?" He asked, and I looked up at him.

"Just pills, if you see them on the ground or somewhere, I need them," I said as I ran my fingers through my hair again.

"Are you okay? Are you sick?" Do you have a headache?" He moved closer to me, concern etched on his face as my panic didn't subside at all, my heart was racing, it felt as if everything was drowning out. "Elona?" I felt his hand gently against my arm.

"Um... I just need them. I take them every day, I just need them," my breath nearly hitched as I said the last part when the dull ache made itself known in my lower abdomen. I walked away toward the bus and searched there. But they were not there either. Why was this happening to me now?

"I will look inside the bus," Tristan walked towards me with the bus keys in his hands that he got from the bus driver who was not on the campsite with us. I let out a slow breath, trying to calm myself down as I stood behind the bus. Cris didn't bother helping me look as she sat on one step of a small building as she was on her phone far across from me. I waited for Tristan, and then eventually he came to the back. "There are no pills," he said.

"I must've left them at home, thank you," I responded.

"Are you sure you're okay?" I just walked away from him all the way back to the campsite. How could I be so irresponsible? Now I will suffer the consequences of leaving my pills at home. Hopefully, I get home in time to take them tomorrow.

As we made our way to the campsite, Miss Jennings was gathering everyone around. This distracted me a bit, but it didn't lessen the dull ache that I was feeling. I hugged myself as I stood with everyone else. Cris and Tristan were there too.

"We will be playing volleyball. Everyone will participate. Boys and girls will be teamed up together. Mr Crane, you're on our team–"

"Oh, for fucks sake," I heard him mutter further away from me as some students giggled at his response. My ache was not helping much. I hugged myself tighter. I closed my eyes. *Please, just let me get through this camp.* I said to myself in my mind.

"Elona, you're on Team B!" Miss Jennings snapped me out of it.

"You're with me then," Cris stood beside me now as everyone else went to their teams. The net had already been set up, so we were already on our side. "Are you okay?" Cris asked.

"Yeah," I replied softly as I tied my hair up into a high ponytail.

"Just let me know if you aren't." She was concerned about me.

"I will," I forced a smile.

Miss Johnson and Mr Adams were on our team. My gaze found Tristan's, concern etched on his face as he watched me intently, and then I broke eye contact as we got into position. The ball started flying over the net back and forth. I took a deep breath as I saw the ball flying my way, pushing aside the discomfort as I focused on the game ahead. It wasn't too bad, just a dull ache that I could bear for the time being.

My muscles moved with fluidity as I dove for the ball and sent it soaring back over the net. With each movement, I felt the pain in my abdomen intensify, but I refused to let it slow me down. Tristan watched me from the other side of the net, his gaze filled with concern as he noticed my slight grimace. I offered him a reassuring smile, silently willing myself to push through the pain.

As the game progressed, I found myself growing stronger, the adrenaline pumping through my veins driving me forward. Despite the discomfort, I fought with everything I had. Miss Jennings nearly fell to the back and Tristan caught her in time. She held onto him with a smile as he helped her to stand up straight and to check if she was fine standing on her own. She was perfectly fine, I just did not like her one bit. I hugged myself again with the pain.

"Another round!" Miss Jennings called out and got into position, but Tristan was still watching me intently with concern.

The ball was flying over the net again, but this time, it came straight to me, and I wasn't prepared. But as I lunged for the ball, a sudden shove from behind sent me crashing to the ground with my face nearly in the sand, leaves, and twigs. I had landed on my front, squeezing my eyes shut as pain sneered through me. Stunned, I lay there for a moment, the breath knocked out of me as I tried to make sense of what had just happened. But the pain was getting worse by the minute. I tried to breathe.

"Elona, are you alright?!" Tristan called out from the other side of the net.

"Are you hurt?" Cris was now beside me as she gripped my arm and helped me up. It was a bit difficult to breathe, but I sucked it up as I stood up straight, and then I saw the culprit. It was Grace who shoved me, her eyes filled with jealousy and resentment. Anger flared within me, but I forced myself to remain calm, refusing to let her actions dictate my response.

As I got into position with Tristan's concerned gaze fixed on me, I took a deep breath. Ignoring the pain that shot through my body, I was not going to let Grace push me down. I won't allow her to ruin my day any further than it was already ruined. Tears stung the back of my eyes, but I blinked them away. I just needed to get home.

Despite the setback with each volley and each spike, I poured all of my energy into the game, refusing to back down in the face of adversity. As the final point was scored and the game came to an end, I felt a sense of pride wash over me. Despite the challenges I faced, I persevered, proving to myself and others that I was stronger than I ever imagined. We won.

As I walked away from the volleyball court that they had created in their way, Tristan approached me, a look of concern still etched across his features. "Are you okay?" he asked, his voice filled with genuine concern.

I smiled, nodding in reassurance. "I'm fine," I replied, the adrenaline still coursing through my veins. "Just another day with some classmates." I walked further ahead of him as I wanted to breathe and be alone.

"You don't look fine to me," he caught up to me.

My breathing was heavy, still from the game. "I will be fine."

"Did she hurt you? I'll have a word with her because that was the second time she has done that," Tristan said as I took a seat on a log of the tree. He crouched down in front of me, holding a water bottle in his hand. "I brought this for you," he held it out to me.

I took it from him, "Thanks, I'm fine. Just in a little pain but I'm fine," I looked up into his gaze, there was so much worry in them. I uncapped the bottle and gulped down some water, and then capped it closed again.

"If you need anything, please let me know. I'm your boyfriend and I want to take care of you. I don't want anything to happen to you. I saw you in pain before the shove, and you happened to look for pills, so if those are painkillers, you need to tell me. I can get some painkillers for you."

"I only use those specific pills, but I'll be fine," I gave him a small smile.

"I think you should get some rest," he suggested.

"I think so too," I said.

"Mr Crane! You are needed!" Miss Jennings' voice echoed in the air.

"I wish that she could just leave me alone. I wish I had never signed up for this, but here we are." He hissed, and then his expression softened as his gaze found mine again. "Will you be okay?" He asked as he placed a hand on my leg.

I nodded, "Yes, I'll be fine. Go see what she needs help with, otherwise, we won't hear the end of it," I smiled weakly, I just wanted to be alone so that I could deal with the pain on my own.

"Just let me know if you need anything. Or let Cris know."

"I will," he leaned in closer but stopped himself as we were not alone on the campsite. He stood up and then walked to where Miss Jennings was.

I was still in pain, so I took a deep breath and drank the water that Tristan had given me. The cool air blew against my skin, which was damp with sweat and dirt from the sand. I needed to wash myself in the bathroom facilities later, but I hoped that sleep would make this pain go away. How could I not pack those pills in? They were very important.

Pool Party

Elona

We were on our way home in Tristan's car. The bus dropped us off at school earlier. I slept the entire journey back. In fact, I had to ask Cris to get some painkillers for me last night and I slept through most of the night, not interacting with anyone on the camp. Tristan was too occupied with helping everyone else to check up on me. But at least, I could sleep. I sent him a text as soon as we had signal this morning to wish him a happy birthday. Cris was most of the time on her phone as she received tons of texts, so I left her to it in the bus and I slept.

We pulled up in the driveway to my house, there were a few cars and I knew what this was. Tristan's surprise party was being held at my house. We all got out of the car. I had a dull ache, but the painkillers managed most of the pain. I swung the strap of my backpack over my shoulder.

"Are you okay?" Tristan asked with concern laced in his voice.

"I'm okay," I forced a smile as I lied, and then walked into the house.

Cris was already inside, she was speaking to my dad. I heard some voices coming from the backyard. "Thank you so much, Uncle David, for pulling this off without me," she said quietly so that Tristan would not hear anything when he entered.

My father's gaze fell on me and his brows furrowed a bit, "Are you okay? You look a bit pale," he said.

"Yeah, I'm good. If everyone could stop with that same question," I said as I walked up the stairs and then Tristan entered.

I went to my bedroom, closing the door behind me. I dropped my backpack on the floor and went to my vanity cupboard. I opened the drawer, rummaging through the contents, and I found it. As I looked at the dates on them, I skipped a few days, but I took one out, and then I picked my backpack up from the floor to get my bottle of water. I took my pill. This has to help with my cramps.

I took a deep breath. I needed to make sure to take these every day. I heard cheers outside in the backyard and I moved to the window. Looking down, there were people, probably from Tristan's company and perhaps, who were friends with him and my dad. I spotted Tristan, and they all sang Happy Birthday to him. I'm not even there to sing along with them. He turned around, and I could see a forced smile on his face as Cris went towards him with a cake and candle. His smile widened because of that, and then he blew out the candle. His gaze caught mine as he looked up at me through my window. He smiled at me, and then he smiled at everyone else surrounding him.

I moved away from the window, and then I changed into a bikini, with a white sarong around my waist. I had my flip-flops on, and I tied my hair up into a messy bun at the top of my head before I went downstairs. Cris was busy in the kitchen when I entered.

"Need some help?" I asked.

"No, it's okay. Spooky is helping me. You aren't well, so you need to just enjoy the day. Your father is keeping everyone else entertained in the backyard, but I do need to get changed," she said as she threw some potato chips into a bowl.

"Of course. I'll be in the backyard," I said as Spooky entered.

"Your father doesn't seem to be happy about this," he said to Cris.

"He will never be happy about his birthday being celebrated," she rolled her eyes, "I'll get changed," she walked out of the kitchen.

"I'm going to get into the pool, it's a hot day," I said, even though I was still fighting against the dull ache.

"Enjoy it," Spooky smiled as he continued where Cris had left off. As I walked out into the backyard, Tristan's eyes caught mine, and then he walked towards me.

"You look stunning," he said softly, "I'll be changing into whatever swimwear I have. Cris packed it without me knowing," he grinned, and then he went into the house.

I continued my way to the sun lounger and I unwrapped my sarong, draping it over the sun lounger. I kicked my flip-flops off, and then I stepped into the pool. The water felt so good. Some joined me inside the pool, but I made sure to keep a distance because I didn't really know these people well enough.

After a while, Tristan got into the pool and he came my way. I was chilling at the edge of the pool. "How are you feeling?" He asked.

"I will not answer that question," I smirked.

"I take it you're feeling better," he stated as he studied my face and then his eyes fell on the swells of my breasts. He reached up and traced them with his index finger.

"We have to be careful," I said.

"I'll wait until they leave because I don't think I can wait to be inside you. Besides, we haven't tried the pool yet," he smirked.

"I'm sure you will have fun with me," I smiled.

We were interrupted as our lunch was ready. We got out of the pool and joined the rest of the others.

* * *

After my lunch, I went back to the pool. Eventually, the people left. I was so happy that Maggie was not here. As I leaned against the edge of the pool, Tristan came back. It was only Tristan and I. My cramps were still dull, but bearable.

He caged me in with both of his hands on either side of me. His green eyes had that hunger within them, and he leaned in pressing his lips against mine. He deepened the kiss as I moved my hands around the back of his neck. "Anyone can find us like this," I said against his lips.

"We will be quick, and they won't notice since we are in the pool. Besides, what a way to have birthday sex, my best birthday gift," he rasped. He moved his hands into the water and cupped my ass, lifting me up as I wrapped my legs around his waist. I sucked in a breath as the dull ache in my abdomen was back...stronger this time. My back pressed into the edge of the pool as he reached between us and freed his cock, and then he moved the fabric of my bikini bottom to the side, aligning the tip of his cock at my entrance.

"This will hurt," he said softly, and then he plunged into me and I gasped. Pain sneered within me as if all the air in my lungs had been punched out of me, he was all the way inside of me. "Are you okay?" He asked.

"Yes," I breathed, and then he started to move slowly in and out of me. I held onto him so tight as he picked up the pace, plunging in and out of me at a rapid pace, I rested my forehead against his shoulder as the pain continued. I tried to breathe. This was too painful for me to handle. I don't know what was wrong. Perhaps it was my flare-up. But it was painful to bear.

"I'm going to cum," he gasped. I was relieved as I nearly gave up and asked him to stop, "Fuck," he groaned as he bit on his teeth, filling me up with his fluids, and I squeezed my eyes shut the deeper he went inside of me. He stayed like that for a little while, his chest heaving as he came down from his climax.

"I-I need the bathroom, please," I breathed.

He pulled away from me. "Are you okay? Did I hurt you?" He asked, concern in his eyes.

"I need the bathroom," I repeated, and he pulled out of me. I moved the fabric of my bikini bottom in place before I got out of the pool, placing a hand on my lower abdomen as I walked into the house. The pain was more intense now, I tried to breathe.

I went to my bathroom and dried myself. After I used the toilet and wiped myself, there was blood on the toilet paper. Great. I flushed the toilet and went back into my room as the pain was not getting any better. I put a sanitary pad on and then denim shorts with a cropped top before I went downstairs at a slow pace.

I reached the lounge and Tristan was there as Cris and Spooky were busy tidying up the kitchen. "I hope you had a great birthday, Dad," Cris said from the kitchen.

"Thank you for the surprise. You didn't have to do any of this," he replied to her.

"We had to do it," she said as I moved to the sofa. He came my way. I hunched over, the breath knocked out of me as I held my belly, and the pain increased severely.

"Elona?" Tristan was by my side. His hand was gentle on my back. I tried to speak but all I could do was focus on breathing. But even that hurt. "Talk to me." Panic laced in his voice. I moved onto the sofa and I lay down on my side, curling up into a fetal position just hugging myself. "Did I hurt you?"

"Elona?" My father appeared, and he crouched in front of me. Tears streamed down my face as I tried to breathe, "Is it happening again?" He asked as he rubbed my leg as a way of comfort.

"It-it h-hurts to breathe," I whispered as more tears ran down my face. Tristan just stood there not sure what to do, he had panic and concern written all over his face.

"Okay, let's get you to the hospital," my dad scooped me up into his arms. "Tristan, please keep an eye on the house, I'll be back when I can," my father said.

I buried my face into his chest, my hand grabbing a fistful of his gray t-shirt as he hurried with me out of the house. I just wanted the pain to go away. Hopefully, it will soon.

Concerned

Tristan

I was still standing on my spot as David rushed Elona to the hospital, my heart was beating at a rapid pace. I wasn't sure what was going on. I know that she was in some sort of pain or not feeling well on the camping trip, but if it got to this extent then why did she push herself through it and have sex?

Shit, was it because of me? Was I too rough? Did I hurt her that badly?

"Dad," Cris snapped me out of my trance as she gently placed her hand on my arm. "Can we go to the hospital please?" She asked softly, panic laced in her voice. When I looked at her, I could see panic. Huge eyes looking at me.

"You can go, I'll finish tidying up over here," Eric stepped into the lounge.

I nodded, "Thanks," I told him, and then my gaze fell on Cris again. "Of course, let's go," I said, and then we both hurried out of the house.

The ride to the hospital was silent as I weaved through the traffic. I wanted to get to Elona as soon as I could as panic was still coursing through my body. We pulled up into the parking lot of the hospital and then we hurried down the corridor, stopping at the receptionist.

"We are here for Elona Everett," I said impatiently.

"On the sixth floor," the receptionist said. Cris and I jogged towards the elevator, stepping inside just in time before the doors closed. The elevator ascended. Cris was fidgeting with her hands. She was nervous. I exhaled slowly through my mouth as I waited impatiently to get to the sixth floor.

The elevator finally stopped on the sixth floor. As soon as the doors opened, Cris and I hurried down the corridor. David was talking to a doctor further down. Cris and I didn't want to intrude, so we took a seat on the two chairs available. I ran a hand over my face.

"Dad, I know how much you care about her, it's clear. Sometimes I think that you prefer her over me-"

"Now is not the time to talk about this and you're my daughter. Stop thinking that I have a favorite because I don't," I said impatiently. I most certainly don't have time for this right now.

"I saw the jacket that you left in the bathroom by Elona's house. I could smell your scent on it. She told me that it was Uncle David's."

"Well, it is. We wear the same scent sometimes," I lied.

"I also happen to see you both have wallpapers of the two of you, so I don't know what to think of that. You don't even have a picture of us on your screen. Ever since mom died you have stopped doing those things with me."

"Cris, can we please not do this now? You're my daughter, and I love you. I'm Elona's guardian when she doesn't have her father around. I'm there to take care of her too, the same way as David would be there to take care of you when I'm not around or if something had to happen to me-" I held her gaze.

"Don't speak like that, I can't lose another parent." She looked down at her hands that were clasped in her lap.

"You won't lose me. Let's focus on Elona."

"You're right. I'm sorry," she apologized.

"You two didn't have to come all the way here," I looked up at David who was standing in front of us now. His hair was disheveled. Sadness was evident in his eyes.

"We wanted to be here, Eric is keeping an eye on the house. How is she? What's wrong with her?" I asked. I was even afraid to know what might be wrong.

He let out a heavy breath, "She's in surgery."

My heart stopped at the mention of that word. "Surgery?" I furrowed my brows in confusion.

"Um... I don't think that I can say more. Elona and I have kept this between us for a long time. I don't think that it's my place to say anything when she made me swear to never tell a soul." He was battling with it. He needed someone to speak to but nothing was wrong with pushing him to tell me what it was.

"How am I supposed to know what's going on when no one is informing me about this? I'm her guardian. If you're not around, I need to know these things. I need to know what to do," I held my gaze on him. He nodded. It was difficult for him.

"She was diagnosed with endometriosis a few years ago. She must've stopped taking her birth control pills, which she never missed at all. But this is a first. They help with her pain and discomfort. It's basically tissue that grows where it doesn't belong. It grows outside the uterus and ovaries..." He had a difficult time with it.

"So... the surgery can cure that, right?" I asked.

"It can relieve pain, but it can return. It's a chronic condition that she has. It can spread to her other organs, so if surgery is what is needed every time to help with her pain or try to stop it from spreading, then surgery is what she can have. I hate to see her in this kind of pain," tears welled up in his eyes. "I just- I just wish that I could take all her pain away," a tear ran down his cheek.

Cris let out a gasp as she covered her mouth with both of her hands. "So... so there is no cure for this at all?" I asked. My world was now completely shattered upon hearing this.

"No cure at all. It might be difficult for her to fall pregnant and carry to full term one day if she does fall pregnant, but that all depends on her condition and how far things have progressed with the endometriosis. It can affect her fallopian tubes as well, so it will be difficult. And I might never become a grandfather one day." A tear streamed down his face, and he wiped it away with the back of his hand as he tried to pull himself together. So that could be the reason why she said she didn't want to have kids either. At least we are on the same page on that. "I'm just reminded of her mother and I just don't want my daughter to suffer like this. I've seen her mother suffer and I just... wish to make things better for her." He wiped a tear away with the back of his hand again.

"I need the bathroom," Cris said, her voice breaking a bit as she walked past us.

"I-I'm sorry that you both have to go through this. I'll always be here whenever you need me. I will leave work in case of an emergency, and you have my word," I said, even though this broke my heart.

"Thanks," he said. "I need to go for a walk if you don't mind. This just came suddenly when she was doing so well over the years. But her missing some of her pills just has me concerned. Perhaps she has a lot of stress with the final year of school and modeling. I will have a talk with her regarding that. Please call me when I'm needed here," he said.

I only nodded, I didn't know what else to say and then he left me all alone in the corridor. I leaned forward, resting my elbows on my knees. Staring at the floor, trying to soak this in. I wished that she had told me about this. I'm her boyfriend, maybe she was afraid of what I would think, but this was something serious that had no cure.

My Support

Elona

I stirred with pain and discomfort, squinting as the light blinded me. I groaned as I rubbed my eyes. The events of what happened came rushing back to me as I now took in my surroundings. I was lying in the hospital bed. I placed my hand on my belly. I had to make sure that I took my pills, but I forgot. Now, I was here because of that.

"Hey," I heard a familiar voice and I looked to my side to see Tristan lean forward in the chair that he sat in beside me. He took my hand in his. I swallowed my throat feeling dry. "How are you feeling?" He asked, concern evident on his face.

"I feel like crap. Some pain and discomfort," I sucked in a breath.

"You had surgery. I know what the issue is. Your father explained to me because I asked him to since he put you in my care. If something had to happen like this to you, and he was not around, I needed to know. So, don't be angry with him that he told me. More importantly, I'm your boyfriend. You could've told me," he squeezed my hand gently.

I let out a slow breath, "I didn't want anyone to know about this since my father and I found out about it years ago. I was irresponsible by forgetting to take my birth control pills, which was a massive help with my pain." I licked my lips to moisten them.

"You also could've fallen pregnant easily by being that irresponsible," he said with disappointment, and when my eyes met his, there was a bit of disappointment.

"I'm sorry. I just... I'm not even sure if I would ever fall pregnant. That's a good thing for us both, so relax." I tried to reassure him.

"What if you didn't have this condition, and you forgot to take those pills?"

"But that's not the case with me. You know it. Sorry if I have disappointed you in that regard." I was not happy with where this conversation was going.

"As long as you're okay, your health is the top priority, and we know what's going on, then there is nothing to apologize for," he let out a breath as he caressed the back of my hand with his thumb. "Just know that I'm always here for you and you can tell me anything."

"Thanks," I said. "Where's my father?" I asked.

"He went for a walk, I did text him that you were out of surgery. I've been here by your side ever since they brought you back in." My heart fluttered that he was by my side the entire time.

"Thanks for being here," I said.

"I'll always be here for you. From now on, you tell everything whether you have pain or discomfort. If I had known what was wrong with you at the camp, I wouldn't think twice about taking you back home. You were very pale, but somehow you were strong through it all. So, from now on, you will tell me, okay?" His expression softened.

"I will," I replied. I looked at the door, "I just hate to go through this. I don't wish this on any woman. When I'm in pain, I keep asking myself, why is this happening to me? Why me? I don't like to have my father go through this with me, because I know that it reminds him of my mother. I don't want these things to trigger him. I have no cure and I had to make peace with that. Some doctors would say that painful periods are normal, that it's all in my head as if I was crazy. My father clearly saw that it was not normal for me. He fought to get the right doctors. The doctors that I'm under at this hospital are amazing. I can only do things that will relieve the pain and discomfort and surgery. I just... don't want you to be in this situation either if this is something that will also trigger things inside of you that... that might remind you of loss or anything. But I'm not going anywhere. If you want to support me through this, then, you need to be sure to stick by my side, no matter what. If this is not something that you want to deal with, then you are free to leave," I looked at him as he continued to caress the back of his hand. It hurt to say it.

"I'm in this for the long haul. I'm not leaving your side...ever. You're stuck with me forever. I don't want any other life without you in it. I only want you because you make my life complete. I may be feeling sad about what you're going through, but we will get through this together. I'm your strength whenever you are weak. I'm here to lift you up when you are down and to be that little push when you need it. But I will not go anywhere," he gave me a little smile.

"Promise me that you won't grow tired of me and this condition... ever," I said.

"I promise. I will never grow tired of you and this condition. You make my life colorful. As long as you do whatever it is that you need to do in order to feel better and from here on out remember to take your pills, we will be fine."

"I ruined your birthday." I felt down that I had ruined it.

"Stop that. You didn't ruin anything. I hate celebrating my birthday. But maybe in the future when we're married, then I might just be able to celebrate my birthday again." He smiled. That concern was no longer visible on his face.

"I will surprise you with breakfast in bed and whatever you want," I smiled.

"Well, that depends on what kind of breakfast you're talking about," he stated in thought, smirking.

"Whatever breakfast you want," I continued to smile. "What's taking my father so long?"

"He should be here any minute, or he hasn't read my text. But I'm able to get more time alone with you before he enters. Cris went to the cafeteria. She should also be here." He explained.

"I feel like Cris knows something is going on between us, but she's taking it as if you are choosing me over her in a father/daughter type of way." I was worried about that.

"Don't worry about her. I told her that I was your guardian and that was all that it was. Also, the jacket of mine that I left by you. I had to lie and say that it was your father's jacket, and we wear the same scent."

"So many lies to keep up with, what if we eventually slip up?" I asked.

"We will take it one day at a time. We should try not to make things obvious, especially in front of Cris. She's a clever girl and I hope that she will be okay with us when the time comes," he said with worry etched on his face.

"Me too."

All we could do was play it safe and make sure that we could keep up with all these lies until we told them. My priority right now is to get better and recover. My biggest secret is out with regards to my endometriosis, and it felt like a weight had been lifted knowing that Tristan wouldn't go anywhere and to be my support.

Another Breadcrumb

Tristan

I'm worried about Elona, and it crushed me that she had to go through something like this. She doesn't deserve this at all. I would do anything to be by her side, even if that meant spending most days at home and doing my work in the comfort of my study room. I let go of her hand as I leaned back in the chair. I felt bad about having sex with her when she wasn't feeling well. It was ripping through me on the inside.

"I really feel bad that I just went ahead and had sex with you. You should've told me you were not well. I was selfish." I let out a shaky breath.

"It's not your fault. I wanted to satisfy you. I love to satisfy you and I had to bite my tongue through the pain, it was like the breath in my lungs was punched out of me. It was excruciating, and it was the first time I had sex while in pain. It was a lesson on my side too. I just... I just wanted to make you happy." She looked down. That made me feel even worse.

"Sex doesn't satisfy me, and it doesn't make me happy. You're the only person that satisfies me because I love you. You make me happy. I can go days, months, and years without sex. I went three years without it when Estelle passed away. It's mind over matter. I won't even mention the one-night stand I had with Maggie because I was trying to get you out of my mind. But never think that you have to satisfy me with sex because I don't care about that. I care about you. If you're not feeling well and if you're in pain, please tell me so that I also know that sex is off-limits, because your health is my priority and I don't want to put you in pain. I'm so, so sorry that I was selfish," my voice nearly broke, but I held it together.

"You were not selfish and stop blaming yourself. I will inform you next time as long as you stop blaming yourself. It was not your fault, you didn't know, and it was a lesson for myself," she reassured me and I nodded.

The door opened. "Hey, how are you feeling?" David rushed to her side, and he leaned down, placing a kiss on her forehead. "I only saw the text now, thanks," he stood up straight as he looked at me.

I nodded in response as his gaze fell on Elona, "I have some pain, but that's what always goes down, right?" She let out a sigh. I still can't believe that this strong Elona whom I have always known and saw grow up with my daughter, was in pain, and she tried to be strong, which was admirable.

"Hey," Cris entered, "Uncle David got me along the way and told me that you're out of surgery. I'm so sorry about this. I didn't know that you had this condition. Am I even allowed to say it?" Cris asked. Her eyes were still huge as if she didn't get over the initial shock of the news earlier. She stood at the foot of the bed.

"Cris, it's nothing. This is something that I'm used to dealing with on my own and with the help of my father, but I was careless and this happened." Elona said, wincing as she tried to sit up.

"Is it okay for you to even sit up?" I blurted out, concerned because she had just got out of surgery, I was now on the edge of the chair, my arm reaching out to her, ready to step into action if anything went wrong in this moment.

"Relax," Elona smiled.

"With Elona's surgery, she had a laparoscopy. They only make some incisions close to her belly button, and work through those little incisions to remove whatever tissue of the endometriosis. However, she will be discharged later. This surgery doesn't require her to be kept in the hospital." David smiled, and then I shifted in the chair again, getting comfortable.

"Okay, I suppose I need to learn these things...for whenever you're not around," I said to David.

"Yes, you do." He replied.

"I guess I need to do research too. If you need anything, then we are here for you, or you can sleep over by us whenever Uncle David is not around," Cris shrugged.

"No," Elona blurted out.

"That's a brilliant idea," I said, furrowing my brows at Elona who just stared at me for a brief moment before she looked at her best friend.

"That would be great. I won't take no for an answer," David chimed in.

"Okay, I guess I will be sleeping over when my father is not around," Elona finally agreed.

"Awesome!" Cris was happy about it, and it only made my heart swell more. "So, this means that I'm never going to be an aunt," Cris seemed sad about it and I looked down at Elona's belly, which was covered with the hospital sheet.

I'm reminded of how badly Cris wanted a sibling. She knew that she wouldn't get one. Now she thought that she would be an aunt, Elona and I decided from the beginning not to have any kids, so in this case, the endometriosis is a reason for Cris to understand that Elona can't have kids. I do hate to see my daughter being sad, but we won't be giving her those titles of big sister or aunt.

"Unfortunately, you won't be an aunt. I don't want kids at all. I have gone through so much pain and I don't think I can do that. It's something that I decided years ago. I won't even try and, please, don't encourage me to try because you're not in my shoes, you should have respect for my decisions," Elona said. That's my girl for standing her ground on her decision as an individual and with me as a couple.

"I totally understand. I'm sorry for bringing it up," Cris was quick to apologize.

"You are both learning." Elona smiled at Cris and me.

"Does anyone want coffee or something to eat?" David asked.

"I just came from the cafeteria, but I won't say no to more coffee," Cris smiled at him. But there was something that I had noticed about the way that David was looking at my daughter. A look that I had not seen before. Was he into her? Was it my daughter that he was talking about? My heart picked up its pace, almost sending me into a heart attack.

"Tristan?" I snapped out of it when David looked at me, expecting an answer. "Would you like coffee or anything?"

"Um...no, thanks," I replied. David and Cris left the hospital room, leaving me alone with Elona. "I'm sorry for the questions and statements from Cris. She could come across as insensitive when asking about these kinds of things. She only cares about you and she's worried. I can see it in her eyes," I said.

"It's okay. I have to get used to it because my father and I have kept this a secret for so long. So, it's not a big deal," she smiled.

I stood up and leaned over her, pressing my lips against her forehead before pulling away. "I love you, always remember that. You are my strong angel that came into my life when I had least expected it," I smiled down at her.

"I love you too, thank you for being my strength," she returned the smile.

"We have to lean on each other when times get tough. Whether it's when one of us are sick, or when we are down and angry. I want to be that person for you. I know I'm an ass, but I'm trying to be the man that I used to be before I had built up my walls." I stroked her hair.

"You are showing that side of you even more. I love you more and more for the person that you are and are yet to become in a better way, but I don't want you to change the person that you really are. I love you for who you are," Gosh, she was so wise with those words.

"You surprise me," I smiled and leaned down one last time to place a kiss against her forehead.

My phone started to ring, and then I pulled away, taking my phone out of my pocket. It was work and I answered, "Crane."

"Mr Crane, we have another lead, which is a breadcrumb of the hacker. If you don't mind coming in...it seems as if it could be coming from a building close to The Dakota Agency."

"Fuck," I muttered under my breath, "Stay on that, and I'll be there soon," I hung up and turned back to Elona. "There was a lead for the hacker. I'm needed, but if you are home later, I will pop in."

"Please, go and find that hacker. I'll text you later."

I kissed her before I rushed down the corridor, bumping into David and Cris along the way, telling them my reason for leaving so urgently. I hope that this hacker was found and put behind bars after this.

Telling The Truth

Elona

It had been two weeks since my surgery. Tristan was amazing, he was supportive and made sure to be there for me even though my father was around. But I had this constant feeling within me that was nagging me the entire time. That feeling was telling me to inform Tristan about the truth.

Now I stood in front of his front door, knocking. Cris was at SNT because she had to go on another outing program with them for the weekend. The door swung open and Tristan was on the phone. Sadly, they didn't find the hacker because that hacker was constantly on the move. It was just weird for me that it was tracked that the hacker was close to The Dakota Agency building.

"I will call you back," he hung up and opened the door wider for me. "Is everything okay?" He asked as I stepped inside, concern laced his voice.

"I know that you might be busy with work, but I wanted to come over to tell you some things," I said as he closed the door behind me.

I turned around to face him, his brows furrowed, "Okay? Let's go sit in the kitchen," he gestured for me to go first, and I did.

I pulled a chair from the dining table and took a seat. He sat across from me, "This might not be an easy thing, but I think that you should know about this." I leaned back in the chair, taking in a deep breath.

His green eyes were brighter today, and they were so gorgeous I could stare into them the entire day. I swallowed. "What is it? Is it the endometriosis?" He asked as he now placed his phone on the table.

I shook my head, no, "No, it's something else that I lied-" his phone rang,

325

stopping me from saying anything further.

"It's work. We are quite busy, especially with the hacker constantly on the move. I feel as if this person is playing me like a fool. This hacker took some money from the company yet again." He said as his phone rang again. "I need to take this," he said as he answered the phone.

As he had his conversation on the phone, barking orders, I was slowly losing the will to tell him the truth. I took another deep breath, willing myself to not back out from this. This was important for our relationship if I wanted to have a future with him. I don't know how he would react, but I can't keep up with the lies. There was so much of it, I just needed to get it over with.

I fidgeted with my hands in my lap as I found his eyes already on me as I took a nervous breath. "Yeah, can I call you back, I have something important that needs my attention now," his eyes never leaving mine, they were burning into me, and it was like that first day that he stared at me over the glass of juice that he drank, which made my crush for him explode into more. "I'll call you back. Let me know if there is anything else...thanks," he hung up and placed his phone on the table again.

I shifted on the chair, this was now or never, "What is it? Is everything okay? You can talk to me... I won't bite," I looked at him. He smirked a little.

"Well, this won't be easy, but it needs to be said."

"Okay, I'm all ears," he pushed me a bit further.

I need to just dive into this and get it over with, "I lied to you about being a virgin and I lied about having experience with things. I was never with another guy. As Cris said before, I'm a saint and I was keeping myself for someone that I wanted to have that moment with. I have always had a crush on you over the years, but that one day in the kitchen when you stared at me over the glass, it made me feel like more than just a silly crush. I couldn't believe it when you returned my feelings. When we ended up having sex that night for the first time, and you asked if I was a virgin, I said no because I didn't want you to stop and have us wait. I wanted to have sex with you at that moment. I just didn't want to wait because I was a virgin. More lies came up when you asked me if I had any experience. I had no experience at all, but I tried to satisfy you," I looked at him as he continued to burn his gaze into me, which wasn't making things easy for me. I didn't know if he was okay or not.

"So, all this time you lied to me about that?" He finally asked.

"Yes, those are the only times I lied. It won't happen again," I bit my bottom lip. I was nervous.

"Okay... I guess women just like to do whatever to get into my pants," the corners of his lips curled up as he looked down at his phone. But they were gone as quickly as they curled up.

"It wasn't like that for me, I swear. It's more than sex for me," I blurted out, which was true.

"I would've worshiped your whole body, I wouldn't have been rough and made you bleed the way that I did. A virgin doesn't need to have sex roughly, I would massage the nerves out of you before I had even been inside of you because a virgin needs to be relaxed." He finally looked up at me. "That's what I would've done. If you really wanted sex that night, if you had told me the truth right there, that is what I would've done. I would've made sure to listen to you and make sure that you were okay. I would've been gentle, the same way I should've been before you were rushed to the hospital for your endometriosis. I don't just fuck, I worship too. I just need transparency from now on. No secrets or lies at all. I hate lies, I do have feelings too."

"I promise this won't happen at all. That's everything that I lied about. You know about everything now," I said.

He nodded, "Good, because now... I will show you just the way I would've worshiped every inch of your body as if it was that first time." He leaned in closer to the table, his eyes dark with hunger. My core throbbed. This wasn't how I had expected this to go, but it turned out great. I could finally let out a sigh of relief.

His phone rang, and he had to answer it as he stood up and walked out of the kitchen. I looked down at my hands, they were trembling from the nerves that I had while I told him the truth. I literally thought he would have a fit about it, but I was wrong. That didn't destroy us, we were still strong. After a while, he came back. "Sorry, but I need to take care of work. I'm not sure how long it will be, but this is important. I feel bad to be doing this."

"It's fine, I'll text you later," I stood up and walked to him. I leaned in, and he rested his hands on my hips. He placed a light kiss on my lips, "I love you, never forget that," he said against my lips.

"I love you too," I replied as I pulled away, and I moved out of his grasp and then I went back home.

I understood that he had work to do that was important regarding this hacker. I didn't want to stand in the way of it. As long as I knew that we were still going strong, there would be nothing that would come between us now and that made me happy.

Doorstep Surprise

Tristan

I was sitting in the lounge, going through documents from my company. I worked late last night and I do not know what time I went to bed. Some money had been taken from my company by this person, and I'm trying to keep track of everything. I do not want to lose what I have because of this person yet again. Who the hell is this hacker? The investigation was also a flop. We could've had the fucker by now.

I spent most of the night thinking about the lies that Elona had told me. I hate lies because that ruins a person's trust. It did hurt me a little bit because those were lies. I'm grateful that she told me the truth and I have to believe everything that she will be saying in the future. She's a brilliant person, but it took one lie from the person you love to shift that trust. With Elona, I'm giving her the benefit of the doubt. This also doesn't change the fact that she's suffering from a painful condition, and it doesn't change my feelings for her. I still want all those dreams with her and to make her Mrs Crane one day.

My phone rang. It was my IT.

I answered, "Yes?"

"This person is definitely moving around a lot, and it may be difficult to find him or her, but are there any other enemies or rivals?"

"I don't have any rivals that I'm aware of," I replied, was there anyone out there that had something against me?

"Can you check anything to do with Maggie Roberts? She might be the one, or she might have someone doing this for her. She might be after my money.

Um... The Parkers down the street from me is a possibility. Those are ones that I can come up with that could have something against me," I said.

"I will look into this. I know that the professional investigation didn't go as planned, but I have someone that I know who might be of huge help."

"I hope so. I cannot lose anything more. I have poured years into this company. So, please do everything that you can to find this person," I let out a huge breath.

"I will, Sir," he hung up.

I decided to text Elona.

Me: I'll be busy for the entire day and night. I'm trying to find the hacker because the investigation went down to shit. You can come over tomorrow. I'll make time for us. I love you.

I didn't want her to think that I was avoiding her after she told me the truth. I just have this situation to sort out or else I would end up with nothing. Before I placed my phone on the coffee table, my phone chimed. It was a reply from Elona.

Elona: I completely understand. I'll see you tomorrow. I love you more.

After placing my phone on the coffee table, I continued to go through the paperwork. The companies that I'm working with and the investors... searching for who might be on the list, so far I have none. It's like working on something that had nothing to do with my situation. I've been with these people for years and this hacking only started recently, so I doubt it could be any of them. I scrubbed my face with my hand, letting out a frustrated sigh. There was a knock on the front door. I stood up and opened it.

"What the fuck are you doing here?" I hissed.

"Well, we need to talk, and that's not the way to greet the mother of your unborn baby," I don't know if blood boiled within me or if it was shock.

"What?" I asked impatiently.

"You heard me, Tristan. I'm pregnant, and the baby is yours." Maggie was sure about that.

I scoffed, "Really? I don't trust you and I hate lies. I used condoms, so nice try," I was about to close the door in her face, but she stopped me from doing that, by pushing it open again. "Woman, just leave before I call the cops on you," I hissed.

"Did you forget that one condom broke on that night? I never slept with anyone else after that because I was too determined to have you, and you don't have to believe me, but David and I never fucked each other when you told us to at the gallery." She hissed back. I don't know what kind of woman you take me for, but I'm a woman who is pregnant."

*****Flashback*****

I pulled out of Maggie, it was our fourth round and Elona still kept invading my mind even though she was in Cris' bedroom. But as I pulled out, my fluids were everywhere, and they were starting to drip from Maggie.

"Shit."

"What is it?" Maggie sat up straight as I was on my knees on the bed.

"The condom broke," I said, remaining calm.

"I will get the morning-after pill," she replied.

"Didn't you take the morning-after pill that you said you would?" I scowled at her.

"I forgot to take it."

I shook my head in disbelief, "You are so unbelievable, was this your way of tricking me?"

"I swear that I never planned this. I forgot, honestly." she seemed genuine about it, but I did not trust her one bit. "I don't even know if you're lying to me right now."

"If you don't believe me..." she took something out of her handbag, "Here." She shoved an envelope and a stick against my chest. I grabbed it before it fell to the floor. "I hope you are sorry after the way that you have just treated me," her voice broke and she stormed off.

I closed the door and now looked at the envelope and the pregnancy test that showed two lines on it. I walked into the kitchen and I pulled a chair out from the dining table, taking a seat as I opened the envelope. I took out the image, after placing the envelope on the table and the pregnancy test on top of it that I was still holding.

I focused on the image, it was an ultrasound of a tiny little... I can't even think of it as I sat here, my heart was just breaking, because this was not what I wanted, and not even with this woman that I love. I stared at the ultrasound, sucking in a deep breath, this can't be happening to me. Was this a dream, a nightmare?

Reminders of the baby Estelle and I lost resurfaced. Anger boiled within me along with shock and disappointment. I don't want this, but this was a life. I just wanted to explode with all the emotions that I was feeling as I continued to stare at this image. I scoffed, shaking my head, I don't even have this with Elona but why am I being punished for having a baby with the woman I despise? Maybe my punishment was for the one-night stand that I had and the fact that I didn't want any more kids. A tear ran down my cheek. I don't want this to be my life. I just can't do this with Maggie.

Something Not Expected

Elona

It was a stormy day. Tristan was busy for the entire day. He only read my texts but never responded. I wanted to see how he was doing seem that he had to deal with the hacker. He had been there for me with my condition, and now I want to do the same for him. I slipped on a light blue hoodie, my black leggings and sneakers. My father was at work, so I didn't need to lie about where I would be going. Since Tristan wanted me to come over today, that was where I would be headed.

I jogged down the street in the light rain, the hood of my hoodie over my head. I knocked on the front door of Tristan's house. I waited a while for the door to open. Tristan must be in the shower, or working if he wasn't hearing me. I knocked some more, but still no answer. His car was parked in the driveway, so he was at home. I just hope that everything is okay with him. I knocked again as I started to get worried about him.

The door finally opened, and he seemed to be in a bad mood, scowling at me, his hair was disheveled, and I could smell a little alcohol and I get it. This hacker thing is taking a toll on him.

"Are you okay?" I asked as he moved out of the way, opening the door wider as I entered. I removed the hood from my head. He walked past me into the kitchen and I followed after him. "How is work? Any word about the hacker?" I asked as I pulled a chair out, but my gaze fell on the half-empty glass of Whiskey and the half-empty bottle of Whiskey on the table. This must be serious, which made me stand instead.

He stood across from me, he looked at the table, his jaw clenching. "What is it?" I pushed.

"We need to talk," his gaze met mine, they were dark. Clearly, something serious was going on.

"Okay..." I furrowed my brows and hugged myself as I was not sure where this was going.

"Um... I'm going to become a father."

"Wait...What?" My heart sank. Am I hearing this correctly?

" I will be a father. Maggie showed up yesterday, and she has proof that she is–"

"How do you know that you're the father?" I asked. I was determined to know that Maggie might be trapping him and lying to him about him being the father of the baby.

"I'm the father. Everything adds up because the condom broke. So, I really needed to tell you," he looked at me with no emotion at all.

"So, you want to become a father?" I asked, my heart was breaking.

"Do I have a choice?!" He raised his voice, which made me crawl back into my shell. "I have decided to raise this baby with her and... we will have to break things off between us. I know this is...not what we had planned, but that is what I've decided for the sake of my baby. I'm not going to abandon my own child. I'm not that kind of person," that was a knife through my heart.

"So, it's goodbye to us, everything that you had said to me about marrying me was all for nothing. That you would always be by my side was all for nothing. That you loved me was all for nothing," tears welled up in my eyes, my voice breaking, "That everything we had planned to do together just went down the drain. Why date me in the first place?" I was trembling. His expression changed from hurting briefly to someone who was livid.

"All of those things were true and you know it. Shit happens and now things have changed. I have to be there for my child whether I like it or not," he hissed at me. I took a deep breath.

He raked his fingers through his hair, letting out a heavy sigh, "You don't mean that, we can still be together, and you can just support the baby."

"I'm not going to live like that! I don't trust women that easily anymore.

Maggie was the biggest one and you...you lied to me about being a virgin, about someone who broke your virginity and kept a massive secret about your endometriosis to yourself and even missed taking your birth control pills. Now it's difficult for me to believe that you were not trying to trap me either," he held my gaze and I fought hard to keep it together. This was a punch.

"Yes, I lied, but with the birth control pills, I forgot to take them a few days in a row. You know it will be difficult for me to fall pregnant," I argued.

"Well, It's still unprotected sex against pregnancy." He barked at me.

"I'm not pregnant," I raised my voice even though my heart was breaking.

"I just can't. I can't deal with women who lie and drop shit on me. That was the whole purpose of me not getting involved with anyone else. I was fucking fine on my own after Estelle passed away. I only had my daughter and my work. I should never have listened to your father at the bar that night when he smeared Maggie onto me. I hate the fact that I did it to forget about you, now I'm being punished," he hissed.

"I thought that we were okay after I told you the truth," I was hurting badly.

"I was trying to be okay ever since Maggie showed up and made me realize everything." His gaze never left mine.

"I'm not all women, so don't put me in the same category as Maggie. So what is happening now?" I asked. Hoping that we could get past this and move on.

"I've decided to break it off between us. We will no longer be dating. I'm going to support my unborn child," he said, and he seemed tired as if he hadn't gotten any sleep.

My heart was being badly hurt in all kinds of ways and I felt like ripping it out of my chest. "We don't have to break up."

"I have already decided, so leave," he demanded, his jaw clenching. This was not happening.

"No," my voice broke even more as I tried to be strong.

"Leave, get the hell out of my house! Leave," I remained in my spot. He wanted me to leave, he was throwing me out with his words. "I said Leave!" I jumped at his tone which I had never experienced this side of him before, "Leave!" He dragged it out as if someone was in so much anger and pain, but that did not stop my heart from breaking into ten million pieces.

"I hope that you're happy with your decision. You won't see me ever again," I said, and I stormed out.

Heavy rain poured on me as I ran back to my house. Tears were streaming down my face as I just wanted to bury myself in bed and not see the day of light ever again. He broke me into millions of pieces. I rushed into the house, my back against the door and I just sobbed the most gut-wrenching sob I ever cried, screaming because he ripped out my heart and kept all the pieces. I sank down on the floor and I pulled my knees up against my breasts, wrapping my arms around my legs. I tried to control my sobs, but they were too much to handle.

I moved into a fetal position, lying against the cold tiled floor and I sobbed until I was tired enough for darkness to consume me. Maybe sleep would keep my heartache away because I don't know how to put those pieces of myself that he had back together again. He was my first, my everything, my crush, my whole world, and he took that all away.

The Issue

Tristan

I hate that I had done that to Elona, the hurt written all over her face. She tried to hold it all together, but I knew that I had destroyed her heart. It destroyed mine too... But I needed to do that. I don't want her to be part of this mess, she deserved better, and I had to let her go. The lies that she told me about wanted to resurface as a negative aspect to motivate me to move on. I never imagined that we would end this way.

I took the glass filled with Whiskey and I brought it to my lips, taking a sip as I sat at the dining table. I don't know what to do with myself. So I buried myself by drinking alcohol. It helped me to break up with her. I placed the glass on the table, and then I took my phone that was lying beside the bottle of half-empty Whiskey. I went to Maggie's blocked number, and unblocked it, then pressed it on, bringing the phone against my ear, waiting for her to answer as her phone rang.

"Hey," Maggie answered, but she didn't sound as excited about hearing me as she usually was.

"I will be making an appointment with the doctor for tomorrow. I need to know if I'm really the father. I will get you at your place tomorrow. I'll text you the time of the appointment." I said.

"Well, what doctor are we going to? I have my own."

"I will not let you see your own doctor. I will take you to mine. I think it's better that way. Bye." I hung up before she could say anything else.

I placed my phone on the table with a sigh, "I heard what happened," I looked up to see Eric walking slowly towards the table, he pulled a chair out and took a seat.

"What part?" I asked.

"The break-up and the pregnancy," he said carefully as if not trying to step on my toes.

"Well, I'm being punished. One night with Maggie and that is what I got. I'm taking her to the doctor to make sure that I'm really the father of that baby. I lost Elona in this regard. It doesn't make it better when the words she confessed to me that she lied about being a virgin and being with someone else before just find their way into my head, further fueling the fact that I made the right decision," I was breaking on the inside. "I wanted a life with her, and she made me happy. Now, I'm back to being this person who just blocks himself off from the world. I just need today to think things through and then, hopefully, I can focus on my company."

"She lied that she was a virgin and had been with someone else before. Why?" Eric narrowed his eyes.

"She didn't want to wait to have sex if she had told me that she was a virgin, it's just that... I would've been gentle with her, not rough, and I could kick myself for that...and then not knowing what else she might lie about in the future, and that is a feeling that I don't want to have that will probably make me question if what she says is true. I can't believe I'm telling you these things," I let out a sigh.

"You're afraid that the trust might be broken," he nodded in understanding. "But knowing Elona, you can trust her, don't do this to her." He pleaded with me.

"I have a possible baby to take care of and this is just the way things will be right now," I said, I just wanted time to myself.

"Don't bury yourself in alcohol, it's not healthy. On a different note, thanks for the opportunity that you made for me to be part of The Dakota Agency, the photography training went well."

"You deserve that," I replied. I had to make a way for him to achieve his dreams, and what way to see him happy with this internship at The Dakota Agency.

The front door opened, and I knew that it was Cris. "Hey," she walked towards us, her eyes falling on the Whiskey and her gaze found mine. "What is up with that?" she gestured to the Whiskey.

"We need to talk about something," I said.

"I will give you both some privacy," Eric said as he stood up from the chair and walked away. Cris took a seat on that same chair across from me.

"So, what is it?" She asked, her brows furrowed.

"Maggie is pregnant, and I might be the father." I blurted out.

Her eyes went huge, "Really?!" She squealed.

"I want to make sure that I'm the father."

"This is something that I've wanted forever, and now it's finally coming true... I'm so happy," she stood up from the chair.

"Cris, I don't even know if I'm the father."

"Well, by the looks of it..." her eyes moved to the alcohol. "I think that you are, I'm being positive and this will be great for us, Dad." she smiled, she was so happy about it. It broke my heart because it's not what I want. I want to yell, but I can't until I know for sure.

"How was SNT?" I asked, changing the topic because I could no longer talk about it. If I do, it will make me explode at the wrong people.

"It was great, there is progress. I cannot wait to work for them once the internship is over and when graduation is done," she smiled. "Let me go and text Maggie to congratulate her. I'm sure that she's ecstatic, and I do think that you should give her a chance. I don't mind that she becomes my stepmother, you have my permission, Dad," she said, hopefully.

I scoffed, "I doubt I would marry her," I shook my head as I took the glass of Whiskey and I gulped the rest down,

"Don't say that, Dad. Trust me...you will be married to her. You also need to slow down with that, it will not make anything better, and you have a baby on the way, you need to be with Maggie. I cannot wait to share this news with Elona," My grip on the glass tightened as I placed it back on the table with a soft thud, biting on my teeth as the anger boiled within me. I know that this was not Cris' fault for being hopeful, but it's not what I fucking wanted and I wanted people to respect that. "Let me call Maggie," she said, and then she walked away.

I raked my fingers through my hair, letting out a frustrated sigh. Maggie would give me hell, and it would be agony to be with her, especially to have a baby with her. What the fuck have I done? Thanks to David for encouraging me to have that one-night stand with Maggie in the first place, but I gave in just to get him off my back and forget about Elona. Now I'm being punished for that. My heart was tearing apart inside of me, and it's a pain that I couldn't face. So, the next best thing for me to do was drink myself into a stupor until I got the results of who the father was.

My Best Friend

Elona

I was curled up in bed, tears streaming down my face. I didn't even bother to change into my pajamas last night. It was still storming today. My father came home late last night, so before that, I had dragged myself up to my bedroom. I managed to sleep, but it was like I had this pit of hurt in my stomach that wouldn't go away, and it made me feel nauseous.

Tristan was going to have a baby and, of course, he would choose his unborn baby over me. He chose that woman over me. That hurt a lot. I grabbed my pillow, burying my face into it. I let out the loudest scream that I could, and I just sobbed all over again. Why does this have to hurt so badly? He was my first love, my crush, my first everything.

What also hurt me was when he threw the lies I had said back in my face as if he really didn't move on when I told him the truth. He made me believe that he was okay with it. Every word that he said to me, professing his love to me and wanting to marry me one day, was now all down the drain and I can never get that back. He chose his life forever and that does not include me. That hurt me even more.

I reached for my phone, there were texts from Cris.

Cris: I'm back home and my father looks like crap... Alcohol, as you know. But there's an exciting reason for that.

Cris: Hellooo? Anyone home?

Cris: I guess you're sleeping.

Cris: So, my father's in a bad mood, but I'll be coming over in a few minutes. I have something to share with you.

That was sent a few minutes ago. I scrolled through mine and Tristan's text conversation thread before our break-up happened. He loved me, but now that was not the case anymore.

Crane: I love you.

Crane: You are beautiful.

Crane: I cannot wait to wake up next to you one day when you are Mrs Crane.

Crane: I'm never leaving your side.

Crane: You drive me crazy.

Crane: You are my fresh start. You keep me alive, you are the brightest light in my world that was once gray.

Crane: I will take care of you. You don't need to go through this condition alone. I will be a hands-on boyfriend. This won't scare me away. I love you so much.

Fresh tears ran down my cheeks as I read those old texts. Then there was pounding on the front door. I placed my phone on the bed and I mustered up the strength to sit up. Wiping the tears away with the back of my hands before I dragged myself out of bed.

I looked at myself in the mirror, my eyes were all puffy from crying so much that they even gave me a headache. I sucked in a deep breath as I walked out of the bedroom. I felt hollow inside. My father must've left early for work. I went down the stairs and opened the front door.

"I was just about to text you again," Cris was on her phone, and then she looked up at me. Her brows furrowed. "What's wrong?" She stepped closer and then my lips trembled, I just couldn't keep my sobs under control, and then, as I let them out, she wrapped her arms around me, holding me in the doorway. I held onto her for dear life because she was part of Tristan, the closest connection that I have to him.

"Hey, I'm here... Shhhh," she comforted me, rubbing my back gently. I tried to stop, but slowly I managed as I pulled away. She cupped the sides of my face, "Everything is okay," but I shook my head.

"It's not."

"Okay. I'm all ears, okay? Let me close the door," she let go of me to close the door.

I moved further into the lounge, but I stood, I just couldn't sit down. Cris remained standing too. She was worried. "I'm sorry that you have to see me this way," I said, wiping my tears away with the back of my hands.

"I swear you and my father are going through the motions today. If it helps, I'm going to be a big sister. My father just told me the news. I never thought that he would be with Maggie again, he despised her. But I guess things changed." I didn't want to hear that. It was crushing my heart even more. "I guess that didn't help."

I sucked in a breath, "Your father and I were secretly dating, and we planned on telling you and my father when we graduated. We kept on lying to you both and everyone else. I love him, and now I'm broken because he chose her." My voice broke.

Cris just looked at me as if she was thinking about all the times that Tristan and I were together. "So, I was right about his jacket, the wallpapers, you both spending so much time together, and also the fact that you both didn't want kids... I mean with your endometriosis...he was always around you at The Dakota Agency to protect you and being your guardian. All the time, I thought that I was crazy and that it was nothing, that he chose you over me as his daughter. I felt jealous that he couldn't even do that for me. But it all makes sense now," she said as she held my gaze.

"I'm sorry that we lied." I was more worried about her reaction right now. It was scaring me.

"I finally get to be a big sister, and I believe that my father is doing this with Maggie. I-I need time," she said as tears welled up in her eyes.

"I love him."

"It's an infatuation-"

"He loved me too," I interrupted.

"I saw the way that you made him come to life, but let him be with someone that can give us a family. You probably can never give us that." That crushed my heart.

"But I'm like family, Cris," a tear streamed down my face.

"I need time," she said, and then she stormed out of the front door.

I fell to my knees on the floor, burying my face in my hands as I sobbed. Nothing could take this pain away. I lost my best friend too. I know I have lost her. I don't think that she would ever want to face me again. I could not breathe, my heart was already in pieces, so how much more could it break?

I lost the two people in my life that I love so much, and I don't know what would make this any better. I don't think that I can go through this. I can't. I just want this heartache to stop, but when will it end? Clearly, Cris was on Maggie's side because she was going to be a big sister, with her being on Maggie's side was everything that just crushed me even further, and I don't think that I can get back up. I don't ever think that I can get past this.

To Be Continued

Playlist

Right Now- Danity Kane

Redemption- Besomorph, Coopex, RIELL

Animal-Jim Yosef, RIELL

Dance With Me-Besomorph, RIELL

Stubborn-RIELL

Over The Edge (Radio Edit) –RIELL

3 Months- RIELL

Better Off- RIELL

Bad Things- Nation Haven

Dirtier Thoughts- Nation Haven

Butterflies-Isabel LaRosa

Without You- Isabel LaRosa

Older-Isabel LaRosa

Eyes Don't Lie- Isabel LaRosa

Tears On The Dancefloor-UPSAHL

Cornfield Chase-Piano Version-Hans Zimmer, Alex Gibson (Moment when Tristan played the piano)

You can find more to the series playlist on Spotify-'My Best Friend's Dad-PLWaites'

Acknowledgements

Thank you, readers, for sticking around until the end of Sweet Torture, I hope that you'll be back for book two. My fiance has always been encouraging me to do what I love and telling me to go for it, and this is what I'm doing. To some of my friends and family members and my mother, thank you for the support and listening to me when I vent about things and also encouraging me to take breaks when I do everything at once, yet you all find me doing something because I just cannot sit and do nothing. Thank you Sierra Winson for being my Beta reader and editor. I appreciate your help and you are wonderful to work with. Thank you to my sprinting buddies, Becca Swan, Hannah Armitage, Tina Tyr, Ruby K, Amanda Layne, Samantha O'Maker, Eve Marcoux, Aurora Moon, Charlotte Deehr, Morgan Butler, Anne T. Thyssen, and more, you all have pushed me in these writing sprints, especially on those procrastination days. To my very early readers, who get to see me write each chapter raw, K-Bear, Florence Fassou, Bubbles, Fluffydiva869, April Walters, Ischneickert, aBlack3026, AnoniMas, Mercia Hendricks, Desmine Davids, Xpressions by Scotty, Jessica Heap, Debbie Poirier, Phionah Namukwaya. You all are amazing. Jessica Scott and Kelly Diedericks, I look forward to working with you both on amazing things for this series. Tamera Hon, thank you for always being so supportive and always bringing in new readers. To my South African Arc readers you are amazing, there are too many to name. Crestina Besario, my Facebook group admin, my reader and friend, and the one who gets to hear most of my ideas first, thank you for the support and the sweet person that you are. Thank you to everyone for the support and for being on this journey with me.

Much love!

P.L Waites

A Little Story

This book came from my own inspiration as my fiance and I are in a ten-year age gap relationship with him being older than me. We first started dating when I was eighteen and I was halfway done with high school, he was twenty-seven at the time. We had known each other for a very long time before that but then one day with just eye contact, we were being pulled towards each other like a magnet.

He is sweet and respectful, he even asked my mom for her blessing to date me and she gave her blessing because she knew the type of man that he was. We've been dating ever since and have been going strong for ten years.

We cannot help who we fall in love with and who we spend our future with. So, my own age gap is unique and this was my inspiration for Sweet Torture and many of my other age gap books.

From experience, I didn't care what anyone said about the relationship even though it hurt. I proved to them, I wasn't going anywhere, and to this day we are still going strong.

I hope you enjoyed my little story.

Much love!

Stalk Me

Facebook Page:
Author P.L Waites

Facebook Reader Group:
Straight To The Forbidden Point–P.L Waites

Instagram:
PL Waites

TikTok:
Author PL Waites